Priscilla of Alexandria

BY THE SAME AUTHOR

The Marvelous Story of Claire d'Amour
The Call of the Beast
The Angel of Lust
The Mystery of the Tiger
The Poison of Goa
Lucifer
The Blood of Toulouse
The Albigensian Treasure
Jean de Fodoas
Melusine
The Brothers of the Virgin Gold

Priscilla of Alexandria
and Other Stories

by
Maurice Magre

Translated, annotated and introduced by
Brian Stableford

A Black Coat Press Book

Visit our website at www.blackcoatpress.com

ISBN 978-1-61227-667-0. First Printing. September 2017. Published by Black Coat Press, an imprint of Hollywood Comics.com, LLC, P.O. Box 17270, Encino, CA 91416. All rights reserved. Except for review purposes, no part of this book may be reproduced or transmitted in any form or by any means, electronic or mechanical, including photocopying, recording, or by any information storage and retrieval system, without permission in writing from the publisher. The stories and characters depicted in this novel are entirely fictional. Printed in the United States of America.

TABLE OF CONTENTS

Introduction

This is the third volume of a twelve-volume set of translations of Maurice Magre's prose fiction. It contains translations of the original version of the story collection *Vies des courtisanes*, first published in *Les Oeuvres Libres* XXIII (1923), as "Courtesans' Lives" plus the additional story added to the version of the collection published in volume form in 1925, and the novel *Priscilla d'Alexandrie* (1925), as "Priscilla of Alexandria."

Volume One, *The Marvelous Story of Claire d'Amour and Other Stories*, contains translations of early short stories, including the collection *Histoire merveilleuse de Claire d'Amour suivie d'autres contes merveilleux* (1903) and six other stories from various sources, published between 1901 and 1913.

Volume Two, *The Call of the Beast and Other Stories*, contains translations of his first three works of prose fiction in volume form, *Les Colombes poignardées* (1917), as "Stabbed Doves," *La Tendre camarade* (1918), as "The Tender Comrade" and *L'Appel de la bête* (1920), as "The Call of the Beast."

Volume Four, *The Angel of Lust*, contains translations of the novella, *La Vie amoureuse de Messaline* (1925), as "The Love Life of Messalina," the novel published as *La Luxure de Grenade* (1926), as "The Angel of Lust," and the chapter from *Magiciens et illuminés* (1930) entitled "Christian Rosenkreutz et les Rose-croix," as "Christian Rosenkreutz and the Rosicrucians."

Volume Five, *The Mystery of the Tiger*, contains translations of the novella *Le Roman de Confucius* (1927), as "The Story of Confucius," and the novel *Le Mystère du tigre* (1927), as "The Mystery of the Tiger."

Volume Six, *The Poison of Goa*, contains translations of the novel *Le Poison de Goa* (1928), as "The Poison of Goa," and the prose poems contained in *Le Livre des lotus entr'ouverts* (1926), as "Lotus Blossoms."

Volume Seven, *Lucifer*, contains a translation of the novel originally published under the same title in 1929 and the novella *La Nuit de haschich et d'opium* (1929), as "The Night of Hashish and Opium."

Volume Eight, *The Blood of Toulouse*, contains translations of the novel *Le Sang de Toulouse* (1931), as "The Blood of Toulouse," and the chapter from *Magiciens et illuminés* entitled "Le Maître inconnu des Albigeois," as "The Secret Master of the Albigensians."

Volume Nine, *The Albigensian Treasure*, contains translations of the novel *Le Trésor des Albigeois* (1938) as "The Albigensian Treasure," and the collection of vignettes "Communication avec la nature" from *La Beauté invisible* (1937), as "Communication with Nature."

Volume Ten, *Jean de Fodoas*, contains translations of the novel *Jean de Fodoas: aventures d'un Français à la cour de l'empereur Akbar* (1939) as "Jean de Fodoas" and the chapter from *Magiciens et illuminés* entitled "Le Mystère des Templiers," as "The Mystery of the Templars."

Volume Eleven, *Melusine*, contains translations of the novel *Mélusine, ou le secret de solitude* (1941) and the collections of vignettes "Le Côté d'ombre des âmes" and "Révélation des mondes invisibles" from *La Beauté invisible*, as "The Dark Side of Souls" and "The Revelation of Invisible Worlds."

Volume Twelve, *The Brothers of the Virgin Gold*, contains a translation of the novel *Les Frères de l'or vierge*, first published posthumously in 1949.

Vies des courtisanes was initially published in volume XXIII of the periodical *Les Oeuvres Libres* in 1923, where it was classified as "variétés inédits" [previously-unpublished miscellanea]; it consists of a collection of thematically-linked short stories. That original version was headed by a prefatory essay entitled "De la supériorité des courtisanes sur les autres femmes," here translated as "On the Superiority of Courtesans to Other Women." The six stories in that version were "Hermanossa, auteur du traité sur les moyens pour orienter vers le divin la volupté de l'amour physique" ("Hermanossa, author of the treatise of the means or orientate the sensuality of amour toward the divine"); "Priscilla d'Alexandrie" ("Priscilla of Alexandria"); "Jeanne la Pautonnière" ("Jeanne the Lascivious"); "Lorenza la Vénitienne" ("Lorenza the Venetian"); "Bagawali" ("Bagawali"); and "Julia la dompteuse" (Julia the Animal-Tamer"). The six stories all adopted the form of brief fictitious biographies of sexually voracious women, ranging far and wide both historically and geographically, thus marking a radical new departure from the three works featured in Volume Two, all of which are contemporary novels.

The author went on to expand the second item in the collection into the full-length novel *Priscilla d'Alexandrie* (1925), which greatly elaborated the sketch of eponymous heroine's life contained in the short story, transforming it significantly in the process, and interwove it with sketches of the careers of several fictitious contemporaries. Although the novel does recapitulate the major events of the short story, it alters them very considerably, and becomes a markedly different narrative. It therefore seemed appropriate to include a translation of the earlier version in the present volume, in order not to spoil the integrity of the original assemblage, even though the author removed the story from the version of *Vies des courtisanes* published in volume form in 1925 by La Nouvelle Revue Critique. In that version, the missing wordage was made up by inserting a new penultimate item entitled "Hiao la Coréenne" ("Hiao the Korean") but it clearly does not belong to the set, being a story of a different narrative type, although it does include a brief encounter with a sexually voracious woman; it gives the appearance of having been developed from the opening chapters of an aborted novel.

Of the six women in the original collection—one (Jeanne) is born sexually voracious, three (Hermanossa,

9

Lorenza and Julia) acquire voracity and the other two have it thrust upon them. The story that the author elected to expand, presumably having found it the most fascinating, belongs to the third category and is, unsurprisingly, the oddest and most perverse of them all. It became even odder and more perverse in the retelling, and considerably more fascinating in consequence.

The year in which the *Oeuvre Libres* version of *Vies des courtisanes* was published was the year in which Magre's marriage to Jeanne Rosen ended in divorce, although it had effectively fallen apart some time before. In his biography *Maurice Magre: Le Lotus Perdu* [Maurice Magre: The Lost Lotus] (1999), Jean-Jacques Bedu makes no connection between that divorce and the fact and the fact that Magre was diagnosed at some time in the early 1920s with syphilis—an infection that progressed far enough to cause him serious complications thereafter, eventually costing him the sight of one eye. As with his marriage and the child born of it, Magre never mentioned in any of his autobiographical writings that he had suffered from the disease, and thus gave no indication of the effects it had had on his life and ideas, but it would be surprising if those effects were not profound and permanent. The fact that he discovered that had contracted syphilis is surely a significant factor in the sharp change in direction that his literary work underwent in the early 1920s, when he published a sequence of luridly erotic but deeply ambivalent historical fantasies, of which the works in the present volume represent the first of two phases.

With the aid of hindsight, it is easy to read echoes of the unwelcome revelation in "Jeanne la Pautonnière," the most fantastic of the stories in *Vies des courtisanes*, which is almost allegorical in its manner and formation, and grimly excessive in its representation of obsessive sexual voracity. Jeanne's métier as a the operator of a ferry enables her to become the nucleus of an epidemic of venereal disease, which kills off her entire family and disfigures her horribly before her life reaches its strange climax. Although the short version of "Priscilla d'Alexandrie" shows no evidence of any such effect, the novel version certainly does, graphic images of the ravages of a hypothetical venereal disease being added to the description of Priscilla's career in the brothel in Constantinople, and the odyssey undertaken by the philosopher Aurelius including a gruesome account of the effects of an epidemic of the plague.

Some of the stories in the collection were probably written before Magre received his life-changing diagnosis, and they exhibit a very different attitude to erotic matters, resplendently displayed in what is probably the earliest unit in the set, "Hermanossa." The introduction to the previous volume in the present series observed that when Magre began to characterize himself in the years before the outbreak of the Great War, as an essentially divided being, in which a bestial inferior self orientated entirely toward physical pleasure was in constant competition with a superior self striving toward a higher spiritual ideal, his initial reaction was not to attempt to excise or suppress his carnal lusts in order to concentrate on the higher ideal, but to attempt to use the carnal as a means of attaining the ideal: specifically, an attempt to discover in sexual intercourse, especially in the crucial moment of orgasm, a kind of portal to the spiritual, to the realm of the divinity.

Looking back on that phase of his endeavor in *Confessions sur les femmes, l'opium, l'amour, l'idéal, etc...* [Confessions Regarding Women, Opium, Amour and the Ideal, etc.] (1930), Magre made that statement explicitly and straightforwardly, but its reflection in his fiction is muted and oblique, partly because he did not publish any fiction during that period in his life. It is, however, ironically echoed in the prefaces to *Les Colombes poignardées*, the first item of long fiction he produced after that phase of his life had ended, and again in the preface to *Vies des courtisanes*, as well as being developed explicitly and extravagantly in "Hermanossa." The story in question might have been written some time before its publication, but it might simply have been looking back from a distance at a philosophy that the author had once entertained but no longer took seriously.

Although the fascination with Greek courtesans exhibited by several writers associated with the symbolic movement date back to the heyday of the movement, when significant melodramatic reference points were posted by Anatole France's *Thaïs* (1890) and Pierre Louÿs; magisterial *Aphrodite* (1896), the attitude and tone of Magre's stories has much more in common with the sarcastic skepticism of Marcel Schwob's *Vies Imaginaires* [Imaginary Lives] (1896), which Magre references in his later collection of imaginary biographies *Le Côté d'ombre des âmes*. It is, however, possible that he also took some inspiration from Nicolas Ségur's *Naïs au miroir* [Naïs in the Mirror] (1920), to which "Hermanossa" might almost be seen as a sarcastic response.

As well as its wholehearted enthusiasm for carnal joys—an enthusiasm echoed more ambivalently in the other five stories in *Vies des courtisanes*, and ultimately fatal in every instance—"Hermanossa" is also breezier in its comedy, which is considerably more buoyant than the ironic humor featured in "Lorenza la Vénitienne" and "Julia la dompteuse," and contrasts sharply with the violent sardonic tragedy of "Bagawali." In spite of the enthusiasm and comedy, however, and the ingenuity of her treatise, Hermanossa does not actually succeed in converting the skeptical Pausanius to her way of thinking, and Magre appears never to have had had much faith in the project of employing the carnal as a route to the spiritual, even with the aid of slight opium intoxication. He did not need the revelation of the legacy of disease bequeathed to him by his promiscuity to generate his skepticism, but it certainly provided a cruel confirmation of it, and occasioned a significant transformation of his attitude to carnality and his inferior self.

The long version of *Priscilla d'Alexandrie* not only features graphic echoes of disease and depictions of death in its garish melodrama, but, more importantly, offers extravagant narrative scope to the perceived antidote to dangers of carnality and the enmity of the inferior self: the consolations of philosophy. The account of the death of Hypatia is greatly elaborated, an extra dimension being added it in the long version of

the story by the hypothesis of a prelude in which Hypatia de-
cides to forsake the chastity that she has previously adopted in
order to give physical expression to her own eroticism. The
three exemplary philosophers with carefully contrasted ap-
proaches to the attainment of spiritual enlightenment, on the
other hand, all take it for granted that the suppression of the
carnal is an essential prerequisite of success in the quest.

In the specific case of Aurelius, however, that conviction
is compromised, not only by remorse regarding the love he
once had for Priscilla's mother—whose continuing consequences are utterly horrible—but his belated realization of his
love for Touta, whose reciprocal affection for him also has
tragic consequences. Although the novel is unrelenting in its
association of sex with horror and death, it is also poignantly
regretful about that fateful connection. That confusion of its
emotional core contributes enormously to the novel's narrative
force, and also serves to make Priscilla a more complicated
and more interesting character in the novel that she was in the
short story. Although she was originally invented merely as a
case study in sexual liberation, her case is not simply expanded in the novel version but drastically altered, her career following her escape from the brothel in Constantinople taking a
significantly different shape, no longer orientated toward care-
less promiscuity, as it is in the short version.

The six female protagonists featured in the present volume—Hiao does not count, being only a minor character
viewed from a distance—represent more than fifty per cent of
those featured Magre's entire *oeuvre*. Aline had previously
been given the opportunity to voice part of her own story in *La
Tendre camarade*, and at the very end of Magre's career
Malvina de Noussoulens' thoughts were brought into moderately close focus in the early chapters of *Les Frère de l'or
vierge*, but the only female protagonists whose consciousness
Magre subsequently placed center-stage in works of fiction
were Messalina, in *La Vie amoureuse de Messaline*, Rachel
Jehoudah, in *Le Poison de Goa*, and the narrator of *La Nuit de
haschich et d'opium*. The first and third of those works were

probably written to commission, and the former is essentially a belated addition to the *Vies des courtisanes* sequence, but Rachel Jehoudah is a very different character, recapitulating Priscilla's mission of revenge from a distantly displaced standpoint in terms of her attitude to sex and her behavior, and the narrator of *La Nuit de haschich et d'opium* is even more different, parodic and risible in her conventional prudishness.

There is a sense, therefore, in which *Vies des courtisanes* and its spinoff represent a terminus to the promiscuous phase of Magre's literary life, and that beautiful women, seen as objects and incarnations of desire, changed their position in his literary consciousness thereafter, distanced from his eagerness, and perhaps even from his capacity for imaginative identification. It is arguable, in consequence, that Priscilla remained, and still remains, the most intriguing of all his female characters, and perhaps the one of whom Magre was most likely to say, as Flaubert once famously said of Madame Bovary, "C'est moi!"

Priscilla d'Alexandrie was a contender for the Prix Goncourt, but the jury eventually decided, after the customary fierce controversy, that they could not award the prize to the novel, because it was simply too shocking in its imagery, its violence and its amorality. It is, however, precisely those qualities that make it a masterpiece, and its determined perversity can now be seen without any difficulty as a virtue as well as a remarkable achievement. It is, in essence, a horror story, and a story whose composition was motivated by real horror; it retains its power to shock even now, when the relentless effects of melodramatic inflation have raised the stakes in generic horror fiction very considerably.

The translation of Vies des Courtisanes and its supplement was made from the London Library's copy of *Oeuvres Libres* volume XXIII and a copy of the 1925 Nouvelle Revue Critique edition. The translation of *Priscilla d'Alexandrie* was made from a copy of the 1925 Albin Michel edition.

Brian Stableford

14

COURTESANS' LIVES

Preface

On the Superiority of Courtesans to Other Women

"It is necessary to have three kinds of women: hetaerae, for the sensuality of the soul, concubines for the satisfactions of the senses, and matrons to give us children of our race and to keep our houses," said the greatest orator in Athens during the finest days of Greece.

We have a very different idea of women, alas. The logic, intelligence and true purity of the ancient Greeks are no longer within us. We must have attained an age of inconceivable materialism to consider that it is shameful to sell one's body. If the mind is superior to the body, as everyone agrees, then it is the mind that it is necessary not to sell. Why, then, honor so many men, especially writers, who prostitute their sublime mind for money, and despise a prostitute who sells that humble servant of the mind, the wretched shell that is the body?

In antiquity, courtesans were, for men, a spiritual aide, the physical beauty of the flesh that is the privilege of the feminine element on earth. They had the foremost place in society then, and that was justice. Civilizations only exist and develop because of them. They are the secret mechanism, the drop of perfume that fills the atmosphere and enables one to progress with intoxication. Sensuality, the love of amour, exalts all those who provide support to activity or thought, whether they are artists, inventors or men of war; it would exalt priests if they had a more accurate comprehension of the range of their role.

Christian morality has fixed a formula of perfection from which sensuality is excluded, and in which it is even considered to be a sin. It is at the moment when that morality invades the earth that the glory of courtesans declines and the light of the mind also palpitates. They are struck with anathema, rejected from society, become fallen beings. Their history is the history of their martyrdom. During plagues, famines and great calamities they are expelled and killed, to appease the anger of the gods. They have different legislations. In many countries they do not have the right to marry and in others they are parked in ghettos. In Rome, under Paul IV, young nobles believed themselves dishonored if they did not set fire to a house of women into which they penetrated. In Toulouse, one who had committed the crime of entering a convent was hanged. In Beaucaire, every year, they were made to run naked around a hippodrome until they were breathless. In Mantua, a prostitute who has touched an object is obliged to buy it, for she is considered to be impure, and in that same city they must wear a little bell around their neck, like lepers.

And yet, even when they have forgotten their past grandeur, even in their abasement, they remain the vestals of an imperishable flame. What has subsisted through the centuries of the spirit of the ancient courtesans has remained the fecund element of society.

I have tried to sketch in broad outlines a few courtesans' lives, a few lives of women who, by their energy, their activity and the wide abandon they made of their bodies for their own pleasure and that of others, appear to me to have been creators of joy and beauty, to have brought more perfection to humanity than many illustrious generals or venerated pontiffs. Condemned and decried, they have been obliged to live on the margins of societies; they have skirted crime and sometimes fallen into it, for the bringing of pleasure, like that of pain, is often tainted with blood. But they have lived, they have traced the design of their life forcefully on the changing picture of things, in which good and evil are mingled, and in which amour has had the principal role. That is already a great deal.

I firmly believe that a time will come when courtesans will recover the place among women that is their due, which is the foremost. For the moment, a false conception of morality is triumphant. An insurmountable wall has been raised between all those who have sought and received the title of wife, who are sheltered by the formidable fortress of faith, and the others, those who have more desires, less money and more fantasy and have remained in the plain of life, and it has been decreed that there is virtue on one side and dishonor on the other. That has been transmitted to children, carefully and religiously, as a sacred principle; their souls have been spoiled so thoroughly that the idea in question seems to form part of them, to be an indisputable verity, which they will also transmit faithfully.

Chastity does not have that importance. It is not sublime in essence. Beneath the frock-coats of hypocritical clergymen, behind their plastrons of congealed habit, like breastplates of virtue, conventional men, the powerful and pitiless directors of opinion, proclaim it in vain. The matrons of yore might have triumphed and stood tall, aureoled by their children, they might have glorified their chastity as if it were a virtue to be chaste, but the reason and the sense of life tell us loudly that the truth is in the free gift of oneself, in the offering of the carnal splendor received from nature. To nourish and bring up her children is not the only, nor even the primary, duty of a woman. It would be better if there were no children and humanity were to perish than to live without the beauty and the sensuality that raise the spirit equally.

No, family, pleasure of the hearth, crown of virginity secretly woven by pious hands, you are perhaps an egotistical form of happiness, but you cannot be the ideal. A slow but victorious law rises above all beings and bears them toward greater intelligence and greater amour. Even if it requires countless centuries, woman will one day be the equal of man. She cannot be that as long as she is captive in the gynaeceum, the harem or the boudoir where one takes tea. She cannot be that as long as she is not granted, like a man, the absolute right to dispose of her body to whomever she pleases and as often as she pleases.

Glory to the courtesans who were the first to dare to liberate themselves, to dare to climb one step higher, to replace the task devolved to women with a higher one, to be, instead of the vegetable that nourishes, the lily of the field that has only cultivated perfume and color. Many those of today who live without esteem, those to whom no honors are rendered, have recovered the consciousness of their role. Let them immolate their pride in the temple of the beauty they create, just as the courtesans of Corinth offered their hair in holocaust to Venus in order to obtain the victory of the Greeks. But let them remain courtesans, without going backwards, for they will radiate, with the perfection of faces and the harmonious lines of bodies, the purest light of humanity.

Hermanossa

Author of the Treatise on the practical means
of orientating the sensuality of physical amour
toward the divine.

What is known about the life of Hermanossa of Corinth
has an uncertain character. It seems that the surest fact is that
she was raped during her fourteenth year at the foot of a pine
tree on a sandy slope that inclined toward the sea, and even
that is doubtful.

The poet Andronicus said on that subject:

"I raped her when she was an adolescent and a virgin because she spat in my face. I punished her for her pride. She
chewed in rage a lump of resin detached from the pine that
sheltered us. When I left her, having enjoyed her, she rolled to
the bottom of the sandy slope and was slightly bruised by the
shingle of the sea. She complained about that and I shouted to
her: "Go on, little swallow, I've made a more durable mark on
our flesh by taking you by force, for that one won't be effaced
from your memory. Bruised vanity is not like the skin of the
body, it never scars."

It is not certain, however, that the poet Andronicus told
the exact truth about the rape. This is an epigram addressed by
Chereas to Andronicus:

"What a singular form pride has in your soul, Andronicus. You take pride in having knocked down a little girl and
taken her by force on the sea shore. She, on the contrary,
claims to have given herself to you freely. You glorify your
strength at the expense of your power of seduction. Are you,
then, so weak in the body as take pride in what ordinarily a
matter of shame?"

And there is this in a poem by Hermanossa:

"When I was a child I chewed a lump of resin in order not to cry out or ask him not to do me harm. I saw the branches to the pine tree agitating above my head and I clutched it as I had seen the flute-player Phylotis do in a similar case. When I slid in the sand it seemed to me to be softer than usual, and when I walked into the sea water I thought that Aphrodite was protecting me."

Hermanossa must have been from a good family in Corinth, since she was locked up and beaten when she first manifested the desire to share the existence of the cynic philosopher Ammonius. Was that already by virtue of the liking for philosophy she had later? Was it because of the habit that the cynic philosophers had of making love in public? Hermanossa was to give subsequent evidence of that curious penchant. The feasts that were held in her home when she was rich and famous never ended without all the guests, stripped of their garments, coupling in front of one another by the light of lamps carefully filled with oil by the slaves.

It is most likely that it was in the company of the philosopher Ammonius that she acquired the habit from which, she claimed, she was subsequently to derive such a great source of pleasure.

Ammonius was ugly and powerfully built. He lived in a wretched house in an outlying district of Corinth. He was no longer a young man when he was loved by Hermanossa, but he was not old. He lived with other cynic philosophers and prostitutes of the lowest class.

They must, it seems, have led a joyous life. Wine and nourishment were abundant by virtue of the money that the women brought to that sort of community. Often, too, a rich citizen or a fortunate hetaera would invite them to spend the evening in their home, in order to provide entertainment and hold forth, and would send them away laden with jugs of wine, pullets and vegetables. They criticized amour when it provoked jealousy and exclusive desire, reproved modesty, and passed their women on to one another. They also rejoiced in the pleasures that the latter could obtain between them, but always before their eyes. They mingled with all these material enjoyments and excesses of physical amour the highest speculations regarding the origins of life, the immortality of the soul and its indefinite course through successive existences

Hermanossa's parents went to find Ammonius and to beg him to deflect their daughter from the amour that she had inspired in her. Doubtless they would have given him money. Ammonius came to their house and, which apparent honesty, described to the young woman the evils that awaited her in his company. A fragment of that dialogue has survived, reported by Aristophanes of Byzantium:

"Our way of life, Hermanossa, is different from that of other men, because philosophy is our principal attraction. We go to sit down at night on the bank of the river Hexamilia, and when the heat is extreme, those who are silent have to listen naked to those who speak, for the beauty of the body gives lightness to eloquence. What will you say, Hermanossa, when Hierocles, who always emerges unsatisfied from a brothel in the port of Lecheum and joins us at dawn, throws himself upon you and bites your belly and your breasts, perhaps without injuring you but forcefully enough to make you moan? What will you say, Hermanossa, when Philemon the Theban, who is enormous and hairy and to whom the gods have given the prodigious power of always being in a state of desire, torments you with a caress that only hunger or the need to sleep can interrupt, and who can even fall asleep without quitting you? What will you say, Hermanossa, to being like one of those lyres that all the musicians take in their hands at public festivals and cause to resonate in turn?"

Doubtless the cynic Ammonius was being hypocritically sincere, and only evoking images capable of tempting the young woman rather than deterring her. Perhaps Hermanossa's parents were extremely severe in her regard and any other existence seemed preferable to her to the one that she was leading. Perhaps she was at that troubled moment of adolescence when physical desire renders one capable of all excesses and all bodily abandonments. What is certain is that she quit her family and went to live with the cynic philosopher Ammonius. She could not have had a more complete education as a courtesan at the beginning of her life.

After some while, Ammonius trimmed his beard and hair and became an object of scorn among his companions because of the elegance he affected. He grew thin and old.

We have, unfortunately, no details of Hermanossa's nights on the bank of the Hexamilia, and in the little houses on the road to Cenchreae, among the cynic philosophers and their free companions. She retained a favorable memory of it, for she saw her old friends afterwards with pleasure and sometimes found an unoccupied night to spend in the arms of a cynic. But she was too beautiful to remain among them.

Ambition doubtless comes to her. She becomes celebrated in Corinth. She has composed a series of epigrams to Andronicus that everyone quotes. Now she lives with the rich sculptor Apollodorus.

He has been banished from Athens for his violence; he has been nicknamed "the madman." It is his genius that enables him not to lose his liberty. His friend, the sculptor Silenion, who has made his portrait, has represented him with the bulging eyes and contorted mouth of a furious madman.

He sculpts the naked form of Hermanossa untiringly, but as soon as he has finished it, he hurls himself upon his statue and breaks it into a thousand pieces. It is a miracle that the model is not broken too. He drags her by the hair and whips her. Once, it is necessary for physicians to come.

Hermanossa says in a poem, with regard to that part of her life, "that there is no greater voluptuousness than fearing death at the moment when one is loved."

An epigram by Andronicus informs us that, although Apollodorus was violent by nature, that violence could only increase during the nights he spent with Hermanossa.

"Why, then, Hermanossa, if you desire the amour of the two Athenian dancers Theon and Lysimachus, do you not go to find them secretly at Cenchreae, where they have the same room and the same bed? Why must your lover contemplate them in your arms, and what is the love of delirium, and perhaps death, that drives you to give yourself to him immediately after them?"

It was, no doubt, during one of the scenes to which Andronicus' epigram makes allusion that Apollodorus struck a young man on the head with a stool, who remained an idiot in consequence. He was obliged to leave Corinth. He did not leave a bust or a statue of Hermanossa. He even attempted to destroy his house with a hammer.

But for that departure, Hermanossa would probably have been killed by him, and yet, that curious woman wrote on his subject:

"Only a great artist knows how to see. It is said that he was violent, and perhaps it is true. He destroyed what he had created. I could not reach an understanding with him because, when we walked by the sea shore, he always wanted to walk rapidly and I adore walking slowly."

Those little things played a large role in Hermanossa's life—and, in fact, they play a large role in all human amours. She broke with the physician Antiphanes because the latter only ate a single dish, always the same at every meal, claiming that one can live for two hundred years on that diet, because the variety of dishes is the cause of all maladies. When he died, still young, a short while thereafter, she displayed an extraordinary joy, and let it burst forth—which proves the extent to which an unimportant dispute had impassioned her.

She did not want a Prytanis, very rich and very influential by virtue of his position, to be brought to her because she had seen him in the Agora and, according to her, he laced his cothurnes badly.

She broke with young Lycias, whom she called her beardless goat, because, like the sculptor Apollodorus, he walked too quickly while out for a stroll, and she also broke with a young man whose name has not reached us because he had a habit of leaving a few drops of wine at the bottom of a bowl from which he had drunk.

She dismissed a faithful maidservant because she woke her up too early, and for a few days, she had a caprice for an old man devoid of attractions and riches because he was almost bald but knew how to comb the little hair that he had very well.

Hermanossa's other liaisons are unknown to us. We know nothing more about her except the dread she had of growing fat that gripped her at the age of twenty-five, of which she was to die, and her love for the young philosopher Pausanius.

The man whom Socrates calls the magician and Sappho calls the weaver of chimeras, the man, who, according to the poetess of Lesbos is both bitter and sweet, the man who gives her dolor and amour, strikes the courtesan Hermanossa and gives her an incurable wound.

It is the moment when her orgies are celebrated in Corinth and throughout Greece. She has brought young men from Macedonia who know new fashions of sensuality. An old woman from Persia sings songs during her banquets whose magical rhythm is aphrodisiac and which cause people to fall into a kind of amorous trance. Powders have been brought to her from India that trouble the mind when one respires them, and perfumes that multiply the spasms during intercourse.

It is also the moment when she devotes herself with the greatest ardor to poetry and is most occupied with problems of philosophy.

The sudden disappearance of one of her companions in debauchery, who must have been one of her lovers, the Alexandrian adventurer Naucrates, and the connection made between that disappearance and a grave in her garden under the turpentine trees, caused her to be accused of murder, but the Prytaneis, although severe judges, did not trouble her, or, if they did trouble her, exonerated her easily.

How did she come by that amour for the young philosopher Pausanias. What we find in Hermanossa's writings explains it to us.

The young man has spent a single night in her arms, and has remained cold, according to her. That is an offense to her beauty and her science as a courtesan; but that offense she has immediately forgiven him. By virtue of that fatal morning when at young man has quit her roof without pleasure, when that young man draws away under the porphyry colonnades, when he goes down he marble steps, at the very instant when the insult is so recent, when the bed is so cold and so orderly, he could come back if he wanted to, he would find Hermanossa docile to caresses and even more amorous. But no, he draws away forever.

Either because he does not want to risk a further defeat for his pride, or because, in truth, the most beautiful daughter of Greece does not inspire any desire in him and he prefers to speculate about the immortality of the soul, he will never return.

Hermanossa will search all explanations in vain. To please him, she will change the color of her hair and will acquire the dye made from Scythian wood of which one makes use to redden the tresses. An ancient tradition, that Pliny will report later, said that Phaon was loved by Sappho because he had been able to find the male root of the eryngo plant, what had the magical power of inspiring passion. She offered gold lavishly to anyone who could recover traces of that eryngo plant, and doubtless went to find the old naturalist Phorcos, whom she had known with the physician Antiphanes, and he must have explained to her that the eryngo plant was only a vulgar aphrodisiac, infinitely less powerful than natural desire.

She had Pausanias offered, by turns, little girls, little boys and, in despair of the cause, money.

After long reflection she convinced herself that there were two possible reasons for Pausanias' disdain.

The first was that she had grown fat and that he liked thin women. The second was that the spiritualist in question, imbued with Pythagorean ideas and turned toward the divine, feared the physical closeness of a woman, the pleasure that he might obtain from her, as a force contrary to his designs, susceptible of recalling him to the matter that he wanted to escape.

She resolved, therefore, to get thinner, and then to write for Pausanias the treatise in which practical means for orientating toward the divine the sensuality of physical amour.

It appears that at that moment of her life, her fatness was only the fear of getting fat, and that her body could claim, on the contrary, the perfection of proportions. No matter! She chewed herbs that were given to her by an old woman from Thessaly. She had herself woken up at two-hourly intervals during the night in order to run around the garden twelve times.

A slave who served as a model to sculptors, and was molded by them in plaster, told her that she had noticed a certain thinning effect in consequence of that practice, so she had herself molded too, but that was during an excessive heatwave; the plaster dried prematurely and they had a great deal of difficulty breaking it without tearing off her skin. She had a pomade fabricated containing the hidden principles of the plaster and remained naked in the sunlight for hours in order that the effect should be more active.

She rallied to her theory a physician from Macedonia who claimed that people ate by virtue of an ancient habit acquired when human beings were savage, but that it was sufficient to drink water in order to live. She followed that regime, and died of it in a very short time.

She had not yet concluded her treatise, the fragments of which she sent to Pausanias as she wrote them. Only a small part of the treatise was recovered, which we reproduce here. What remains is sufficient to enable us to see that the Corinthian courtesan, who mingled folly and sagacity, the love of pleasure and that of philosophy, touched upon the most elevated and most anguishing problem of amour.

Is there a sublime component in the mystery that makes bodies want to join together in pairs? When we let ourselves yield without measure to our sexual desire, are we like animals? In that case, is the enjoyment in question analogous to the pleasure of eating and drinking? And if we develop that enjoyment, is it at the expense of our spirit? Are we retrogressing in the spiritual scale, of which we have climbed a few steps so painfully?

The courtesan Hermanossa resolves that problem. There is an enlightenment in sensuality. It can be a road to perfection, and a road as sure as the effort and impulsion of the soul to reach the gods.

All those who, by virtue of their culture or their religion, cannot help imagining the pleasure of the senses in amour without a taint of sin, will reflect on that conclusion and perhaps draw therefrom, for the quotidian practice of life, a liberating instruction.

And if people say that in writing her treatise, the amorous Hermanossa was less occupied with philosophical verity than the desire to possess Pausanias, if they think that she had already spent one night with him without a useful kiss or a fecund caress, and that, in consequence, she must have loved him at least as much for his mind as for his body, that nevertheless remains the most perfect form of amour.

Fragments of the Treatise on the practical means
of orientating the sensuality of physical amour
toward the divine

In the same way that Corinth has two ports, one that opens on the Gulf of Saronica, to the east, and whose waters are slightly bluer, and the port of Cenchreae, which seems to have ashes in its waves because it is orientated toward Phocis, from which mists come, so I have two souls, the one that is turned toward the light of the sun, and the one that contains ashes because it is avid for terrestrial pleasures.

...The little shadow that the sculpted wood of my bed makes on the violet mosaics frightens you as much as the darkness of Hades. You fear caresses as one fears a contrary wind on one's route because it slows progress. You claim that the spirit alone ought to be taken into consideration and that the pleasure we draw from our body prevents it from developing and growing. Perhaps, Pausanias, you simply lack experience. When all the wine has been drunk and one no longer sees anything of it but traces on torn chlamydes, when there is no sound in the garden but that of turpentine trees brushed by the bodies of lovers, when one has on one's shoulders and breasts the imprint of fingers that have caressed them, when one's loins are aching from embraces and one gazes over the sea at the first light of the rising sun, then, from the lassitude of debauchery a kind of paralleled lucidity emerges, a surge of the spirit, a comprehension and an amour greater the highest wisdom that comes from study and the most profound philosophy has ever provided.

...All that you have said on this subject is not vain. Pleasure is a horse that it is necessary to tame, because it might carry you away in the Thracian forest, where the trees are so densely packed that there is no longer an issue. But if one masters it and guides it, it can carry you lightly along the luminous road that has no end.

Everyone has his truth, which he must find, and there is a method for every man. The mariner of the port who smells the sweat and is unaware of the perfume, who drinks wine and goes to the brothel to sate himself with women with sagging breasts, is not accessible to what I shall tell you. There is also a truth for him, but I do not know it. I knew it once, and I have doubtless forgotten it because truths annihilate one another as one attains them.

Not everything that you have said on this subject is vain. There are spasms that prevent you from thinking. There are spasms that bring you back in a sensible fashion toward humanity, to the point that one desires get down on all fours, to bark and gulp like a dog. There are fatigues that engender disgust. Disgust in unproductive. It is not transformable. It is necessary to vanquish it. But it is the desire that it is necessary to manage cleverly. One does not know when one first draws upon it. The first men must have been very surprised when they learned that one could obtain subtle fire from gross pieces of wood.

Plato says: "Perfection is acquired by the possession of a lover in accord with one's soul." Even more than happiness, we ought to seek perfection. We must find, in order to attain it, the lover in accord with our soul. There is no veritable amour but that which is simultaneously physical and spiritual, since we are both a body and a soul. Insensate is the man who wants to make one dominate in amour at the expense of the other.

You wanted me, Pausanias, to take off everything but my bracelets in order that I should be naked, as entirely naked as a rose in the sunlight, as naked as a pebble polished by the sea, and you lay down beside me. I put the palms of my hands behind the nape of your neck and designed my breasts on your breast. All that my body experienced then collaborated in stimulating the heat of my mind, but I sensed in you neither the grossness of desire nor the fury of the satisfaction whose effects you feared. A spark would perhaps have been sufficient then to ignite a purer fire than all those that have ever burned in the sanctuary of your soul.

The ideal is a vague expression that, in common human understanding, signifies perfect happiness. In a more elevated sense, the ideal signifies happiness with something more, with an adjunction of thought. The ideal has a third meaning for those who strive toward knowledge. It is direct communication with the gods. It is by means of ecstasy that one communicates with the gods, and one can arrive at that divine state by various paths. One of those paths is the physical sensuality of lovers.

"My son," said Theophrastus of Tarentum, "there are two kinds of initiation. There is the initiation that teaches you the secret of men and the initiation that teaches you the secret of the gods. But the one that teaches you the secret of men is far more divine than the one that teaches you the secret of the gods." The disciple of Pythagoras meant that, since we are human, it is necessary to scorn nothing that is human, but, on the contrary, to know it and make use of it.

Between the moment when the stars appear and that in which they go away, everyone has the possibility of arriving at the most divine state that a human can know. It is necessary for that to be next to a being that one loves, that one has the assent of the other's thought, in default of their amour, and that one can freely enjoy the body of the other in all the modes appropriate to it. I say "in default of their amour" because reciprocal amour favors ecstasy greatly, but is not absolutely necessary. I say that it is appropriate that the enjoyment of the body be absolute because the body cannot communicate the flame if a single caress is reserved or forbidden to it. All caresses have the same purity, since they represent the gift of the body and they concur in the voluptuous state from which the divine is born.

This touches the most secret information of the doctrine of Pythagoras. One can obtain ecstasy with any being who does not resist, who gives themselves. But ecstasy is easier to obtain, and goes further into the unknowable and is more splendid. if it is obtained mutually. It is more splendid still if it is created by two beings who love one another. It attains an even higher degree if the two beings who love one another have already known one another and loved one another in previous existences. The difficulty of those beings finding one another again is certainly great, and that is the central problem of our lives. There are several means for that, which I shall indicate subsequently.

It is curious that we carry in our sexual conformation a sign that permits us to recognize, in the moment of pleasure, that the lover from whom we are obtaining enjoyment has already been in our arms, in a different form, in a past life. We also have within us a hidden sense, a personal intuition that we can develop, and which informs us of the presence around us of those beloved brethren. With them, ecstasy is obtained all the more easily because it has probably been attained already, under other skies, in other times, by another physical form.

Plato says that perfect lovers are two halves, the active principle and the passive principle, that have formed a unique whole, originally separated, and that those two halves aspire to combine again and find their true nature, which is to be one. If that theory corresponds to the truth, there would only be one being on earth with whom we could realize divine ecstasy. When I think of what I have experienced next to you, Pausanias, I am tempted to believe it.

But on reflection, I prefer the teaching of Theophrastus of Tarentum and my master Andreas, and think that with a superior will, and by realizing a few conditions, one can attain it with anyone. It is true that our life is always dominated by a single lover whom we pursue, at first without knowing them, with an irresistible fury, when we have approached them once.

31

But I believe that that one is only a more fraternal brother, the companion most frequently rediscovered in the course of anterior existences, the one with whom we are most closely linked by the indissoluble bonds of pleasure and dolor.

Rays of sunlight are not favorable to ecstasy—to that of which I want to speak, of course, for there are others, such as those of the Syrian Barkis, the contemplator. It is necessary to wait for the end of dusk, and it is in the recumbent position that one obtains the best. There is, it appears, far beyond Persia, a community of men and women who claim that one can only procure it on a bed made of the leaves of a tree named Ban. Doubtless that tree, unknown in Greece, favors ecstasy, and is even indispensable to those Asiatics, but here, it is sufficient that, softly extended, we can give our body the most comfortable position.

When the moon is only a thin crescent, ecstasy is scarcely possible. When it is full, one finds such an aid in its light that it seems that one is on a gilded slope, and only has to let oneself slide down it.

It is necessary to be naked.

It is necessary even to have taken off one's jewelry, for the contact of metal objects on the skin, especially the contact of gold, is contrary to ecstasy.

There are perfumes that intoxicate, but all are not equally favorable. Incense caries the spirit but reflects the body. If it is burned it is also necessary to burn musk or the essence of wild mint. And reciprocally, the aphrodisiac of the body ought to be accompanied by that of the mind. A liquid is made with the juice of the poppy, which some drink and others burn in order to breathe in the smoke. It is the only substance that stimulates the body and mind at the same time and orientates them toward ecstasy. But there is a mystery in the dose to employ, for a small quantity elevates, a greater one debases, and an even greater one enables you to communicate mysteriously with the ecstasies of other men, which are written in the air.

Men and women coming together to eat have more pleasure by the fact of their number and the joy that circulates around them. If they give themselves to love near others their sensuality is augmented. Similarly, if they have come together for ecstasy, they will obtain it more easily and it will be greater

Two women obtain ecstasy through sensuality as easily as a man and a woman. It is the same for two men, for the amour of bodies and minds has nothing to do with the law by which beings reproduce, and a caress is no less beautiful because it is infecund, and is perhaps as productive in an invisible domain.

It you want ecstasy, Pausanias, take in your arms the woman you desire, extend yourself upon her in such a fashion that your breast crushes her breasts, that your knees lean on her knees and that your mouths are mingled to the point that your teeth touch, and above all make your left hand squeeze the nape of her neck lightly where the hair begins. But at the same time as you squeeze her neck, make a subtle effort of thought and imagine with the greatest possible clarity the double image, living, active and rhythmic, of your two beings, which are fused, which are melting into one alone, until that image, instead of being double, is unique.

And when, in your thought, the image of your body and the one whose skin you are penetrating, and from which you are drawing a delicious enjoyment, is no longer any but the image of a single being, especially if you can make that vision coincide with the amorous spasm, then you will have attained the divine ecstasy of amour, you will touch the unknowable, you will have joined not only the soul of the woman stuck to you, but the Unique, that of which you are a fragment: the divine.

And all that I am telling you about these things only consists of allusions to hidden knowledge that the signs of writing will never be able to reproduce. This knowledge is related to the four elements, to the movements of the stars, to the unity. It is transmitted orally by the mouths of those who know. The items concerning amour were given to me by the philosopher Andreas, who came from Egypt and returned there. They come from the teachings of Damo, daughter of Pythagoras, who obtained them from her father, in whom the gods placed all wisdom.

Priscilla of Alexandria

When Priscilla was fifteen years old her breasts flourished, her skin acquired color and men became troubled in her presence, as if they had respired a dust of sensuality that escaped from her. Many people were astonished by that, because she was a Christian and had chastity for an ideal, and it seemed that it ought to be a logic of nature only to give the voluptuous beauty of the body to those susceptible of making use of it.

Desire prowled around her, in the onyx halls, in the paved atrium, and in the garden of sycamore and dates that descended toward the sea. Her brother Marcus—a degenerate with long ears, ridiculously deployed—strove to get into her bedroom when she was undressing there. A certain Peter, a sort of dirty Hercules, who was both a servant and secretary to Bishop Cyril,[1] had once attempted to tip her over, but she had been able to escape. The only caress she had known thus far was that of a young boy who had come to play with her brother and other children like her. Slowly, he had run his hands over her body and he had kissed her lips for scarcely a second.

---

[1] Cyril of Alexandria was the Patriarch of the city from 412 to his death in 444. He remains notorious as one of the instigators of Christian mobs, led by the so-called Parabalani, including the one that murdered the philosopher Hypatia in 415, and for his fierce opposition to the followers of Nestorius, the Patriarch of Constantinople, whom he condemned as heretics. According to the early fifth-century *Historia Ecclestiastica* of Socrates of Constantinople, the mob that murdered Hypatia was led by a lector named Peter, about whom nothing else is known; the license permitted by that ignorance for the inventions of the present text is employed much more prodigally in the novel version.

Priscilla remembered a perfume of honey and acacia and the light charm of his fingers on her breasts. But the young boy was the son of Phrasilas, a notorious pagan, and she had not seen him again. In any case, she already knew that sin takes the perfume of a kiss and the form of a caress in order to soil the soul more easily.

Priscilla was the granddaughter of the Diodorus who had perished so wretchedly twenty years before in the course of a popular riot. He had been reproached, one day when he was supervising the construction of a church, for having had several children who were playing nearby seized by his slaves and having amused himself by cutting their hair, claiming that long hair was a certain indication of paganism. When people in Alexandria learned of the death of the Christian emperor Constantine[2] the idolaters rose up and massacred the most unpopular of their persecutors. Diodorus' house had been invaded and he had been seized, not to kill him but to render him the same treatment to which he had subjected the sons of pagans. Unfortunately, the man who tried to cut his hair had no scissors. Then again, it is difficult to subject an old man who is almost bald to such an operation. He had removed all the skin from the cranium with his knife while the crowd shouted joyfully. Diodorus had died of it. He could not be counted in the ranks of martyrs because the debauched life he had led was too well-known in Alexandria.

Priscilla had often heard the story of her grandfather's death, and the horrible image of it was engraved in her mind. But times had changed. Bishop Cyril was the master of Alexandria. He imposed all his decisions on a weak and timorous prefect. He spoke seriously about the destruction of temples. He did not hesitate to spread money in profusion among the dregs of the people, who were now Christian, in order to incite them to demonstrations against the pagan cults, and even to murders.

---

[2] This reference is anachronistic, Constantine II having died in 361, while this part of the story is set in 415.

Priscilla's father, Diodorus, had been nicknamed Cyril's golden arm. He was stupid, but it was his immense fortune that paid for the Bishop's intrigues. He represented the Christian aristocracy, made of the purity of the blood and the antiquity of convictions. So, when the time came to make the glory of God shine forth over Alexandria, Bishop Cyril asked of his friend Diodorus that his two children should be at the head of the just and pious men to whom a holy mission had devolved.

The "just and pious men" were emigrants from all points of the Mediterranean, the rabble of the port, whom Christendom enrolled for a little money. They were mingled with fanaticized honorable inhabitants, and monks from numerous convents that surrounded the city, who did not blush to have tatterdemalions and thieves for companions because, they said, what is important is not the quality of the instrument but the sanctity of the result.

The rendezvous had taken place at the Gate of the Sun. There, while waiting for one another, many had drunk copiously at the sleazy taverns that bordered the avenue sloping toward the city. Peter knew the approximate hour of the morning at which it was necessary to set forth in order to arrive at the right moment. When spirits were heated, the air was filled with the singing of canticles mingled with vociferations and obscenities, and they were beginning to stop passing chariots in order to make the conductors kiss the cross, Peter gave the signal to depart and the cortege started walking toward Hypatia's house.

Hypatia's celebrity was then very great. She taught mathematics and philosophy. In Rome, Athens and Byzantium there was no young man inclined toward matters of thought who had not come to hear her. She combined, the Greek philosopher Damascius said, the beauty of the visage with the luminous clarity of speech. She was the torch of neoplatonism, the hope of all those who saw with alarm in that stormy century the Christian shadow extending a little further every day over the ancient wisdom of philosophy.

Even more than her influence, Cyril could not forgive her for a personal insult that her disciples had inflicted on him. A few days before, his chariot had arrived outside Hypatia's house at the moment when numerous young men and women who had come to hear her were companying her and acclaiming her. Having recognized him, they had shouted: "Down with the Bishop!" and he had been forced to retrace his steps.

"I shall also make her turn back," Bishop Cyril had said, that evening.

Events occur less by virtue of the human will than a curious concurrence of circumstances that seems to have prepared them. When the procession that Peter was leading arrived at Hypatia's house, perhaps nothing would have happened if Hypatia, at that precise moment, had not just closed her door and mounted her chariot, which was waiting to take her to the Library.[3] She straightened up and gazed at that howling crowd that blocked the street.

Perhaps nothing would have happened if the driver had whipped his horse and set the chariot in motion. The Christians would probably have stood aside and contented themselves with insulting Hypatia. But the driver was a very young man. Either because he had read the gravity of the situation in the fury of the gazes or because he was gripped by an inexplicable panic terror, he dropped the reins, leapt down from the seat and fled.

Hypatia was standing in the motionless chariot. The Christians had surrounded her but, impressed by her calmness, they formed a circle around her. Even Peter recoiled. Nothing might have happened if a Greek idiot, whose name has not survived, had not been in the front rank of the crowd. He was laughing and shouting without comprehension, divided between joy and rage. He advanced and delivered a blow of his staff to Hypatia's head with all his might. It appears that he hit

---

[3] Another anachronism; as the longer version makes clear, the library of the Serapeum had already been destroyed when Hypatia came to Alexandria.

her on the jaw, which explains why she did not pronounce a syllable until the moment of her death.

She tottered and fell on to the front of her chariot. Immediately, no longer retained by the magnetism of her courage, the Christians rushed forward. Peter seized her by her legs and dragged her on to the pavement of the street.

"Take her to church!" said a voice. "Let her ask God's pardon for her sins!"

Peter and another man seized her and dragged her along the street. The Church of Caesarea was nearby. They arrived there. Hypathia was thrown brutally on to the stones of the threshold. Her head collided with a step with a dull sound. Her hair came undone. She recovered consciousness and got up, her jaw hanging down.

"Let her ask for pardon!" someone cried.

Peter, striking her in the small of the back, put her on her knees.

But then, suddenly, in a second, an obscene fury was unleashed. The Christians rushed upon Hypatia and tore off her clothes. Fifty hands groped her body. A monk with an ascetic face threw himself on the assailants and howled: "Beware of the demon!"

They might have treated him roughly, but, standing on the steps of the church, he said: "It's necessary to stone her." And he added, travestying the thought of Christ: "Let someone who has never sinned cast the first stone!"

Then someone pushed Priscilla forward, and put a stone in her hand. "This is Diodorus' daughter. She's a child. She's never sinned."

Priscilla, overwhelmed by horror, was a few paces away from Hypatia, naked and soiled. She distinguished the imprints of fingers on her shoulders and breasts. A little trickle of blood departed from the temple and ran all the way down to the lips. Behind her, through the door of the church, which stood ajar, the face of a priest appeared, animated by innocent curiosity. It seemed that a great silence fell around her and she had a great deal of trouble detaching her thoughts from the ridiculous shadow that the sun made of her brother's wide-spread ears.

Had she ever sinned? Yes, if she had taken pleasure under the sycamores of the garden in the kiss of a childish mouth scented with honey and acacia. It was necessary for her to say so and recuse herself. She was about to do so. But someone pushed her.

"Well! Priscilla, in the name of Christ!"

She raised her arm, devoid of strength, with difficulty, and threw the stone, which hit Hypatia in the neck.

The martyr's eyes opened wide and fixed themselves on Priscilla. They were large, bright, cold, intelligent eyes that expressed astonishment and the desire to comprehend that had always animated them. A single flash, and that light vanished. Stones rained down from all sides, and the spirit of the neoplatonist at least owed to the fury of the Christians that it escaped without an excess of suffering into the region of which she had weighed the shadows and measured the mystery while alive.

Priscilla fled. The Christians had a long debate around Hypatia's body. A few wanted to carry away her body in order to burn it in the fields. Others, armed with knives, strove to butcher it, saying that it was appropriate, by way of an example, to parade the pieces triumphantly through the city. The former had difficulty winning the argument. Thy transported what remained of Hypatia, the trunk and the head, to a place called Cinaron, and delivered it to the flames.

The prefect only made a simulacrum of investigations in order to punish the guilty parties. Peter disappeared shortly thereafter in order to avoid reprisals. A cobbler near the Diocletian column flattered himself until he died for having conserved one of Hypatia's desiccated hands, which he had cut off with his work-knife.

Because of her fortune, Priscilla was the most sought-after young woman in Alexandria. She refused all suitors, in spite of the exhortations of her father and those of Bishop Cyril, who dreamed of giving her in marriage to an adventurer named Antagoras, whose zeal he wanted to reward. She had not forgotten Quintus Moschus, her brother's friend, and the unique kiss of pleasure that had touched her lips. But those who had remained faithful to the ancient gods of the Empire and the Christians were now too profoundly separated by religious hatred. She no longer had any opportunity to encounter him.

She only saw him again once.

She was coming back from Pharos on the heptastadion at dusk, followed by two negro slaves. In a violet cloak hastened by an emerald clasp, his hair parted at the front, the young Moschus was sitting on a stone bench facing the sea. He was sitting beside a young man of his own age, singularly beautiful and pale. His left arm was negligently placed on the other's shoulder, and his entire face had the animation that intellectual conversation gives

She was tempted to go to him. But at the sight of her they turned away and they were talking in low voices. She heard Moschus say to this companion: "That's Priscilla, who took part in the stoning of Hypatia."

An expression of disgust was in the eyes of the two young men.

Priscilla continued walking along the heptastadion, but from that moment on it was as if a door opening to a beautiful domain was forever closed for her.

At that moment of her life she had the dream that was to decide her destiny.

She was walking along a road on either side of which were cripples, lepers and people covered in lesions and ulcers. In the distance, a woman wearing a luminous robe was making signs to her. She tried to reach her, but as she advanced along the road the cripples threw away their crutches, the lepers lost their scabs and the bearers of ulcers were healed. She, on the contrary, sensed her muscles shriveling and all the wounds that had disappeared as she passed came, like birds, to settle on her.

She thought on awakening that the woman who had beckoned to her in her dream was the Virgin Mary and that it was necessary, in order to reach her, to assume, to the extent that she could, the sins of humankind.

Her life changed. She no longer thought of anything but prayer. She cut off her hair by way of penance. She wanted to go into a convent and wrote asking an abbess she knew to come and intervene with her father in order that he would permit her to withdraw from the world.

Old Diodorus loved his daughter too much to hear anything of the sort. He even asked Bishop Cyril to indicate to his daughter, with all his authority, that there were several possible paths to her salvation and that the one permitting her to accomplish family duties was as certain as that of retreat and the convent.

The path that Priscilla chose thereafter was new, and unexpected by everyone.

A sort of prophet named Sosymus came to Alexandria and was very fashionable for a while. His enemies claimed that he came from a Greek monastery, from which he had been expelled because of his unnatural mores, and that he belonged to one of the richest families in Athens. He spoke in the evening at crossroads, and people of the best society came to listen to him, as they might have listened to an actor. He was clad in rags. He never devoted any care to his beard or his hair. He expressed himself with a kind of savage fury. He preached the necessity and love of suffering. Prayer, good works and religiosity, were futile. The essential thing was to suffer, in the flesh and in the soul equally, to suffer every day and as much as possible.

One evening, Priscilla went to hear Sosymus, who was speaking in the quarter known as Rhacotis, where the sailors' hovels were. He was standing on a trestle of planks set up against a brick wall. Around him, the houses of the poor and the noxious streets formed a kind of perspective of misery. A man holding a torch lifted it up, so that his face could be seen, and the gesture he made in parting his rags to show a wound in his chest. His conviction radiated from him like a palpable atmosphere, and many of those who were listening were penetrated by the desire for immediate suffering.

There were men who tore out their beard, others who cut themselves with their knives. One woman fell to the ground in convulsions, begging the people surrounding her to pierce her hands and feet with nails.

It was before the prophet Sosymus, in the tremulous torchlight, among the prostrated wretches avid to add further to their misery, that Priscilla found the directive idea of her life.

What could be the greatest cause of suffering for her? At the moment of her adolescence, Pricilla had not felt awakening within her the physical desire for amour. "She's as cold as the tomb," her brother Marcus said of her. The sexual appeal of men, which she sensed round her, inspired an invincible disgust in her. There could not be any image more frightful for her than representing herself in the process of submitting to the lust of a man. And that image was so cruel and so redoubtable that, by virtue of a sort of obsession, it returned to her eyes incessantly. She could not get rid of it.

She saw herself delivered to the most abject individuals, like the martyrs whose stories had cradled her infancy. She imagined he violation of her body with a great acuity of vision and the presentation of the most trivial details. She indulged herself above all in imagining it accomplished by the men who inspired in her the most vivid disgust or the greatest terror. She saw herself in the arms of her brother Marcus because the sin of their incestuous union appeared to her to surpass in its horror all the others. She indulged herself by imagining the monstrous body of Peter, and sensing his murderous hands squeezing her delicate neck or her perfumed armpits.

She woke up at night, bathed with sweat, not because she had dreamed during her sleep but because she was gnawed by the irresistible desire to dream while awake. She then imagined, forcefully, what her torture would be. She clenched her teeth in order not to sense noxious kisses on her mouth. She moaned and begged. And sometimes in the morning, there were the stigmata of embraces on her wrists and thighs.

For a long time she had thought that those images were inspired by the demon and she had begged God's pardon for them. But after she had heard the prophet Sosymus she discovered that the Lord was showing her by means of those obsessions the path that she had to follow, and she was singularly comforted by that.

At that point in her life an event occurred that was to hasten her resolution further.

She was coming back one evening along the quay that led from the port of Eunostos, which was deserted at that hour. A beggar, who had been sitting amid the debris of ropes and boats and whom she had not perceived, ran toward her to ask for alms.

She was afraid. And, as he stood before her with a bizarre grunt, she called out to the two slaves who were two steps behind her. Believing that their mistress was being attacked, they struck the beggar with their staffs, and he collapsed.

When Priscilla leaned over him she saw that his jaw was broken and his skull split. He stammered, and died within a few minutes. She recognized the idiot who had been the first to strike Hypatia in the jaw with his staff as she was standing in her chariot.

She felt remorse at having caused the death of that wretch. She wept for him bitterly. The emptiness of her futile life appeared to her more forcefully. And it was shortly thereafter that she quit Alexandria.

No one knows how she did it, how she was able to escape the authority of her father and that of Bishop Cyril, and why the investigations made to find her were fruitless.

What is certain is that the daughter of Diodorus, who was then in the full splendor of her beauty at the age of eighteen, knocked one evening on the door of a certain Spartacus, a renowned brothel-keeper in the Cynegion quarter of Byzantium. He kept a brothel for soldiers and the lower classes under the fortifications, in a place once constructed for food shops, which had been disaffected and abandoned to prostitution.

Spartacus was a good Christian and a good citizen. He paid heavy taxes, for the best part of the Empire's revenues then came from innumerable brothels. He was also a lover of tradition, and, in accordance with an old Roman custom, a copper plate swung over his door, on which was painted: *Hic habitat felicitas*.[4]

Certainly, when he saw the svelte body of Priscilla standing before his threshold at that crepuscular hour, when he looked at the clear oval of her face, her large bistred eyes and the heavy brown tresses overflowing the hood of her cloak, he thought he was in the presence of one of the angels he had admired in the Church of the Holy Purity, the cupola of which extended its shadow over the paved street as the sun set.

He bought slaves, sometimes very dearly, in the markets of the Golden Horn. But not all of them were equally apt for prostitution. There were some who fled without having redeemed their purchase price, others who were sick and others who died in brawls. He often thought that his métier was very hard. Now, Priscilla immediately gave him a thousand drachms. He was dazzled and in, exchange, immediately installed her in the most comfortable of his rooms. He also offered to dispense with the custom by which every prostitute gives herself, once, on arrival, to the keeper of the brothel, but she refused, and it was him who took her virginity.

Priscilla was inscribed in the register of women under the name of Fabrilla, because there had been a Fabrilla some time before who was much in demand among spatharii and the gladiators of the circus. A placard bearing that name was placed over the door of her room. She turned it round herself when a man came in. In addition to her youth and beauty, the

---

[4] "Here resides happiness": an inscription made famous after being found on a phallus on the wall of a bakery during the excavation of Pompeii.

confusion with the original Fabrilla ensured that as soon as night fell until a very late hour, she got scarcely any rest.

Her room's only furniture was a wooden stool, a little earthenware trough, a stone bed on which there was a straw mattress, and an extraordinarily soiled carpet. By day she wore the yellow robe of prostitutes and a square bonnet of the Assyrian form that was customary among women. In the evening she took her place in the common room where people drank. She never showed any preference. She threw herself on the bed and endured all caresses. Doubtless she ended up learning them. Nothing, from what is known about her seems to indicate, during this period of her life, the excess of suffering that she expected, which was to lead her to God.

Did she think that she would succeed by another route? Did she discover an unknown beauty in Spartacus' narrow cell with its low ceiling, the obscene inscriptions of the wall and the vermin that inhabited her mattress? Did she hear, in the drunken voices of street-porters and sailors, in the insults of men who played dice for her body and disputed the possession of it, knife in hand, a music as sweet as that which ought to charm the ears of the elect? Or rather, by virtue of one of those mysterious transformations of which nature has the secret, did the alarm of obscenities and the lacerations of her body a hundred times violated become for her attractions, her dolor changing into pleasure?

She became coquettish, she took an interest in the life of the brothel, she comported herself there not like a martyr but like a woman. She formed a close friendship with a daughter of Egypt named Seso, young and quite pretty, who occupied the room next to hers, and whom many men acquired the habit of possessing at the same time as her because of the intimacy that linked them.

It was forbidden for prostitutes to have images in their rooms of any religion whatsoever. Those who infringed that prohibition could be whipped and a heavy fine imposed on the brothel-keeper, but in fact, the presence of gods above beds of pleasure was tolerated; it was sufficient that a little curtain should hide them from sight.

Priscilla had placed on her wall, behind a piece of black silk bought for that purpose, a little wooden cross. Perhaps, during hours of conversation in the afternoon, she was subject to the influence of the pagan Seso. Perhaps it was the deceived hope of martyrdom, the observation that human joy was replacing divine joy, that caused such a profound revolution in her soul. What is certain is that when a judge visited Priscilla's room after the crime she committed, he found behind the little black curtain not a cross, but a statuette representing the goddess Isis.

And the crime was this.

A new collector of taxes, followed by two soldiers who made his demands respected by force, penetrated one evening in the common room of Spartacus' house. He demanded the register in which the names of the women were inscribed, with their ages and the date of their entry to the house, in accordance with which the sum to be paid for the chrysargirus tax would be determined. Then the collector, who had already drunk a great deal in other places, drank more. He perceived Priscilla and declared that he would make a better calculation if he were allowed to enjoy that girl right away.

Priscilla, who had her back turned, felt her shoulder seized by a strong hand. She looked around and, openmouthed with amazement, she recognized Peter. It was him, even more monstrous than before, the man who had caused the death of Hypatia.

She often thought of him with horror, as often as she remembered the scene forever engraved in her memory of the chariot, the threshold of the church and the stone thrown by the little girl without sin; and that memory came back every day. Spartacus had no need to give her an order. Everyone knew what was due to a tax collector. She got up meekly and preceded him upstairs, helping him to climb up, because he was unsteady on his feet.

Did Peter recognize her? Undoubtedly, because, before she was able to decide anything in her mind, without waiting for her to turn the placard on the door round, he had hurled himself upon her, thrown her down on the bed and possessed her by force. Then she ceased struggling and became hypocritically complaisant, for the thought of punishment had just appeared in her mind. And what she wanted to punish was not the possession of her body, soiled so many times over; it was the old crime, the great crime.

She therefore caressed the individual that she hated, she took off all his clothes, and she did it so effectively that, at length, he fell asleep.

She had a weapon in her room, a large knife forgotten by a man passing through. She only dealt him a single blow, which caused him to die immediately. She regretted not having made him suffer, but it was necessary that he did not utter a single cry, for she wanted to have the chance, albeit slim, of escaping. The blow was so violent, in the throat, that the head was almost entirely severed. As the blood flowed abundantly and might have passed through the crack under the door, she had the presence of mind to staunch it with one of her garments.

When they had no more water for ablutions, the women sometimes went down with their pitcher to go and fetch it from the fountain in the street. She did so noisily and ostentatiously, and went back upstairs with her full pitcher. It was only then that she watched out for the opportunity to get out without being seen by anyone. She succeeded, and lost herself in the immensity of Byzantium. She was not found, in spite of active searches. Perhaps she hid in the home of a street-porter who came every week and paid Spartacus dear in order to spend all night with her.

She had jewelry and money, but above all the love of life that she had acquired, and which gave her ingenuity and courage. It was doubtless her love of life that ensured that no more mention was ever heard in Byzantium of the prostitute Fabrilla, who cut the throat of the tax collector of her quarter one night for no reason, after having given herself to him for a long time.

Priscilla surfaces again in Corinth, a city that Christianity had not yet submerged. Those who remained attached to the old gods were more numerous there than elsewhere, and they had conserved their temples there.

She is rich, she represents herself overtly as a courtesan, and the elite society of Corinth aspire to the honor of being invited to her house She has as a titular lover the poet Caius Aurelius, then at the apogee of his glory, and she sometimes deceives him with other young men, if accomplishing an action with the assent of the person who is being deceived, and sometimes in his presence, can be called deception.

She is no longer a Christian. She goes every day to the altar of a temple raised to Minerva, she places her forehead on the stone and she asks the goddess to grant her intelligence. Is it really of the goddess that she is requesting it? Priscilla is well versed in philosophy. She says that she is a neoplatonist, she has read Porphyry and Plotinus, and it is doubtless toward the great universal thought, the pure logos of ideas, that she raises her spirit. She strives to penetrate the more abstract writings of Hypatia: the commentaries on the astronomical canon of Ptolemy and that on the conic sections of Apollonius of Perga.

She has acquired everything related to Hypatia's works and to her. She talks about her with admiration. But among those who know her, no one dares ask whether she knew or saw her when she was a child in Alexandria, for then her face is veiled by a sadness that is only dissipated with difficulty.

But the poet Caius Aurelius was found dead in his bed one morning beside a drunken adolescent. Priscilla scarcely regretted him. A short time afterwards she learned of the death of her father Diodorus and she decided to return to Alexandria to collect his vast fortune.

She found her brother there, whose intelligence seemed to her to have diminished further and ears to grown longer, and who had complete confidence in devotion. He welcomed her joyfully, in spite of what he might have been told about her life, because he still desired her.

Did she give herself to him? It is not certain, but if she did, it was rarely. It seems likely, however, that it is only by means of the pleasure of the senses that she could have gained an empire as absolute as the one she had over her brother. She gradually dismissed all the servants and only took into her service idolatrous negroes. She expelled the priests and monks who came incessantly to extort sums of money and she replaced the images of Christ and the Virgin with a statue of Hypatia.

She always had a whip in her bedroom beside her bed, for her brother made the same attempts at night as he had when he was a child, but did not allow himself to be sent away as meekly, either because of his age or because she now granted him, albeit at rare intervals, a few favors. He showed the traces of the whip on his body and his face without any shame, and even laughed and them, saying with a certain pride that it was his sister who had struck him. In spite of his lack of intelligence, with the authority that the name of Diodorus gave him, he permitted Pricilla to establish herself in Alexandria without scandal. A few years later he had a fall from a horse that nearly killed him instantly. When someone came to pick him up he spoke his sister's name, and died immediately.

Once only, Priscilla wanted to see Hypatia's house again. Alone, she went down the narrow street that she had descended as a child in the midst of the Christians' ferocious cries. A tree had grown above the wall of the narrow garden since then and its foliage extended over the street; and Priscilla remarked that it was a laurel. Behind it there were turpentine trees and maples, which exhaled a breath of spring.

She knocked on the door. In the marble vestibule, ornamented by mosaics, she found herself in the presence of a woman with gray hair and a visage desiccated by solitude. It was Hypatia's sister, who was welcoming to the admirers who sometimes came to visit the martyr's house.

There was a courtyard behind it, with colonnades of porphyry and a fountain from which no jet of water rose up.

"Here," she said, "are the bronze busts of the philosophers that she loved. This is the courtyard where she strolled, the basin in which she watched the goldfish and the jet of water. Now I no longer maintain either the goldfish or the water jet. What would be the point?"

And she told Priscilla the story of her sister's death, which she doubtless must have done a thousand times. She had just gone out and was standing on her chariot...

Oh, Priscilla knew all that!

But when, at one point in her story, she said: "Someone demanded that someone who had never sinned should throw the first stone; there was a little girl of fifteen there named Priscilla...," Priscilla interrupted her, thanked her, and left.

And it was from that day on that she thought incessantly about Bishop Cyril, who was the first cause of the crime in which she had participated, and who still lived, unpunished and glorious.

Patriarch of Alexandria, vanquisher of the heresy of Nestorius, whom he had had condemned at the Council of Ephesus, Cyril had just expelled forty thousand Jews by violence and stripped of their property, to the scorn of all justice and all humanity. He was growing old in an increasing perfume of sanctity, the renown of which flew all the way to the boundaries of the two Empires.

From one of her negro slaves Priscilla heard mention of a sorceress who lived in the Rhacotis quarter. There the dregs of the port swarmed, prostitutes and thieves, all that the villages of the Nile and the African deserts had cast up as debris in the great city. Guided by her slave and clad in a poor costume, she ventured into the labyrinth of the back streets of Rhacotis one night.

The slave held on to her with one hand and agitated a stout stick in the other, and yet she heard many propositions, and hands palpated her breasts and legs. They reached a red-painted door that gave access to a triangular chamber. There was an old woman with a pale face, braided white hair and a fat belly. She was cutting up a slice of pressed dates that made a paste in a wooden spoon. There was a straw mattress beside her and heaps of rubbish. Nothing was suggestive of magic except, perhaps, a few pieces of wood painted black and crudely representing a vague human form.

When Priscilla had explained what she wanted and the sum of money was fixed, she said: "I'm a sorceress of Bubastis, but my tradition doesn't come from Phoenicia or Thessaly like that of the other witches of the city. So it isn't Eshmun to whom I pray to summon the power hidden round us that is death. I know secrets that come from the South, from places where all the men are born black, like the sacred races that preceded us. There the Nile appears, less broad than the palms of my hands, and there are mountains so high that the stars touch the stones there. There lives a negro king wiser and more knowledgeable than the Solomon that Arab magicians invoke. I have no need of philters, charms or incantations; the rhythm of the seven syllables and the harmony of the seven movements are sufficient for me. Nevertheless, to strike a living man as you desire it's necessary that you bring me an object that has touched his body directly, and that you come back to see me seven times."

Priscilla saw a great difficulty there. She never saw Cyril. It was only out of regard for her father that he had done nothing against her.

She remembered, however, that once, when she was a child, he had given her a little golden cross that he had worn on his chest, a venerable champion of the faith. But where was that cross? Twenty years had passed. She turned the house upside down and finally found it in the little ebony casket where she had once placed it herself. It was a flat cross, with the sign of the crucified Christ, similarly flat, sculpted on it.

She ran to the sorceress that evening. A smile lit up the latter's toothless face. With a long nail she traversed the metal cross; then she took a piece of black wood in human form and, after hesitating for a second, nailed the golden cross on to the

52

simulacrum of the head. Having put that in the middle of the room she asked Priscilla to "concentrate her life" on the piece of wood.

Priscilla did not know what that meant but, at hazard, she fixed her thought on the object, imagining Cyril dead, for the sorceress repeated to her: "See! See!"

Then the old woman, in spite of her paunch, started dancing, or rather, miming attitudes, sometimes slowly, sometimes rapidly. While doing that she uttered guttural and rhythmic cries that did not appear to have any meaning.

That took a long time, which seemed interminable to Priscilla. In the end, droplets of sweat were running down the witch's face and her body was trembling. She fell to the ground. She made a sign to Priscilla to come back the next day.

Patiently, for seven days in succession, Priscilla returned to the witch's house and the same rites were accomplished; the seven syllables were chanted with the same interminable dance around the wooden simulacrum whose forehead bore the nailed cross.

On the seventh day, the weary Priscilla had ceased to believe; she regretted the time wasted and the comedy played.

When the sorceress fell, she said to her: "It's done. Now, he's dead. There are thirty-nine ways to make a man perish without touching him, but this one is the surest. Go. You have no need to come back to tell me that I've succeeded, for I have the proof of his death."

It was not until the next morning that Priscilla learned that the Patriarch of Alexandria had died the previous evening, at the same hour when she had been in the home of the sorceress of Bubastis.

After the evening meal he had wanted to accompany the Bishop of Ephesus, who was his guest. He was on the threshold of his palace when he had suddenly fainted. The Bishop of Ephesus had tried to catch him but had not been able to prevent him from falling heavily on his nose, which was slightly crushed. He was transported to his bed, but he was already dead. The physicians attributed his unexpected death to the abruptness of his fall. There was a little red swelling at the back of the head, almost at the nape.

With the death of Bishop Cyril it seemed to Priscilla that a sort of hidden goal of her existence had been attained. She was happier. She was scarcely forty years old. She was still beautiful. She had desires but she was not in love. It was claimed that she went to Rhacotis by night in order to prostitute herself to slaves in hovels.

It is known from her letters that she had the curiosity of seeing again the Quintus Moschus whose kiss perfumed with honey and acacia had troubled her childhood. She sought him out and invited him to come to see her.

There are men, she wrote, *who have grown old before their time for lack of taking care of themselves. He had a beard and rotten teeth. I kissed him on the lips because of the memory I had of his old kiss. Instead of the breath of spring of which I had thought so often, there was a taste of decomposition, and the odor that one senses near cadavers on hot days.*

One day, feeling ill, Priscilla had herself carried in a litter to a villa she had on the edge of the sea. Children who were sitting by the roadside uttered cries as she went by. She raised herself up slightly and looked at them. Either in play or because they were Christians and had recognized her, they threw stones in her direction. One stone, thrown by a little girl, struck her on the temple.

Pricilla uttered a cry of joy and fell back. When she arrived at her villa, with blood on her cheek, it was as if her face were illuminated. She did not want the wound to be bandaged. Her fever increased and she became delirious during the night. But she had calmed down in the morning. She had herself carried to the sea shore, under a clump of centenarian pines whose needles rained down on her scattered hair. She asked for tablets and wrote before dying the words that she wanted engraved on her tombstone:

I thank you, O goddess, for having permitted me to be punished in this life for the bad actions I have accomplished therein. Thus, in my next existence, good or bad, I shall arrive virgin of sin and will not bear any burden of the past on my shoulders. And in that way, I shall be among the true elect, those who, having been able to throw far away the black stone of chagrin and the red stone of evil, are susceptible of perfection.

Jeanne the Lascivious

This is the story of the daughter of a ferryman, almost exactly as it is told in an old chronicle of Provence.

Jeanne the lascivious lived with her father and her two brothers in a miserable hut on the bank of the Rhône, in a place where there had once been a bridge but whether there was now nothing but a broad, flat boat to take travelers over. When she was very small she wrapped the rope round the post when the boat reached the shore; when she was fourteen she helped her brothers strike the water with an oar, or push against the river-bed with the gaff.

As far as her memory could recall, she had had a flame in the body that drove her to lie down beside men and to have pleasure with them. In the evening she escaped, ran along the river bank and made signs to boatmen descending the river to come and find her among the reeds and the vegetation. Then she gave herself to them all in turn, and her joy was all the greater the more numerous they were.

The hut of beaten earth in which the ferrymen lived was closed by a wooden door, and only had one room, like the huts of the very poor. There they put the provisions that travelers gave them in exchange for the passage; there, they armed themselves; there, they got drunk when they had wine; there they slept, one on top of another. And Jeanne the lascivious was, according to the hazard of the night, the wife of her father or her brothers.

When she approached her twentieth year, she complained of sharp pains in the groin. An old woman from a nearby village, who was renowned for her knowledge of plants, prepared her a cataplasm, which did not cure her. But with time, her malady attenuated, and her face acquired a singular beauty that it had not had before. Her eyes became more profound, her complexion paler, and her hair grew with an unusual abundance.

The men who passed from one bank to the other admired her, and sometimes wanted to take her with them. If they pleased her, she spoke to them in a whisper and arranged to meet them in the evening and satisfy the desire they had for her. But she did not want to quit her profession, her father and her brothers, and above all the river, which she loved because of its color, its immensity and its movement.

The river had waves that varied according to the light, sparkling pebbles, and fish that swam and were alive; it was similar to her in a way, she found in the flow of the water and its lapping of the bank the regularity of her own desire.

Now, it happened that, almost simultaneously, the bodies of Jeanne's father and brothers were covered with red blotches, moist at first, which then became pustules and abscesses. Their eyes became round and protruded from their orbits; their ears shriveled and their cheeks swelled; pieces of their lips came away; their voices became hoarse and they were no longer able to articulate words because of lesions in their throat. After some time they died, and Jeanne buried them herself in the sand not far from the river.

She was alone henceforth in plying the oars. She acquired a great strength in her arms thereby, and her body became more beautiful in becoming more powerful. In spite of the harshness of her métier, she did not want to quit the boat because she thought that she would not find a variety of men elsewhere as great as the one that the river crossing procured her. She communicated her disease to hundreds of creatures who carried it away, destined to transmit it to thousands of others.

One of them once made a long journey to avenge himself on her. For several days she saw him on the opposite bank, where she dared not land, waving a sword and threatening her. His left hand was a frightful stump and his head had become so enormous that one could not receive the human features beneath the pale blisters. She showed him to a group of soldiers, telling them that he was the son of a demon and a woman, and that he was persecuting her because she had refused him, and the soldiers killed him.

The years passed, and by a singular jest of nature, it was not until Jeanne the lascivious had gown old that the disease she had within her manifested itself externally. Her hair and eyebrows fell out, crusts covered her skin, and her tongue became deformed to the point of preventing her from closing her mouth.

She became an object of horror for men and she suffered from their privation. She could only have them by the favor of darkness, or by refusing to let them cross over unless they yielded to her. People spoke of her far and wide as an example of debauchery punished by the Lord. Gradually, no man any longer came who had not been warned, who kept her at bay with a weapon and threw her the fee for the crossing from a distance. While the boat cleaved the water, until it was knotted to the post on the bank, even they saw the face of the terrible oarswoman smiling at them in an engaging manner, and staring at them with bloated eyes.

The desire that Jeanne had within her was not attenuated by time. By night, she set a plank beside her, which she hugged in her arms; at dawn she ran over the stones and among the cork-oaks uttering guttural cries that were amorous appeals. She exposed herself naked, lying on the ground, as if a ray of sunlight might have been able to possess her.

People threw stones at her from a distance. The boatmen descending the Rhône avoided her boat with disgust A priest had cursed her, but she did not expect anything from the future life.

One evening, when the sun had almost set, she thought she heard the voices of her father and her brothers calling to her; she thought she saw them shaking their heads, ruined like hers and making signs to her with their fingers, which lacked phalanges.

Then she shivered, thinking about the chill of the damp sand in which it would be necessary to repose.

The Rhône had flooded; the wind and the water were splashing not far from Jeanne's hut.

Someone knocked at the door, and she was very frightened, because she did not know how Death presented herself. She went to open it, however, and she saw on the threshold a young and handsome man with a radiant face. He did not recoil in horror at the sight of her. He did not draw his sword to threaten her. He smiled at her sympathetically and asked her to take him to the other bank, in the same tender voice that men had had when she was twenty years old.

She rejoiced in her soul at the flooding of the river, which was about to prolong the short journey, and the remains of the twilight, which would permit her to contemplate the contours of youth.

She only looked at the traveler timidly; she did not draw nearer to him, for old age and ill treatment had worn away her audacity.

She made him a sign to sit on the bench facing her, and rowed with all her strength; but when she was in the middle of the river she stopped, and she thought that after the great wealth that she had possessed and lost, after one last joy, she would do well to let herself fall into the river.

Then it happened. The man took her his arms passionately, kissed her frightful mouth, caressed her ulcerated breasts and laid her down on the planks of the boat.

The boat drifted away. Jeanne the lascivious did not get up again to take the oars. She savored the man's embrace endlessly. And the river-dwelling fishermen who were taking their evening meal were astonished to see a flat boat passing by, which seemed to be empty, but which was pitching, rising up and down on the waves, not because of the waves but by virtue of an interior shaking which, for all eternity, was to sway with the regular and powerful rhythm of amour.

Lorenza the Venetian
nicknamed the Immodest

Khair Eddin Barbarossa,[5] who was to become Sultan of Algiers, had the custom of saying, when talking to Lorenza the Venetian, nicknamed the Lewd: "What I commenced by seeing of your body wasn't the face, and that's what I've loved the most."

These are the sanguinary circumstances in which it was given to him to see immediately what women are accustomed only to show after a few difficulties, and in any case, when one already knows their features.

Dragut the corsair,[6] taken prisoner by the Venetians, had spent six years in the galleys. Ransomed at the end of that time by his brothers in arms, the two Barbarossas, Aroudj and Khair Eddin, he had returned to the isle of Djerba, which was the center of Muslim piracy, and had equipped three brigan-

---

[5] Khizir Khayr ad-Din (c1466-1546), nicknamed Barbarossa [Redbeard], was a great mariner of the Ottoman Empire, the younger brother of another famous mariner Arudj Reis, also known by association as Arudj Barbarossa. The latter was proclaimed Bey of Algiers in 1516 by pirates, and pledged allegiance to the Ottoman Empire, for which he and his brother—who replaced him as Bey after his death in 1518—fought in a long war against Spain, then ruled by the Holy Roman Emperor Charles V. Lorenza is fictitious.

[6] Turgut Reis, also known as Dragut (1485-1565), followed a career path very similar to that of Barbarossa, progressing from pirate to Ottoman admiral, and similar serving a term as Bey of Algiers. He did spend four years as a Spanish galley slave in the early 1540s, but the present story is set in a much earlier period of the two men's careers and the allegation here is anachronistic.

tines. He was drunk on vengeance and had declared that he required as many Christian lives as the thrusts of the oar that he had given.

His first prize was an Italian galiot that was going from Naples to Cadiz. It was navigating under an unlucky star. There was only a semblance of resistance, for the captain, a certain Felipe de Menarga had been seized, on leaving the port of Naples, by such a violent colic that it was thought he was about to die of it. He did not die of the colic but of a torch that had been paraded over his body in order to make him tell his captors, so as to avoid a long search, where he had hidden the gold and silver that the galiot was transporting.

All the men were hanged. The women, twenty in number, were to be shared out among the corsairs. They had been grouped on the deck at the moment of the capture. During the hanging of the men it happened that a pistol shot departing from the group of women was fired in the direction of Dragut. The pistol had been dropped immediately, and in the confusion that reigned, it was impossible to determine which of the women had fired it.

A few of them declared that it was Lorenza. She was the youngest among them. She did not appear to be eighteen years old. She had at that time an extraordinary ingenuousness in her dark eyes. With her milky pink skin, her golden-red hair and her aristocratic hands she had a beauty that would have struck any man whom vengeance had not blinded entirely.

She was trembling with anger and not with terror, and that might have encouraged the belief that she was the author of the pistol-shot, an insensate action that guaranteed her a certain death. She kept quiet, and her extreme youth made Dragut doubt.

He reflected. He declared that all the women belonged to him because of that pistol shot and that he would avenge himself on them on arrival at Djerba for his six years in the galleys. They were all Italians with the exception of five young nuns, who were Spanish.

At Djerba, not far from the shore, there was a tree that had seen many hangings. Under that tree, Dragut stripped all the women naked. The pirates opened their dresses with their knives, and sometimes the blade cut their breasts. They were suspended from the branches by the feet, with their legs apart, and Dragut tried to cut them in two with a single stroke of his sword. By the time he reached the twelfth, his sword was chipped and he asked for another.

While one being brought to him Khair Eddin arrived. The twelfth woman was Lorenza. Her arms were hanging down and her long hair was trailing on the ground. As Dragut got ready, with a mechanical or desperate gesture, she took her hair and threw it in such a way that it fell over the part of her body where Dragut was about to strike. The latter started cursing, but Khair Eddin intervened, cut the cords that bound Lorenza and deposited her on the ground. He asked Dragut to grant her mercy. The latter shrugged his shoulders, dropped his weapon and signaled to his men to untie the survivors.

"I won't kill her," he said, "but I want her to remember me."

That evening he had her come to his bedroom, and he kept her with him all right.

It was that night that she had to forgive him, no less than the fear of death and her suspension by the feet. She was, however, in the course of her adventurous life, to know many others as painful. She explained her rancor later by declaring that there is no greater dolor in the world, when one is a woman, than to be treated, in spite of herself, like a young boy.

It was to the pleasures of that night that Dragut owed a visit, after his bath in the palace of the Sultan of Algiers, whom he was visiting, from a barber whose razor was poisoned. A presentiment made him take the razor, with which he cut the barber's hand slightly. The hand swelled up immediately, went violet, and the barber fell in convulsions and died without saying on whose behalf he had brought death. It was also to the pleasures of that night that he owed, as he was returning through the Bab-el-Oued gate, a shot from an arquebus that wounded him in the heel, like Achilles. He thought that it was better to have himself cared for on his ship rather than in the palace of his friend Khair Eddin, and he never went back to Algiers again.

Khair Eddin could have asked Dragut to give him Lorenza as a slave after having saved her, but he did nothing of the sort. Certainly, he had found her beautiful, but she had not impressed him unusually—at least, he thought so. He drank with his companion Dragut while the latter waited for Lorenza and chatted with him about the stupidity of women in general and the slavery in which they ought to be maintained. He wished him a great deal of pleasure when Lorenza appeared, and quit him, laughing.

It was only some time afterwards that he perceived that the gaze and beauty of Lorenza were floating in the ocean of his soul. The image of her marvelous body, which he had seen entirely naked, and the expression on her face after he had preserved her from death, began to haunt him. That was the moment when he and his brother were commencing, by virtue of their audacity and their victories, to become masters of the seas. Khair Eddin returned to Djerba and asked about the Italian slave that belonged to Dragut.

He learned that Dragut had departed without giving precise orders regarding the women that he had spared. Lorenza had lived with the Spanish nuns and their conduct had scandalized the virtuous Turk Azim, who cultivated a part of the island and nourished livestock for the usage of the pirates. A little later, after a quarrel, Lorenza had almost killed a nun. She had been locked up and, Dragut having returned, he had sold her to a slave-merchant who had gone to Tunis.

Khair Eddin is not discouraged, and goes to find the Sultan of Tunis, Muley Mohammed, with whom he maintained the most amicable relations. Not long before, he had obtained the right of refuge in all his ports for all the vessels flying his flag, and after a victory over the fleet of Charles V he had made an almost triumphant entry into Tunis.

Muley Mohammed promises to search for the slave Lorenza. She is not found. Khair Eddin's desire is exasperated. He returns to Tunis several times. Finally, it is learned that she was in the harem of the rich Aboulferes, one of the most important individuals in Tunis, because he serves as the Sultan's banker. Khair Eddin offers to ransom Lorenza. Aboulferes refuses and replies, laughing, that he values her all the more because she has tried to flee his palace several times.

The Sultan intervenes. In order to set aside the ransom proposal Aboulferes fixes the fabulous figure of twenty thousand gold coins for the ransom. Khair Eddin immediately accepts that figure and Aboulferes cannot go back on it. Lorenza is taken away on the flagship of the most celebrated mariner in the Mediterranean.

The adventures of Lorenza had not commenced at the moment when she embarked on the galiot going from Naples to Cadiz. She was only eighteen years old then but she had been married twice and was already animated by the desire that was to be the absurd goal of her existence.

Captain Alonso de Contreras[7] records in his memoirs that when he was in Palermo with his company he was noticed by the widow of an oidor who was young, beautiful and rich. Contreras was, according to the portrait he made of himself, "a youthful soldier, extremely handsome and gallant." He excelled in naval warfare. In Malta he was known as "the friend of the Maina promontory" because, after quarreling with the local inhabitants over a cartload of wheat, he rendered himself justice by attracting their leader on to his frigate, having him given a hundred lashes and dousing him with salt and vinegar, in spite of his quality as a Christian, all the more respectable

---

[7] Alonso de Contreras (1582-1681) was a Spanish adventurer who was by turns a privateer, naval captain and soldier; he became famous after his death because of the historical importance of his oft-reprinted autobiography, whose two manuscripts date from 1628 and 1645.

because he later became a monk. On the Tripolitan coast he was known as "the cutter of noses and ears" because, after exchange of gunfire with the Moors of the coast, he took twenty of them prisoner, cut off their noses and ears, and threw the fresh pieces to their companions on the shore. But he lacked a knowledge of the heart of women and it seems that, in order to please them, he was too respectful and too tender.

Lorenza provoked him with sidelong glances; he wrote to her, knew her and married her.

"The respect that I had for my wife," he wrote, "was such that sometimes, outside the house, I did not want to cover my head before her, so much did I hold her in esteem."

It was that exaggerated respect that was doubtless fatal to the handsome captain. Fatality, for him, was to take the form of two men, his friend Juan Cabrera, to whom he would have entrusted his very soul, and his page Rodrigo, who was Spanish and only fourteen years old.

One day, when Captain de Contreras was absent, the page knocks on the door of Lorenza's bedroom.

"Come in," says the latter, who has already cast her eyes upon the page and who has recognized his voice. He goes in. She is naked on her bed. He tries to withdraw. She calls him back. She makes him sit down beside her, and strokes his hair, promising him a golden ducat—but the page is still timid. He is troubled, he stammers, he leaves the room.

Lorenza conceives a resentment against him. In addition, she needs to distract herself. She becomes Juan Cabrera's mistress; he is an accomplished man, full of experience, with whom things are not dragged out. But the pretty face, youth and naivety of the page are still in her thoughts. She wants to make him jealous and is foolish enough to take great liberties with her lover in front of little Rodrigo, one day when they are both sitting on a bench in the garden of her house.

The page Rodrigo must doubtless have made confidences to comrades on the subject of the visit he made to his mistress in her bedroom, and told them how he was received by her, naked soon her bed. He must have been called an imbecile and given advice. He does not know how to take it. One evening, when his mistress goes past him on the staircase, he pinches her unexpectedly, in a vulgar manner. Surprised, she gives him a formidable slap, which makes him fall down the stairs. He wants to avenge himself.

"Is it the custom here in Palermo," he goes to say to his master, Lorenza's husband, "for men to help women adjust their garter? It isn't in Spain."

"Why are you asking me that question?" says Alonso de Contreras.

"Because the other day, in the garden, Lord Juan Cabrera had his hand on Madame Lorenza's garter."

"It is, indeed, the custom in the vicinity to Palermo," replies the Captain, "but refrain from talking about it."

A few days later, Alfonso de Contreras, having made a semblance of going away, returned unexpectedly and surprised his wife and his friend together in his own bed. The dagger-thrust he delivered to his friend killed him instantly. Doubtless his hand was less firm in striking Lorenza; he touched her near the neck. She fell, almost without uttering a cry, and he believed her dead.

"God has them in his heaven if, in that fatal moment, they repented," Alfonso added, simply, after narrating those facts, without perceiving that he had scarcely left the guilty parties the time to repent.

Lorenza was cured of her wound after a month, and the form of her repentance was manifest by an imperious desire to see the page Rodrigo again. One might think that it was with the aim of vengeance, but no; she did not have the slightest anger against him. She asked what had become of him. He had fled on the day of the drama and had not reappeared.

Her husband had returned to Spain, and, although he had not killed her, he considered her to be dead. She was, therefore, free. She spent a great deal of money picking up Rodrigo's trail. She finally learned that he had returned to Cadiz, his homeland. She did not hesitate to embark for that city, in spite of the dangers of the sea, on the galiot that the corsair Dragut was to capture.

She then commenced an agitated life, of which the page Rodrigo was to be the goal, in spite of the fact that she only knew him by virtue of hair caressed in vain, a slap and a dagger thrust of which she had nearly died.

But in the same way that maladies that are benign if they can follow their course become fatal when they are impeded, there are desires that pass immediately if they are satisfied but which take on a singular force, burst forth and multiply in the soul by virtue of being unsatisfied.

Charles V's army, commanded by Diego de Vero, had just been crushed under the walls of Algiers. The Turks, emerging from the city, had penetrated into their camp, had set fire to it and carried out a great massacre. The Spanish standard, of which a negro had taken possession, had been thrown in front of Barbarossa's horse, which had trampled it underfoot.

Aroudj Barbarossa had taken Algiers with the Arabs of the Sahel; he had strangled Sultan Salem personally and had had himself acclaimed Sultan by his janissaries. Vanquisher of the Spaniards, he thought about consolidating his authority. He appealed to his brother Khair Eddin, who was in Tunis and disposed of five hundred resolute and disciplined Turks, and offered to share power with him. The latter accepted; the entry was solemn, for it was a matter of impressing the Arab and Moorish population.

Khair Eddin matched at the head on a horse covered in a white fur from the Caucasus in spite of the extreme heat. He wore an immense Persian cloak in emerald green silk brocade and a Russian bonnet with a plume attached by an enormous diamond . His son Hasan was to his right. Then came the ulemas and the imams, and then the janissaries, in closely-packed ranks behind their agas. Their breastplates sparkled in the sunlight. They had short coats of garnet cloth on top and leaned on very long canes in imitation of the janissaries of

Constantinople. Behind them, surrounded by a guard of negroes, in a litter curtained in blue silk, Lorenza was carried.
She could not be seen and was not allowed to show herself.
She was veiled like the Muslims, for she had been instructed
in the law of Mohammed. Sometimes, she moved the curtain
aside in order to look at the unfamiliar city and the unknown
people. Although a captive, she felt like a queen, and savored
the intoxication of a triumphal entry.

Now she is in Khair Eddin's palace. Aroudj, the latter's
brother, has just been killed at Tlemcen and his head has been
sent to Spain. Khair Eddin is now the unique Sultan of Algiers. He has a mad passion for Lorenza.

In spite of the difficulties caused by rebel tribes and the
Spanish fleet, which might appear outside the port of Algiers
at any moment, he has constructed around his palace, at great
expense, gardens with flower-bed, fountains and pavilions,
modeled on those found in the palace of Soliman at Constantinople.[8] Like the cadines, or favorite wives, of the latter,
Lorenza will have mutes, eunuchs, twenty peiks clad in golden
cloth to guard her, an ichokadar who will attend to her ward-
robe, a kalib who will write letters, and dwarfs who will carry
them. He buys three hundred precious cashmere shawls for
her. And when he traverses the harem to find her, he wears, in
imitation of Soliman, babouches studded with silver, in order
that the sound they make on the paving stones will warn the
other women to look away and not meet his gaze, all of whose
flame he want to keep for the woman he loves.

She knows the secret that permits her to make his desire
burn incessantly. She has belonged to other men, he knows.
She talks to them about him, either to regret them or to curse
them. She makes him live with memories of lust. She has even
invented some in order to torture him. She makes use of that
for personal vengeances.

---

[8] Suleiman I (1494-1566), commonly known as Suleiman the
Magnificent, ruled the Ottoman Empire from 1520 until his
death, so this reference is slightly anachronistic.

In Tunis, the Jew Aboulferes, in order to humiliate her and to enjoy the spectacle, had her taken by force by one of his negro slaves; she was whipped if she resisted. Khair Eddin sends men to Tunis with the mission to abduct Aboulferes and his wife secretly, to put them on a ship and bring them to him. They come back without having been able to succeed. Khair Eddin then sends his companion, Hassan the Bald, who had a grudge against Aboulferes, putting ten thousand gold ducats at his disposal. Hassan the Bald returns two months later with the two prisoners.

Khair Eddin has them imprisoned and keeps them for several months, treating them reasonably enough. He awaits the return of an Arab chief who has promised him a great ape in a cage. When the ape has arrived, Khair Eddin sends for Aboulferes. He takes him to the animal's cage, into which his beloved wife is introduced before his eyes. She dies in the embrace.

"I am like you, Aboulferes," says Khair Eddin. "I take pleasure through the eyes."

The name and portrait of Alonso de Contreras are sent to all the corsair captains in the Mediterranean with a promise of a thousand ducats if they capture him alive. On the island of Djerba he has Azim killed because he had been to virtuous with regard to Lorenza and had punished her for what he called her bad conduct with the Spanish nuns, and he also has the slave-merchant who sold her in Tunis killed, because he had not been virtuous enough with her.

In spite of such an amour, and perhaps because of the fatigue caused by such an amour in a violent and brutal man, Lorenza only thinks of fleeing. She wants to flee because she is nostalgic for her homeland, the men of her race, and also because she thinks incessantly about the page Rodrigo.

It seems improbable that the Sultana of Algiers, enjoying all the attributes of power, and enjoying them all the more because she has such a great power of enjoyment, has been able to regret a child whose hair she has barely caressed, whom she slapped and whose death she nearly caused, but the root that generates the desire of women is deeply plunged into the soul and the flesh, and its origin is unfathomable. And all of them willingly give their lives a distant objective, which they call their ideal.

There was then in Algiers a very large quantity of Spanish and Italian slaves, whose numbers were increased every day by Khair Eddin's captures at sea. Some lived wretchedly in a vast prison known as the Steambaths; others labored under the rods of bachis on the ramparts and ditches of the city; finally, others more favored, were bought by individuals and were well treated when they fell into the hands of good masters. The Fathers of Mercy came three or four times a year on vessels bearing the Sultan's safeguard and negotiated the ransom of slaves for gold siphoned from bequests and given to them by the families of prisoners.

Lorenza thought that she might escape easily, thanks to them. But they showed mistrust. They had been suspected of facilitating escapes. They feared a trap on the part of a woman who had embraced the Muslim faith. They replied that they would compromise their renown forever by enabling Lorenza to flee, and might be prevented from ransoming other prisoners for a long time.

She nevertheless obtained an assurance from them that they would enquire about Rodrigo in Spain, at Cadiz, and she gave them a letter as well as five hundred gold coins that they were to transmit to him. She explained to him the dignity she had attained, the desire she had to see him and asked him to come to Algiers with the Fathers of Mercy, where she would make his fortune, provided that he consented to embrace the Mohammedan faith.

The Fathers found Rodrigo in the house of his father, who was a cook in Cadiz. They brought back a vague and embarrassed response from the young man. Even with great hopes, one does not venture to the lands of infidels like that, especially when one is summoned by a woman who has nearly caused one's death. He thanked her enormously for the five hundred gold coins and exhorted her to return as soon as she could to Christian soil.

Cruelly chagrined, Lorenza thought about distracting herself while awaiting a favorable opportunity.

She often went to the Batistan, which was the bazaar where slaves were sold. She also watched those who were laboring outside the city. She did her best to ease their condition. She sought confusedly to encounter a known face that would be agreeable to her.

For preference, however, she went to a terrace that overlooked the courtyard of the Steambaths. In that courtyard were the prisoners who belonged to noble or rich families and were awaiting the arrival of their ransom. One day, she noticed a very young man there—for it was always the very young men who impressed her the most. He had reddish blond hair like her own, an effeminate manner and hands that would have been beautiful if they had not ceased to be manicured. He was playing with a cup-and-ball that he had fashioned himself in wood, and Lorenzo saw immediately the advantage she might obtain from that cup-and-ball.

For greater surety, she told Khair Eddin about her desire to play that game, with which she was unfamiliar. He agreed that she could have it explained by the young prisoner, who seemed to excel in it. That did not appear extraordinary. She sent one of her eunuchs to fetch the young man.

Her first concern, when he appeared before her, was to send him to her baths. The prisoners slept heaped together in narrow stone cells that were never cleaned, on rotten straw, and vermin were abundant there. The principal preoccupation of those prisoners who were not working was to destroy that vermin during the day.

She learned that the young man was eighteen years old, that his name was Ruy de Azevedo, that he was the son of an old family from Valencia and that he was waiting for his ransom.

If he taught her to play cup-and-ball, she taught him to play other games, as soon as their first interview, because she

71

did not know than whether she would have the facility of bringing him back. She was able to do to almost every day, but it does not seem that she had conceived a great attachment for the young man, at least on the evidence of what followed.

A Turkish eunuch named Giafar was charged with the administration of the harem. He came to tell Lorenza that the Sultan was beginning to view with a jaundiced eye the excessively frequent presence of a young Spaniard. He no longer dared take it upon himself to introduce him, but as he desired to remain in Lorenza's good graces, he deliberated with her as to the means to employ to enable her to have Ruy beside her. Giafar thought that Khair Eddin would no longer have any objection if, on the one hand, he converted to Islam and if, on the other hand, he submitted to the operation of castration.

Those two conditions, even the second, did not appear to her to be exorbitant—which seems to indicate that she did not have an overly passionate love for the young Spaniard. She took charge of persuading him with regard to the conversion, but they decided that it would be better not to warn him about the matter of the eunuch condition, and that he would be castrated by surprise against his will.

That was what was done. Ruy de Azevedo proclaimed the unity of God and felt the blade of the knife, one evening when he was promising himself a very different caress. His pain was great but he was healed. He became paler and more effeminate. Lorenza swore to him that everything had happened unknown to her, and they strove to console one another by means of incomplete embraces.

Lorenza had not failed to remark that she had a curious resemblance to Ruy de Azevedo. To be sure, their features were different, but there was a similarity in their large dark eyes and the color of their hair. Furthermore, they were almost exactly the same height. Once, to amuse herself, Lorenza put on Ruy's costume, and it was then that the stratagem that would permit her to flee was formulated in her mind.

Ruy's ransom had been long delayed. Lorenza told Giafar to warn her when he ship carrying the Fathers of Mercy entered the port, and above all to inform her as to whether it was bringing the young Spaniard's ransom.

That day finally came. Giafar announced to Lorenza that the ransom had been paid to the functionary charged which receiving it, and that various supplementary fees had also been paid, such as that of the pacha's kaftan, that of the harbormaster, that of the bachis and others. Ruy de Azevedo had no more to do than to board the *Nueva Granada*, which was due to leave the port the next day.

In order for the plan that Lorenza had made to succeed, it was necessary to wait for the last moment. She charged Giafar with warning the Fathers of Mercy and the captain of the *Nueva Granada* who was to transport the ransomed prisoners that Ruy de Azevedo, escorted by one of her mutes, would only arrive at the moment when the vessel hoisted its sails, which was to take place at dawn. Such orders, coming from her and transmitted by Giafar, could only be respected.

The evening before, she instructs her mute Ali to be at the bronze door of the harem that gives access to the gardens shortly before sunrise, and entrusts him with the mission of conducting the Spaniard as far as the *Nueva Granada*. She has prepared a costume similar to the one that Ruy wears and has knotted in a cashmere scarf as many gold coins as she can carry and all her jewels—which represent a fortune—enveloped in silk to that they will not rattle.

How has Ruy, imprisoned in the palace, learned that the Fathers of Mercy had brought his ransom? Doubtless he was secretly corresponding with other prisoners and they have informed him. He comes to see Lorenza, suspecting that she wants to prevent his departure. He begs her, and then threatens her. She cannot use violence, for it is necessary that it is believed until the next day that it is the Spaniard who is going.

She begs him in her turn. She tells him that she loves him, that she cannot do without him. She asks him for a few months more. His ransom is now paid, he has nothing to fear. She swears that she will let him depart with the next convoy of ransomed prisoners.

The insensate consents to that, and in the morning, draped in a Moorish cloak that hides her face, holding in her hand a part of the treasure of Algiers, Lorenza opens the bronze door where the mute Ali is waiting. She reaches the *Nueva Granada* without difficulty, which a favorable wind carries away from the port rapidly.

She is not without anxiety during the crossing. Khair Eddin's vessels will surely be launched in her pursuit. Everything depends on the moment when her flight is discovered. Then too, her companions treat the young Ruy de Azevedo very badly, who is a renegade and is known to have enjoyed the Sultana's favors. Misfortune has embittered the souls of the best and there are men of all sorts among the prisoners. It is necessary for her to watch over her fortune incessantly. By night, the men sleep together, beside one another, on the deck.

A prisoner who has forgotten the taste for women in the Algerian galleys comes to find her at night, taking her for the young man whose costume she wears. She repels him, but not soon enough to prevent his first gestures, which have permitted him to observe that she is a woman. He reveals it the next day. There is no talk of anything but that aboard, and he captain puts her in irons for that deceit.

But finally, the *Nueva Granada* reaches the port of Valencia.

Then Lorenza is forced to deploy all her powers of seduction and all her qualities of deception. Ruy de Azevedo's relatives, people of great nobility, are awaiting the young man impatiently. They are on the quay when the *Nueva Granada* arrives. They learn that Ruy is not there and that a woman has returned in his stead. Explanations are difficult at first, but Lorenza is informed of the actions and deeds of the Azevedo family and a thousand details of all its members by virtue of the conversations she has had with Ruy. It is easy for her to prove that a great intimacy has connected her to him and to give guarantees of Ruy's affection for her.

She also tells them, almost exclusively truthfully, a part of the end of the story. She represents herself as a victim of the Sultan. She has been able to save Ruy from the wretched fate of prisoners. She has done so. She has loved him. But he was dying of a disease when his ransom arrived. He died, she said, on the eve of the day when the Nueva Granada was to quit Algiers, and it was then that the idea came to her to substitute herself for him, an idea that luck has permitted her to realize.

She was, in any case, only mistaken by a matter of days regarding the death of Ruy de Azevedo, for Sultan Khair Eddin, convinced that he had been Lorenza's accomplice, had him impaled after having his hands severed.

Lorenza's stories were plausible, and they were believed. In order to remove doubt, she brought with excessive precision the last will of the young man, imagined by her, as well as words of farewell for his cousin Isabelle, to whom he was betrothed.

Ruy's uncle, the head of the family, old Gomez de Azevedo, was smitten with her, and offered her a palace in Valencia. She did not care about that, for, having consulted a Jewish jeweler as to the value of her jewels, she had learned that her fortune was immense She only took the time to buy dresses, underwear, a carriage and mules, and the time to reconvert with a certain ostentation to the Christian faith; it was known from the prisoners that she had denied her religion and it was necessary not to become suspect to the Inquisition.

She departs as soon as she can for Cadiz, for she is still illuminated by the same obsession. But a sharp disappointment awaits her there. Rodrigo has renounced the estate of page some time ago and that of man of war for which he was destined. He has embraced his father's profession, more placid and safer, and he is a cook—a cook in Genoa, in the house of a great nobleman of that city.

But an unrealized desire has an incalculable power. No matter! Whether he is a page or a cook, it is him she wants. She waits for a ship departing for Genoa and, in spite of the dangers of the sea, and the fear of being recaptured by Khair Eddin, she embarks thereon.

She arrives in Genoa without encumbrance, installs herself in the Swan Hotel with great ostentation, and immediately summons the cook Rodrigo. Because of his functions he can only arrive at a late hour. She waits for him, full of impatience. The hotel servants have been paid to receive him with honor. He finally arrives.

Ten years have gone by since she last saw him. During those ten years, she has been able to consecrate herself to her beauty. She has lived as a Sultana. Power has given nobility to her physiognomy. She is twenty-eight years old and has never been as beautiful.

But things have worked out very differently for him. The desirable little page has become a big man, extraordinarily bloated and fat. He is so broad that it seems to her, at first, that he will be unable to pass through the doorway. His jaundiced face his expanded by a stupid smile. He is holding his cap in his hand and turning it awkwardly. Lorenza has the sensation of an odor of sauce that is spreading through the room. She considers the light and low cut Venetian dress that she has put on, the large four-poster bed that she has bought and had transported in haste to the bedroom in order to embellish it, and the cook who finds himself in her presence in the light of candelabra, and about whom she has been thinking for ten years.

Her first thought is to take a dagger that she has in a chest and to strike him with it, to punish him for having become so ugly and not having warned her about it. But she does not yield to it, and the comical aspect of the situation appears to her. She laughs. She laughs until she weeps.

And when she has laughed a great deal before the stupefied cook, she tells herself that it is in the logic of her character and her life always to go on to the end of things, to attain the goal that she has fixed.

She opens the curtains of the bed brutally and orders the cook to undress and lie down. She speaks as a Sultana and his refusal would certainly cost him his life. He obeys. She lies down beside him and shuts her eyes.

She sends him away in the morning, paid and content.

She will have him beaten some time after, because he has boasted about his adventure. She quits Genoa and goes to install herself in Rome, and then Naples.

She has lovers. She becomes famous because the story of her captivity and her escape has spread. She has been nicknamed the Sultana, and also the Immodest, because she has the custom of receiving her lovers naked—to cut short the preliminaries, she says. She has had Moorish baths constructed in her palace. Her servants are Arab converts to Christianity. The Inquisition watches her because of the perfume of Islam that hovers around her.

Khair Eddin Barbarossa has not forgotten her. Several times he has messages transmitted to her by prisoners that he ends back without ransom for that purpose. He begs her to come back. Sultan Soliman has invested him with the title of Captain Pacha and he is, according to him, the most powerful individual in the Barbary States, with which François I of France has just made an alliance.

But she rejects his propositions with disdain. She finds that one dies too abruptly and too easily out there. The principal reason that keeps her away from Algiers, she says, is that one cannot spend a single night with a young man there without exposing him either to castration or impalement.

She has a liking for young men. She has been obliged to quit Rome because she had seduced and received in her bedroom at the same time the two young nephews of Cardinal Campanella.

In Naples she organized nocturnal feasts where there were only adolescents, and to which she succeeded in making a young woman of great beauty come, who had a reputation for virtue that, naturally, she lost.

It was her love of young men that were to cause, by turns, Lorenza's salvation and doom.

She went to install herself in Fondi, because at that moment Giulia de Gonzague lived there, who was married to Vespasio Colonna, and the renown of whose beauty had caused her umbrage. There, she made the acquaintance of Colonna's young brother, who was only fourteen, and was smitten with him. Giulia and her husband talked about having her expelled from the city. In order to get her revenge she left Fondi one evening, taking the boy with her, and returned to Naples.

In the meantime, Khair Eddin Barbarossa was ravaging the Italian coasts with his ships. He learned that Lorenza was in Fondi. He resolved to recapture her by force. At the same time he would take possession of the celebrated Giulia, of whom he intended to make a gift to Sultan Soliman.

He disembarked secretly by night some distance from Fondi and had the city surrounded by his troops, who were able to advance without being seen under cover of orange and olive groves. It was only when they set up ladders on the ramparts that the alarm was raised. Khair Eddin's janissaries began the pillage of the city, but they searched for Lorenza in vain; she had left that very morning.

Giulia, woken up from her sleep, only had time to leap on to a horse in her night-dress and, conducted by a young squire of her husband's household, was able to flee. The Algerian cavaliers pursued them for a long time. They were able to lose them in the Abruzzi, where they knew the roads.

Giulia's troubles were not over. She camped with the young squire under the trees of a forest, but she was only clad in a light linen chemise, which had been torn during the journey. Either because he had desired her for a long time, because he thought that he merited that recompense or because of the disturbance that combats cause, he was unable to resist the sight of a woman of such great beauty almost naked, the young squire threw himself upon her and raped her.

She had him killed in arrival in Rome and he claimed as he died that she had been "consenting and very willing."

Vespasio Colonna had been able to escape the massacre in Fondi but his palace had burned and his fortune was lost. In Rome, he learned simultaneously about his wife's rape and Lorenza's abduction of his brother. All his enemies were laughing about it loudly. He became furious, and set out with four servants for Naples in order to look for his brother there and take his revenge.

Lorenza's palace was on the road to Vesuvius. He entered it by violence and almost without resistance. A single servant received a sword-thrust. For the second time in her life Lorenza was surprised in the arms of her lover by a man avid for vengeance. They were both naked and there was nothing over their bodies but a large crimson silk sheet, under which they appeared in the light of a torch when the door opened. They must have gone to sleep on one another's shoulder, and in their surprise, they remained in that attitude.

Vespasio ran toward Lorenza calling her a bitch and an infidel, and dealt her a mighty blow with his sword that traversed her heart, after which he seized her by the hair and dragged her cross the floor, while stamping on her. But she was dead. A great flood of blood had sprung forth, entirely inundating the young man, who was still clinging to Lorenza's body and started howling and calling to her by name.

It was necessary for two of Vespasio's servants to tear him away by force and take him to the road. He was tied up, as he was, on a horse, and they departed, for it was in the destiny of that family to ride without garments along the roads. The local inhabitants, woken up, saw with amazement cavaliers passing in a whirlwind, with a naked adolescent in their midst who was screaming incessantly: "Lorenza!"

As she had given great riches to churches when she was alive, Lorenza was buried with great pomp. An artist engraved on her tombstone a Venetian stiletto, a rose and a turban with a Moorish fastening.

Bagawali
with the lotus-blue eyes

Bagawali with the lotus-blue eye was born of a woman of the Carnatic province named Gubrukh and the god Vishnu himself. That sublime parentage is an established fact. Gubrukh made no secret of the circumstances in which she had known that marvelous connection. She did not take any vanity from it, any more than her husband, the vaisya Lakkha. Both were simple and modest. Lakkha was a man of feeble temperament who never went any further than the field that he cultivated with two sudras. Gubrukh was sterile and wanted to have a child. She therefore went to the temple of Tirupati where, by virtue of the sanctity of the Brahmins and the efficacy of their prayers, the god did not disdain to engender.

She had come at the time of the annual festival, in which the statue of Vengatta Souara is paraded through the streets.[9] She had been noticed by the Brahmin Farhad while she was at prayer. He had approached her and had touched her shoulder. What did she want of the god? A child? He would give her the means to have her prayer granted.

At nightfall, in accordance with the Brahmin's indications, she had come to a little square in the depths of the city. There she had found herself before a wall of sparkling whiteness where there was a minuscule ogival door surrounded by floral faiences. That door gave access to the temple gardens.

---

[9] The first reference to this mysterious and probably fictitious festival appears to be a letter of protest written in English by a clergyman in India and printed in the *Catholic Spectator* in 1824, which appears to have been the basis for a more colorful description in French published the following year by Jean Antoine Dubois in *Moeurs, institutions et cérémonies des peuples de l'Inde*, copied in several subsequent texts.

She had gone in, had traversed the garden and penetrated into the temple. As the Brahmin had told her to do, she had taken off her sari and uncovered her legs and belly completely, leaving little bells in her hair, which she agitated at intervals.

Guided by the sound, the god had come, groping in the darkness. Gubrukh had felt him on top of her, and his caress, she said, was exactly similar to that of men, just as brief and perhaps a little more brutal.

Bagawali was born within a year.

Out of gratitude, her mother often took her when she was young to the temple of Tirupati. The Brahmin Farhad saw her, noticed her beauty and appreciated it. He told the simple Gubrukh that a new favor was reserved for her. He recognized in Bagawali a predestined child who ought to be consecrated to the divinity. He had no difficulty in obtaining that she became a priestess of Siva and entered the school of sacred dancers.

According to the story of Bagawali's life that we have via the letters of Dupleix's secretary,[10] she had always had an aversion for the Brahmin Farhad. He raped her on the third day of her entry into the temple, and to succeed in that he had been obliged to lock her up and deprive her of nourishment. It was him who tattooed the image of a lingam on her thigh, as was customary with girls consecrated to Siva, and, she said, he prolonged that operation in such a fashion that she suffered more than the others in undergoing it. He whipped her often and when she refused to give herself to him he threatened to imprison her in a sandalwood pagoda in which the serpents of Vengatta Souara were kept, where, he told her, she would have to endure caresses more penetrating than those of men.

Eventually, he attempted to restore, for her, a practice whose cruelty was so great that the Brahmins of Siva had renounced it long before. In fact, in more ancient times, every young girl who entered the college of Siva had to receive in

---

[10] Joseph-François, Marquis Dupleix (1697-1763), was the Governor General of French India from 1742 to 1754.

her body an emblem of the god in the wood of the Sisu tree, of proportions so enormous that many died after that possession. Would Bagawali with the lotus-blue eyes spare herself that ordeal?

She affirmed that she would.

In September 1746, when the French fleet commanded by La Bourdonnais[11] took possession of Madras, the most celebrated person in the Carnatic province was the dancer Bagawali. The priestesses of Siva were then in India what those of Dionysus and Aphrodite had been in Greece. The pleasure of amour and veneration for the gods were mingled in the honors rendered to them. Simple individuals watched their dances and had them afterwards in the temples. The richest men had them come to their homes. The sum to pay was fixed, and collected by the Brahmins.

Offers for Bagawali arrived from all over southern India. She was obliged to refuse the greater number of them. Some desired her for her beauty, others for the perfection she brought to the art of dancing, others for her knowledge of all caresses and her manner of practicing them. Every new moon, the Nabob of Arcata, a singular man who never showed himself to anyone, sent a cortege of a dozen elephants caparisoned in silver in search of her, whose mahouts, golden robe, were seated under vermilion parasols.

"The renown of such a beauty had wakened my curiosity greatly," recounted the Chevalier Pierre de Landrecy to Monsieur Tilloy, who was Dupleix's secretary. "Not a day went by when I did not go on horseback in the direction of the temple, which had been pointed out to me, in spite of the extreme danger, posed by snakes as much as men. My comrades preferred to savor mediocre pleasures in Madras. I thought that he contemplation of the natural beauties that it had been given to me

---

[11] Bertrand-François Mahé de La Bourdonnais (1699-1753) became head of the French fleet in Indian waters in 1740; he relieved the besieged Dupleix at Pondicherry, but the two quarreled thereafter, fatally for La Bourdonnais.

to see while seeking human beauty was a sufficient satisfaction. I could not help having the certainty that I would encounter Bagawali, and that was an obsession."

Pierre de Landrecy, an officer on the *Phénix* in La Bourdonnais' fleet, was to encounter Bagawali.

He had been riding through the forest for a long time. It was March. There was such an outburst of verdure and flowers, with perfumes so heavy, that it made him dizzy. The hooves of his horse disappeared in the profusion of petals. He arrived in a place where the great trees gave way to spinneys and he found himself among crimson asokas in such great number that nature seemed to have been stained by blood.

As he continued on his way he suddenly perceived a kind of perfectly round pagoda, constructed in red wood, almost the same color as the asokas, with a blue dome. At the sound he made, a woman appeared in the doorway and stood there, motionless. Instinctively, he leapt down from his horse and advanced toward her.

A conversation was engaged. He only spoke French, which she did not understand. In consequence, they only expressed very simple things, by gestures. At hazard, however, he pronounced the name of Bagawali, indicating her. Then Bagawali, for it was her, let an infantile joy burst forth. The idea that her celebrity had even reached the French, the masters of Madras, intoxicated her. She picked up her cymbals and started to dance, to Pierre de Landrecy's great surprise, while he sat down familiarly on the mat of the pagoda.

She danced with her breasts and hips more than with her legs. Sometimes she braced herself and fell backwards, and then spun, bent down and crawled. Sometimes she raised her arms toward the heavens, in a pose of invocation, as if to take invisible powers as her witness. She gradually became excited. A sensual frenzy seemed to take possession of her body. In the end, she fell to the ground and remained there, with a breathlessness that caused her to shake.

Pierre de Landrecy gazed at her in admiration. But he perceived that she raised her head and that there was a hint of surprise in her lotus-blue eyes, which became a hint of disappointment. He did not know that the dance was the one that the bayaderes perform to prepare themselves for amour and that, when they fall down at the end, that is the precise moment when they have brought their bodies, by means of the rhythm, to the highest degree of desire. Their fall is only a fashion of offering themselves to the man for whom they are dancing.

Pierre de Landrecy did not know that, but the solitude, the perfume and the color of the crimson flowers, and the beauty of the woman contributed to informing him of it. In a matter of seconds, he had understood, and he remained in Bagawali's arms until the evening.

He acquired the habit of coming back at the same time every day, and every day he found her again. They made love in the pagoda of red wood, in the sunlight of the clearing, and at dusk, when the crimson asoka flowers rain down more abundantly and have a more powerful perfume. And that lasted until the time when all the flowers had fallen and were strewn so abundantly on the ground that Bagawali did not hear the hoofbeats of her friend's horse on the path when he arrived.

Then, one morning, Pierre de Landrecy was sent by La Bourdonnais to Pondicherry to carry a message to Dupleix, the Governor General of the French establishments in Hindustan. Perhaps La Bourdonnais had been informed of de Landrecy's amours, feared for his life, like his friends, and wanted to force a separation. He left without having been able to warn Bagawali.

For a long time the latter waited in vain on the path that led to Madras. A month had not gone by when she fell into an extreme despair and renounced the hope of seeing her lover again.

Doubtless the other temple dancers, Farhad and the Brahmins had penetrated the mystery of those amours, had been indignant in consequence, and prepared ambushes against the foreigner. To the sound of tambourines, flutes and trumpets, the twelve silver elephants with their gold-clad mahouts had traversed the villages and had returned to Arcata without bringing the nabob the desired dancer. What a loss for the temple revenues! The perpetual languor in which Bagawali lived threatened the Brahmins with poverty.

Doubtless they took advantage of her dolor to force her to make an oath to renounce an ingrate and to participate, as a guarantee of that oath, in the mystery of the goddess Shakti, in the same place where she had given herself to the foreigner. There is no doubt that Bagawali loved Pierre de Landrecy with a great and faithful amour, even though she had not been able to exchange any comprehensible words with him. Great amours are not based on words.

It is only by the intervention of the Brahmins, and by the mystery of the goddess Shakti, that the scene can be explained of which Pierre de Landrecy was the witness when he finally returned at nightfall, on the very day of his return to Madras, to the pagoda where he had made love to Bagawali so often under the asokas the color of coral.

Having tethered his horse to a tree, he walked over the putrescence of vegetation and fallen flowers that the nascent summer decomposes. A slow, plaintive, heart-rending music stopped him. He crouched down among the clumps of asokas and watched anxiously.

In the twilight, in front of the red pagoda, there were a great many men and women, at least thirty, perhaps fifty—he could not count them. Some were sitting, other standing; almost all were naked.

A few had the instruments he had heard, which were unknown to him. There must have been tambourines and flutes, and sometimes strange sounds resounded the like of which he had never heard before. Many of the people he saw were delivering themselves to contortions, punctuated with guttural cries, and took an ocher paste from jars with which they rubbed their bodies. He guessed, on seeing the parts of the bodies that they rubbed for preference and the effects that resulted therefrom, that the paste must be an aphrodisiac. There were others who were drinking something similar from a large bowl that was passed from hand to hand.

A terrible curiosity animated Landrecy. He was seized by vertigo. The asokas seemed to him to be bleeding in a sinister fashion. In his eyes they took on the color of blood, and the entire landscape was a landscape of death.

A circle had formed now and a human form was dancing in the middle of the watchers, themselves agitated by intoxication, quivering in a kind of hysteria. With horror, Landrecy recognized Bagawali. She appeared to be prey to a furious delirium. Next to her, a naked old man with long braided hair, was howling a sort of incantation.

Suddenly, Bagawali lay down on the ground, arms open, in the pose of a woman offering herself. Leaning forward between the bushes, Landrecy saw her trembling with desire. The naked old man extended his hands, appeared to be making a kind of consecration over her belly, and with a cry resembling the wail of a jackal, threw himself upon her. Some of the watchers did likewise. The others embraced one another.

Pierre de Landrecy often expressed regret at not having gone away silently, at not having remounted his horse and come back to Madras with no thought of returning. But he was a man of extreme violence, who did not know how to master his first impulses. It is also necessary to remember that he was strongly attached to Bagawali, that he had acquired the habit of thinking of her as physically his, that he had been traveling for a month while evoking the image of the pleasure that awaited him on his return. It is necessary, finally, to imagine what that young and ardent man might have felt on seeing the woman he desired prey to so many men. It was only later that he was to learn that the scene was the celebration, on the fourteenth day of the month of April, of the orgiastic rite of Shakti, simultaneously obscene and sacred. That knowledge, in any case, would not have diminished his dolor, his rage, or his imprudence.

He stood up, took his pistols from his saddle-holsters and discharged them at the men who were before him. Then, having thrown them away, he drew his sword and rushed forward uttering cries of death. He had lost all consciousness of himself. The sole thought that animated him was to destroy by violence the frightful image that he had before his eyes. He struck at random individuals whose surprise and intoxication rendered them defenseless. Blood flowed. He aimed a great blow in the direction of Bagawali, whose lotus-blue eyes he perceived for a second, exorbitant with terror. He had the sensation that with the cutting edge of his blade he severed an ear and gashed the cheek of the naked old man with the braided hair, who was probably the Brahmin Farhad.

A single furious man could destroy a thousand if they were animated by rut. In a few seconds, the worshipers of the goddess Shakti, with howls of terror, fled in all directions. Pierre de Landrecy, haggard and bloody, returned to reason. He had plunged his sword into the body of a young man agitated by somersaults, so profoundly that he was obliged to put his foot on his breast in order to pull it out. A woman, ridiculously fat, was walking on all fours, her breasts hanging down at a trickle of blood running down her face.

Bagawali had disappeared.

He was gripped by an immense lassitude. He had a desire to let himself fall into the blood he had spilled. He was not a man to have remorse. He often declared, subsequently, that he had done nothing but punish criminals. But it was disgust that was overwhelming him. At any rate, he decided to leave,

Having returned to Madras he fell into a profound prostration from which he did not emerge. His friends became anxious about him and, as much to remove him from a probable vengeance as to cure him, they obtained permission from La Bourdonnais for him to return to France on the *Neptune*.

No more mention was heard of Bagawali. Perhaps the Brahmins, attributing that violation of the mysteries of the goddess to her, imprisoned her in their temple. Perhaps they sent her to another city in India. Perhaps, in the confusion of the scene, she had been killed by the man she loved, under the asokas the color of coral that had been witness to their caresses.

The Siva Bakta, worshipers of Siva, contrary to the rites customary in India, do not burn their dead but bury them. One of the beggars who live on the threshold of pagodas, and are known as sanyassis, interrogated on the subject, reported that one night, approximately at that time, he had seen a cortege of Siva Bakta, recognizable by their red robes bordered in yellow, heading toward the forest, carrying a corpse. Was that Bagawali? As the Siva Bakta do not put any stele or exterior sign on the place where they bury one of their own, and even efface any visible trace of it, it has been impossible to determine.

Julia the Animal-Tamer

Julia the Animal-Tamer, who was celebrated throughout the south of France toward the end of the Second Empire, is known to us via the memoirs and correspondence of Madame de Lestang[12] and also the memories of a few men still alive who were, in their early years, the gilded youth of Marseilles, Montpelier and Toulouse.

She sometimes told her lovers that her real name was Julie de Trécoeur and that she was from an old and noble family of Rouergue. No one believed her because of the common character of such fables, but it was true.

"The old dowager de Trécoeur," reports Madame de Lestang, "often told me that her granddaughter incessantly formed the project of becoming a nun. I did not want her to do that. She was a very beautiful brunette child of fourteen, with gray-blue eyes, who did not seem to be made to consecrate herself to God. Fortunately, it is to donkeys that she devotes herself presently. The Trécoeurs have two charming ones in their stables. Little Julie adores them and occupies herself with them to the point that it is a true folly."

It certainly seems that her love for those two charming donkeys left a vivid impression in the soul of the woman who was later to become the beautiful Julia. She never ceased, in the course of her life, to talk about them, to describe them and to regret them. We know nothing about their history and it is probable that they accomplished their donkey destiny obscurely. Julie de Trécoeur has not informed us, via those of her

---

[12] Not the singer and pianist Paule de Lestang (1875-1968), who was not alive during the Second Empire; an earlier person of that name to whom several oblique references can be found in sources from the 1860s, perhaps her mother-in-law, remains somewhat obscure.

words that have reached us, of any particularity of their life except for the love she had for them.

We are better informed regarding Fauvette, the beloved bitch, because we know of one sublime feature of her. Fauvette was Julie's inseparable companion. She slept in her bed and show a vivid jealousy if anyone came near her mistress. But when Julie was eighteen her taste for religion had developed singularly and her parents did not raise any objection to her entering a convent. It was the house of the Carmelites established in the Rue Saint-Michel in Toulouse. Julie wanted to take her dog with her, but the rules of the Order forbade it. She quit her tearfully when the carriage that was taking her away went down the slopes of the chalky plateau, heading for Najac on the way to Toulouse.

It is a long way from Najac in Rouergue to the Rue Saint-Michel, very far for a young woman quitting her family and the world, and even further for a little dog that does not know the way and has no map to guide her. In spite of that, a few hours after Julie de Trécoeur's arrival among the Carmelites of Toulouse, the convent's doorkeeper heard desperate appeals from the street and found Fauvette, covered in dust, searching the mossy stones of the old house for the lost scent of her mistress.

Julie de Trécoeur remained in the convent for a year, only knowing the sensualities of divine love. It was the roar of a lion that deflected her soul from its path.

In those days the great Autumn fair was installed in the Allées Saint-Michel, which opened at the corner of the old convent, and the last fairground booths were extended in front of the high wall on the Carmelites. The Castaniès menagerie was there, and Castaniès himself, with a square head, an athletic torso, clad in a red shirt, brandishing a snake in his hands, was delivering his patter in a resounding voice.

From the small window through which Julie de Trécoeur still had access to life, Castaniès' face and form could be seen distinctly, but it was not those attractions, which had troubled more than one beautiful daughter of the Midi, and it was not the warmth of the voice and the picturesque setting that that changed the Carmelite's destiny.

The lion roared, either because of anger, hunger or more likely dread—for it was the son and grandson of menagerie lions and it feared humans. It was when that roar resounded that Julie de Trécoeur's heart caught fire. It was a heat that she had not known before, which she thought could never be extinguished.

Castaniès, his enormous neck and his gladiatorial build were only a pretext. The animal-tamer was to have a soul illuminated by the pride of having seduced a young woman of good society. He never knew that it was his lion that had made that conquest.

One night, at the hour when the crowd had ebbed away and the candles were about to be extinguished, Julie understood that the voice that had appealed to her could not remain without response; she let herself down from her window into the street and simply went to offer herself to Castaniès, who shoved her, even more simply, into his caravan.

For several years, Julia the Animal-Tamer astonished the towns of the Midi that the Castaniès menagerie toured. During the preliminary patter, she stood next to Castaniès, whip in hand, with a black mask over her eyes, clad in a pink leotard that allowed perfect forms to be seen, and the crowd pressed forward to look at her.

It was only given to the paying spectators to see her face when she went into the lion's cage. That face then seemed transformed by the exaltation of passion. The lion, which knew its métier as a menagerie lion, roared with a simulated fury, agitated his mane, and did his best to disguise the placid mildness of his soul. He flew like a bird at a signal from Julia's whip, and the latter came to lie down voluptuously between his claws, and put her little child-like head in its mouth.

Moreover, that king of beasts was a slave for her. If she left the menagerie it roared to lament the fact, and he had more powerful roars to express his joy when she appeared. Julia

91

loved him, and her life was completely happy divided between Castaniès and the lion.

But a great catastrophe overtook the menagerie. The exact cause of it was never known. It happened one summer morning in the outskirts of a small village, where they had camped, not far from the city of Foix, to which the menagerie was going for the festival of the fifteenth of August.

Had Castaniès, in accordance with a habit that had become increasingly frequent, drunk too much that evening? Was it necessary, rather, to blame the malevolence of a boy who had been dismissed they day before because of certain nasty remarks he had made about Julia? No one knows.

When dawn appeared in that corner of the Ariège valley, however, a milkman who arrived in his cart was witness to an extraordinary spectacle. There was a cockatoo with multicolored plumage singing on a branch; several young monkeys were playing with stones; a brown bear was climbing a slope with a satisfied sway; further way, a boa was dragging itself through the grass; and along the road, a huge lion was marching at a slow pace, gravely. Before the Ariégois mountains, having the revelation of what liberty could be, he was surprised and sad. He was, above all, frightened and inoffensive. The gendarmes of Foix killed him before Castaniès had time to arrive.

That was the sole loss that the menagerie had to deplore, for all the other animals returned to their cages, but it was the most serious. Julia was consoled with difficulty, and from that day on her métier as an animal-tamer had scarcely any attraction for her.

Castaniès had developed a pot belly and drank too much. Julia was in the full bloom of her beauty. She quit him on friendly terms. He had a large enough sum of money. She took away the skin of the lion and a large chimpanzee that was very intelligent.

Then the brilliant period of Julia's life commences. A rich owner of vineyards gives her a carriage, horses, and a house in Montpelier. She is the cynosure, the splendid and lustful target of all the young men whose ideal is to be the lover of a woman maintained by another.

She realizes that ideal as often as possible and she reveals herself to be a woman of untiring temperament. By a singular particularity of her taste, however, she seeks out most of all men whose bestial physiognomy and certain mannerisms are reminiscent of animality. She ruins a young married deputy prosecutor whom she says resembles an eagle. She remains the mistress for several years of a sculptor with a floating beard and long blond hair, because he reminds her of the lion. She gives herself to her coachman for some time because of his resemblance to the chimpanzee.

Furthermore, that animal never quit her. He was taciturn and faithful. He slept in Julia's bedroom when she slept alone there. On the nights when she had a lover with her it was necessary to appease him with caresses and tender words in order for him to be able to tolerate a night in the next room. He was poisoned by a lover who judged him importunate. He was mourned for a long time.

It would have been in inconformity with a habitual curve of her life, as well as literary tradition, if, when she grew old, Julia had returned to the convent of Carmelites in the Rue Saint-Michel. Nothing of the sort. She never gave it a thought. Rich, and weary of men, she retired with a linen maid named Floria, who was her friend, to a comfortable villa on the road between Béziers and Sérignan.

She had become with age one of those loquacious and eccentric southerners of which the Midi is full, who weep at the slightest excuse, laugh and sing without motive, and do extravagant things, either because the excessively hot summer sun affects their brains or because the quality of their race dictates that they become somewhat irrational at a certain age.

Julia had around her a well-stocked poultry-yard and many domestic animals. She collected stray dogs and always had several around her. For hours on end she went to play with a young calf in a meadow. It was her, personally, who gave hay to her horses in the stables. She was sometimes passionate about some of them, sometimes others. Sometimes she did not quit the pig-sty and at other times she went to sit in the bulldog's kennel, which was large enough for her to lie down full length there.

She had birds of every sort in cages, bees in hives, and even domesticated fleas. She was fond of the fauna of hot countries, bought books on natural history, and marveled at the number and variety of species. She brought a llama from the Andes at great expense, which died of cold the in first winter, and an ant-eater, which deteriorated rapidly and also died, because the fields of the Béziers region did not contain enough ants, its only possible nourishment.

She grew old with the constant thought and love of animals. She said incessantly that they were far superior to humans, less by virtue of their fidelity than because they placed amour above everything else and thought of nothing but that. Perhaps she was right.

Madame Floria, the linen maid, who witnessed Julia's last moments, reported them in these terms:

"She had stopped talking and no longer responded to the questions I asked her except by grunts that imitated those of a pig or a strident cry like the crow of a cock. After two days in that condition, however, she became agitated and started running around the house imitating the braying of a donkey, the roaring of a lion and the barking of a dog. She even walked on all fours, trying to bite. In the end, though, she calmed down and she died smiling, caressing a little gilded cage in which there was a tame lizard."

Appendix
Hiao the Korean[13]

I knew for the first time how unjust the fear of death renders one when the tempest commenced to rage in all its fury and I started to curse my father with a violence almost equal to that of the wind, for the reason that he had allowed me to undertake that voyage. It was me who had wanted to depart, in spite of his pleas and even his orders. He had urged me to marry beforehand the daughter of one of our rich neighbors, who pleased me very much, hoping that that would retain me. Nothing had been able to stop me. I nevertheless rendered him responsible for the danger that I was running, telling myself that he ought to have obliged me to remain with him by violence.

A barrel that had been detached from who knows where rolled over the deck and collided violently with my knee. The sails had been carried away, and the vessel was creaking and trembling as if it were a living being shaken by fever. I went back down precipitately to the passenger cabin. But there, the screams, the invocations of God and the spectacle of human cowardice rendered me a little courage, and I ceased to curse my father.

Only the old gray-haired Arab was calm. He called me "Giaour!" by way of a joke, as he had had the custom of doing since the beginning of our voyage, and then he leaned over to say to me: "Allah is great!" He claimed to have grown rich in the slave trade in the Red Sea and he gave himself, proudly, the singular title of the former chief of the fleet of the Imam of Muscat.

---

[13] Author's note: "We thought that this account of the voyage of a young Dutchman in the last century had its place in *Courtesans' Lives* since it informs us about the Korean Hiao. We are publishing it without changing anything."

We had left Batavia on the first of June 1721, we had dropped anchor at Tay Ouen in the island of Formosa and we were headed for Japan. According to my calculations, we must have been carried by the tempest not far from the coasts of China.

All night and all the following day we were tossed by the waves at hazard. Several Chinamen went to find the captain in order to ask him for permission to throw one of their comrades overboard. They accused him of carrying with him something that they designated by a Chinese term that I did not understand, but which was equivalent to what we call "bad luck" in Europe. It would also be necessary for the ship to draw away rapidly from the place where the man had been thrown, because Chinese bad luck has the ability to swim and sometimes escorts ships.

The Portuguese of noble birth who affected not to address a word to anyone had become extraordinarily familiar and was asking everyone the probable duration of death by asphyxia under water. That problem, which was secretly tormenting everyone, is scarcely pleasant to discuss at such moments.

The Portuguese had a wife of great beauty who seemed scarcely older than eighteen. She had large languorous eyes and it had seemed to me that, during the crossing, she had directed them at me quite frequently. I had been vividly impressed by that. As her husband was running in all directions to interrogate everyone, and seemed to have lost his head, she leaned against me several times in a troubling fashion, mingling her gaze with mine—but I scarcely paid any attention to what would have filed me with joy in other circumstances.

Daylight was about to appear when we heard a cry of "Land!" That provoked a delirious joy from some, who believed that we would soon be saved, and brought to others, better informed, the certainty of their imminent end. The passenger cabin into which we were crowded, and from which hardly anyone had emerged for days, exhaled a nauseating odor. A box belonging to a Chinaman, containing a kind of bird-lime, had broken and the glue had spread. Everyone had some on their garments, with the consequence that we stuck to one another.

I went out and went up on deck. As well as the sails, the launches had been carried away by the waves. The rails had been crushed, and the hatches torn away. Enormous gushes of sea-water were sweeping the deck incessantly.

I asked the first mate, who was passing by, crawling, what he thought would become of us, and whether we could reach port.

He only replied to me with a single excessively vulgar word, by which I felt wounded. I wondered at first whether I ought not to crawl after him in order to strike him, but, as if the insult had had a magic power, I was penetrated thereafter by a extraordinary sentiment of calm. A vague, frightful, indefinable yellow light began to cover the sea and render it similar to a purulent wound that was in motion. Very close to us there was a somber mass, which was the shore.

There was a shock, followed by a howl, in which all the voices of the passengers and crew were mingled, but terror was no longer making me suffer. My mind had been gained by a lucidity that became increasingly great and which combined with a sentiment of almost perfect security. I considered a spectacle from which I was detached.

I saw a few passengers appear who attempted to walk on the deck, which became almost vertical. One mariner stripped completely naked and dived into the sea. Another was pulling a packet of ropes in order to tie planks together, perhaps in the hope of making a raft. I heard the young Portuguese woman shout: "Miguel!" which was her husband's name. I perceived the noise that the water made as it precipitated into the interior of the ship. A wisdom hidden within me drove me, independent of all reflection, to throw myself overboard abruptly.

I had the good luck to be thrown on to the sand. The shock had stunned me, but I only had bruises. I started running to flee the detestable element that had nearly swallowed me.

Then I retraced my steps to discover what had happened to my companions in misfortune, and also to dry myself and escape the cold that was invading me.

The daylight was beginning to appear. I thought at first that I was the only one to have escaped, but I seemed to hear cries among the rocks. My joy was immense on seeing two men dragging themselves over the ground. It was the captain of the ship and a crewman, both Dutch like myself. The sailor was a big red-haired fellow named Otters, renowned on the ship for the violence of his character, and whom people amused themselves by irritating deliberately. As soon as he saw me he repeated several times that he thought he had broken his foot, as well as several fingers. As for Captain Fingham, without perceiving my presence, he vomited up the water that he had drunk and wept without pause for the loss of his ship.

I helped them to draw away from the shore. We lay down on the sand and waited, prey to despair. The tempest calmed down, and when our clothes were dry, we went to sleep.

We woke up toward evening, famished. I went into the rocks and I had the good fortune to find a cask of wine and a barrel of salted meat. With great difficulty, I dragged them out of the reach of the waves, and we ate avidly.

We had seen nothing around us but marshes and desolate heath, and we thought we were on a desert island. We had nothing with which to make a fire and we suffered cruelly from the cold and the apprehension of ferocious beasts.

In the morning, Captain Fingham wept even more abundantly than the day before, which made me think that the emotions he had experienced had attacked his reason. I agreed with Otters that he would stay with him while I went along the shore to discover whether the land we were on was inhabited. That violent man, impressed by his captain's tears and the wound in his foot, had become as weak and gentle as a child. He told me that we were going to fall into the hands of savages who would kill us amid tortures and that it was preferable to kill ourselves immediately. I did my best to comfort him and I left.

I walked for half an hour over sandy terrain, dotted here and there by trees, when I seemed to hear human voices. I continued advancing and perceived two forms in the distance, one of which was lying on the ground and the other bending over it.

As I approached I recognized Omar, the former chief of the fleet of the Imam of Muscat. He had made me signals from a distance but he manifested a certain embarrassment in my presence. A naked woman was lying face down on the ground. It was her who was uttering cries. At the sight of me she stopped, leapt to her feet and ran toward me, imploring my pity and begging me to defend her. She took me by the shoulders, trembling, and did not let go.

In spite of the great difference there is between someone dressed and someone naked, I had recognized the beautiful Portuguese woman. She showed her fist to the Arab. She explained to me in halting words that he had stripped her of all her garments by force and had not ceased to do violence to her all night. She had resisted him on my arrival and begged me to save her and punish the wretch.

I reproached Omar for conduct all the more unworthy as it came from a man with graying hair and who ought not to have added further to the misfortunes of destiny. He replied to me that he had saved the life of the Portuguese woman by pulling her out of the sea and that he had, in consequence, certain rights over her. He had only taken off her clothes because they were wet and in order to reanimate her by an energetic friction, without which she would probably not have survived. The chill of the night had obliged them to cling together tightly in order to keep warm. No man, he added, would have done otherwise, and anyway, when death is so close, what is the point of not taking the final pleasure that it might permit you.

I could not help finding those reasons valid enough. I told the young woman that a common misfortune ought to incite forgiveness, that, in any case, she was sheltered henceforth from the Arab's attempts, and that it was necessary, in order to try to save our lives, that we be united.

She perceived then that she was only clad in her hair, which scarcely came down any lower than her shoulders. She made a modest gesture and wanted to put on her dress—but the dress was in tatters, either because the rocks had ripped it or because of the Arab and his brutality.

Omar declared to us that the wise thing to do was to draw closer to the shore while returning to our companions and to see whether the sea had cast up any cadavers on the sand. We could strip them of their garments and thus remedy the wretched state of our own. That proposal filled us with horror at first, but we accepted it thereafter because necessity is stronger than anything.

After several hours of searching we had found the bodies of some of our companions and a large quantity of objects that might be of great utility to us subsequently. We removed the costume of a poor mariner whose face, already partly eaten away, was painful to behold, and we gave it to the beautiful Portuguese woman.

She washed it in the sea with great care and put it on still wet, for the sun had become ardent. I noticed that, in spite of the grief that she now allowed to burst forth in thinking about her husband, she put a certain coquetry into arranging the folds of her jacket. I had been dazzled by the beauty of her nudity and I regretted being deprived of it.

Our companions showed neither joy nor surprise when they saw me returning with two survivors of the shipwreck. We all ate salted meat and drank a little wine. We decided to spend the coming night in the place where we were and set off the following day marching toward a wooded hill that we could see in the distance, where we hoped to encounter inhabitants.

I learned that the beautiful Portuguese was named Inès de Torres, that she had married before her departure from Portugal, and that she had been going to Japan where her husband was to direct a large business trading in furs, spices and precious wood. She thanked me for having saved her from the man she called the ignoble Arab. She told me that she placed herself under my protection with every confidence. She kissed me on the cheeks to seal our amity. I experienced a delight full of tenderness.

We had dug a hole in the sand in order to be sheltered from the wind while we slept. The night was not as cold, and Inès slept next to me without any fear. In the morning, when we woke up, however she had such aches in her body that she declared herself to be incapable of walking. The wound that the sailor Otters had in his foot had become infected and he could hardly stand. We then decided that they would both remain there with the provisions and the objects recovered from the shipwreck, while I went with the Arab and Captain Fingham to the wooded hill, which ought not to be more than a few hours march away.

We set forth, only taking a little salted meat for our breakfast.

We had not been waking for an hour when we discovered a stream, from which we drank with delight. To our great joy, we saw a bridge, over which we passed. It was made of wood but cemented at its two extremities, which made us think that we were in a country inhabited by civilized men.

Scarcely had we made that observation than we heard several gunshots and we perceived several men who were firing at us with muskets. They appeared to me to be dressed as I imagined the Chinese were dressed. I waved my handkerchief as a sign of peace, but we saw that they were reloading their weapons and were about to recommence firing. We went back over the bridge and retraced our steps.

I was anxious about having abandoned Inès even for a day. I reflected that, if she had consented to it, it was uniquely because of her desire to sleep, and that once that desire passed she would be afraid to be distanced from me. I therefore persuaded my companions to return to the shore. In any case, only Omar had an opinion, for Captain Fingham seemed struck with stupidity.

I acted sagely, but it was already too late, Inès came running toward us. Scarcely had we left than Otters had drunk all the wine that remained in the cask and had lost consciousness of things through drunkenness. He had thrown himself upon her. She dared not say what had happened, but it was easy to guess.

I allowed my indignation to burst forth on seeing Otters, but he was like a madman. I had scarcely called out to him than he threw himself upon me. The wine he had drunk and his injured foot put him in a state of inferiority. I knocked him down easily, but without doing him any great harm. I was still holding him beneath me when shouts burst forth from all sides. We were surrounded by a hundred men.

Some of them were on horseback. Almost all of them had long moustaches and they were wearing fur bonnets. The one who appeared to be the leader continually made signs to the men surrounding us not to do us any violence, and he made us understand that we had nothing to fear. Nevertheless, as he had seen me knock down one of my companions, he gave the order that my wrists should be bound, which was done immediately.

It was in vain that Inès and Omar tried to explain in Dutch, Portuguese and Arabic that it was only a quarrel without importance. Otters himself, sobered up and calmed down, attempted it just as loyally and gestured to them to remove my bonds. It was futile.

Having my hands tied, I told Inès to make a present to the islanders' chief of a telescope that was one of the objects cast up by the waves, which we had picked up. He received it with pleasure and gave the impression of telling us that everything originating from the ship was ours, and that he would not permit anyone to touch it.

Then everyone set forth. Otters was placed on a horse because of his foot. I was treated with far less respect than my companions and one of my guards even sniggered as he looked at me, pointing to my back and making the gesture of beating it with a rod, which was a promise of punishment.

On the way we learned that we were on the island of Quelpart, which is part of the kingdom of Korea.

We marched all day and arrived, worn out by fatigue, when night had already fallen, in the outskirts of a town that was named as Mokso. I was so weary that I scarcely had the strength to look around. The chief, who was on horseback, quit us, having given orders in our regard. We were given a meal composed of boiled rice, which, in the condition we were in, seemed very tasty. Then we were made to understand that we would be locked up for the night.

I had been untied in order to permit me to eat, and there was no question of tying me up again. But it was still supposed that I was dangerous, and I was shoved to one side, in order to be locked up on my own in a kind of narrow hut. I understood that my companions would be imprisoned together.

When she saw that she was about to be separated from me and that she would be obliged to spend the night with men she feared, with reason, Inès begged her guards to put her in the same hut as me, and I joined my pleas with hers. She did not hide, in doing that, the horror that my companions inspired in her—a horror that was susceptible of awakening a spirit of vengeance in them. It was in vain that I told her in a low voice to moderate herself.

The Koreans that were guarding us did not give the impression of being bad men, in spite of their terrible appearance, but they made us understand that their chief had departed and that they were obliged to carry out his orders. They concluded the argument by imprisoning me violently, and I heard them dragging Inès away, and that the Arab was laughing.

The hut where my companions were imprisoned was not far from mine. As I began to fall asleep I was woken up by a cry for help from Inès. A little later, she uttered others, but I could not do anything for her. I imagined the frightful scene that must be unfolding, and I wept bitterly over her fate and mine. I heard her screams far into the night.

We were all reunited the following day in order to be taken before the Governor. Inès made no complaint. I dared not question her, but she told me that she did not want to be parted from me again, no matter what happened.

We traversed the town, which was singular, in that the houses were almost invisible. They were all situated behind bamboo palisades. The majority appeared to me to be made of wood, but there were some in stone that were large and beautiful. The Governor's house was circular in form and had the appearance of a very ancient fortress. Our passage provoked a great curiosity among the inhabitants.

The Governor was old and ill. He had an extraordinarily white face with very soft eyes. He received us lying in his bed. A very small man with a long white beard had been summoned to serve as interpreter. We learned that he was a Japanese prisoner who had learned a few words of Dutch thirty years ago. He had almost forgotten them and the conversation was very difficult.

I explained that we were victims of a shipwreck and we were imploring the Governor for the means to reach Japan. The interpreter explained to us that it was a law of the land, without exception, never to allow foreigners whose ill fortune cast them ashore in Korea to leave. Nevertheless, they were not reduced to slavery, what belonged to them was not taken, and they were allowed to work and beg. We learned that in exchange for the wreckage originating from the ship we would have a hut outside the town where we could live. A ration of salt and cooked rice would be brought to us there for some time. In order to give evidence of his benevolence, the Governor, by reason of the state of our clothes, would have us each given a pair of shoes, a coat and hide stockings.

He had just made a sign that the audience was concluded when Inès, who had not understood very well what the Japanese had said and dreaded spending another night like the previous one advanced, unfastened her jacket and showed her breasts in order to make it known that she was a woman. Then she put her arm round my neck to express that she did not want us to be separated. The Governor's only response was that she would have a woman's dress.

My prudence would have made me repress Inès' gesture had I been able to do so; but it was too late. A tall and very fat Korean who wore rich garments and who seemed to be a counselor of the Governor advanced precipitately as we were being taken away. He passed his hand under Inès' jacket several times and touched her breasts, laughing. Then he made a gesture that seemed to signify: *"Au revoir!"*

The hut to which we were taken was wretched and only had a rickety door. When the five of found ourselves confronted by the rations of salt and rice and the Korean clothing, we became conscious of our poverty and we understood that it came less from our abandonment in a unknown country but from the bad sentiments that we had toward one another.

We agreed that we ought not to think about anything but our escape. It might be achieved by stealing one of the boats we had seen moored on the coast. Captain Fingham, who had recovered his intelligence, assured us that we were only a few days away from the islands surrounding Japan and that we might be able to reach them if the wind was favorable and if we wanted to take the risk. He added that in the meantime, and after what had happened the previous night, Inès ought to be common to all of us. Otters and the Arab agreed with him.

I did not know what had happened in the night, but I could guess all too easily. Anger took possession of me at that odious pretension, coldly formulated. I went out of the cabin and took possession of a broken oar that I had noticed, abandoned next to the road. I went back in precipitately, raising that weapon, and I swore solemnly to break the skull immediately of anyone who dared to renew the proposition made by the captain. That threat changed their ideas. They pretended to laugh, and Otters declared that it was absurd to quarrel over a question of such scant importance.

It was agreed that we would go to see right way—separately, so as not to awaken suspicion—which boat would be the easiest to capture.

Many curious individuals were gathered around the place where we were, but they dared not disturb us, for the Governor had given the order to administer twenty strokes of the rod to the inhabitants who had fired musket-shots at us, and cavaliers had departed to carry out that order.

Scarcely were Inès and I alone than she threw herself into my arms and kissed me on the lips. I sensed that she was in haste to lavish the caresses upon me that she had not been able to refuse the men she hated.

In the evening, Inès picked up the dress give by the Governor in order to put it on. We were all together in our narrow habitation and she did not want to undress in front of four men. I asked my companions to come outside for a few moments with me. Those coarse individuals refused, claiming that it was not necessary to be so ceremonious since they were very familiar with the body that Inès wanted to hide from them.

As night had fallen completely and it was still warm, I told Inès to go out and change her clothes outside. There was no moon and all the curious people had gone.

She put the Korean robe under her arm and went out, smiling at me tenderly and making a movement of the lips that signified that she was soon going to give me the recompense or my solicitude for her.

I was never to see her again.

When she did not come back, I went outside in my turn, but I called in vain in the darkness. No one responded. I found not only the Korean dress but also the mariner's costume she had worn, which made me think that she had been taken by surprise and abducted just as she was about to exchange one costume for the other.

I ran in all directions. I even obtained from my companions that they would assist me in my search. We were outside the town and its gates were closed. The Koreans that we interrogated did not reply to us. One of them threw stones at us and wounded Omar on the forehead.

We went back inside. That night was the saddest of all.

The next day, the Japanese who knew a little Dutch came to find us. He told us not to occupy ourselves with our companion any longer if we valued our lives. She had been abducted by Sun Yen, who was the king's uncle and had more power than the Governor. He was the fat Korean who had touched Inès' breasts the day before. She would become his wife. The Japanese assured us that she would be infinitely happier with him than with us because he was rich and moderately good. The only fault for which he was reputed was lasciviousness—but, he added, with a wink, perhaps she would not complain about that.

Those words and the gold coin he gave each of us, by way of indemnity, made me think that the guards had divulged what had happened the previous night in the prison.

I swore to myself to liberate Inès.

We led a very miserable life. The rice that we had been given was replaced by barley. That barley was stopped. We were obliged to beg in order to live, but the charity of the inhabitants for us was quickly exhausted. We were advised to do what other beggars did, who were not sedentary and who went from town to town, but we did not want to quit the sea shore, which represented for us the hope of escape.

Winter had come and bad weather prevented any attempt for the moment. Our character had become embittered. We had frequent arguments.

Otters and the Arab, in particular, were always on the brink of coming to blows. They only reached an understanding in the evening when we were gathered round the fire in our hut and they talked about Inès. They praised her beauty and boasted about the pleasure they had had with her. They mocked me for not having had it.

To make me suffer, Omar claimed that on the sand dune where he had spent the night with her it was she who, driven by her indecent nature, had woken him from his sleep in order to make advances to him. Otters affirmed that it had been the same for him, and Captain Fingham disparaged her with filthy words. Once I seized a firebrand and threatened to set fire to our hut if they did not stop the flow of their hatred.

One evening, at sunset, four armed Koreans came to fetch us out of our hut rather violently. A closed palanquin was outside the door. We sensed that someone was examining us from the interior. A powerful hand with square fingers passed through the curtain, the wrist of which bore a gold bracelet. Then the palanquin drew away. We were still meditating on that event when the Japanese came to find Otters. He told him that it was on behalf of the governor's wife, Hiao, Manchu in origin, who dominated her weak husband completely. He added that no harm would come to Otters if he conducted himself cleverly.

The latter departed, full of apprehension, for everything now inspired dread in us because of the weakness that misfortune gives the mind.

He came back the following day quite satisfied, with a sort of superior conceit. He refused to tell us anything, on the pretext of the terrible punishments with which he had been threatened if he talked. We noticed that he had bruises on the right eye and the neck.

He went out during the day, as he had the habit of doing, in order to go and beg. But when we came back in the evening he filled the hut with horrible cries. He had been seized and knocked down by Koreans and one of them had crushed his right foot by dropping a heavy mass of iron on it.

We were in the process of bandaging his foot as best we could when the Japanese came and took Fingham away.

The next day, the latter came back, smiling, in spite of the seeming evidence of a punch that he had on his chin. He had the same superior attitude as Otters the day before, and he observed the same silence, in spite of my questions.

In the day, while I was caring for Otters, I saw Captain Fingham coming back, dragging himself along the ground.

The same thing that had happened to Otters had happened to him. Koreans lying in wait for him had crushed his right foot.

Omar and I begged him to tell us what had happened the previous night in order that we could discover whether there as a connection between the employment of the night and the crushing of the foot. He was obstinate in keeping silent. Otters had a fever and there was no point in questioning him again.

We gave the wounded man the cares of which we were capable and the Japanese appeared again when evening came. It was Omar that he came to fetch.

"We are in Allah's hands," he said, and followed the Japanese.

I saw him come back, like the others, with a tranquil face and with the same conceit. He apologized for not being able to tell me anything because of the horrible punishment with which he had been threatened in the case of indiscretion. But he assured me that, in his opinion, there could not be any connection between what had happened during the night and the torture to which our companions had been subjected.

One of his eyes was in a very poor state. He resolved not to go out all day.

I absented myself in order to go buy a kind of maize that we cooked and which served us as bread. When I returned, Omar was lying on the ground unconscious. His foot was crushed. I brought him round, bandaged him and spent a sad day.

I thought about running away, but where could I go? I would be rapidly overtaken. Then too, I could not abandon my injured companions. All three had a fever and two were delirious. I could not think of making them say anything that might inform me as to what had happened to them and the manner in which I might be able to preserve my right foot.

Then I meditated profoundly, for wisdom is in the hidden part of ourselves, and I began to see a glimmer of truth.

"Only tell me," I said to the Japanese, "whether the Governor's wife has any knowledge of the night that my three companions spent in prison with the Portuguese woman, and the screams that she uttered during that night."

He considered me with an extreme surprise, nodded his head, and added that he would not have believed that I was so intelligent. He left me at the door of the palace.

A Korean armed with a naked sword conducted me along a long stone corridor. We went past a grille behind which a lion was pacing, which seemed furious. The Korean touched his lips with his finger and mimed pushing me toward the lion. That was the punishment reserved for the talkative, which had frightened my companions so much.

Then we traversed several empty rooms, until we reached a chamber covered with carpets, where he left me. There was no furniture except for a tall lamp and a large bed. After a moment, one of the hangings moved aside and I saw a woman appear of almost immeasurable stature. She was wearing a Chinese robe. She was frightfully ugly and I thought that she was laughing. I saw then that her raised upper lip allowed the sight of her singularly long and yellow teeth.

She looked at me without amenity, gripped my shoulder, turned me around, and suddenly, without warning, punched me in the chest. Surprise caused me to recoil, but she delivered two or three more punches to my face, more forcefully applied. I tried to push her away but she started striking me with all her might. Anger seized me and I riposted. Her eyes lit up with joy and I sensed that she wanted to fight. She was very strong. She was now trying to knock me over on to the bed. I dared not strike her with any serious blows, which meant that she had the upper hand momentarily, and she succeeded, by grabbing my legs, in laying me down on the bed.

She started to laugh; her teeth seemed elongated; she pronounced a few words that I did not understand and made an imperious gesture instructing me not to move. She took off her robe and came to lie down beside me. Her violence had given way to the simulacra of a ridiculous affection. She took her head in my hands and placed her mouth on mine. I perceived the cold of her long teeth on my lips and the detestable odor of her breath. Her skin gave me a sensation of dampness.

Then I thought about the unpardonable imprudence of my companions and wondered how they had had the courage to satisfy that amorous woman who needed the stimulus of a fight to prepare herself for amour and who, once satisfied, would inevitably think of recommencing.

I remained inert by her side without difficulty. Then I detached myself, pretending to be uniquely occupied with the pain that the blows I had received had caused me.

She leapt out of bed and put on her robe again. She spat in my face, and as I went to the door she tried to kick me. I went out and she shouted insults at me from a distance, which I did not understand.

I took the same route that I had followed, hastening my steps when I went past the lion. At the door, the Korean who had accompanied me had the kind of smile one had for someone who has had a stroke of luck.

As the gates of the town were closed until the next day, I could not go back to our habitation and I went to ask the Japanese for hospitality.

"Already," he said to me, offering me a little rice alcohol. And he questioned me as to whether my foot would suffer the same fate as those of by companions.

I shook my head. In a country where beggars are accustomed not to remain in the same town, I had not rendered myself sufficiently desirable for me to require an infirmity to oblige me to remain forever close at hand and at the disposal of the powerful Hiao.

My companions healed slowly. As I had foreseen, they were recalled two or three times to the home of the Governor's wife, but the only benefits they obtained from it were the bruises with which she covered their faces.

They suffered cruelly from the jealousy that I inspired in them. When we were together I saw their eyes obstinately fixed on my feet. They could not bear the idea that I had not been subjected to the same torture as them. They were perpetually wondering why.

On evening, on going back to our hut, I noticed an enormous stone near the door hat had not been there in the morning. That put me on the alert. I pretended to be very weary and overtaken by a heavy slumber. My companions got up, limping, went out silently, and I saw them bringing back the stone in order to drop it on my right foot.

I had no difficulty preventing them from doing so. I represented the injustice of their action to them. They made a semblance of renouncing it, but I sensed that they believed in all sincerity that they were the victims of the injustice of fate. The stone remained by the door as evidence of their menacing hatred.

The good weather had returned. I had put off the project of escape by sea because of my hope of rescuing Inès. In addition, my companions' minds had weakened. They had become pusillanimous, they feared death all the more as their live became more miserable.

I had finally had news of Inès. She got a letter to me via the Japanese, who had been charged with teaching her the Korean language. She told me that after long suffering she was beginning to get accustomed to her existence. She was a prisoner in an immense dwelling, but her husband, Sun Yen, was very good to her and adored her. She had just brought into the world a daughter who would always retain her next to him. She exhorted me not to make any attempt to find her. She sent her adieux and the assurance that she had loved me.

I experienced a great sadness and no longer thought about anything but quitting the land of Korea, whatever the risks it was necessary to run at sea.

My companions, while hating me, obeyed by virtue of the action that my will exerted upon them. Our flight was decided and we agreed that we would embark on a small boat moored in a bay near the town.

We chose a moonless night, for three limping silhouettes were susceptible of identifying us to those who might perceive us. We therefore quit out hut carrying two large pitchers full of water, carefully stoppered, as well as a large quantity of cooked rice and bread made with maize.

As we arrived near the boat, a Korean who must have followed us uttered a cry of alarm behind us. Omar retraced his steps swiftly, his knife in his hand. We hastened to prepare the sails in accordance with Fingham's instructions, but Omar came back to the boat and assured us that the Korean would not cry out again.

He was mistaken, for I was to perceive, as we drew away from the shore, the plaint of someone dying.

As we embarked the provisions, Otters dropped a heavy crate laden with rice, which nearly broke my foot. I understood that he had done it deliberately, and promised myself to be careful of my security.

The wind was propitious and impelled us all night far from the Korean coast, with the result that at sunrise, we were in the open sea and could consider ourselves safe from any pursuit.

Toward the middle of the day, a sea-spider started running around the bottom of the boat. Omar claimed, without any reason, that the animal brought bad luck. He seized an oar in order to crush it. I only just had time to jump sideways, because he had aimed at my foot and not the spider.

I seized him by the throat and made as if to throw him overboard. The captain and Otters intervened and the former threatened to put me in irons by virtue of his power as captain. I had snatched the Arab's knife. I replied that I would kill the first man who came near me.

After having been contrary for such a long time, was favorable to us. On the fifth day after our departure we came in sight of land, which we believed to be Japan, and which was the island of Goto. We landed there without difficulty and were greeted by a Dutchman named Guillaume Navi, who had a trading-post. He kept us with him for a few days, enabling us to sleep in beds and nourishing us abundantly. I had given him an account of our adventures and begged him not to confide any heavy object to my companions.

He took us to Nagasaki himself. We arrived on the eighth of October. Our captivity had lasted fifteen months.

The Director of the Dutch Company, who knew my father, offered me hospitality and treated me as his own son. We were the object of general curiosity and the Governor of the city wanted to hear our story from our own mouths.

I spent a month there before embarking on a Dutch three-master that set sail for Batavia. In the meantime I could not go out in Nagasaki without being followed by a few curious people. But every time I heard, at a street corner, an irregular sound of footsteps attesting to the lameness of a passer-by, I turned around swiftly, and ran.

PRISCILLA OF ALEXANDRIA

I. Priscilla, it's you, Priscilla...

A great rumor filled all the streets leading down to the old port of Kibotos. It was a muffled stamping of feet, and the cries of a furious multitude.

Priscilla, who was playing with her brother Marcus, stopped, thinking that the sea made less noise on stormy nights as it broke on the cliffs of the isle of the Pharos.

Suddenly, she perceived the click of the two enormous battens of the solid cedar-wood door of the palace, which had been closed in haste.

"The demons! The demons are coming!" someone shouted.

Immediately afterwards, a desperate howl rose from the interior courtyard to the room where the children were, and that howl became a regular, frightful lament that seemed to be emerging from the throat of a beast rather than a human throat.

Priscilla leaned out of the window and perceived a slave named Mammoea on all fours on the mosaics with an animal expression on her face. She was a Phrygian renowned for her fasting and the Christian austerity of her life. She was reputed to have once seen the Virgin Mary, but she could not hear the syllables of the word "demon" without falling into a singular crisis in which her voice lost any human intonation, as if the demon had entered into her by virtue of the force of the word.

Marcus burst into idiotic laughter and came to huddle against his sister, touching her arm and her shoulder, as he had a habit of doing every time he was close to her. This time, Priscilla did not think of pushing him away. Footfalls filled the staircase.

"Throw the pikes out of the window," ordered a voice.

The door opened and Priscilla saw her grandfather on the threshold. He was simulating calm, and a mocking smile was fixed on his lips. He raised his right hand and waved it, as if to reassure his trembling grandson and a few servants who were waiting his orders in the vestibule and on the steps of the marble stairway. He gave the impression of saying: *I've seen many others!*

Old Diodorus had been twenty years old in the times of the Emperor Julian and he had indeed, as he frequently repeated, seen many others. The pagan populace did not frighten him. At Hamath in Syria he had dispersed with blows of his staff a procession of naked priestesses who were attempting to invade the Church of the Epiphany, to the sound of tambourines, in order to replace a statue of Bacchus therein. He had nearly been stoned alongside Bishop Georgius of Cappadocia.[14] He had contributed under Theodosius to the destruction of the temple of Serapis.[15] He would not allow himself to be frightened by the cries of hatred of the prostitutes of Rhacotis and the thieves of the embalmers' quarter. They had been wrong to bring out weapons and close the door. It was, on the contrary, necessary to open it wide. He would appear on the threshold and the crowd would flee before his gaze...

Diodorus the son held him by the arm and held hard. Although he had inherited his father's piety, he had neither his violence, nor his courage.

"My God! My God! It's necessary to be careful because of my children..."

---

[14] Georgius was the Arian bishop of Alexandria from 356 to 351. He died in 361, two years before Julian the Apostate, which implies that Old Diodorus is presently in his late sixties.
[15] Theodosius I (347-392), Emperor of the East from 379-392 and then of the entire Empire until his death. Notoriously, he did not prevent or punish the destruction by Christians of the Serapeum in Alexandria in 391.

Old Diodorus shrugged his shoulders. "Hide them in the cellars if you're afraid." And he went downstairs and traversed the courtyard, heading for the door.

Voices were rising from the street now, as lugubrious as the cries of wild beasts in the desert, and the sound of sticks hitting the wood of the door was audible. The porter had fled somewhere in the palace, taking away the heavy key. People searched for him and called to him. That lasted several minutes.

Diodorus the son's teeth were chattering. He suddenly made a resolution.

He turned toward Thoutmos and Tehenna, two slaves whose fidelity was proven and who were ordinarily charged with the care of the children.

"Leave with them by the little garden door. Run to the bishop's house. Confide hem to him. Come back when the Praetorian guards have rendered justice. It should be over in an hour, but one never knows."

Fear took possession of Marcus and he started crying. He could not be stopped. Thoutmos rolled him up in a woolen cloak and they all went into the garden.

It was the moment when twilight changes into night. Between the gilded mosaics of the fountain the water jets rose up higher than usual and the orange-trees had a heavier perfume. Priscilla would have liked to sit down on the sand, to breathe in the evening air and not to be obliged to flee the wickedness of men.

The garden door opened into a back street in the Epsilon quarter. It was deserted. The two slaves, each carrying a child, started running. By turning right they could have reached the great Serapeum in a few minutes, but they would have bumped into the crowd that was coming from the western part of the city and feared being recognized as servants of Diodorus.

They made a wide detour. They passed furious bands. Alexandria had been ignited by the setting sun with a fire of the hatred of gods.

As if in a dream, Priscilla watched the long longitudinal avenues file past, some of which were born in the azure-tinted blue of the sea and went to terminate in the ashen pewter of Lake Mareotis. The monuments were innumerable. They were heaped on top of one another like stone fruits in a porphyry basket. Many destroyed temples had become churches, but there were temples that had been allowed to subsist because of their beauty, because they were a wealth for the city. At certain crossroads, they faced chapels like inexorable enemies supported on pylons and threatening them with their monumental doors.

Lanterns were illuminated along the terraces. Priscilla saw in passing the spiral staircases twisting their white steps toward the hill of the Paneum; the pathways lined by sphinxes and sycamores uncovering in their perspectives the mysterious dome of a hypogeum; the long colonnades in the Greek style succeeding monuments of the Ptolemaic era like a procession of young hierophants paused in the contemplation of the past. The ruins of the temple of Isis were compact and terrible, showing like severed limbs their quadrangular pillars with cubic capitals, where images of the cow-headed goddess Hathor still subsisted. Those of the temple of Poseidon were light and white; laurels had grown in the cracks between the paving-stones and invaded the broken altars, and doves had taken up residence in the foliage, making a great flutter of wings there.

There were beds of roses in front of private dwellings, and clumps of mimosas emerging over walls and almost obstructing the roadway. An Osirian colossus overturned during a riot, but which had not been moved because of its weight, had been surmounted by an image of the Virgin. In the triangular plaza where Saint Peter's Church stood there was a forest of obelisks, and the old house of the philosopher Olympios raised up its sculptural accumulation, in which Egyptian and Hellenic art were mingled: emblematic figures henceforth deprived of meaning, which has been covered in places by large white crosses.

Sometimes a torch illuminated the furious faces in passing. Priscilla began to tremble as they passed under the Tetrapylon of Vespasian because its four enormous pillars intercepted the last glow of the sky. They turned into the street of the Sema, but there a man who was clad in a yellow veil in the Syrian manner and who was running in the opposite direction called out to them with a triumphant tone in his voice: "Is it true that Diodorus' house is being pillaged?"

Then they went down the street of the Sema, went past the four porphyry lions of the little temple of Serapis and the twelve bronze winged horses of the Museum. They heard a confused clamor and saw the great stone stairway of a hundred steps that led to the Serapeum encumbered by a menacing crowd.

Bishop Cyril's dwelling was at the top between the three hundred columns of syenite erected by Ptolemy Soter. It dominated the entire city. It had been built, along with the Church of Saint Arcadius, with the sacred stones of the temple of the god Serapis, destroyed some years earlier by the patriarch Theophilus.

Thoutmos stopped, thinking that he could not get the children into the hands of Bishop Cyril without danger. Discouraged, he turned to Tehenna.

"Let's head for the gate of the Necropolis," said the latter. "We can go to my sister's house. The children won't be safer anywhere else than they will in her house."

Thoutmos hesitated. He never saw his sister-in-law. He knew that she prostituted herself in the Rhacotis quarter. She was married to a strange individual who was known as "the man who believes in nothing," and who exercised the decried profession of embalmer.

"What will the master say when he finds out?"

But Marcus, whom he had set down on his feet, suddenly started running hither and yon, uttering cries. It was necessary to catch him.

"Jesus! Jesus! Protect us!" Tehenna started repeating.

"Oh well, let's go to your sister's house," said Thoutmos.

They made a detour, skirted the Rhacotis quarter, arrived at the gate of the Necropolis, and penetrated into the district of the same name.

It was a mass of side-streets in which all the artisans of métiers relative to embalming and the ceremonies of death had once lived, but since Theodosius had forbidden the embalming and also the incineration of the dead it was only legal simply to bury them in the ground. The Necropolis quarter had been partially deserted and had become the refuge of ambulant merchants, prostitutes and thieves. A few embalmers still remained there, and those who had not renounced the ancient Egyptian rites transported the cadavers of their relatives to them, in order to come back and retrieve them when they had become mummies. That was the profession that Thoutmos' brother-in-law exercised.

In order to reach his dwelling it was first necessary to cross a narrow bridge over the canal that connected Lake Mareotis with the port of Kibotos. The water was stagnant, and an insipid odor charged with miasmas emerged from it. The two slaves made the sign of the cross as they passed over it. Near that bridge, a few years before, the centurion Septimus, responsible for watching over the Necropolis quarter, had had his soldiers throw into the water a number of mummies found in the home of an embalmer, and their plaintive and irritated doubles, it was said, had remained trapped in the putrescence of the waters.

After the bridge there was a long narrow street with a few shops. That street was calm, and those who lived there seemed unaware of the agitations of Alexandria. Women were sitting doorways; a beggar was rooting through the rubbish piled up at a crossroads.

The children walked alongside the slaves, but when the road curved and Thoutmos went into a narrower street that descended a steep slope, it was necessary to carry them again because they sank into soft things and an emaciated dog sometimes frightened them by coming to sniff them.

Thoutmos pushed a wooden barrier. The traversed some waste ground between two cracked walls and found themselves in front of a narrow door with a disjointed judas grille that let a vague light filter through.

Before Thoutmos had knocked, the door opened, and they saw on the threshold the man who believed in nothing.

Priscilla was very glad to know that there was no longer any danger, that they would soon have news and that they would doubtless soon be taken back to their father's house.

Tehenna had installed her beside her brother on a large woolen cloak. Sleep! She certainly had not slept. On entering that low-ceiling room where a heavy odor of myrrh and cassis hovered, she had had a very strange sensation.

"Priscilla! Priscilla! It's you, Priscilla!" an invisible breath, an inanimate voice, had whispered in her ear.

No, it was not that tall man with the triangular beard, with bushy eyebrows so thick that one could not distinguish his eyes, and it was not that woman with the ravaged face sitting on the ground, huddled up, who could have murmured her name so close to her. The perfumed air was full of human presences, and a mysterious activity that was not perceptible to the senses filled the atmosphere of the room.

Who had spoken Priscilla's name—or, rather, what illusion had made her think that she had been named?

The room, which was only illuminated by the smoky glow of an oil lamp, was cluttered with all sorts of objects. In the corners there were heaps of curved tongs, short knives, metal tubes and little saws, as if the master of the place practiced the art of torturer. Full sachets were piled on top of one another, and a bitter odor of spices emerged from one of them, which was open. A set of wooden shelves supported a long row of sealed bottles of blue, yellow and green liquids, and behind them there was a series of little colored masks, some made of cloth, others of gold-lined paper, almost all of them devoid of eyes. Large canopic jars in onyx and alabaster were lined up at the back, bearing on their bulge, in hieroglyphs, prayers to Isis, Nephtys, Neith and Serket, and on their lids the head of a hawk or a dog. Those canopic jars framed a low door, singularly obscure, that seemingly must have opened to the most important room in the house.

Sebek, the embalmer, listened in silence to what Thoutmos and the two women said. He rarely spoke and he never prayed to any god. He belonged by heredity to the inferior sacerdotal caste of Paraschites, but that caste had declined. A kind of malediction floated over embalmers. Sebek was a man scorned in his quarter, firstly because of his profession, and then because it was known that his wife went to prostitute herself in Rhacotis, and that he tolerated it, either out of weakness or because the constant handing of dead bodies gave his mind a bleak indifference to the things of life

"It was bound to happen," said Khepra, the embalmer's wife, shaking her head and making her fake earrings and necklaces rattle. "The gods of Egypt will resuscitate. Is it not shameful that the dead have to be bought here in secret and one had to hide in order to embalm them? The Christians glorify rotting in the ground! They'll rot there!"

Thoutmos made her a sign to shut up on that subject because of the children, but she stamped her heel and repeated: "They'll rot there!"

However, she stared at Priscilla's face with admiration. She even got up to look at her more closely.

"Isn't she beautiful?" said Tehenna, proudly.

"And they're capable of making her a virgin moldering in a monastery!" said Khepra, leaning over.

Priscilla saw above her face enormous glaucous, moist eyes, with large bistre circles, a fleshy mouth, features hollowed out by pleasure, reposing on a fat, almost milky neck. She felt the woman remove the Arab shawl with broad green stripes from her shoulder, and that she set it down over her, doubtless so that she would not be cold; and then, in that warmth, she became drowsy

In that torpor she had the sensation that somewhere, from a shadowed corner, an insect had risen into the air to circle around her, buzzing. It left behind it a wake of gold, which enveloped her. She could not make out the contour of its wings, but she sensed that it was a dangerous insect, of a bizarre form, with a black head, whose sting must be redoubtable. She was afraid of it; she would have liked to chase it away, but a sort of unhealthy attraction prevented her from moving.

The insect brushed her skin and suddenly alighted between her two girlish breasts. It was heavy and cold, and Priscilla's entire little body stiffened, prey to a delicious well-being.

She woke up, and retained herself from uttering a cry. Suspended around her neck by a golden thread there was a little black stone, which she palpated, and the contours of which seemed inexplicable to her. She knew that there were talismans against which it was necessary to protect oneself, because they communicated sins that certain impure beings had stored within them. She took it off immediately and threw it away, wondering whether it was not to the contact of that stone that she owed the moisture that was covering her and the disturbance by which she had been gripped.

She looked around. Tehenna and Khepra were asleep, side by side. The two men must have gone to find out what was happening in Alexandria.

She got up, set aside the blanket and the shawl that covered her, taking care not to wake her brother, and took a few paces across the room, very quietly. She was intrigued by the stifling perfumes and the singular objects that surrounded her.

She had reached the door at the back and perceived that the door was only pushed to, and that there was another room behind it, the grandeur and emptiness of which she perceived by the tremulous light of a vacillating lamp.

The door yielded without grating and Priscilla, obedient to her curiosity, crossed its threshold.

"Priscilla! Priscilla! It's you, Priscilla!"

She heard that whispered appeal again in her ear, so close but which seemed to be coming from very far away. The tone was plaintive, and she had heard it before, but where and when? Her memory could not pin it down.

To her right, stone sarcophagi were lined up, which seemed to be full of a bluish liquid, and a star whose light filtered through a skylight caused sapphire scintillations to run over it periodically. Facing her, there was an almost equal file of oblong wooden cases, encrusted with stones of all colors. And Priscilla, who had taken a few steps into the room, perceived then that she was in the midst of the dead.

They were not all in the same stage of their journey. Those to the right were reposing in natron water, rubbed with bitumen, stuffed with myrrh, cinnamon and aromatic herbs. They waited there for forty days before being impregnated with gold and wrapped in bandages, before receiving on their faces the masks with enamel eyes, in order to take their place for eternity in a hieroglyphic coffin, amid the symbols of all the gods, and to confront, motionless, the great course of time.

Priscilla did not experience terror. The voice that had named her had too much sadness and benevolence. She leaned over a single mummy, for while one is still in childhood, one retains a certain clairvoyance. On the base of the coffin she read the name *Theodula*.

That was the name of a pious old lady who had been a friend of her mother and had always had a great affection for Priscilla. She lived in a small house surmounted by a cross and surrounded by a garden full of currant bushes, not far from the sea, in the part of the Bruchium that touches the Macedonian Acropolis. There, conducted by Tehenna, Priscilla had gone to see her almost every Sunday. The old lady waited for the child in an interior courtyard, and when footsteps resonated in the corridor, at the habitual hour, she invariably got up and said: "Priscilla! Priscilla! It's you, Priscilla!"

She had attached herself forcefully to existence at the end of her days, although she had apparently received few pleasures in life. She had consulted a priest of Osiris to discover in what measure the rite of embalming permitted the double to subsist after death and continue to know physical joys. Priscilla recalled having heard her grandfather Diodorus wax indignant at those returns to ancient superstitions, and even affirm that Theodula would be damned for it, in spite of a life of piety.

Priscilla gazed at the black, shriveled, unrecognizable form that old Theodula made for a moment. There was nothing frightening about it; it was more conducive to pity. Priscilla recalled the bright garden where she had walked among beds of irises and carnations, and where she had handed her clusters of currants with astonishingly slender white hands. She would have liked to be able to offer her fruits in her turn. But no, never again! Old Theodula was now staring at her, from behind her golden mask, with enamel eyes circled with bronze; her hands were crossed over her breast, enveloped in sheaths of porcelain, and a little terracotta scarab was in the place of her heart.

But was her soul in the paradise of Jesus or was it beginning its peregrinations in the immense fields of the Amenti?

Thoutmos' face was grave when he reappeared, followed by the embalmer.

"Jesus has protected us in bringing us here. It's him who has saved these children!"

Marcus groaned, complaining about being woken up, and buried his head under the blanket.

Priscilla understood from the words exchanged that they were now going back to Alexandria peacefully, but that something had happened that no one dared say. She stepped on a hard object and saw on bending down the stone that she had earlier found around her neck and had thrown away. It was an ancient priapic emblem, eroded by time.

"The little princess didn't want to keep the god Khem," said Khepra softly, fixing her large glaucous eyes upon her, "but it doesn't matter. The god only needs a second, during sleep."

Then Priscilla remembered the burn between her breasts and the frisson that had run through her, and she experienced a great repulsion throughout her flesh.

The return seemed infinitely long. There were legionaries at all the crossroads, and the street where Diodorus' palace stood was full of them.

In the courtyard, slaves were standing immobile with torches, having the obligatory sadness in their features that is the rule in funeral ceremonies.

Then Priscilla noticed, with surprise, that two of the four marble vases that were in the corners of the courtyard had been smashed, and their debris scattered. A slave kneeling on the floor was washing the mosaics with water. A sticky red patch soiled a column.

She did not have time to be astonished. As Thoutmos set her brother down, still half-asleep, on his feet, Bishop Cyril appeared at the door of house, holding her father Diodorus by the shoulders, who was with him, bent double, his eyes half closed, his thin mouth forming the arc of a circle, livid and trembling.

"Courage!" said the Bishop, untiringly. "Come on, courage!"

He stopped when he perceived the children.

"Your grandfather was a saint," he said, raising his voice with an artificial solemnity, as if he were speaking as much for the slaves and the soldiers, and as much for posterity, as for Priscilla and Marcus, to whom he was addressing himself. "God wanted to recall him to his side. He has given him the glory of dying a martyr to his faith. Remember his example and be champions of Jesus all your life, like him."

Priscilla was immediately struck by the conventional character of those words. She loved her grandfather and she would subsequently feel a deep remorse at not having felt a sharp dolor immediately. Her sole thought now was to prevent her simple-minded brother Marcus from starting to laugh stupidly or say something incongruous in front of the Bishop, and all those who were looking at them curiously. She took him by the neck and embraced him abruptly. He struggled, but she was able to hold him against her until her father, having shaken the Bishop's hand, weeping, and escorted him as far as the street, had taken them back into the house.

That night, Priscilla went to sleep to the murmur of chanted prayers, and it was not until the next day that she found out what had happened.

Old Diodorus, while supervising the construction of a church the previous day on land that belonged to him, had perceived children playing, some of whom had long and curly hair. He had seen that as an indication of paganism, a sort of bravado against the simplicity of Christian fashion. He had had them seized by slaves and their heads shaved before him.

That had aroused the indignation of the pagan families to which they belonged. The news had spread from quarter to quarter. After the temples, they were attacking children! A dog-clipper had incited the mob while waving enormous shears and shouting that it was necessary to do the same to Diodorus. That idea had taken hold. The rabble of the port had followed the dog-clipper and had come *en masse* to surround Diodorus' house

Misfortune had determined that the irascible old man, confident in the majesty of his person, had opened the door wide. He had been knocked down. The dog-clipper had come too far to do nothing, but as Diodorus was extraordinarily bald, desiring nevertheless to show the crowd a trophy, he had attempted to tear off the skin of his scalp with the point of his scissors.

Diodorus was dead. The soldiers had arrived just in time to prevent the pillage of the palace by the pagans.

The funeral was celebrated with extreme magnificence. All the monasteries in Egypt were represented there. The news of a new martyr having penetrated into the deserts where the solitaries lived, several of them, with their hirsute manes and their animal skins, had set out on the march to attend the burial of the pious Diodorus. Several days after everything had been concluded, they were still presenting themselves at the gates of the city, covered in dust and mud.

Priscilla prayed with such fervor that her knees ached by dint of being folded, and she could only stand up afterwards with great difficulty. The frightful death of her grandfather inspired a horror in her of everything that was not Christian.

She often looked between her two breasts to see whether the little priapic stone that she had had around her neck while she slept had not left traces of a burn.

II. The Convent of Thirst

The convent of Zenobia the Syrian stood amid the sands on a stony hill, far into the desert beyond the last human habitation and the last anchorite hut. It was not on any caravan route. In order to reach it, it was necessary to go alongside Lake Mareotis, on the road that Alexander had taken several centuries earlier when he had gone to the temple of Ammon,[16] and then turn left on to a scarcely-visible sandy trail and plunge into a region bristling with rocks.

From a distance, it looked like a fortress, but at closer range one could see that it was only formed by a circular white wall surrounding an area of rather mediocre grandeur in the middle of which was a chapel without a bell-tower.[17] About fifty cells opened on to that space, and those cells only saw daylight through a narrow opening in the form of a cross cut out of the door. The chapel was juxtaposed with hangars in which there was wheat, barley, oil and a stable for camels.

That convent was known as the convent of thirst because it had no well, and in order to reach the nearest one it was necessary to travel for two days. Every week, a few nuns departed on the back of camels in order to go and fetch the provision of

---

[16] Accounts of Alexander's visit to the great temple of Ammon at the Oasis of Siwa in 331 B.C. are preserved by numerous ancient sources, all of them published after Alexander's death and based on rumor; the geographer Strabo claimed to have obtained the information from Ptolemy and Aristoboulos, who were allegedly at Siwa at the time, but that attempted justification only makes his account seem more dubious to skeptical eyes. The present text embellishes the myth considerably.

[17] It is unsurprising that it was not equipped with a bell-tower, as bells were not introduced into the Christian Church until 400 A.D. and their use was not officially sanctioned by the papacy until 604.

water that was to serve the community for seven days. They set forth before dawn, for even showing diligence, they could not return before the next evening but one. Some had been devoured by lions, others had disappeared in sandstorms. Others had gone astray on the return journey in spite of the bell that Zenobia rang herself all night long, and had wandered into the desert never to reappear. But no matter! Zenobia was a saint with a firm heart. She gladly offered to God the lives of her ewes as well as her own life, and when the well was dry and the convent had been suffering thirst for several days, she claimed that a purer prayer emerged from lips cracked by lack of water.

Every year, Priscilla and her brother, under the guard of majordomo Longinian, set out for the convent of thirst. That distant expedition was a great joy for the two children. The joy in question commenced several days before the departure when the tents were taken down to the courtyard and the slaves checked their canvas, their metal fittings and hooks. It continued when the sacks of provisions were prepared and the large jugs of wine.

It was a marvelous minute for the children when their father kissed them before they were hoisted on to the most vigorous of the camels of the caravan. But what pleased them most of all was the company of a few soldiers that Bishop Cyril had put at the disposal of Diodorus to protect them in the desert. They admired their weapons, theirs stature and the words they pronounced.

They traversed fertile plains, intercut with canals, where wheat grew and where he houses made golden patches. In the fields, they saw naked bronzed men swarming, picking cucumbers and sowing cotton. Sometimes behind a clump of palm trees, there was a village made up of mud cottages covered in straw and reeds, and a few stone houses, which resembled white hexahedra with flat roofs, in which a door and windows had been pierced. Those hexahedra often bore a smaller one, and on top of that there was a third. They were painted different colors in bright shades, which the sun made flamboyant, and Priscilla pointed them out to her brother from a distance, with exclamations,

The halt after the first stage was the less agreeable because they stayed overnight with an employee of Diodorus who supervised the large cotton plantations that he owned there. He was an austere and tedious man who lived in a large dilapidated palace dating back to the time of the Ptolemies. The wind made a sinister noise there and the large quadrangular room where the children spent the night was surrounded by red-tinted bas-reliefs that became impressive under the mobile light of the lamp.

An extended canvas divided the room into two, but Priscilla did not like spending the night with her brother. Marcus was showing signs of degeneracy. His intelligence only awoke slowly. He sometimes laughed idiotically and inexplicably. As he had grown older, his ears had fanned out immeasurably, his nose had become too long, his lips had thickened and, with his slightly hunched back and his enormous hands, there was something of the animal about him. His sister exerted an unhealthy physical attraction upon him. He could not be beside her without squeezing her neck, palpating her arms and caressing her skin. She had sometimes been obliged to strike him in order for him to let her go. So, in that room, where Marcus was more frightened than her, she feared that he would come to find her. She spoke to him to reassure him and looked for a long time, on the sheet that separated them, at the shadow that he cast, sitting up, with his ears like two ridiculous wings.

But the following evening, Priscilla savored the great emotion of beauty that the magnificence of nature procures children when it is mingled with dread.

They camped not far from a pool at the bottom of a circus of sand, near two stunted palm trees. The slaves ran hither and yon to light the fire, unroll the tents and pitch them, and make the camels drink. The soldiers lay down on the ground, and when the moon appeared in the sky, it made little gilded lights dance over their armor. Some of them threw their javelins into the distance to amuse the children. They formed a great circle to take the meal.

Then, by the light of the fire, like a phantom emerging from the darkness, an old anchorite appeared, who had a white beard down to his feet. He raised a little wooden cross and blessed everyone, even those soldiers who were not Christians, who knelt down like the others. Afterwards he sat down, and did not disdain to eat, drink and laugh. He stared at Priscilla with extraordinarily intelligent, laughing and benevolent eyes, and recounted marvelous stories of miracles while extending his hands toward the fire. Then he left the camp and disappeared, as if he had returned to another world.

They sometimes heard the roar of a lion, but when Priscilla expressed anxiety for the old man, she learned with admiration that in order for the wild beasts of the desert to come and lick the feet of solitaries they only had to extend the middle finger while keeping the others closed and murmur the name of Christ.

Late into the night, a soldier, a native of a northern country, intoned a long melancholy chant that evoked the passing of great rivers through forests of firs, villages obliquely illuminated by low suns, and smoke swirling over snowy valleys. Priscilla fell asleep to that chant, her heart deliciously gripped by anguish, and clutching in each hand a fistful of the warm sand of the land of Egypt.

It was not without apprehension that the majordomo Longinian and the soldiers of the caravan approached the convent. They gazed from afar at its terrible silhouette of stone outlined on the horizon and wondered whether it might not have become a college of dead women. That place of penitence had become famous in Alexandria. The tortures contained in its walls and the dangers by which that solitude was besieged were known, and the pious admiration that it provoked was mingled with a little pity and a little horror.

For not all the penitents were voluntary. Noble families had sent young women there possessed by the demon of lust and husbands had taken adulterous wives there. Face to face with the fiery sky and the bleak extent of the desert, burned by thirst, the sinners were bound to find repentance of their sins. And many, in the narrow cell that they could not flee without going to the certainty of death, had ended up resigning themselves to it. But not all! There had been frightful revolts that had only been appeased by the energy of Zenobia.

The peasants who renewed the convent's food supplies four times a year had heard many laments and many appeals, and they drew away making the sign of the cross, being uncertain, in their simple hearts, that so much suffering could be agreeable to God.

Every year, in accordance with an unchanging ritual, Priscilla and her brother accomplished their visit to the convent of thirst. The caravan camped at the base of the hill. Longinian climbed the narrow, winding path that led to the convent door with the children, whom he held by the hand. Three slaves marched behind him, laden with bananas, dates and olives, the only gifts that Zenobia consented to receive. Invariably, she was standing at the door. She did not smile and scarcely spoke. She conducted the children across the courtyard.

Then, from a cell facing them, a woman emerged, with immense eyes full of tears and a face whose features were a little more drawn every year. She kissed Priscilla and Marcus by turns, especially Priscilla, with all her might. That only lasted a few moments; it could not last any longer, by virtue of a pact that was doubtless accepted, but was still very cruel. Every time, the woman made an imploring gesture; Zenobia, making another, remained as mute as divine justice, and she took the children away. She accompanied them to the door, and expended her hand to bless them.

That was all. That long voyage had had no other objective than that interview of a few seconds. They set out for Alexandria again.

The children submitted to all the events, strange as they appeared to them, as the result of a fatality they could not change. Priscilla reviewed the acts of the drama, but she only connected them vaguely and did not understand their original cause; nor could she understand their cruelty.

She remembered a distant time when life had changed abruptly in the house of Diodorus. She had been told at first that her mother was ill and confined to bed in the room. It had been forbidden for her to go and embrace her. A few days passed. Priscilla had noticed that none of the usual physicians had come and that only Bishop Cyril had made frequent visits to her grandfather. Her father wept incessantly, and Priscilla had heard Cyril say to old Diodorus, indicating him, that he was the one that it was necessary to save.

Her mother was ill, but it was her father who was in danger. She had not understood.

While playing in the garden, however, she had perceived her mother at the widow of her room. She had never seemed so full of life. Never, either, had her great splendid eyes stared so desperately at the blue of the sky. Her hair, in heavy tresses, hung down over the nape of her neck like vivacious plants. Her milky neck and the blonde birth of her shoulder were radiant with the richness of her blood. That visage of desire was framed by sycamore branches; it seemed to be drinking the afternoon sunlight; it gave such an impression of youth and amour that Priscilla remained dazzled by it.

She had been woken up the following night by the heart-rending voice of her mother. That voice was mingled with that of her grandfather, dry and inexorable. Footsteps descended the staircase. A horse whinnied in the courtyard. Priscilla had got out of bed, had opened the door of her bedroom and had leaned over the stone balustrade.

She had not grasped what was said very clearly. Her mother was begging. She repeated her name and her brother's. She was asking for something that was not granted to her.

"You'll see them once a year, I swear before God," her grandfather had said.

"Have pity on me! Have pity on me!"

Priscilla was about to run downstairs. An inexplicable dread had held her back.

Oh, why had she not gone down those stairs? She was to reproach herself for that a thousand times in the course of her life, to ask herself a thousand times by virtue of what force she had not done it. In that second, the destiny of her family, and her own, had been decided. If, obedient to her instinct, she had suddenly appeared in her long night-dress, like the angelic savior for which her mother doubtless hoped, her grandfather's will might have weakened, pity might have intervened, thanks to her. But no. She had not dared. She had crept back to her room. She had listened again. The main door had closed. She had gone to sleep.

Priscilla knew that it was her grandfather who had done everything, on the advice of Bishop Cyril. Her father had only wept and obeyed. The first time she had departed for the beautiful and terrible journey, she had heard old Diodorus give his instructions to the majordomo Longinian.

"I promised that she would see them once a year but I didn't make any promise as to the duration of the meeting. You'll let her see the children for the time of a glance, no longer." And as Longinian remained standing before him in the attitude of a man who has a phrase on his lips that he dare not pronounce, he added: "It's the Patriarch himself who has decided it thus."

Diodorus had spread the rumor that his wife had retired voluntarily to a convent following a mystical crisis. Those who knew her had not believed it. A rich Alexandrian with whom she had sometimes been seen had disappeared at about the same time, without anyone making a connection between that disappearance and her departure for the convent.

Years had passed. Everything was forgotten.

Priscilla was accustomed only to see her mother out there for a few moments, under the burning sky, in the abode of stones and sand. She was accustomed to seeing her pure and bright visage, ravaged by the torment of thirst, lose its beauty year by year, becoming more haggard at every visit, more desperate and more similar to the bleak desert.

What had happened that year? Had Priscilla and Marcus emitted a more attractive life? Are there, in the resignation of souls, unexpected surges of revolt, like a tidal wave suddenly swelling a calm sea?

Everything had happened as usual. Longinian and the children had climbed the little winding path, the slaves had deposited the fruits on the threshold and a few silent women had carried them to the hangars behind the chapel The annual kiss had been given, the tears had been shed, and Priscilla, as she drew away across the courtyard, had carried one away on her cheek, so quickly dried!

The door had closed again, they had gone back down, the camels had stretched out their necks, and they had departed.

Then a strange cry had been heard. It was not someone calling to tell the caravan to stop and wait; it was not a human plaint; it was a hoarse sound like the cry of a beast, a instinctive voice coming from the utmost depths of being: a frightful, prolonged sound that did not evoke dolor but something worse, unnamable, surpassing the known measure of horror.

A form had been seen to descend, a gesticulating form that was running so rapidly through the stones that everyone, unable to believe their eyes, remained immobilized. An unkempt woman with frightened eyes raced down the slopes, letting herself fall into the short cuts. She reached the bottom of the hill and advanced into the sand. Everyone understood, for the story of Diodorus was known in Alexandria, and everyone watched, consternated.

Longinian gave orders to a few soldiers.

It was necessary to take the mother back to the convent, willingly or by force; it was necessary to move the children away.

The savage and terrible being was now clinging on to a large leather bag suspended from the flank of a camel, without ceasing to utter her inconceivable cry. To that cry, by virtue of a power of communication that no one could explain, another, almost identical, responded. It was Marcus who uttered it, in spite of the fact that his stupid face denoted incomprehension of what was happening.

There was a minute of extraordinary disarray. Priscilla had let herself slide down to the sand and had attempted to join her mother. Longinian had been able to stop her and she struggled in his arms. Then, one of the soldiers, a man who was called the barbarian, a simple and taciturn man with long blond hair, without anything enabling the gesture to be anticipated, drew his sword and delivered a forceful blow to the head of one of his comrades who was trying to detach the woman's arms by force from the leather bag to which they were clinging. He was pale, and his limbs were agitated by a tremor. His blow, launched at hazard, struck the soldier's helmet, and did not inflict any wound.

The barbarian was surrounded. He repeated: "It's necessary to have pity on her! I've had children too!"

All that was very brief, but it was to remain engraved in the minds of the witnesses. Zenobia the Syrian finally arrived. Other nuns accompanied her, but they were unnecessary. Priscilla's mother, very meekly, at a slow pace, like a child that had committed a sin and is afraid, started walking back to the convent, hunched and shrunken, bent double in her torn veils, like a bundle of rags. All the energy of several years had been expended. She did not even look back.

Old Diodorus had been killed the same year. His son was a poor, weak man devoid of will-power. He became even more timid and uncertain and acquired the habit of not making any decision, and not having any precise thought, without reference to Bishop Cyril.

The latter decided that the children would no longer accomplish their annual visit to Zenobia's convent. The scandal that had occurred had annulled the promise made.

Diodorus attempted a few objections.

"It's for your children, and in the interest of the unfortunate sinner herself," the Bishop replied.

When the following autumn reddened the palm trees of the desert and the land exhaled heavy vapors, forerunners of the season's simooms, the unfortunate sinner gazed for many days at the cross that let a little light into her cell, the cross that never brought her any more hope.

III. Hypatia

In the stifling heat of the afternoon, the tamarisks of the garden were immobile. Clusters of wisteria seemed to have been painted on the azure of the sky. Bees were buzzing around.

Then, for no reason, Priscilla tilted her head backwards, her gaze lost in the distance, and, as if she were expressing a thought already ancient, she said: "I'd like to see Hypatia."

At that name, the face of Majorin, who was playing the role of tutor with regard to Priscilla and her brother and was in the process of giving them a history lesson, took on an expression of sad hatred. His eyelids were creased, his complexion jaundiced. He was afflicted by a disease of the liver, and irritations and bad sentiments were immediately reflected in his features.

"Is it true that there isn't a more beautiful woman in Alexandria?" Priscilla added.

"The wicked are never beautiful," said Majorin, giving his lips an expression of disgust. "Everyone conceives beauty differently. On the rare occasions that it has been given to me to encounter that woman, I have had the sentiment of the most abject ugliness, that of the soul, and I fled immediately. The limited pagans who delight in lies can appreciate her face and find beauty therein. If there is any, it is given by the basest vices. Perhaps the line of her mouth is regular, but when I have seen that mouth open to speak, it made me think of the drains of Bruchium that carry the filth of Alexandria to the sea."

Skeletal in his black robe, Majorin was sitting facing the children on a stone bench in the shade of the palm trees in the garden.

Behind him, a gardener was holding a large watering-can at arm's length, with which he was watering the mimosas. The water, spreading out in a fan through the broad head, sur-

139

rounded Majorin with a luminous silver aureole that brought out the yellow color of his skin, his thinness, his wrinkles, and his hidden malevolence, and rendered him similar to a caricature of a saint.

Hypatia! She was for some the glory of Alexandria, for others its opprobrium. Never, either in Athens or in Rome, had a woman professed philosophical teachings publicly. It was an unprecedented novelty that shocked and excited opinion at the same time. Her great beauty, the austerity of her life and the slightly theatrical ostentation she put into making the most of both added further to her prestige. The prefect Orestes asked her advice.[18] Synesius, whom the city of Ptolemais had just proclaimed Bishop because of his justice, called her his sister, mother and mistress in spirit.[19] The poet Palladius compared her to Astraea and Minerva and addressed hymns to her in the model of those the Greek poets composed in honor of the gods.

She battled against the authority of Bishop Cyril in Alexandria, and the increasing number of students who came to hear her lectures at the Museum caused her partisans to say that through her, philosophy would triumph over Christian ideas in Egypt. Many men had loved her, but she had neglected amour thus far. She gave her black hair the undulation of waves and wore a large green jewel therein, made of an unknown substance, which was said to be a magical stone once possessed by Iamblichus, which gave spiritual power. She had rare essences brought from Arabia to perfume herself, and her garments were made of a cloth so fine that they adapted to her

---

[18] Orestes was the Roman governor of the province of Egypt in 415, when he clashed with Cyril over the latter's attempts to exert ecclesiastical authority over secular matters. He was forced to leave Alexandria after Hypatia's murder, and history lost trace of him thereafter.

[19] Synesius (373-c414) was a neoplatonist philosopher whose Christianity had seemed rather lukewarm until he was appointed bishop of Ptolemais by popular acclaim in 410.

body and allowed all of its harmonious grace to be seen when she walked. She lived with her father, the mathematician Theon,[20] in a little house not far from the Church of Caesarea, whose threshold was surmounted by a stone owl, the emblem of Athene. Its garden was small and no plants other than laurels grew there.

Majorin's gaze expressed the irritated scorn of his entire being. Marcus was dozing quietly, his mouth open.

"However," said Priscilla, "there are many philosophers and professors who come from Corinth, Antioch and Rome to hear her. It's said that the Museum has never known an influx as great as when she speaks there."

Majorin burst into bitter laughter. "Philosophers! Professors! Professors of what? Of lies! What do they teach? The three hypostases of Ammonius, the Sophia of the Gnostics. It's risible. Bad times are those in which we live. Error is allowed to propagate. People forget that there is a hidden force that makes it spread more easily than truth, and that the demon lends it wings. We have our hands bound. It's necessary for there to be another prefect!"

"Even if only once, I'd like to see Hypatia," murmured Priscilla, who was no longer listening.

Majorin shrugged his shoulders. He was about to criticize the impropriety of that desire and affirm that it would never be realized.

A little caterpillar, as yellow as a drop of gold, dropped on to his black robe and made a living stain there. He stood up in order to shake it off. That made a diversion. He was in a bad mood. Marcus was completely asleep. Priscilla laughed. He interrupted the lesson and went back up to his room, which was under the eaves.

He did not suspect that the mysterious law that connects events and enables great events to stem from tiny causes,

---

[20] The historical Theon (335-405) was dead by the time this part of the story is set (415), but the present text prolongs the life of the character somewhat.

would put his pupil in the presence of Hypatia before the end of the day, and that it would only be the first scene in a great drama that was in preparation.

Priscilla was now fifteen years old. Her breasts had flourished, her flesh had colored, her eyes had acquired a singular profundity, and men were troubled in her presence, as if they had respired a dust of sensuality that escaped her and trailed behind her footsteps.

Many were astonished by that, for it seems that there ought to be a logic of nature only to give a voluptuous beauty of the body to those who are susceptible of making use of it.

Priscilla was inclined toward religion with all her ardor. Naturally, the daughter of the richest man in Alexandria had had a thousand aspirants for her hand, but the news had rapidly spread that her tastès pushed her toward the monastic life. The narrow amity of the Patriarch of Alexandria and Diodorus confirmed that opinion, for Cyril considered that the renunciation of a great fortune for retreat into a convent made the power of Christ more glaringly evident. He also saw it as a source of profit for the Church.

At the moment of puberty Priscilla had been struck by human desires like so many arrows plunging into her flesh. Her modesty had triumphed over the initial curiosities that one experiences at that age, and a perpetual suffering had come to her, from which she could not protect herself. That suffering came from obscene inscriptions that she saw involuntarily on walls, certain words that she overheard, gestures that she glimpsed whose meaning she divined, and certain expressions in gazes audaciously fixed on her.

When she passed through the port, the wind martyrized her because it stuck her garment to her torso and uncovered her ankles. She lowered her eyes because of the nudity of the negroes unloading merchandise along the quays, but even when she could not see it, that nudity, close by, offended her. She could not pray in church if a man was kneeling beside her. When she opened her window on spring mornings she respired something sexual with the pollen and the vegetal dust of the garden, which made her faint with disgust.

She was subject on the part of her brother to attempted caresses that, although rare, were odious to her. Marcus' intelligence had not developed with the years. He had periods of almost complete imbecility. He laughed constantly then, and thought of nothing but getting close to his sister. When he found himself alone with her, either in a room or in the garden, he would suddenly seize her in his arms and hug her to him, until she was able to escape his embrace by force. At other times he kissed her neck, breathing the perfume of her skin forcefully, or laughed endlessly while enveloping himself in the embroidered mantle that she wore, and in which he perceived something of her. Strictly speaking, all that did not surpass the manifestations of affection that a brother can permit himself with his sister, but Priscilla, rightly or wrongly, sensed an obscure impulsion therein, a love of her flesh that had the violence of sin and by which she was dolorously traversed.

A certain Peter, lector and caretaker of the Church of Saint Mark, who was Bishop Cyril's man of confidence, often came to see her father. He was a kind of Hercules who panted as he walked and emitted an odor of garlic and old linen. His short-cropped hair was born almost over his eyes, which were very small, and he seemed to have no forehead, and with the pointed form of his head, his prominent jaw, his bad teeth and he greasy pallor of his hops he evoked the idea of a monstrous pig. His hands, by virtue of a particular infirmity, gave off a sticky liquid, which did not prevent him extending them to people he encountered with such frank force that one was obliged to shake them.

Peter was dominated by a continual desire for coupling. In the evening he prowled deserted quarters in order to knock down and take by force the women the encountered, or, sitting in front of the portal of Saint Mark's, he whispered propositions to those who came to pray alone. He sometimes employed threats, and sometimes promises. A black woman from

Rhacotis had attempted to kill him out of jealousy. It was said that he had once been condemned to the mines as a thief. No one knew the origin of his elevation.

For Priscilla he was the symbol of the material ugliness by which she was surrounded. His presence was an insult to her chastity. He remained apparently respectful, but stared at her with his blinking eyes, undressing her, considering her body from the roots of her thick hair to the tips of her delicate feet. She saw his mouth trembling imperceptibly then; that movement was the sole sign of his desire, but she was obliged to flee under its pollution.

When she was all alone in her room, before going to bed, when she had recited all her prayers, she sometimes wept in front of the large bronze mirror at the foot of her bed, in considering the receptacle of evil, the vase of sin, that her slender and excessively perfect body was.

Majorin was never able to explain what happened. There was a crowd outside the Museum. A large number of young men stationed around the twelve winged horses that framed the portal were waiting for the emergence of Hypatia, in order to acclaim her.

Followed by Priscilla and Marcus, he had advanced quite a long way along the street of the Sema when he saw a chariot turn round and retrace its steps because of the density of the crowd.

On that chariot was Bishop Cyril. His lips were taut, his immense forehead was deeply furrowed.

"I too ought to turn back," he murmured.

Majorin thought that it was appropriate to act like Bishop Cyril and not to mingle with the crowd of pagans, where his ecclesiastical appearance was beginning to provoke jeers on the part of the injurious young men.

"Come on, come on, don't remain among there people. Follow me."

Doubtless neither Marcus nor Priscilla heard him, for they continued walking past the Museum while he turned back with great strides. When Majorin perceived that he was alone and tried to catch up with his pupils, a stir in the crowd prevented him from doing so.

Then Priscilla knew for the first time the light of a gaze that was not devoid of softness.

A young man who was marching beside her looked at her, smiling. His hair was parted at the front and the regular features of his face were calm and handsome. He was dressed with care. His mauve chiton was pinned at the shoulder by an Egyptian jewel. A cloak of a deeper mauve was thrown over his shoulder and trailed behind him. There was something negligent, easy and cheerful in his gait. Priscilla noticed, with surprise, that he was wearing several bracelets on his wrist.

"If it's Hypatia you want to see, come with me; I'll introduce you to her." He said that as if Priscilla and Marcus were old acquaintances. "Let's get out of this crowd. By going this way we'll arrive in a matter of minutes."

And, without waiting for a response, certain that his proposition would be accepted, he went into a narrow street to the left and plunged into ancient Bruchium.

He had affected to address Marcus directly, like a familiar comrade, but he had judged him with a glance.

Her desire to prevent her brother making a ridiculous response, and also the desire that she had to see Hypatia, impelled Priscilla to stammer a few words and, uncertainly, she turned with her brother behind the young man.

"I'm from the family of Azarias and my name is Telamon," said the latter, not without a hint of pride. Then, on the way, he explained that his father had had a gymnasium built, on the model of that of Ephesus, in the vicinity of the public gardens, not far from the ruins of the Macedonian Acropolis. There, a few young men, smitten with ancient Greece, met at dusk in order to discuss philosophy, take baths and devote themselves to all the games of old.

"Hypatia is particularly fond of throwing the discus. You could compete with her if you've already had a little practice," Telamon went on, darting an ironic glance at Marcus. "There's a stadium for running and a xyste for wrestling. My sisters engage in combats there like true athletes. But perhaps you'd prefer to drink sorbets while listening to the discourses of philosophers. There are very arduous ones. It's true that it's permissible to imitate Antagoras and listen without understanding. Proclus is there almost every day, and also Isidore of Gaza.[21] He's the most interesting because he recounts the visions he has had and explains dreams. Perhaps last night, one or other of you had a curious dream whose symbolic meaning you'd like to know?"

Oh, yes, Priscilla had had a dream: a terrible dream, which had woken her up with a start, leaving her damp with sweat.

In an endless avenue bordered by cypresses, obelisks and stone sphinxes very small and very pale, she was walking alongside the monstrous Peter, the sight of whom, when he came to see her father, caused her such a complete repulsion. He was holding her by the hand and she felt her palm and fingers impregnated by his sticky grip. She was his thing, his property, his slave. He was not dragging her. She was walking beside him meekly, of her own free will.

To the right and the left, faces that she knew were considering her with horror, but as they went along she acquired a lightness. A nauseating odor emerged from her companion, and he sometimes uttered a bestial grunt. They went quickly toward the goal that was designated in the distance beneath a lunar glow, and that goal was a poor chapel that resembled the one that she had seen several years before in the midst of the sands, between the cells of the convent of Zenobia the Syrian.

---

[21] The historical neoplatonist philosopher Isidore of Gaza could not have been in Alexandria at the beginning of the fifth century, as he was the leader of the Athenian school near the century's end. He was a friend of the historical Proclus, who was born circa 412, and also could not have been in Alexandria while Hypatia was alive. The characters bearing those names in the present text are, therefore, fictitious.

On the threshold of that chapel, Jesus Christ was standing, but he was not the Christ of the churches, the one who
was paraded in processions, the one who was worshiped over
tabernacles. This one was neither radiant nor splendid. He
wore a triangular beard in accordance with the custom of the
Essenes of the shore of the Dead Sea. He had one shoulder
higher than the other and knock-knees, and on drawing closer
Priscilla saw that his entire body was deformed. Beneath the
rags that covered him she distinguished traces of leprosy,
moist pustules and hideous lesions. A swarming life animated
his body. Beasts were climbing his legs, lice were circulating
in his hair, and worms were eating his abscesses.

She understood that this was the true Christ of men, the
one who had assumed their sins and miseries in order that the
spirit might be saved; and she fell to her knees to adore him.
But then the horrible Peter, the ignominious companion who
had brought her here, shook her forcefully and handed her a
stone in order for her to throw it at the sublime Christ. She
perceived that the liquid sweated by his hand was blood,
which had stained her arms and her white tunic, and had
dripped behind her all along the great avenue.

She knew that it was necessary, in spite of herself, to accomplish the greatest crime, to throw the stone, and, with all
her might, she threw it.

But how would she dare to recount that dream, and who
could explain it?

"We've arrived," said Telamon. "Look at the bas-relief
above the door. It's my father who recovered it. It ornamented
the temple of Apollo at Delos and it's by Phidias."

The first courtyard was paved with large orange-colored
mosaics and was surrounded by busts of Socrates, Plato and
the most famous Greek philosophers.

After having passed through a marble portal, the young
people penetrated a second square courtyard planted with
palm trees, surrounded by a double portico, and in the middle
of which was a statue of Hermes. Sitting on stone benches,

several individuals formed a semicircle and were chatting while respiring the first freshness of dusk.

"Hypatia has preceded us," said Telamon, joyfully, and he pushed his two companions ahead of him.

She was, in fact, there.

Priscilla contemplated the illustrious neoplatonist with amazement.

The oval of her face was perfect. The large green jewel that she wore in her undulating hair put an emerald reflection into her immobile features. Her eyes were immense, changing and limpid, and one could not say whether they were green, like the jewel in her hair, or blue, like the necklace of sapphires that she wore around her neck. She was enveloped by an Oriental garment whose fabric was a darker blue than her sapphires, the blue of a stormy sea in the dusk, spangled with bright silver gleams that made it shimmer and sparkle, like a wave sown with stars, like the zaimph of a miraculous divinity.

"I was waiting for you," she said, getting up. "You know how to throw the discus well, you're my preferred partner."

And with a gesture of a slightly theatrical grandeur she extended her minuscule hand to Telamon, smiling as she added the formula of salutation of the ancient Greeks, which the Hellenists of Alexandra had adopted: "Rejoice!"

Telamon could indeed rejoice. Hypatia's face only took on that vivid animation, the active gaiety that it had suddenly acquired on seeing the young man, for ideas that were dear to her. A tall and robust individual covered in jewels, who was sitting beside her, had certainly perceived it. That was the rich poet Palladius. He reddened with surprise and wounded vanity. Beneath his fleecy and curly hair he was reminiscent of a great pink sheep, easily irritated. He thought himself the most handsome and intelligent man in Alexandria and he had a natural pride so great that an amicable gesture or an amiable word addressed by a woman to another man in his presence appeared to him to be a personal insult.

148

"What a beautiful young woman!" said Hypatia, considering Priscilla and moving slightly aside the veil that the latter wore on her head, which hid a part of her face.

For a second, Priscilla saw the philosopher's marvelous gaze fixed upon her. There was a sincere admiration therein, a little spontaneous tenderness and perhaps the hint of envy that a woman of thirty always experiences in the presence of a girl of fifteen.

They stood facing one another, almost equal in height, and they offered the image of feminine beauty in its double aspect of knowledge and ingenuousness.

"Child, child," murmured Hypatia, in a low voice, more for herself than Priscilla, "take as much advantage of existence as you can. Perhaps there is a wisdom that escapes sages, which only those who know nothing possess."

Everything that she saw and heard thereafter was, for Priscilla, a strange dream from which she would have liked to escape. But how? Marcus was laughing very loudly with two or three young men, amused by his protruding ears and his long nose. She had followed Hypatia and Telamon into the xyste, and imagined the terms in which she would confess, the following day, the sin into which her timidity was causing her to plunge ever deeper.

The xyste was long and narrow, with two rows of plane trees, the crowns of which were illuminated by the setting sun. Two negro slaves who were crouching by the threshold got up and picked up the metal disks attached to a strap that they had beside them.

With a natural gesture, without hesitation and without embarrassment, Hypatia had removed the great blue veil with silver spangles that was wrapped around her body, and then she had taken off a tunic of a paler blue that she was wearing underneath. To Priscilla's great amazement, she appeared almost naked, in silk shorts and a transparent tunic of a blue that was almost white, which exposed her shoulders, part of her breasts and her legs. Tranquil and splendid, without thinking about the body that she had just unveiled almost entirely, she

149

took a discus from the hands of one of the negroes and advanced in the sunlight.

Telamon had done likewise. He was bronzed, muscular, broad-shouldered, and his ankles were remarkably delicate. Priscilla remembered words heard in sermons on the morals of pagans and their immodesty. The latter term had remained mysterious for her. She understood it now. The surge of sympathy that she had felt for Hypatia was transformed into fear. What was this creature, who did not hesitate to show, before a man and a woman, the forms that God had created for evil and whose shame he ordered to be hidden?

Telamon and Hypatia took turns to throw the discus; they ran to see the distance at which it had fallen; they uttered bursts of laughter; their complexions became animated; their movements gave rise to an aureole of innocent life.

But that only lasted for a few minutes. Abruptly, without warning her partner, Hypatia dropped the discus at her feet and disappeared in three light bounds behind a door that opened to the right and was that of the loutron where cold baths were taken.

Telamon must have been accustomed to such caprices, for he too pushed the door to the men's bath, which was facing it.

"Don't be annoyed, little girl," Priscilla heard, amid a splash of water. "It's only when you know mathematics and philosophy that you'll understand the sensuality procured by throwing the discus and cold water on warm skin. But perhaps no sensuality is important to you?"

If she had been certain of finding her brother right away, perhaps Priscilla would have departed at a run for the exit of the gymnasium. The fear of being ridiculous, and an obscure attraction for this society, so new for her, retained her.

In any case, a group had just invaded the xyste and surrounded Hypatia, who emerged from the bath in her garment the color of the sea.

A thin man with illuminated eyes, who was raising a feverish finger toward the sky, was gesticulating and talking loudly. That was Isidore of Gaza, one of Hypatia's closest friends, who was even reputed to be betrothed to her.

He was expressing himself with an extreme rapidity.

"There are correspondences between the dreams of individuals linked by a bond of sympathy. What the invisible world designs for me during sleep it also designs or others of whom my mind has formed the image before going to sleep. The dreams complete one another, and if one succeeds in grasping the relationships that exist between them one can read the future as easily as the past. I can affirm that I am in the process of making oneiromancy an exact science. Would you like me to give you a striking example? I haven't consulted Hypatia. I haven't seen her all day. I'm going to tell her what she dreamed shortly before dawn, which is the moment when dreams are almost always symbolic."

"Well?" voices around him said.

He turned toward Hypatia. "There appeared to you in a dream," he said, "and with extreme clarity, I'm sure, a lion crouching between two empty urns, not far from a ruined tower. And I'll add that there were black birds above the tower."

Hypatia smiled and declared that not only had she not dreamed anything similar, but that she had not had any dream at all.

"Recall your memories," said Isidore.

No, her sleep had been profound and exempt from dreams.

"That doesn't change anything of what I'm advancing," said Isidore then, casting a glance at his audience full of the joyful delight that only absolute faith can give. "The image existed, but the sleep was too profound for consciousness to be able to retain it. I've contrived to see almost all of Hypatia's life unfolding before me. I know that she will soon return to Athens and that she will speak in Rome, and will also live for a time in Syracuse. And what longevity! I know that she will attain her hundredth year..."

"Many thanks!" said Hypatia.

They started to walk under the plane trees.

Priscilla heard Isidore affirm that when he was able to publish his treatise on the correspondences between nocturnal images, everyone would know his future, and because of that, would be able to make better usage of the present. She looked at him with terror, because he was one of the magicians that the Church reproved.

Telamon leaned toward her and, showing her a man of about thirty who was now conversing with Hypatia, he said: "That's Proclus." But that name was unknown to Priscilla.

"He was initiated in Chaldea," Telamon added, with admiration. "Minerva appeared to him twice during his childhood."

The setting sun was spreading an inexpressibly soft light. The exclamations and laughter of young men were audible, coming from the stadium, and the sonority of their voices was musical. Others, in white mantles, were debating under the porticos. The group that Priscilla was following penetrated into a garden whose sandy pathways were ordered with clumps of spindle trees that had just been watered and where brilliant droplets were shining like as many little pearls.

Jets of water swayed in onyx fountains surrounded by white laurels.

Priscilla understood very little of what she heard and her remorse increased because she was conscious of experiencing pleasure in meeting Telamon's gaze.

Proclus' face reflected enthusiasm. He had devoted himself to divine matters and he lived in an atmosphere of the marvelous that his imagination created around him. He had been admitted in Babylon as an epopt to the mysteries of the great Hecate. He communicated by intuition with superior intelligences and genii. He practiced the lustrations customary in the Orphic mysteries, he observed the auspicious and inauspicious days, like the Egyptian priests, purified himself in honor of Vesta, fasted in honor of Astarte, and recited prayers in honor of the sun at dawn and dusk. All forms of adoration were familiar to him, and all rites were dear to him.

"Jesus was merely an initiate who was mistaken," he said to Hypatia. "He betrayed the mysteries. He revealed them too soon for them to be profitable to humans. We are only seeing the commencement of the deadly results of his error, but we cannot know what disastrous consequences might yet flow from the hatred of culture and scorn for intelligence and beauty that are preached in his name. But it is necessary not to manipulate forces whose range one does not know and cast over the world a flame of which one is not the master. It was Apollonius of Tyana who was in the right when he went from sanctuary to sanctuary to unify religions and teach that the same God inhabits all temples. It is the same for initiates as for other men in other branches of life. It is never the greatest who carry off the palm. Renown wears a blindfold, and a certain portion of popular mediocrity is even necessary to attain the hearts of men."

"Apollonius certainly had the advantage over Jesus for the grandeur of his thought and the teachings of his life," replied Hypatia, turning aside to dart a long glance at Telamon, as if she wanted to take him as a witness., "but he was wrong to work miracles like him. He cured the sick, he prophesied, he rendered himself invisible and resuscitated the dead. What good did it do? Only the truth matters. It's not in vain that it is always represented naked emerging from a well. Woe betide the sage who dresses in the robe of the magician and the miter of the mage. His work will perish."

Proclus' eyes sparkled. He considered Hypatia's hair, undulated with so much care, the folds of her pallium, so artistically draped, and her harmonious movements, as if her person were a living contradiction of her words.

"Do you believe that your beauty does not add to the force of your teaching and does not serve to propagate the truths that you express? It is, at any rate, a gift that has only been made to you with that goal by the intelligences that rule us. But do not those intelligences make themselves concrete in material forms in order to reach the vulgar human mind? Pallas Athene really exists and will exist as long as we are enveloped in such a demanding material body. Do you not take account of the inconceivable stupidity of men, their baseness, and their reckless love of matter? What a time for an idea to grow! What an ocean of darkness in which we are trying to make a spark shine! For a long time yet it will be necessary for the sage and the charlatan to resemble one another. Jesus did well to reawaken Lazarus publicly. Apollonius did well to announce the death of Domitian at Ephesus. And I am following their example by composing a magical globe, with the aid of which I will be able to make rain at will and cast into astonishment men who could only believe in my wisdom afterwards."

While talking, the group had made a tour of the garden and had arrived at a door that opened to the first courtyard of the gymnasium.

Hypatia paused for a moment on the threshold, pensively.

"Yes, as Plato said, the last veil that the sage strips away, the one he removes with the greatest difficulty, is that of personal pride. I do not flatter myself with having gone so far. But I believe that your magic ball, if it makes rain fall from the sky, might make error fall into minds. Men are avid for tricks, for proofs, for miracles. So much the worse! Reason ought to present itself entirely pure and cause its light to spring forth without material proof. Only for a small number, assuredly. Truth intoxicates the ignorant and gives them a taste for killing. It is not in vain that in the temple, secrecy was always the first principle of higher knowledge. The world will suffer from Jesus' error and his pride."

Behind Hypatia and Proclus, Priscilla was about to cross the threshold of the portal and emerge from the garden, now deserted, where the shadow was beginning to fill the pathways and to veil the jets of water and the pallor of the laurel. Abruptly, but gently, Telamon drew her toward him. He had taken her by the shoulders and he inclined his smiling face toward her. Without haste, tilting Pricilla's head with his arm, he placed his lips on hers and caressed her momentarily.

She did not have time to defend herself against such an unexpected action. She awakened, respiring in the young man's mouth a slightly inebriating perfume of honey and acacia that left her faint.

Telamon was now looking at her without emotion, with a slightly affectionate glint of victory in his eyes. She was a fruit that he had bitten, a cup of precious wine from which he had taken a sip, nothing more.

Priscilla straightened up, her eyelids fluttering, but in the movement she made, a little golden cross given to her by Bishop Cyril, which she had around her neck, emerged from her tunic, under which she had hidden it.

Telamon looked at that jewel in surprise, and even touched it to make sure that it was a cross.

"You're a Christian!" he said.

She did not have time to respond affirmatively. Telamon's smile had become bitter. He pulled the young girl to him with an almost savage movement and kissed her again on the lips; but it was a different kiss, long and profound, which parted her lips, which she felt on her teeth, while two hands clutched her breasts and ran audaciously over her entire body.

She struggled and escaped the young man's embrace. She felt a horror all the greater because sensuality, unknown to her until then, had penetrated her with a frisson, and she believed that she had experienced a physical pain.

She suddenly remembered that the Angel of Evil borrows for his temptations the form of the most beautiful children of men. Satan was standing before her in a garden full of enchantments, with the slim upper body and the perverse face of an adolescent coiffed like a Greek of the time of Plato.

The landscape changed for her. She glimpsed beneath the climbing roses inscriptions more obscene than those in the port of Kibotos. In the fountains, the faces of demons stared, sniggering, at the sexual design of her loins, which the folds of her garments no longer seemed to shelter. Living warmth, like wings, glided through the air and descended along her back.

They were forms agitated by coupling that were making the white laurels quiver.

She went through the door, ran into the courtyard, where she recognized the ogival exit among the busts of the philosophers. Her brother was there. She seized him forcefully by the arm and drew him away.

Outside, she started to run. She felt withered and desperate, but she believed that she was only bearing away the pollution of the kiss, the demonic mark of the beast upon her.

Only a little later was she to discover that nothing is more dolorous for a virtuous soul than the nostalgia of the inferno glimpsed and voluntarily forsaken.

And that evening, at the hour when, before the bas-relief of Phidias, the philosophers exchange the formula of vesperal farewell, a great flight of birds made a white streak on the obscured sky. They came from beyond Thebes, and were migrating from Upper Egypt with the spring, heading for a less fiery region.

Suddenly grave and silent, the young men clad in white, with a single impulse, raised their open right hand toward them. The birds were flying toward Greece; they were going to brush the golden cupola of the Temple of the Sun in Corinth, the Doric columns of the Parthenon in Athens and its dome, as blue as Minerva's buckler. Perhaps they would pause to drink at Delphi in the marble basin where the pythoness dipped her hands and moistened her immortal lips. They would pass everywhere that the philosophers sent their pious thoughts from afar.

For a long time they remained immobile in the twilight, until night had covered with its shadow the two white groups, the one on the ground and the one in the sky.

IV. The Blood of Christians

That evening, old Amoraim was hastening toward the Jewish quarter.

He had just been haggling with a merchant in Rhacotis over a purchase of wax for the candle shop that he had in the side-street in the Delta, and he had probably never been so late returning home.

He had just gone around the public gardens when he stopped for a few seconds. Should he turn left on to a narrow street that rose up in a straight line and was rather ill-famed? He usually avoided it, for he was a pious and placid Jew and he could not pass the door of a brothel without being internally scandalized. Or should he take the street along the gardens, which was longer, but on which all the houses were respectable?

He did not know that he was deciding in those few moments the life and death of his forty thousand coreligionists in Alexandria.

If he had known, he would have fallen in the dust and asked God to preserve the humility that he had always had, to permit him not to play any role except that of a trader in wax candles in the most modest shop in the narrowest street in the Delta quarter.

But a man is completely ignorant of his destiny, especially when he is as simple and uneducated as Amoraim was.

He did not like having to choose. When two alternatives were offered to his mind, it was always the one that was to have unfortunate consequences for which he opted.

As far as he went back in his memories, he saw bad luck installed by his side and following him like his shadow. As a child, he had broken his leg playing and had remained lame. When he had gone in pilgrimage to Jerusalem he had been gripped by a malign fever at Joppa, where he had just disembarked. He had spent three months lying in a fisherman's hut, which had caught fire just as he was entering into convalescence, and he had been obliged to return to Egypt without having kissed the spot where the temple had stood.

His wife had died bringing a child into the world, who had not survived. He had been imprisoned for theft because he had been mistaken for another Amoraim who resembled him, and had had great difficulty justifying himself. He was ugly and expressed himself with difficulty. He had possessed a small field in the environs of Alexandria but a singular hail, which had not ravaged the neighboring fields, had destroyed his crop the previous year, limited to his own domain as if God had wanted to mark a creature devoid of merit with special disfavor. Meanwhile, a slave who had occupied himself with the field in question had died, and Amoraim had sold that petty property for a petty price.

He was accustomed to blows of that sort. Every time, he curbed his head with more resignation. He felt that an evil force accompanied him. So he did as little as possible, because of the consequences his actions might have. He rarely went out. With a sort of anxious dread he sold his candles to his clients, who were not very numerous, and only did so while pronouncing an internal prayer that their light might only illuminate his neighbor's wellbeing.

He had remained good and gentle. He was ignorant of jealousy and derived his joy from being useful. He did not measure the injustice of his destiny. But sometimes, he attempted innocently to dupe fate. That was what he did that evening.

"I've decided to take the street of the Gardens," he proclaimed, almost loudly.

And he took it. But scarcely had he taken two or three steps than he went back, thinking that he had deflected the hostile forces, and went directly up the high street, at the extremity of which the Jewish quarter commenced.

He stumbled and almost fell. He put his hand out and had a sensation of moist warmth. He touched a beard, a neck, a human form. By the uncertain light of the stars he saw blood on his hand. Someone was lying there, motionless.

He leaned over and recognized the face of a certain Hieros, a notorious Christian of Alexandria, who had a school and taught theology.

Amoraim's first thought was to flee. Surprised by a patrol of soldiers next to that man, who had probably been murdered, how would be defend himself against the suspicion of being the murderer? The Jews were only judged by their ethnarch for what happened within the strict limits of their quarter, and in any case, the murder of a Christian reverted to the imperial tribunals, and a Jew who was implicated was always condemned.

He was therefore about to go back down the high street when his name resounded in his ears, pronounced by a severe voice: "Amoraim!"

He had voiced it himself.

Almost everything that he did turned against him; he had made it a law only to accomplish what his conscience deemed just, in order to be without regret.

It was not just to leave a dead man with his head in the gutter.

Around him, all the windows were closed. In any case, it would be a Christian house on which it was necessary to knock in order to obtain help. With great difficulty, he loaded the corpse on to his back and started going back down the street. He had remembered that the Church of Saint Mark was not very far away and that there was a small red brick dwelling beside it which served as the caretaker's residence.

Hieros was a tall, stout man and Amoraim, who was not very strong, staggered under his weight. He walked slowly and quietly.

"It's for your sins, Amoraim, that God has just placed this burden on your shoulders. You have not been pious enough, or humble enough."

Something trickled into his ear that seemed to be warmer than his own sweat, He thought several times about renouncing his task and setting the body down along a wall. He remembered as he walked that Hieros had hated Jews and had spoken against them in public several times.

"Amoraim, go on Amoraim!"

How far away the Church of Saint Mark was! It retreated into a tenebrous horizon. It seemed to him now that it was spinning around him in the midst of a farandole of colonnades and obelisks.

"Courage, Amoraim!" Accomplish the good deed that is preparing the misery of your people. It is necessary this evening that a just old man carry the heavy burden of a cadaver, in order to enable injustice to triumph.

Before a narrow window Amoraim almost let himself fall. He breathed in deeply. He straightened Hieros' upper body. Then he knocked on the shutter. He knocked for a long time, because Peter the church caretaker must have been profoundly sleep.

In the end, Amoraim heard a human grunt coming from inside the house. The shutter opened and Peter's enormous, redoubtable and hairy head was framed in the window.

But that was more than Amoraim could bear. Not that man! He knew his reputation. He would always retrace his steps rather than cross his path in a street. He was afraid of him, afraid of the pollution of his breath, afraid of the evil that radiated in the gaze of his little eyes.

In any case, had the Christian not been helped? Was he not on the threshold of a church, in the hands of another Christian?

"Hieros! It's Hieros, whom someone has killed!" said Amoraim to the stupefied Peter. And with all the speed of his legs, multiplied tenfold by terror, fleeing the evil destiny that had just been rendered forever inevitable, he started running and disappeared into the night.

Peter, as he opened his door, had the time to distinguish that it was a limping man who was running away, and, seeing his sleeves as broad as wings and his square bonnet, he said: "It's a Jew!"

Bishop Cyril mingled in his soul ardent faith, profound mediocrity and an unlimited liking for wealth. He was eloquent, for it is not necessary to have ideas to be a orator, and he was easily enthused because, with his tall stature, his long beard and his bulging blue eyes, he resembled the image that people had of Christ's first apostles. He had no sensuality, although he had a sanguine temperament, and because of that he was ravaged by sudden tempests of anger in which the violence of his nature was given free rein. He hated forcefully and he was devoid of pity for those who did not think as he did. Gold exercised a physical magnetism upon him that he had never been able to master.

Bare-headed, in the light of the torches that his six armed servants were carrying, he took great strides, holding on to the arm of his companion, who was having difficulty keeping up with him.

Peter was repeating his explanations.

"There must have been a whole band. Doubtless they killed him. After which, by derision, they carried him to the church. I heard them blaspheming and laughing when they ran away."

"Yes," said Cyril, "that's it. Hieros had singular habits. He went out late at night, and alone. And see where it led him!"

And he darted a severe glance at Peter, who also sometimes wandered in Rhacotis and the back-streets of the port for the same reasons as Hieros.

"I picked him up in the street and laid him down in my bedroom. He appeared to me to have a wound in his head and another in his breast. Our bodies must contain a lot of blood, for the three steps of my door were entirely red."

Cyril followed his train of thought and was excited.

"The Church will perish if she doesn't defend herself with the same weapons hat used to strike her. Neither Constantine nor Theodosius has dared to go on to the end, and that's why we're where we are. Tolerance is a crime, since it engenders crime. Pagans and Jews are ready to put Jesus on the cross again, if they could. There's no Emperor, there's no Pope; there's only the strength of those who believe. Everyone must act in the measure of his means. God has confided to me courageous and passionate men whom I've contributed myself to inflaming, I'll make use of them to defend him!"

He clapped Peter on the shoulder; the latter bowed his head respectfully.

"The moment has come," Cyril said, as if struck by a sudden idea. "Three hundred and seventy years ago the Christians were expelled from Alexandria. Where did they go? Into the deserts of Libya and the Thebaid! Just retribution! Those who have struck with the sword will perish by the sword. Since the Jews are murdering ours, we'll send them to the places where the Christians of old went. They'll discover the blackened stones where our martyrs once lit their fires and they'll drink from the same wells, if the wrath of Heaven doesn't desiccate them."

Suddenly, it was as if Cyril's mind was illuminated. He imagined the Jewish quarter when its inhabitants had been expelled by force. That quarter was not immense, although it sheltered a population of forty thousand people, because of the singular faculty the Jewish people had for crowding together. But it contained enormous wealth. Cyril knew the ancient traditions that said that when the Emperor Hadrian had burned Jerusalem two and a half centuries before, the powerful families of the Gamaliels and the Hillels had divided up the treasures of the Temple, those of Herod's palace and those of the Antonia fortress. The Gamaliels had gone to the banks of the Euphrates, but the Hillels, who were more numerous and who had taken charge of the greater part of the treasures, had come to Alexandria, had established themselves near the Eastern necropolis, and had founded the Jewish city there.

Cyril knew a legend that circulated among the mariners of the port and the poor people of the outlying districts. A century before, a Carthaginian pilot had got drunk and had set out after sunset to traverse Alexandria. Without really knowing how, he had reached the Delta quarter and had wandered at hazard through the little streets that intersected there. Those streets were so narrow, it was said that sometimes, by extending both hands, he could touch the opposite walls, which permitted him to support himself when he staggered.

A door had opened in front of him in a place that he could not find again subsequently, and he had crossed the threshold. He had the sensation that a feast, or perhaps a funeral ceremony, had attracted the masters and servants to a certain part of the house, and he seemed to hear a murmur of voices similar to that of a large number of people praying together. He went down a stairway that he encountered and stopped, contemplating an unexpected spectacle.

Three candelabra disposed in a triangle illuminated a quadrangular room which seemed to him to be entirely covered in golden plaques. He perceived in large bronze jars heaps of coins of all lands, making dull piles. Camel-skin gourds were swollen by gold powder, and in places that powder had overflowed, strewn on the floor like sand. There were ingots of a darker gold that obstructed the entrance of a gallery at the back, where gold spangles palpitated as far as the eye could see. To the right and the left, suspended from the walls, attached to the ceiling and covering the floor, objects of singular form, the hilts of swords, mirrors, disks, massive balls, thick necklaces were heaped in disorder in a palpitation of yellow light, mingled with life-size statues with gold visages, golden robes and pedestals of the same metal.

All those objects framed a sort of altar, before which a resplendent candelabrum with seven gold branches was set. And on the altar, as if on a sacred tabernacle, reposed a worn ark, rounded by time, enriched with blue sapphires, with four stout gold rings on its sides and having at the extremities of the lid two solid gold cherubim, facing one another, with their wings deployed. And that ark was dense, ancient and miraculous, in green-tinted gold, gold a thousand years old, so polished by centuries of adoration, conflagrations and travels, that it did not give any reflection, and yet exhaled a mysterious glow of sanctity,

The drunken mariner, suddenly sobered up, had thought about the risk he was running if he were discovered in that room, before that fabulous treasure. He had gone back upstairs silently and had been able to reach the street.

Afterwards, he had disappeared mysteriously. That end had given credit to his improbable story. It was thought that the Jews had killed the man who might know the location where the Hebrew fortune reposed.

Cyril remembered that story. It confirmed other things he knew. The sanctuary of the race of Moses, the Holy of Holies for which King Solomon had had the sacred Temple built in blocks of porphyry linked with lead on the hill of Moriah, the ark that contained the law, which the sun of the south had burnished in exile, which the waves of the Red Sea had moistened, might now repose within his arm's reach, in a cellar in Alexandria.

He shivered at the reality of the dream. Herod the Great had combined the formidable riches of Arabia, bequeathed by his father Hyrcanus,[22] with the riches of the Asmonean dynasty. Cyril could follow the destiny of the Jewish treasure during the siege and destruction of Jerusalem under Titus, until the moment when Hadrian had burned the Temple for the last time. It was not impossible that the Carthaginian mariner had penetrated one evening into the house of the Hillels, where the Holy of Holies of King Solomon reposed obscurely among the riches of Herod.

The gold could belong to him. He had no remorse about desiring it so ardently. He would employ the greater part of it for the defense of the Church, the maintenance of convents and the edification of cathedrals. In any case, he was only one with the Church. As Patriarch of Alexandria, he had the right

---

[22] Herod the Great was actually the son of Antipater the Idumaean, an official who served under the ethnarch Hyrcanus II.

to take in order to protect his own and build their shelters. The gold was necessary to the religion. It was necessary to maintain the flow of monstrances and pyxes. The mystical wine needed a chalice of unalloyed metal, divine metal. Like the Aphrodites of Corinth and Byblos, the Virgin Mary ought to be carved in single blocks of gold.

His vision was so clear that, like the Carthaginian mariner, he was almost blinded by it. He tottered like him in a yellow light. He had the sensation of plunging ankle-deep in strewn gold powder.

"Be careful," said Peter, "one walks on blood here."

They had arrived. Bending down, Cyril saw that his sandals were soiled.

He's lying behind the door," said Peter, with a certain embarrassment, standing aside to let Cyril pass. But he uttered a cry of surprise. The cadaver was no longer on the flagstones where he had left it.

Peter's room was very large and illuminated by a single candle, which the wind, blowing through the open door, caused to vacillate. It was dirty and untidy. Cobwebs garnished the corners of the ceiling and hung down from an iron lantern suspended from a hook. A dirty rag was placed in evidence on the table. An open wooden chest containing old linen and detritus had been dragged into the middle of the room. A thousand feet wandered over the black tiles, among the remains of a meal that had not been swept away. And at the back, enormous, splendid and full of gilt, with four sculpted columns and an awning in crimson Damask velvet, was a Babylonian bed of monumental form, from which animal skins, lacerated precious furs and smoke-blackened silk cushions were overflowing.

Cyril did not have time to be astonished by the contrast between the dirtiness of the room and the sumptuousness of the bed. Before being struck by that image of ecclesiastical debauchery he had perceived, facing him, against the wall, a livid human form, a pale imitation of what the professor of theology Hieros had been, a bloodless specter with a face like a host with eyes, and transparent hands, and in which, in a blue mist, the design of bones was floating.

He recoiled in terror to the door. But the form deprived of blood, exhausted by a supreme effort, collapsed upon itself, agitating the milky fragments of wax that were its lips.

Then Cyril understood that it was Hieros himself, and that if he had attained that degree of phantasmal fluidity, it was because all the blood he had shed was about to turn into gold, for the greater glory of Christ.

He advanced, avid to collect the certainty of the accusation, and he knelt down beside the dying man.

Peter had followed him, and lifted the shaky head.

"It was the Jews? You've been murdered by the Jews? Speak."

The head, still animate, moved from left to right, in a gesture of denial.

"I'm Bishop Cyril. I'll give you absolution for your sins. Tell me who struck you."

The waxy mouth palpitated and formed a few slight sounds. That vibration of scarcely-sketched syllables reached the ears of the two men. It was only a breath, but in that breath they perceived names, a semblance of a sentence.

"No! Not Jews! Christians! Nicanor the Ephesian, his mistress Olympe...at the bottom of the high street. They were the ones who killed me..."

The head agitated again before immobilizing completely. Cyril was muttering the formula of absolution mechanically when the door opened and a man appeared on the threshold.

He was tall and strong, with a bird-like head whose smallness was disproportionate with his body. He advanced hesitantly and irritatedly, looking alternately at the standing Peter and the kneeling bishop, the sordid room and the sumptuous bed. It was the Prefect Orestes, whom Cyril had sent someone in haste to inform. He was rubbing his well-manicured and ring-laden hands together nervously.

There was a clink of weapons in the street.

"Well," he said, "Hieros has been murdered. I've always thought that it would happen. The procurator of Rhacotis told me, a few days ago, about the danger there was to a man of his reputation..."

He did not finish. Cyril had stood up abruptly. His resolution was made. In any case, did not the grandeur of the Church, the victory of Christ, justify any lie?

He raised his hand in a theatrical gesture. "It's the Jews who killed him. He just told me so, as he died. In any case, Peter saw them. If imperial justice is impotent to defend us, we'll arm ourselves and defend ourselves."

The Prefect made a weary gesture. For a long time, the Christians, organized by Cyril, had formed militias of fanatics, more numerous and better disciplined than his own soldiers. He lowered his head, fatigued in advance by all the annoyances that he glimpsed, the weight of decisions to be made, the injustices in which it would be necessary to participate. He draped himself in his toga in a melancholy fashion and delicately, almost with respect, with the tip of his silver-laced cothurne, he crushed a spider that was about to reach the dead man's face.

In the narrow redoubt behind his shop where he slept, Amoraim considered his garments, laid out on his meager bed. His only robe of almost-new black cloth and his broad belt were soiled by the impurity of Christian blood. Having examined them carefully he made a little heap of them in order to burn them the next day.

He certainly did not aspire to elegance, but when one is old and alone, one has few joys. The solidity of a robe that hangs well, the suppleness of a belt that holds warmly were petty quotidian satisfactions of which he would be deprived henceforth. He thought that he no longer possessed anything to cover his body but a few miserable rags.

Bur no matter! He accepted that new humiliation without bitterness. He had escaped a great danger while accomplishing that which seemed to him to be just. Old Amoraim would have the appearance of a beggar, but he would wear a fine vestment of duty accomplished. Then again, was there not in what had just happened a sign of a small protection? Perhaps God was about to commence showing a little more clemency to a pious old man?

And he repeated, before going to sleep: "You have always sinned out of pride. Be humble, Amoraim!"

V. The Three Philosophers

Aurelius allowed the book that he had just reread for the hundredth time fall from his hands. It was the life of Apollonius of Tyana by his disciple Damis.[23] He traversed the interior courtyard of his small square house and appeared in the midst of the accumulation of white roses that grew in his garden and climbed the colonnades of his terrace.

His ever-sorrowful face had just brightened. He had drawn himself up to his full height, and the two patches that the graying of his temples made in his thick hair gave the impression of two roses detached from one of the bushes posed to either side of his forehead.

Once a day, only, he emerged from his reading or a somnolent ennui. It was when his slave Touta returned from Alexandria, where she had gone to the market—for he lived near the Canopic Gate, outside the city wall, beside a little wood of sycamores that extended along the shore of Lake Mareotis.

---

[23] *The Life of Apollonius of Tyana* was actually written, more than a hundred years after the philosopher's death, by Philostratus, who claimed to have obtained the information from a probably-non-existent disciple names Damis. The book is a confection of fantasies, which represents Apollonius as a miracle-worker, in an attempt to establish a reputation rivaling that of Christ, employing the same strategy as the latter's adherents. Magre apparently took the account seriously; the first chapter of his *Magiciens et Illuminés* (1930) is devoted to Apollonius, based on Philostratus, and it formed one of the foundation stones of his fanciful history of a secret wisdom transmitted through the ages, which he first elaborated in the present chapter, and which forms the backcloth to many of his novels.

Every day he interrogated Touta with his gaze, and she, while lifting vegetables, oil or fruits out of her wicker basket, almost always gave him the same response.

"I encountered her alongside the apostases. I had to wait a long time because she came out late. She was with her father this morning." And she almost always added: "Priscilla is certainly the prettiest young woman in Alexandria.

That was all. Aurelius' gaze lost its gleam, the interest that he had in living vanished; he went back to sit in his library in the midst of the scrolls of papyrus in their wooden cases, written in all languages, and half-effaced tablets that were almost indecipherable.

Those books had been his consolation. Seven years before he had experienced a great and mysterious chagrin about which he had not talked to anyone. Dolor that does not escape in words causes interior ravages. An intimate mechanism had stopped in Aurelius' soul and had ceased to provoke the reactions of his will. He had lost the courage to go beyond the limits of his garden and he had never crossed its threshold again. His friends believed that he had departed on a voyage. Solitude had formed around him. He had dismissed his servants, with the exception of Touta, a young Armenian slave who paid the taxes, went in search of garments and nourishment, and was his only link of communication with the world.

He had devoted himself to philosophy with the ardor of a lover for the body of his mistress. The books he possessed were inestimable. A part of the precious library of the Serapeum had been brought to him by the only two men he continued to see, Socles and Olympios, former friends of his father. Those two old men, who had once professed sciences and philosophy at the Museum, came regularly once a week to sit among the white roses of Aurelius' garden at the hour when the declining sun set the waters of Lake Mareotis ablaze, in order to discuss matters of wisdom.

Twenty-six years before, both of them had played a role in Alexandria in revolution. Emperor Theodosius had just ordered the destruction of the pagan temples, and Bishop

Theophilus, Cyril's predecessor, had pursued the execution of those orders with a furious fanaticism. Olympios and Socles had helped to fortify the ancient temple of Serapis, the palladium of paganism and had attempted to resist the Christian fury. They had tried to defend the intellectual wealth of the library, which was immense, for the Serapeum contained the six hundred thousand scrolls once given by Mark Antony to Queen Cleopatra, which had been drawn from Greece, Syria, Persia and all the countries of the world by Eumenes, the literate King of Pergamon.[24]

In a golden tube there was a papyrus in the hand of Pythagoras, annotated by Ammonius Saccas and by Plotinus, which the erudite only consulted with a pious emotion. There were unknown works by Philo the Jew and a few writings by the legendary Dositheus, who was reputed to have been the master of the legendary Simon Magus. There were works engraved on thin stones, which came from the druids of Brittany. There were some made of parchment impregnated with an oil so persistent that one could still find the fingerprints of a Chaldean mage who had handled it a thousand years before. Others formed a succession of copper leaves and came from India. A jade box contained several pages of the Book of Changes of the Chinaman Fo-Hi. There were some in Zend script, in Devanagari, in cuneiform characters or hieroglyphics; there were some that were composed of primitive trigrams and others written in a language that no people spoke. One little red tablet came from vanished Atlantis.

On the night that preceded the final assault on the Serapeum, Olympios and Socles, foreseeing the destruction of the library, had been able to remove a considerable number of the most precious works and hide them in Alexandria. At dawn, they had witnessed the burning of the books they had not had time to remove.

They had fled in order to escape reprisals, and had not reappeared until the death of Theodosius, when the appease-

---

[24] Eumenes II ruled Pergamon from 197-159 B.C.

171

ment had taken place. Socles had then returned home, but Olympios, having spent a year in the hut of a herb-picker in the marshes surrounding the salt-pans of Shedia, had found that the solitary life was the best possible for a man in search of the truth. Years had gone by. He had not given the lie to rumors of his death. In the image of the anchorites of the Thebaid, he slept on the hard ground, sheltered by a roof of reeds, only nourishing himself on a few vegetables and fruits. Every week, he crosses the fifty stadia that separated him from Aurelius' house, where Socles came to join him. The three men, equally fond of philosophy and solitude, conversed all night about the eternity of the soul, the powers of ecstasy and the mysteries of reincarnation.

With what ardor they pursued the truth then, and strove to demonstrate it to one another! What beautiful hours those sages, almost equally detached from earthly things, lived in the mind! Sitting under the marble portico, they breathed the fresh nocturnal air of the lake, not as soft after the heat of the day as the spiritual breeze born of their words.

Touta sometimes amused herself chasing away the mosquitoes from their foreheads with a large palm leaf, and they smiled at one another as they gazed at her corporeal youth, as if she were a living symbol of the invisible light they sought.

When the star Sothis[25] commenced to pale and the lake turned a more ashen blue, Touta went to sleep, her head on her folded arm, on the mosaics of the terrace. The three philosophers walked under the sycamores, the silver of their hair like a shifting aureole around their head. Their discussion was never concluded, and they promised one another for the following meting an irrefutable demonstration of the eternal verity. A competition was born between them. Each claimed to know a purer source than the others.

It was that competition that had just impelled Socles to undertake a mysterious voyage to the south, from which he

---

[25] The star the Egyptians called Sothis is almost certainly Sirius.

had brought back an element essential to their research. He had not given any further explanation but he had assured his friends that on his return, which would be in exactly three months, he would be able to take a decisive step toward the goal they were pursuing.

Finally, Socles had obtained consent from Aurelius, by means of affectionate pleas, that he would come with Olympios to meet him at Sais, where he expected to arrive on the first day of the month of Choiac. In accord with Olympios he had counted in the desire that Aurelius would have to see him again to vanquish the singular loss of will-power that had robbed him of the ability to leave home. Aurelius had ended up accepting, and Touta, who was also to make the journey, made sure that he did not change his mind.

As she opened the door to the garden on the eve of the appointed day, Touta perceived her master, who was waiting for her on the terrace, as usual. She noticed with satisfaction that his gaze was more assured and his stance more upright.

"Well?" he said.

"I've seen Priscilla, and even followed her into the Church of Theonas,"[26] Touta replied. "An extraordinarily ugly black man accompanied her. She knelt down and almost touched the stone with her forehead."

Aurelius made a melancholy gesture.

In order to deflect his thoughts, Touta hastened to tell the story of everything she had heard at the shops.

Forming small groups, more than six hundred monks of Mount Nitra had entered Alexandria through the Canopic Gate.[27] They had a savage aspect and were hiding weapons

---

[26] i.e., the Church of Saint Mark, formerly the residence of Theonas, the Pope of Alexandria from 282-300.

[27] The "savage monks of Nitra" are said by some sources describing the death of Hypatia to have been summoned by Cyril to take part in that murder, but the reference should actually be to Nitria, which is not a mountain but a monastic site in the

under their robes. It was said that they had come to avenge the death of the Christian Hieros, murdered by Jewish fanatics. It was also said that Bishop Cyril was making inspired speeches in the churches, which he announced that there would soon no longer be a single Jew in the city. He was taking advantage of the opportunity also to hurl maledictions against Hypatia and all the philosophers of the Museum.

But Aurelius listened to that news distractedly.

"Touta," he said, "I've made an important resolution. I'm going to go to India, like Apollonius of Tyana in order to reach the abode of the wise men where he learned the truth."

Touta and the three philosophers, lying in a large flat boat with four oarsmen under and awning of orange byssus, were now descending the branch of the Nile that went toward Canopus and the sea. They left to their right the great mass of red granite formed by the wall of Sais, the tombs of Apries and the Saite kings, and the funerary monument of Amasis. The moon illuminated the muddy waters and caused the boat to glide over a river of ocher.

Socles had not wanted to say anything to his friends about the result of his voyage before they were all installed comfortably to their woolen cloaks and the last songs of the mariners of the landing-stage had died away.

"I'm prepared for my disappointment," said Olympios, smiling.

Finally, Socles spoke.

"Have you ever wondered why, when he had conquered Egypt, Alexander the Great plunged into the desert, at the price of a thousand perils, trying to reach the Temple of Ammon?"

He stopped to enjoy his companions' surprise.

"All the historians report it," said Aurelius. "He wanted to consult the oracle, to receive from the Egyptian priests that

---

Nitrian desert. Magre might have misread the reference, and has also redirected the monks to another mission.

title of son of God, which all the pharaohs had borne before him. But it isn't to ask us that question that you've gathered us together solemnly after an absence of three months."

Socles shrugged his shoulders and went on: "Should he not have remembered that the army of Cambyses had been engulfed by the sands while attempting the same expedition? Did he not know almost exactly, by way of his master Lysimachus,[28] one of the greatest magicians of antiquity, the duration of his brief existence, and had he ever been seen to waste time and effort for an uncertain end? He had been initiated, his armies occupied Canopus, where he was, and the priests of Serapis could have proclaimed him a son of Jupiter with the same authority as those of Ammon. So why did he go? Of what did he go in search, so far away?"

"What do the actions of that warrior matter?" said Aurelius. "You've just said that Alexander was an initiate. I don't believe that. Not because he caused the deaths of a great number of men in battles and futile conquests, for an initiate can be the instrument of a murderous fatality whose design escapes us, but because his life was full of personal violence and crimes inspired by his rancor or his vanity."

"It was in Samothrace," said Socles, "that Alexander was initiated into the mysteries by his master Lysimachus. After that he honored all the gods indifferently with the same fervor. He prostrated himself in the temple of Serapis at Memphis, in that of Hercules in Tyre. He advanced alone, on foot, before Jadduah, the high priest of the Jews, near Jerusalem and fell to his knees. The magi of Chaldea were heaped with riches by him, and he brought back from India, as if he were a king, the old gymnosophist Calamos, who was to burn himself alive to prove how small a price he attached to life.

---

[28] Lysimachus of Acarnania, one of Alexander the Great's tutors, should not be confused with another Lysimachus, who was one of his bodyguards. The details of the biography and thought of this Lysimachus provided by the present text are all invented.

"Alexander knew that it was the same God who was worshiped under different symbols, and it was of scant importance to him whether the appearance was that of Moloch or the bull Apis. That knowledge clearly indicates that he had received initiation. The unity of the world of which he dreamed and attempted to realize by the mingling of races is a further indication. In all the countries that he conquered, did he not think first of imposing marriages? He wanted to unite the victors and the vanquished by blood ties because he saw therein the seeds of a universal peace. Mingle with one another, that was his dictum. Love one another, Jesus was later to say. One employed force, the other sentiment, one united by blood, the other by love, but the objective was the same."

"That's a part of the truth," said Aurelius, "but once again, I don't see..."

"I'm getting to the purpose of my journey. Lysimachus, Alexander's master, was already very old when he taught Philip's son. He has not left any writings, but I have been able to reconstitute parts of his life and his teachings via fragments in the works of later philosophers that mention him. He was a very elevated intelligence, and the great sorrow of his life was to be misunderstood by his peers because of his difficulty in expressing himself and a certain expression of stupidity spread over his face. He traveled in all lands, visited all temples. He spent three years among the Celtic Semnothei, whose sanctuaries were subterranean and formed perfect squares. He studied the art of presages among the Pazate magi of Babylon and the laws of generation in the colleges of Thebes. It was from Egypt that he brought back certain curious information concerning the march of human events.

"He claimed that, through countless ages, wisdom had been transmitted like a sacred torch by a small number of unknown men who were its depositories, and only revealed it in a measured fashion because of the destructive force that wisdom allows to burst forth when it is divulged before time. He knew that some of those elite men, those guides invested with a quasi-divine mission, were to be found in that epoch in the

176

temple of Ammon in the deserts of Egypt, others on an isle lost in the northern seas, and others, finally, in a monastery in India on the banks of the mysterious River Ganges. Did he dream of approaching them and participating in their wisdom? That's probable. What is certain, what is proven by Clitomachus of Carthage at the end of his *Conversations*,[29] is that he was rejected at the temple of Ammon and returned disappointed to Samothrace.

"A few years before his voyage to Egypt he had commenced practicing intoxication by wine. Perhaps it was for that reason that he was not judged worthy of a more elevated initiation and not, as he later allowed it to be believed, for the apparent stupidity of his face, which would not have deceived the conductors of humankind. It was, I imagine, that habit of intemperance that impelled him to recount that which ought not to be spoken, the secret that should only be formulated between the echoless stones of sanctuaries.

"He said that a man, in order to become perfect, has three paths: knowledge action and amour. Three heroes were to be born successively, the first of them, Pythagoras, had already accomplished his task by furnishing the elements of Hellenic thought. He knew by his science of divination that the third would only appear later, in the kingdom of the Jews; but he, Lysimachus, had the honor of instructing the second, the man of war, the one who would drag the races out of immobility, the one who would tempt by violence to make a single people out of all peoples. To tell the truth, he did not profit from that honor, since Philip separated him from his son, because of his increasing drunkenness—but he had convinced Alexander of his divine mission.

"It was to see the spiritual masters of the earth that Alexander went to the temple of Ammon and he obtained, as Lysimachus had asked him to do, a papyrus in which one of them had traced with his own hand a summary of the science of the

---

[29] A fictitious reference, which cannot be to the Clitomachus mentioned briefly by Cicero.

universe. Almost all the portraits of Alexander that historians have made for us represent him with a little chain of green bronze around his neck, from which a somber metal case was suspended. On learning that Alexander had returned from Egypt, Lysimachus, although afflicted by a serious illness, set forth from the depths of Macedonia. He died before reaching him. The precious papyrus remained around the sovereign's neck and later, when he died, we know that Perdiccas, who had received his last will, when the embalming was concluded and the solid gold coffin was about to be sealed, replaced the black cylinder on the breast stuffed with aromatics. It should still be there."

Socles considered his interlocutors. Aurelius, supporting his chin on his fist, was listening with a passionate interest. Touta was blinking her long-lashed eyelids and seemed to be struggling against drowsiness. Olympios was smiling. In the distance, to the left, the lamps had just been lit in several small villages bordering the Nile. The travelers heard a vague rumor of musical instruments reaching them.

"So," said Aurelius, excitedly, "You've attained at the first attempt the goal that I was proposing to attain myself by undertaking a much more distant voyage. I also knew the legend of the initiates and was inspired by it. Apollonius of Tyana spoke about it often and I know almost by heart the parts of his life written by his disciple Damis that deal with his adventures in reaching the monastery of clay near the inaccessible city of Palibothra, under the fabulous palm trees of unknown India, which he called the abode of wise men. I had sworn that I wouldn't die before reaching it. I only wanted to vanquish my weakness in order to go myself along the River Ganges to the place where, as Apollonius reports, seven narrow clay cells with a small altar in the middle form the design of a lotus. Speak. What did the sages of the temple of Ammon say? Are they the supremely intelligent adepts of the fraternity of the elect that lives in India?"

Socles remained silent for a few seconds.

"I promised myself to tell you everything, so I shall do so. I've always laughed internally at the folly of Lysimachus, who, after having accomplished a perilous voyage to reach the most venerable sacerdotal college that has ever existed, had not been able to moderate his intemperance. Our passions are attached to us no less faithfully than our shadow. Sometimes, like him, I have procured mental exaltation by means of wine. I remember that you reproached me for it. So I took care during my voyage not to raise anything but water to my lips. A small gourd of wine was, however, attached to the flank of my camel, for wine can be a precious comfort when one endures excessive fatigue. Exhausted by the final two days of my journey through the sands, when I perceived the mass of shadows made by the oasis of Ammon in the distance, I could not resist the desire to give my weakening body the same satisfaction as my soul. I drank a little wine, which rendered me life with excess. I left my guide by the first well, under the first date-palms, and I ran toward the gigantic columns that I glimpsed through trees, in order to present myself without delay to the hierophants of the temple.

"They caused me a vivid surprise, and that surprise was shared by them. They are clad in animal skins and they are living in a half-ruined temple, which they have no thought of repairing. They receive no offerings from the inhabitants, and nourish themselves on the flesh of game that they kill themselves—which is contrary to the rules of all colleges of priests in all religions. Hunting also seems to be their principal topic of conversation. They appeared to me to be singularly lacking in understanding, and vulgar, and that opinion was not belied by the few days that I spent with them.

"I must admit that when I explained the purpose of my journey, while the wine was acting upon my brain, I expressed myself volubly and did not give the impression of possessing the slightest parcel of the wisdom I was seeking. But I must also admit that they only listened to me distractedly and that their greatest concern was to ask me whether I had brought the wine with me. I gave them what remained in my gourd, and they drank it avidly.

"I wondered afterwards whether they might have wanted to deceive me. Perhaps they were only the servants of the true hierophants and had judged me unworthy of being taken to them. I questioned the inhabitants, but they are half-savage and live in abject huts. I explored the oasis and found no trace of a hidden sanctuary. I arrived at the conviction that the location had been deserted by the perfect men who had once lived there. Nevertheless, my voyage was not futile. I was able to observe in my conversations with the hunter priests that they retained a strong tradition of a time when the temple of Ammon had sheltered beings they called 'the sovereigns of the mind.' They also spoke with pride of Alexander's visit, and they knew that the King of Macedonia had come, not for an oracle, but to obtain a talisman, which he had taken away."

The music of trigonal harps, triangular citharas and tambourines reached the ears of the three philosophers in gusts. The boat had drawn nearer to the left bank. Men were seen running hither and yon, agitating lamps. At the same time, on the opposite bank, other chants were rising, and some sort of procession was visible. Touta had got up and, standing at the prow of the boat, she looked at each bank in turn.

"If I understand correctly," said Aurelius, whose face now reflected the deepest disappointment, "your research has concluded with the certainty that Alexander was the custodian of the supreme verities of the world, that he carried those verities around his neck during his life and that they were placed in his coffin after his death. In accordance with his will, that coffin was transported to Alexandria. But what has become of it now? The mausoleum that contained it, the funerary crypts where the bodies of the Ptolemies were, and the hypogeum that Cleopatra had constructed to shelter her body and Antony's, collapsed thirty years ago, during the last earthquake, which destroyed almost all of the Street of the Sema. The Christians affected to see that as a miraculous manifestation. A chapel of Saint Athanasius was built on the cupola of agate and crystal of Stratonicus' tomb and it is, I believe, the Church of Saint Mark that now stands above the marble hall where Alexander reposed."

"That's possible," relied Socles, "but that marble hall was constructed in blocks so thick that it must have rested the crumbling of the old Alexandrian soil. A celebrated prophecy said that the kingdom of the man who would receive and keep Alexander's body would be stable and flourishing. Ptolemy sent an army to search for the sacred remains in Damascus. The believed in the prophecy, and he had an interest in defending, against men and time, a coffin on which the future of his dynasty depended.

"In any case, there is mention of the thickness of that marble in Strabo, when he reports that Ptolemy IX violated the sepulcher by virtue of cupidity in order to take possession of the old coffin and replace it with a coffin of glass. Those massive walls were also the astonishment of the emperors Augustus, Caligula and Septimus Severus when they came piously to visit the tomb of the hero. We know from accounts of those visits that Alexander's body was respected for centuries. According to the history of Cassius Dio, Septimus Severus even had a certain number of sacred works on the religions of ancient Egypt buried, which he did not want scholars to study but which he dared not destroy because of the reactive force that sometimes strikes the sacrilegious. Very close to us, in the very soil of Alexandria, which we have trodden so many times, is the most inestimable document on the verity that we are pursuing. It only remains for us to attain it."

Aurelius made a gesture of discouragement. That task was impossible. How could an excavation be carried out? How could it even be attempted in soil that belonged to the Christians? For the Christians, the disappearance of the venerated monuments of paganism had been a blessing, a sign of the divine will. They would not permit them to be resuscitated.

He shook his head and said: "It's easier to go on foot across the world to reach he abode of the wise men."

But Socles repeated: "Who knows? Who knows?" And he added: "Menalchos, who lives in Bruchium, not far from the street of the Sema, told me once that his cellar communicates with a subterranean aqueduct that dates back to the earliest epoch of Alexandria, through which water no longer passes. He talked about it at every opportunity, in accordance with his favorite idea, to demonstrate the superiority of our forefathers over us in all material workings. He praised the strength of old constructions, the solidity of the cements employed, and gave the walls of that aqueduct as an example. He offered to take me down there. He had studied its history and he knew that it had been disaffected at the time of the construction of Cleopatra's mausoleum, because the architect had encountered it in digging the foundations. Now, Cleopatra's mausoleum was adjacent to Alexander's tomb. The site of Menalchos' house indicates that the aqueduct must be parallel to the two monuments. By following that aqueduct, which the earthquake hasn't destroyed, since Menalchos talked about it a few years ago, one would certainly arrive at Alexander's tomb. Menalchos' faculties have declined to the point that he scarcely recognizes his friends, but an understanding could be reached with his son to buy his house. It would be easy then to undertake the necessary work..."

Aurelius seemed to be chasing such vain projects away with his hand.

"But why does Olympios, who never stops smiling, not give us his opinion on this matter?" said Socles, turning to his friend.

Olympios replied: "What's the point of going to so much trouble? It is within us that the verity lies, and it's sufficient to look into one's soul to discover it. A man who meditates alone goes further than the temple of Ammon and the River Ganges. I don't know what is written on Alexander's papyrus, and it matters little to me. I prefer to decipher the eternal papyrus that unrolls incessantly within me, and of which the clairvoyance that I'm in the process of acquiring will explain the mute hieroglyphs and the invisible symbols No prophet's words, no sacred teaching of a messiah is worth as much as the little truth that we extract ourselves by the radiance of our interior lamp."

"I'll gladly agree," said Socles, "but what mental force will not be mine if I can reach the certainty that superior beings are directing humankind, and if I can be the servant of their thought!"

"The only means of reaching them and conversing with them is to be immobile and to meditate. You know full well what force there is in meditation. Concentrated thought has such a great power that no law of the universe can resist it. Are not the extraordinary results that I have achieved the striking proof of it?"

It was the turn of Socles and Aurelius to smile, but their faces quickly resumed an expression of gravity. They knew that that was their friend's weakness. Olympios claimed to possess the power that Simon Magus had had, of which certain Ethiopian gymnosophist boasted, of being able to rise into the air by means of the power of the will alone. He was still, he said, in the early stages of his results. He only rose up rarely and not very high—and never in the presence of other men. That was the mystery of the hidden forces that he set in motion; they required solitude. Aurelius and Socles pretended to believe in those powers, and did not ask to verify them.

Touta inclined her loyal face toward her master, as if she wanted to say something, but at that moment, clamors resounded on both banks of the river. The moon had risen high in the sky and it gave a supernatural appearance to the villages, with their lamps, a sycamore wood and a distant monastery. Two groups were facing one another, separated by the width of the Nile, and they were shouting threats of death at one another, while a flock of frightened ibises streaked the sky.

The group to the left was led by an old man who was bowed down under the weight of a white ewe, which he set down by the water's edge. Behind him marched players of harps and tambourines, of both sexes. Young men and women were carrying lanterns, raising them with an alternating gesture, and sometimes uttering a modulation that was sometimes plaintive and sometimes joyful. On the opposite bank, the moonlight suddenly caused the reflection of a huge metal Christ to glisten. A Christian priest, his hands joined, was standing up, leaning over the river. Monks and peasants appeared to be praying behind him, only interrupting themselves to address threats to the group on the other side of the Nile.

The boatmen explained to the philosophers the meaning of the scene they had before their eyes.

The villages scattered on the left had remained faithful to the old religion of Egypt, and continued to worship the goddess Neith, the protectress of that region. On the first evening of the month of Choiac, in accordance with age-old custom, the inhabitants came to the Nile to sacrifice a ewe in honor of the goddess, in order that the river's flooding would not be delayed and would continue to bring fertility. On the opposite bank, however, there was a monastery, and the peasants who lived in its vicinity were Christians. It was necessary to satisfy their taste for superstition. Otherwise, they would have feared that the Nile would only flood on one side. The priest of Jesus, clad in is sacerdotal garments, had therefore come on the day prescribed by the Egyptian rite in order to invoke the river and combat by means of a ceremonial appearance the influence of the priest of the goddess Neith.

"Fortunately, crocodiles are abundant in this place," said one of the boatmen. "Otherwise, both parties would throw themselves into the water in order to come to blows."

The boat glided over the shiny water between the two groups. The pagan priest was now taking handfuls of gem salt out of a bag, which he threw high in the air and which fell back, making a rain full of silvery incandescence. The incense burned in profusion on both sides swirled and rose up in a double spiral, which the breeze united in the sky.

"That's the image of the error of the entire earth," said Socles. "People hate one another because of their different religions, but at a certain height their confused prayers are no more than a single breath, which is lost in the unknowable."

Almost at the same time, a cry resounded on the two banks. The Christian priest and the monks fell to their knees beneath the huge metal cross, which swayed as if struck by terror. Opposite, the handfuls of gem salt launched with so much precipitation made broader luminous circles. The movement of the lamps raised at arm's length and the noise of the trigonal harps became hectic.

Christians and pagans alike were staring at the boat, the cadence of whose oars caused it to move downstream majestically. The wooden sides hid the philosophers and the oarsmen from their view. They only saw Touta standing at the prow in her white tunic, slightly agitated by the wind, and under the ocher moonlight, in the thousand parcels of light reflected by the waves, that feminine apparition on a dream-like boat had something miraculous about it. The uttered cry became a prayer, and the same effusion toward beauty curbed both enemy groups at the same time.

"Touta is the Virgin Mary for one party," said Aurelius, "the goddess Neith for the other, but she's only a servant to us." A few seconds later, he added: "Can there be a man for whom she would only be a beloved woman?"

VI. The Statue of Aphrodite

Leaning on the balustrade of the terrace, Priscilla gazed at the sea. It was not yet dusk. The heat was scorching and the air still. An implacable mildness came to the shining waters.

Behind her extended the immense gardens of Diodorus' villa. The villa stood facing the sea, far beyond the western Necropolis and the catacombs of Alexandria. It had been constructed a century before by the most ostentatious of the Diodoruses on the model of Roman villas. It was surrounded on all sides by colonnades, with large porticos where statues of all the gods of Athens and Rome had once stood. Priscilla's grandfather had had them removed and replaced by statues of saints and martyrs, too large or too small, which seemed solemn and out of place under the liberty of the marine breeze. Apart from that, the splendor of the dwelling had been conserved intact. No one had dared touch the mosaics of the Atrium, which represented celebrated scenes of mythology, the painted murals, the azure cupolas or the large pools in the middle of the rooms, into which one descended by means of onyx steps, and where jets of water deployed the mysterious poetry of the pagan sensuality that was in their fluid surge.

To the left extended the thermes, the apotheca where wine was pressed, the compluvium where livestock was bathed, the habitation of the procurator and the vilicus, the slaves' lodgings, the cowsheds, the sheepfolds, the beehives and the poultry-yards. But to the right was the mass of gardens with their expertly designed flower-beds, their baskets of multicolored flowers, their pathways sprinkled with coral pink powder, their irrigation channels and their pavilions with painted domes, for repose and reverie.

Priscilla's great-grandfather, who had begun the cultivation of the gardens, had had a mania for singular flowers and rare shrubs. Enriched by speculations in grain, to the profits of which had been added those of his cotton-mills, he had spared no expense to bring plants from all the countries of the world, which had never been seen in Alexandria, with the soil in which they had grown, and even the fluid of their natal rivers to water them.

For him, travelers had gone as far as he was able to suppose that there was soil with vegetation. He had had Assyrian, Hindu and Persian gardeners, who had planted, cultivated and grafter. He had been able to exhibit a pale pink flower in the form of a sun, with animate bloodsucking tentacles like those of cephalopods, which an Ethiopian had brought back from the mysterious sources of the Nile, and he had rejoiced in sitting in the shade of a tree with great palms, which only grew in the inaccessible mountains of the realm of Magada and bore the magical characters of a vanished language between the fibers of its bark.

Priscilla shuddered. Lost in her reverie, she had not heard the sound of the oars of a galley going along the coast and making a black patch against the first tints of dusk. It was emerging from the port of Eunostos and heading for Cyrene or Carthage. Songs and laughter filled the deck, reaching as far as the young woman. Priscilla saw that it was transporting an ambulant troupe of mimes and dancers.

They must be Greeks. Some of them were naked to the waist, with effeminate faces and curly hair, and wore red skirts like the women of Syria, at the extremity of which hung stones of all colors. Hands on hips, agitating their bellies and raising their knees, they were dancing in an equivocal and grotesque fashion, to the discordant sounds of a lute, in order to make the mariners laugh.

A Jewess with enormous breasts, who was only clad in a transparent loincloth, was also dancing, waving a tambourine over her head, which she was striking rhythmically.

Priscilla distinguished the coarse faces of the oarsmen, their expressions of bestial gaiety, and the movement they made to hoist themselves up on their benches in order to get a better view of the improvised spectacle. She also distinguished, at the rear of the ship, two forms lying against the rigging, who were gripped by a feverish enlacement. It seemed that a magnet had attracted them forcefully, stuck between them in an immutable caress that ought to last for an eternity

For a few seconds, Priscilla, her head forward, gazed with a passionate curiosity. Then she knew that she had to turn away and flee the vision of evil. She went along the terrace, down a few steps and followed a path.

But a new sensation ran through her body. She had a desire to cry out, to start running, to exteriorize a warm force that was burning her without her being able to specify how. She perceived that the bushes and flowers around her had brighter colors and more emphatic forms, a language whose terrible meaning she understood for the first time.

A pistil brushed her hand and left a kind of gray semen on her skin, which she experienced as a pollution. She saw a yellow droplet in the heart of a flower whose rigid stem emerged from a bush and seemed to be reaching toward her. Plants were exhaling seeds, pollen and moisture all round her, which inspired disgust in her. Stamens vibrated with desire, calices sweated enjoyment, corollas displayed themselves lewdly.

Certain flowers affected the form of an erect egg, others reproduced female and male sexual parts, the generative organs of animals. There were strange vegetal pumps that absorbed the life of the dying light. A fecund respiration caused the lungs of lilies to rise, inflated their bulbs, and descended into the lowers layers of plants, making them palpitate all the way to their roots.

And that circled around her like a terrestrial rainbow, quivering, embalming and moistening, running light frictions over her as she passed, intoxicating her with insipid aromas. Abruptly, under a solitary oak, a little acorn was detached and ran between her breasts. It was round and warm. It slid down her abdomen and she took a few steps, her head buzzing, with the sensation than an audacious beast was about to bruise her with an unsuspected caress.

Feeling faint, she leaned against a parasol pine, and, her hand having encountered an outflow of soft resin, she withdrew it, sticky, as if she had touched he stupor of the trees.

Then she collected herself. She had just known temptation. Like the anchorites of the desert, it was necessary for her to sustain the struggle. She had read the story of the combat that the saints had delivered a hundred times over. She knew what diverse forms the demon was able to take, his power of becoming, by turns, a man, an animal or a plant. It was him who had appeared on the crespuscular ship with the obscene visage of those dancing actors. It was him who was now swaying in the velvety roses, putting the milky juice into the umbels of the euphorbias, extending the darts of the cacti, causing the large white nympheas to burgeon like crushed flesh on the water of the pools, gripping the basins with the unfurling of crimson ipomoeas. In the nearby wood, it was him yet again who was making, with the knots of trunks and the gestures of branches, caricatures of legs, hairy stirrings of deformed arms.

Why was she the victim of that enchantment? She had prayed, as usual, she had driven away evil thoughts, she had repented of the kiss that her mouth had enjoyed in spite of her.

And suddenly, she was able to understand what the force of temptation was that was surrounding her. Lightly, she started to run, going alongside the villa, and reached a little house with a flat roof backed up against the baths. There was a workshop there in which an old man labored. He had just tidied away his tools and folded up his leather apron.

"Give me a hammer," Priscilla said. "A heavy hammer."

And, without waiting for a response, having spotted what she needed, she took it away.

Beyond the flower-beds, a large green meadow extended, irrigated by streams. Priscilla traversed it and went into a wood of parasol pines, which she also traversed. A path descended beneath interlaced branches toward a part of the garden at a lower level, whose cultivation had been renounced, and where a luxuriant vegetation blossomed in disorder.

Priscilla parted the branches of the tamarind and turpentine trees and uncovered a marble form lying under the vegetation.

It was a statue of Aphrodite.

She had remained marvelously white in spite of the rain and the vegetable parasites. She unveiled an impeccable shoulder and a hollow back, in accordance with the poem of human form. Her legs were partly buried in the soil, as if to testify to the eternal relationship of the earth with the symbol that she represented. Her mouth retained an ineffable smile, by which the sculptor had tried to indicate the enigma of amorous attraction.

Then Priscilla, with all her strength, brought her hammer down on the marble smile; she smashed the narrow forehead, the sightless eyes, and then the breasts and the rounded legs. She struck with the energy that the certainty of a virtuous and profitable action gives. She felt full of delight.

When the work of destruction was complete, she was hot and she was weary. A vague melancholy was mingled with her sentiment of deliverance. She wondered whether she might not have incurred a vengeance on the part of hidden powers, of which she had only been able to reach the image.

She raised her head, and on the slope opposite the one she had come down, she perceived a young woman between the branches of the turpentine trees, a few paces away, who was looking at her.

She knew her face. She seemed to find in her dark eyes, that bright oval filled with ardor, anxiety and goodness, the features of a slave scarcely older than her, whom she often encountered when she went out, and who followed her with a gaze full of affection. She considered her for a second, and did not find the same expression in the depths of her eyes. She found there, on the contrary, reproach, and almost fear. The evening made the flesh of her shoulder glisten. Beneath the veil, the breast seemed form and harmoniously designed. The beauty that emanated from her was that of the goddess. Priscilla had only struck the material form, but the living carnal goddess, the Aphrodite who did not perish was before her and about to strike her in her turn with an invisible spell.

The image of Aphrodite made a movement of the hand. She was about to advance and speak.

Priscilla dropped the hammer she was holding and, driven by a panic terror, she fled.

Touta watched Priscilla's silhouette disappear under the pines in the twilight. She saw her again in the meadow, where she was gliding, charming and rapid, like a fleeing hope.

Then Touta returned slowly, the way she had come, through the wild plants. Anyway, exactly what she would have said, she did not know. A vague inspiration had impelled her. Aurelius, her master, was about to leave Alexandria for a voyage from which he would not return. She wanted to retain him at any price. She had thought about the only link that retained him to things of the world, his affection for that young woman, whom he had only glimpsed when she was a child, and to whom he had never spoken.

Touta had often gazed, in her master's library, at a cameo representing the head of a woman who had Priscilla's features, with a few years more. She had often surprised Aurelius in contemplation before that portrait, and she had made a connection between that sorrowful contemplation and the news of the young woman with which she was charged with reporting every day.

She did not want him to go. She had traversed Alexandria, and launched forth along the road that ran along the coast, all the way to Diodorus' villa in order to reach Priscilla, the only creature able to retain the philosopher. She had intended to throw herself at her feet, to tell her that a very wise and very good man who sometimes wept while looking at a cameo in which there was her mother's face, needed a word from her, or even less, a gaze in passing, of which he would have made the great light of his life.

She had felt a marvelous force of persuasion. She had slipped through a breach in the wall of the flower-garden and had watched for part of the afternoon. Hazard had taken Priscilla to the most solitary place, the most propitious for a conversation.

But Touta had witnessed the murder of the statue. She had seen the charming Priscilla, her forehead furrowed and her lips taut, strike with all her strength the image of the beauty that was an object of veneration for her master.

What unexpected differences there were in souls! Was it worth the trouble of appealing to that one? The words had caught in her throat.

Touta arrived at the place in the wall where she had climbed over. She darted a glance at the garden, which the sun was illuminating with splendor, before disappearing. The parasol pines gave the impression of cups extended toward the sky for offerings by dolorous supplicants. The flower-beds formed enormous iridescent sheaves in which flames were brooding. The jets of water rose up incessantly and perished untiringly against the crimson of the setting sun.

Oh, how far some people were from others!

She leapt on to the road and set forth in the direction of Alexandria.

VII. The Monk Simon

Among the monks of Mount Nitra who had just arrived in Alexandria, Simon was surrounded by a sort of admiring veneration. He was scarcely twenty years old. He was thin and fair of face. It was said that he had come to the convent as a beggar and that, if he had knocked on the door one evening, it was because he had seen from a distance a miraculous cross of fire designed there.

He spoke rarely and always gave the impression of emerging from a dream. Sometimes he advanced toward one of his comrades in the convent and, without any reason, while looking him in the eyes, announced an event concerning him that was about to occur. It was as if what he said were pronounced by another mouth than his own, having the semblance of a message that he was charged with transmitting.

One night, he had woken up the superior of the convent because he had witnessed a shipwreck somewhere at sea and was suffering from the laments of the drowned. They had learned the next day that a ship full of passengers coming from Carthage had sunk not far from Alexandria.

Another time, he had suddenly approached the old porter of the convent, whose path he had crossed in a courtyard, and said to him: "Start praying quickly, I've heard Death setting out on his way to collect you."

The old porter, who was a pious man, had said his farewells, and then ran toward the door of the convent, for he had made a vow to die beside that door, which he had opened and closed for years. He had knelt down, and had not got up again.

Simon also said things that appeared to be devoid of meaning, and many people merely estimated that he did not have all his reason.

The monks of Mount Nitra were warriors as well as peasants. Sometimes, a marauding tribe from the desert attacked the convent and it was then necessary to take up arms and fight. They were also regimented and disciplined, they had decurions and centurions.

Simon had started to laugh the first time someone had handed him a pike, and he had thrown it away. Nor did he seem to understand how to handle a bow. One evening, when he was walking along a path at the extremity of the crop-fields, several monks worthy of faith certified that they had seen a jackal at his heels, which followed him as if he had domesticated it, and which stopped at intervals to lick his feet.

Simon had the habit of turning his head abruptly to the right, as if someone had spoken beside him, and his face then took on a blissful expression. Those who liked him said that it was his guardian angel, who was informing him of divine matters.

The monks of Mount Nitra had been lodged in various convents in Alexandria. The group of which Simon was a part was camped under the porticos of a courtyard near the Church of Caesarea.

That morning, Simon was walking slowly back and forth. His comrades watched him in surprise. Since his arrival he had lost his serene tranquility. He was not smiling softly, as usual, and his gaze sometimes had a sudden expression of dread.

In the midst of the buzz that filled the courtyard, an appeal rang out: "Simon!"

The monks talking among themselves pointed him out.

Someone was asking for Simon! It was Bishop Cyril who wanted to see him!

He did not realize the honor that had fallen to him, for he started to tremble in the presence of the Patriarch's emissary. That was Peter. He loomed up before him, gigantic, and looked at him with scornful pity.

"Follow me," he said.

He drew him outside, and they started to walk rapidly.

It's with a very wretched individual, Peter thought, on the way, *that the Bishop wants to converse. He can scarcely keep his feet, and the most complete imbecility is inscribed in his features.*

Simon had, indeed, changed his appearance. He was livid, he was weak. He looked in all directions, as if he were searching for someone. As they went past the Church of Saint Mark in the street of the Sema, without paying any attention to his companion and before the latter could stop him, he went into the church and immediately fell to his knees in prayer on the flagstones.

"Bishop Cyril is waiting for us," said Peter, who had followed him, nudging him gently with his knee.

Simon made no response. Then Peter reflected that he could give him a few minutes to pray. He took advantage of it to assure himself of the exactitude of the caretaker, whom he paid and for whom he was responsible. Sometimes, the caretaker, after having opened the door at the first hour of the day, went to sleep in a corner of the church. Peter thought about the pleasure of waking him up with a few kicks, and set forth to make a tour of the nave.

He perceived a slight sound in the part that was behind the altar. There was a narrow iron door there, to which he alone had the key, which opened on to a stone stairway. That stairway communicated with vast subterrains that extended beneath the church and far beyond it, through old Bruchium, destroyed by the earthquake. The subterrains had been blocked up and only two rooms had been retained, where religious objects were stored.

Peter saw a form crouching in front of the iron door, examining the lock. It was a woman. As the sound of his footsteps she stood up and tried to run away. But in the presence of any woman, Peter carried within him the instincts of hunting and violence, which precipitated him forward and caused him to seize her around the waist.

The rising sun only cast a faint light through the stained glass windows, He grabbed the head, which was moving away, and dragged it toward his own. He uttered a grunt of joy on recognizing Touta.

She was only a slave, but the most beautiful of all those he knew. He had often encountered her at the market of the gate of the Sun, to which she came every morning. He had pursued her with propositions and obscene words, but she had always drawn away, silent and scornful, along the road that descended outside the city wall toward Lake Mareotis. He had desired her forcefully and had sometimes gone to prowl, in the evening, around the villa full of white roses, in order to try to drag her into some remote place.

Now he held her in his arms like a palpitating bird.

"What are you doing here? Why were you looking at that lock?"

To his great surprise, however, Touta did not manifest any terror. She did not even try to get away. She looked him in the face, half-smiling. He sensed her warm body against him, and here was a hint of abandonment in its movement that made him quiver with desire.

"I thought I might encounter you," said Touta. "I was waiting for you. The church was deserted. It's impossible for me to come at any other time. I have a severe master, and I don't know what he'd do if he saw me with a Christian."

Peter had relaxed his grip. Touta did not flee; she even put her hand on his shoulder with a spontaneous familiarity.

"You know that there are gold monstrances and pyxes at the bottom of the stairs," he said. "There are also relics, and certain demoniac pagans try to take possession of them for profanations."

She burst into laughter whose echoes resonated under the vault. Peter did not distinguish the exaggeration in that hilarity.

"Silly! I'd like to see all those riches with you, and how the relics are made. There are some, it appears, that give life-long good fortune if one touches them. Can you enable me to touch them? Oh, say yes! You won't refuse me. Take me down with you into the subterrains..."

No, he did not have the key on him. Bishop Cyril was waiting for him. It wasn't possible right now. But if she wanted to come back..."

"Come back! I should think so. I've been thinking about meeting you here for a long time. You frighten me a little, but I can see that you're not nasty. I'll come back this evening, if you wish, but swear to me that you'll let me touch the relics?"

Peter was suspicious. Touta might perhaps have been trying to steal, and, having been surprised, she was making promises in order to get away. He drew her to him and placed his thick lips on the pure design of the Armenian's mouth. He ran his hands over her firm breasts and her hips. Stuck to him, she returned his kiss.

His powerful build and his brutal manner had been worth much vulgar good fortune to Peter. Touta's disdain, when he had encountered her, might have been feminine feints. That happened sometimes. One pleased women, but they only let one see it later.

"Well, this evening," he said. "I live in the little single-story red brick house beside the church. I'll wait for you there at the first hour of the night." He laughed coarsely and significantly. "Do you like the wine of the Sais hills? It's the best in Egypt. I have a few bottles that we can open together."

Touta smiled, and her eyelids, in creasing, consented more eloquently than any response.

Then Peter let her leave and went back to the young monk. He was obliged to lift him up by the shoulders to extract him from his prayer.

Bishop Cyril was pacing back and forth in the large square room of the Serapeum where he slept and worked.

Possessed of a narrow faith, he believed himself to be the champion of Jesus Christ, the man chosen to make his religion triumph against the pagans. But he suffered because no celestial sign designated him to the world. He believed in miracles but he had never witnessed one. On the eve of a decisive action he was waiting for a marvelous event, a prophecy, something to indicate to him that he was following God's path. And as he was a violent man, anger was mingled with that expectation. He aspired to sanctity with all the more force because he knew that he did not have the right to claim it, and if he could, he would have imposed his title of saint by force.[30]

A servant came to announce to him that the monk he had asked for had arrived. He ran to the door, shouting "Send him in!"

Then he changed his mind. He went to lean on his priedieu, which was surmounted by a tall oak cross, in such a fashion that the cross loomed up directly above his head.

The rumor had run round Alexandria that Simon had announced certain events in advance, and a legend, contradicted by some and reported admiringly by others, floated round his name. Cyril had the vague hope of provoking a favorable inspiration for his projects.

He started with surprise. Peter had just pushed in front of him a sickly, frightened child, who fell to his knees, his hands joined, as he had been told to do, and as any other monk in his place would have done.

The Bishop lifted him up indulgently. He was not displeased to inspire that respectful dread, but for once he would have liked something else.

He started to speak to Simon. He told him that he knew of his influence over the monks of the convent of Nitra. He was counting on their courage, and their discipline. The times were difficult. Christianity had never been subjected to such an assault. Combat was necessary. Blood would perhaps be spilled. Had Jesus Christ not shed his own?

He looked at his interlocutor from the corner of his eye. God sometimes made use of the simple to make himself manifest. But he had the sentiment of talking to the void. Simon was not listening to him. He was turning round, and had the

---

[30] Cyril was, in fact canonized—by no means the first vicious mass-murderer to receive that honor, and certainly not the last.

appearance of searching for someone to his right or behind him.

And suddenly, he wept miserably, like a beggar who is hungry, like a culpable caught at fault.

"I'm alone, I'm all alone," he repeated. "God has abandoned me."

Then Cyril, irritated, made a sign to Peter to take him away.

The most singular rumors were the circulating in Alexandria.

An inhabitant who had spent the night at the corner of the apostases and the street that led to the Church of Caesarea claimed to have been witness to an extraordinary spectacle.

He had found himself in the presence of an enormous catafalque that blocked the entire width of the street. Young men and young men crowned with blue flowers were carrying a transparent blue-tinted stone coffin, by the weight of which they seemed overwhelmed. Lying in the coffin he had perceived the form of a woman with sapphires as scintillating as the stars on her feet, her hands and her head. Behind the coffin walked a man, full of nobility, who resembled Plato as he is represented in all his busts. He was surrounded by philosophers and sages, whom he recognized by their costumes as belonging to the most different countries and the remotest times. All of them had an expression of infinite sorrow on their faces.

Chilled by horror, he had stopped, and the cortege had turned the corner of the street silently, to disappear like a dream.

When he told the story of that vision he found several people who affirmed that they had also seen the mysterious funeral pass by.

The same night, a little before sunrise, the centurion who was on guard on the old Macedonian fortress saw, clearly, coming from the sea, a flaming sword, with its point directed toward Alexandria. It floated in the sky for a few minutes, and he had time to wake the legionaries who were nearby, and they saw it too.

But what brought the terror to a peak was the apparition of a comet. It was livid, as if desperate. In the popular quarters, outside doors and on terraces, people stayed awake for a long time contemplating it.

The following day, there were people who left the city, and as many of the shops remained closed, the Prefect was obliged to make it known officially, via the criers, that it was only a celestial phenomenon foreseen for a long time by the calculations of astronomers.

As there was no talk of anything but dreams and presages, Diodorus came to find Cyril and confide to him that his daughter Priscilla said that she had had a singularly precise dream the previous night.

In front of the Church of Cesarea she had seen Hypatia streaming with blood and trying to speak, but the jaw was moving, rising and falling, without allowing any words to escape.

Diodorus knew that divination by dreams was contrary to the teachings of the Church, but he had thought that in these troubled times the Bishop might perhaps derive some indication from that dream.

He was not mistaken.

Cyril was radiant. Was it not the sign for which he was waiting? He thanked his friend warmly, and as Diodorus as about to withdraw, struck by a sudden idea, he placed his hands on his shoulders and said to him gravely: "Send your children to me tomorrow with Majorin. It's necessary, to set an example, that they are at the head of those who strike." And as Diodorus interrogated him with his gaze, anxiously, he went on as he turned away: "Don't worry. There won't be any danger that day."

VII. A Perfume of Crushed Mint

The Gymnasium was deserted. A warm reverberation rose from the mosaics of the xyste. In the garden, the earth was cracking and the flowers, weighed down, exhaled more powerful odors.

The day before, Hypatia and Telamon had agreed, almost without saying so, that they would come earlier than usual in order to throw the discus, before the time when the Gymnasium was populated by its usual guests. They had been surprised by the extreme solitude of the place. They had undressed, only retaining their under-tunics. But then the heat had seemed to them to be too great. The slave who picked up the discuses when they had thrown them was not yet there. There was only a negro so profoundly sleep that they started to laugh, and with a common accord they decided to walk, both equally troubled by the silence and the stillness of the heat-wave.

They walked along a path lined by sycamores, whose dense shade protected them from the sun, and they perceived for the first time that they were more to one another than companions in games.

Telamon picked a sprig of mint and crumpled it in his hand, and said, for the sake of saying something: "How much more penetrating the scent of mint is when the weather is very hot!"

And he extended his hand to Hypatia, and leaned toward her slightly.

For a second, that hand brushed Hypatia's mouth and the young man's shoulder touched her bare shoulder. The mint embalmed her, she felt dizzy and recoiled. Then, ashamed, she smiled, and leaned on Telamon in order to prove to herself that she remained the mistress of her instinct.

Then they resumed a conversation they had had before, an endless conversation. "Why? Oh, why?" said Hypatia, looking into the distance. "Perhaps because I've always thought that sensuality is the most absolute form of the slavery of women with regard to men. Perhaps because my efforts have turned toward the development of my mind, and I haven't had the time to think that that mind is enveloped by a form of flesh. How many joys would have been lost to me if I hadn't been chaste! The intoxication of work, a faint delight one has on waking up that is untroubled by any aftertaste of desire, a more perfect admiration of beauty because intelligence alone participates in it."

"Perhaps the contrary is also true," Telamon replied, with a musical softness in his voice, fixing his large, dark long-lashed eyes on Hypatia. "The philosopher who voluntarily renounces sensuality is an eternal solitary. He does not communicate with nature by the means that she has given him, which he judges arbitrarily to be vulgar. I even defy him fully to admirer the laws of art. How can one understand the marvel there is in the hollow backs of beautiful statues, in the delicacy of their legs, if one does not imagine the movements of physical love and the harmony of tenderness and the vigor with which the artist has dosed the lines? Do temples not symbolize by their eurhythmia the divine mixture of mind and matter? Is there not in the surge of columns, the curve of arches and the caress of architraves and ineffable poem that is not exempt from something carnal?"

"And yet," said Hypatia, "it was in Syracuse, when I was twenty years old—when I was your age—before the little temple of Minerva outside the city on the edge of the sea, that I swore not to belong to any man. That evening, there was a rain of shooting stars, the laurels embalmed the air, the sea had never been as blue, and never had life seemed so sweet. I remember that I was sitting on the worn steps of the threshold. I thought that Pythagoras and Plato must have sat down in the same place, for that temple of Tyche is one of the most ancient in the world, and I wept with emotion, touched by a ray of the intelligence of those pure minds."

"The oaths that one swears to oneself can be revoked by the new being that we are a few years after having made them..."

Telamon stopped.

They had arrived at the very spot where, a few days before, while Hypatia and Proclus were going through the portal leading to the courtyard, he had taken Priscilla in his arms and had kissed her on the lips.

And he went on, as if talking to himself: "It's necessary to put oneself above sensuality, to summon it and dismiss it like a slave, to play with it as we play with the discus."

But Hypatia, seizing him by the arm, said to him imperiously: "Come on, let's not stay here." And she drew him backwards into the sycamore-lined path they had just quit.

She started to laugh, but there was a hint of bitterness that pierced that laughter.

"Do you think that I didn't see you the other day? You were playing with sensuality, weren't you? I turned round when you were pressing that young girl against you. You stuck your mouth to hers. Do you see her again, sometimes? Does she please you that much? Well, answer me!"

Telamon considered Hypatia's animated face with surprise. He had never seen her thus, and had never found her as beautiful. The color of her nipple appeared beneath the transparent fabric like an incarnadine droplet, and her teeth shone between her redder teeth. There was a slight quiver in her nostrils.

They were walking rapidly. They had gone along the path. They sat down at hazard on a stone bench.

"Something very curious happened within me," said Telamon, with his habitual slowness. "Certainly, you don't resemble that girl named Priscilla. But when I kissed her, it seemed that it was you that I was kissing and that it was your body that I was holding against mine. And for a second, I possessed you in spite of you."

He looked her full in the face, projecting over her, like a living fluid, the desire by which he was animated. Hypatia looked at him too, wondering whether she ought not to get up and go away, whether she ought not to reproach him for such a brutal confession, or even become indignant at what she could consider to be an insult.

Rapidly, she reviewed previous gazes and gestures on Telamon's part. How young he was, in sum! He had never shown the elevation of mind of a Proclus. He scarcely took part in philosophical conversations. He never manifested the intellectual admiration that everyone had lavished upon her.

And suddenly, it seemed to her that all her being was inflamed, like a bouquet dried out by the sun that only requires a spark. She had a desire to take the young man in her arms, ripping his tunic. She experienced a fraternity with him so great that their two bodies, without touching became only one. A great mystery was revealed to her in a voluptuous dolor.

They perceived at the same time that the bench on to which they had fallen was at the foot of a small statue of Aphrodite situated in the depths of the garden. They had raised their eyes together and the same thought had come to them in considering the admirable nudity of the goddess.

They too felt naked. Their light tunics scarcely veiled their form. But they looked at one another without modesty, proud of feeling beautiful, inflamed by a common desire, the intoxication of embracing one another.

But they did not do it.

Hypatia, as vanquished as if the young man had possessed her, took his hand gently and raised the palm to her lips. She kept it there, respiring the attenuated perfume of mint in which, for her young amour, the sad charm of flourishing things trailed.

"It's the mint I'm respiring," she said.

"I wish it were my entire being that is evaporating toward you in that odor," he replied.

They knew that they belonged to one another, and they savored in silence the sweetness of that possession.

Telamon made a movement.

"No," said Hypatia, "tomorrow. Today, that's enough."

And as he persisted, by puckering his lips, she repeated: "Tomorrow! It's so beautiful to be able to wait for tomorrow with impatience! And then, if we suffer from that wait, are we not surer that tomorrow will inevitably arrive?"

She did not know how mistaken she was.

And, when Telamon had just gone away, and Hypatia, pensively, had remained on the bench, out of all the minutes in life, that was the minute that the poet Palladius chose as the most favorable to speak about love to Hypatia.

Palladius had an immense vanity, which came less from his fortune, which was considerable, than from his physical beauty. He had a round, pink face and thick curly hair. He was tall, and he strove to put an imperial majesty into all his gestures. He lived in an entirely unrealizable dream of fabulous grandeur.

He dreamed of being a king and building a scaffolding of glory. Some of his relatives, who were in the Emperor's favor in Constantinople, had obtained for him the title of Count of Africa. Thanks to that title and his literary renown, which he believed to be very great, he would group around Cyrene, Carthage and all of North Africa the elements that dreamed of shrugging off the yoke of Rome. He had the basis of an army. A militia of students at the Museum of Alexandria constituted, for him, a counterbalance to the influence in the city of the Parabalani, a militia of warrior clerics under Cyril's orders. He would create similar militias in all the cities of Africa in order to favor the return of paganism. It was on them that he would rely in order to realize what Count Heraclian had once attempted without success.[31]

---

[31] Heraclian, Count of Africa was a general in the service of the Emperor of the Western Roman Emperor Honorius, who led a revolt against his master in 413, two years before the present scene is set, and attempted an unsuccessful invasion of Italy.

Hypathia knew about his infantile vanity and his disproportionate dreams, and smiled at them, without contradicting them. She knew that he desired her, and deflected that desire.

Immediately, however, Palladius pressed her with the haste that one has, instinctively, when one wants to seize something that is escaping.

The time had come to extinguish Christianity by force throughout Africa. That task was incumbent on him. If she consented to be his wife, he would no longer doubt his success. Rome was still filled with disciples of Symmachus.[32] Many senators had remained faithful to the gods of paganism, and he, Palladius, maintained a secret correspondence with those senators. If, like Heraclian, he disembarked with an army in disorganized Italy, he was certain that Rome would rise up for him against Milan.[33] The most beautiful dreams of the Emperor Julian could be realized. But it was necessary that Hypatia be at his side, that she love him, that she marry him!

Hypatia experienced a great need for sincerity.

"Well, no," she said "I have less ambition, and I have more. The reign of pure ideas of which the Olympian gods are only the material symbols will not come yet. It is not by violence that truth can ever be imposed. Every temple demolished by the Christians, every beautiful statue that they break, is reedified spiritually, and the temple is larger and the statue more perfect. And then, listen..."

Involuntarily, she had darted a gaze in the direction of the garden in which Telamon had drawn away.

For a second, she had been invaded by the desire to talk about the new genius of which her body was the receptacle,

---

[32] Quintus Aurelius Symmachus (345-402) was a Roman consul who tried to preserve the traditional religions of Rome when the greater part of the aristocracy was converting to Christianity.

[33] Honorius did establish his court in Milan for a while, but he had moved it to Ravenna in 401, so this reference is anachronistic

that Olympian flame by which she had been burned and which she knew to be sent by the gods.

But she stopped.

"And then, there's Telamon, isn't there?" said Palladius. But he said it without believing it, in order to hear indignant protests, to assure himself that Hypatia was still inaccessible to the sympathy of any man other than him.

She only replied: "Perhaps..." And she fixed her moist eyes upon an absent image.

That was enough for Palladius. He had received an insult that he could not forgive. He was struck by a cruel dart whose poison was about to corrupt his blood. He would have liked to believe that he was mistaken. He considered Hypatia, who was standing before him. He had never seen that hopeful light in her eyes, that impulse in her body to throw herself into arms that were not his. He sensed that she was elsewhere, far away, that she was looking through him at someone else, whose beauty had moved her.

Such a misunderstanding of the superiority that he attributed to himself threw him into astonishment, and filled him with anger. He no longer believed in the intelligence of a woman who was the victim of such an aberration.

He attempted a burst of disdainful laughter. He was very red. He straightened himself, giving his appearance the greatest possible majesty.

"Adieu," he said.

He made the gesture of a king repudiating an excessively amorous woman, who is ridding himself of her importunity, and drew away with a long stride, without the smiling Hypatia having had time to retain him.

IX. Toward the Abode of the Wise Men

Aurelius had gone to say adieu to his friend Olympios.

He had crossed the few stadia that separated his house from the salt-pans of Shedia and had found the sage sitting cross-legged in his narrow hut, between a small heap of bananas and a jug of water.

"Why didn't you come sooner?" said Olympios. "I now arrive easily at the divine ecstasy that Plotinus only knew three times and Iamblichus only once. Then, the laws of matter no longer exist for my spiritual body and you could have seen me, an hour ago, floating in this hut with as much ease as a mist in a globe of glass."

Aurelius knew that the greatest sages have their weaknesses and that it is vain to contradict them. Olympios professed the same tolerance. So, when Aurelius announced his resolution to depart, as Apollonius had done several centuries before, in order to reach, in the depths of India, the abode of the wise men where the Tyanian had found the truth, he contented himself with nodding his head and hugging his old friend.

"We won't be conversing any more with Socles about divine things, in the evenings, among the roses of your garden. For me, the palm that the charming slave agitated over our heads, the blue of the waters of Lake Mareotis, the sweetness of the soul that the warmth of our amity gives, were the last pleasures in which I participated. Perhaps they distanced me from the absolute that I seek, and it's a good thing that I'm losing them...but I sense that I shall miss them, so much do terrestrial things take possession of us without our realizing it. Henceforth, I shall only gaze at the green-tinted waters of the marshes, where the reeds agitate endlessly. If you come back one day..."

But Olympios stopped. He measured the distance, the dangers of the journey for a solitary man, the half-savage peoples that it would be necessary to traverse, and he lowered his head.

"Let's embrace one last time," he said, simply.

When Aurelius looked back, at the place where the path quit the marsh to turn through a grove of palm trees, he perceived his friend in the distance, at the door of his hut, who was still making him a sign, and he thought: *All affections make us suffer. We are torn by amour, we are torn by friendship. May I find out there the secret of the serene verity!*

Socles had come to make one last attempt to retain him, but he had not foreseen the astonishing activity that now animated Aurelius. The latter had gone to the port of Eunostos and had reserved his place on a ship that was about to set sail for Tyre that same day at sunset. He had been obliged to bring forward his departure and put his affairs in order rapidly, because, if he missed that ship, two weeks might go by before he could depart, because of the large number of people who were quitting Alexandria for Greece and all the ports of Syria.

He had just had a long conversation with Mucius the trapezite,[34] whose shop was in the emporium. It was him who received the income from his lands and he had regulated the usage that was to be made of it henceforth.

Socles found his friend clad in his traveling cloak, sitting on the steps of his perron, contemplating the roses of his garden one last time.

The calm that befits a philosopher was not radiating from his person. Immediately, he stood up, and seemed disappointed on seeing Socles.

---

[34] The trapezites (literally "men at tables") were the bankers of ancient Athens, who branched out from money-changing into money-lending. They had disappeared from the Western Empire by the time of the present story, suppressed by the Church's ban on usury, they continued to operate in the Byzantine Empire, where they organized a system of transferable credit.

"Have you seen Touta?" he asked. "Touta left this morning and hasn't come back."

And he explained that it was necessary for him to see his slave before his departure and inform her of the arrangements he had made with the trapezite Mucius in order that a part of his income should be put into her hands. In any case, he was anxious about an absence that had never happened before in ten years.

Socles sat down beside his friend and insisted affectionately that he should renounce his voyage.

"Plotinus also attempted to reach India, following the armies of the Emperor Gordian, and was obliged to turn back. What guide will you have when you arrive at Circesium, the last city of the Empire? How will you traverse Persia, whose language you don't know and where those who speak Greek are hated? Oh, I know what you're counting on: the fraternity of the hierophants of the temples. But times have changed since Apollonius traveled the earth, favorably welcomed everywhere by the priests of different gods, but who celebrated the same mysteries.

"And supposing that, through a thousand dangers, you reach Attock, Taxila and the River Ganges, what proof do you have that you'll discover the mysterious brotherhood of sages whose thought directs the world? They assuredly lived in Egypt in the epoch of Alexander, but I only found half-savage priests at the temple of Ammon. Perhaps they inhabited India in the days of Apollonius and Jesus, but four centuries have passed. Where are they now?"

Aurelius got up, went to the door of his garden that overlooked the road and looked at the horizon to see whether he could perceive Touta's violet garment in the distance.

Then, his eyes lowered, he came back to Socles slowly and said to him in a low voice: "The faculty of cherishing the beings that surround us is almost imperishable within us. I confess to myself for the first time that I'm attached to that slave. I find her beautiful. She's devoted to me. She surrounds me with an atmosphere of affection. Where can she be?"

And as Socles was about to represent the difficulties of the journey to him again, he stopped him.

"I have to go. I shall go like Apollonius, without baggage, leaning on a staff. I shall only differ from him in that I shall carry a few mina in my belt converted into Persian coin by my trapezite. I've determined the Tyanian's itinerary, very nearly. I shall follow it exactly, on foot, like him. If it's given to me to reach the seven clay cells that form the design of a lotus I shall stay out there until I have been instructed in the wisdom. But if I die on the way, which is possible, I count on you, Socles, to watch over Touta, the thought of whom fills me with anxiety at this moment."

Aurelius got up again to see whether Touta was about to appear, and then walked back and forth, agitatedly.

"She's a child," he said. "She knows very little about life. A host of procurers emerge from Rhacotis every day in search of young foreign women whom they entice with promises. Who knows what trap she might have fallen into? But I no longer have time to go to the police commander..."

"Postpone your journey," said Socles. "Touta will come back, and I'll have time to succeed in the discovery of Alexander's tomb. It's ridiculous to go in search of the truth in the depths of India if we have it alongside us, written on a papyrus by the hands of the masters of wisdom themselves. I've been to Menalchos' house. He's almost completely mad. When I talked to him about buying his house he fell into a sort of bizarre crisis. I thought that he was about to leap at my throat. But I saw his son, who is direly in need of money, and I'm on the point of settling things with him. I'm convinced that if you wait a few more days..."

Aurelius shook his head sadly. He did not believe in that chimera.

"Can the swimmer who wishes to traverse a river and is carried away by the current turn back?" he said. "I am that swimmer, driven irresistibly by the desire for knowledge. But I believe that I can go with the joy of hope in my heart. Nothing can stop me. Regret and anxiety will be my lot. I've just discovered an affection of which I was unaware, and affections are tyrants that devastate the soul and deflect us from the path."

He went through the door to the vestibule of the house and listened for a few seconds to the sigh of the water-clock. Then he came back to his friend.

"The captain told me that he would have to depart at sunset because of the favorable breeze that rises at that moment. Doubtless I would rejoice if someone told me that his ship has caught fire or that it isn't leaving, because of some event independent of my will, but that won't happen, and I shall embark at sunset, for my reason must hold sway over my sentiments, or my entire life has been an error."

The afternoon was about to reach its conclusion. The spring roses had a more penetrating aroma, which mingled with that of box trees and sycamores.

What! The gaze of the sage, in embracing the trees and the waters, when evening was about to fall, could reflect such a great anguish, such a human despair?

Rapidly, Aurelius went back into his house and started moving through the rooms. He saw the books in their wooden and metal cylinders lined up on the shelves, as regular and faithful as the evenings of study that he had spent in their company. He saw a cameo before which he had often wept. He saw the room where Touta had slept.

"Touta," he repeated, in a low voice. "A slave, nothing but a slave!"

He went out into the garden again. He picked up his staff and he said to Socles: "The time has come. You can accompany me as far as the port."

He closed the garden door again, and they started walking along the road.

They had covered half a stadion when Aurelius grabbed the arm of his companion. He had to go back. He absolutely had to go back. Socles would wait for him on the road.

He retraced his steps at a run. He climbed the steps of the perron. He went back inside.

Another glance at the books, a glance t the cameo, a glance at Touta's bedroom...

And he started to write: only a few words for Touta. He began thus:

When Diodorus, the father of Priscilla, dies...

He placed the papyrus very evidently. She could not fail to see it. He added a formula of adieu.

Oh, wisdom truly does not give any strength. The water-clock marked the time inexorably. By hurrying, he would arrive at the port of Eunostos just before the departure. When she came back, Touta would read the papyrus, and those few words that he had just added...

When she same back...

But she was never to return.

X. The Tomb of Alexander

Almost soundlessly, the lock opened, and Touta went down the stone staircase that led to the subterrain of the Church of Saint Mark.

She knew now that she would not be surprised. The caretaker had just left, without suspecting that she was hidden in the sculpted wooden pulpit from which the Patriach, on certain days, delivered sermons, It had been necessary for her to take advantage of a favorable opportunity to slip into it, and she had remained there for several hours. But now evening had come. It was the hour when Peter was waiting for her at home, in the house next to the church. She was calm and resolute.

Touta loved her master and did not want to lose him. She only understood very vaguely what the mysterious wisdom might be about which he talked with his friends and dreamed of going to seek in India, but she had discerned in the discussions of the three philosophers that an inestimable papyrus was around the neck of the mummy of Alexander and that possession of that papyrus would fill Aurelius with joy and retain him.

A room of black marble in ground that had collapsed! Who knows?

She had heard mention of the legendary Sema, the magnificent and formidable tomb once constructed by kings who put a talismanic value of royal eternity on their conservation. She knew that next to the Sema reposed, in tombs no less splendid, the family of all those kings, all those constructor Ptolemies who had wanted masterpieces of architecture for their remains as astonishing as the palaces in which they had lived while alive. And that had made an incomparable necropolis, an accumulation of cupolas and mortuary chambers, a forest of columns and porticos, a sumptuous city of the dead. People had admired it, gods had fought their battles around it; Jesus, Jupiter and Osiris had enclosed it in a circle of different emblems and statues, and one day, that funerary capital, by virtue of a natural revolution, had descended mysteriously into the earth.

The pagans had said that the gods had wanted to remove the masters of ancient Egypt from the sadness of the Christian sun. The Christians had claimed that Jesus himself had swept way those excessively splendid vestiges of paganism, and they had edified the vast Church of Saint Mark on the site.

Who knows? Touta had thought. Since the Church of Saint Mark had subterrains, there was a possibility that those subterrains communicated at one point with the buried tombs.

On the day of the feast of Saint Mark, the relics of the saint were exposed in the church near the altar. They were taken out of the rooms where they reposed in their gold and silver cases. Then the host of Christians filled the nave and filed past the relics. Touta had followed the crowd the previous year and she had visited the church, which she did not know. The door behind the altar remained open then, and one could descend into the subterranean rooms. In any case, one could only see an ordinary stone staircase and a vaulted gallery with two rooms to either side, which presented nothing curious, and one of which was entirely filled with candles that people bought for religious purposes.

But Touta, who had gone down there to pass the time, had noticed a wooden door at the extremity of the gallery, which had intrigued her. She had wondered at the time where that door might lead. She had not attached any importance to it, but the memory of that door had returned to her when she had heard Socles talking about the tomb of Alexander and making hypotheses as to its approximate position. And she had conceived the audacious project of penetrating into the tombs via the church.

In case of difficulty, she had resolved to go find Peter and offer herself to him, if he would help her. She did not worry about her disgust. What did the gift of her slave's body matter by comparison with the grandeur of the result?

And she glimpsed a sublime moment. The three philosophers were sitting out there in the rose garden, and she was gently stirring the air around them with a palm. They had just resumed their habitual subject of conversation. Socles was speaking with abundance and conviction. Her master was doubtful and shook his head. But when he repeated: "I don't believe in that papyrus," she, the maidservant, the slave, advanced and said, simply: "I've been to look for it—here it is!"

At the bottom of the stone staircase, Touta struck a briquette and lit a little bronze lamp that she had hidden under her garments. It was an oil lamp that only cast a miserable glow. Behind that drop of light she arrived at the end of the gallery. But then she saw the room where he great piles of candles were heaped. She seized one of the stoutest and lit it instead of her oil lamp.

She examined the door and ran the flame of the candle over the lock. Luck favored her again. The door could not have been opened for years. It was worm-eaten, and the wood was disjointed. The lock was shaky and she saw that it would yield to the iron hook that she had bought even more easily than the lock of the first door.

Her heart beat faster. Destiny seemed to be favoring her expedition.

A few minutes later, the lock fell to the ground and the door yielded to her effort and swung open before her.

Touta gazed into the darkness.

It seemed to her that a damp breath, a subterranean exhalation, was coming from very far away, cold and mephitic: an almost living respiration that died at her feet and tilted the flame of the candle, which she had placed on the ground. It was like the sight of the Amenti where the dead trailed. And there was something melancholy and terrifying in that sadness of another world, exhaled silently by the corruption of that breath.

But Touta had a simple and firm soul that was never tormented by the mystery of the afterlife. She saw nothing but the goal to be attained and she had made the sacrifice of her life.

She secured her briquette preciously in her linen belt, for she knew that the greatest danger for her was being lost in the darkness. She picked up the candle, measured its length with her eye, which would give her several hours of light, and she advanced resolutely into the unknown.

The gallery sloped downwards. Touta walked for quite a long time. She saw, not without astonishment, that the vault and the walls were not very ancient in their contrivance, and must date from the epoch in which the Church of Saint Mark had been built. For her that was a fortunate augury. Her only chance of success reposed on the knowledge that the architects of the church had had of the Sema and the tombs of the Ptolemies. In building the foundations they might have found a part of them and established a gallery enabling them to be reached.

Touta had heard Socles speak abundantly on that subject and emit all possible hypotheses. He said that Johannes of Corinth, the architect to whom the care of building the Church of Saint Mark had been confided, was simultaneously a pious Christian and a scholar passionate about the beauties of antiquity. He could not have edified a church on ground in which the most admirable monuments of Alexandria reposed without carrying out research to find them.

Socles claimed to know that the construction of the Church of Saint Mark had taken an unusually long time and that that time had been employed by Johannes in excavations. He affirmed that Johannes had changed the origin disposition of his plans and modified the orientation of the church in order not to disturb the tombs that he had discovered. He could not have failed to construct some kind of secret way to penetrate as far as the tombs himself. But he had drowned while bathing in the sea at the moment when the last stones of the church were about to be placed. He had left no children or close relatives and it seemed that no one had inherited his secrets.

Touta remembered Socles' speeches as she walked. She had heard him give the measurements of monuments, and specify their position relative to the church with so much exactitude that she was not astonished to see the gallery she was following turn left. It was to the left of the church, she had concluded, that the Sema ought to be found.

To the left! She thought that a few feet above her was the brick house of the wretched Peter, who was waiting for her, and she smiled in satisfaction.

She stopped. In front of her here was a narrow stairway. There was no longer any doubt. Socles' hypotheses were accurate. Works dating from the epoch of the church had extended this gallery and these stairs toward the rediscovered tombs. If that had not been the case she would have found herself in the presence of a chaos of rubble and ruins. She had seen clearly. Perhaps she was about to reach her goal. She felt faint.

A deleterious atmosphere full of miasmas, almost unbreathable, was stagnating in the spiral stone stairwell that she had begun to descend. It seemed to her that she was entering an abode of granitic decomposition, of mineral putrescence, as if down there, far from the vivifying solar light, the dead stones were rotting. She was penetrated by a sepulchral impression so gripping and so horrifying that memories of religious beliefs that dated from her earliest childhood surged forth from the depths of her soul.

Once, in Armenia, she had been raised in the religion of Zoroaster. But since then, as a slave in Syria and Egypt, she had heard mention of so many different gods, had seen so many statues and so many temples that Ormuz with the luminous robe and Ahriman with the three grimacing faces had been effaced from her thoughts.

And now, suddenly, she found herself on the threshold of the subterranean realms, at the door to the Hell that had been described to her when she was very small, on winter evenings in her village in Armenia.

It was just as she had imagined the departure from life. She recognized the funereal entrance, the endless stairway.

She had seen it before in dreams. She experienced the pitiless solitude of the being who will never see daylight again or the faces of beloved individuals. Yima, the master of the dead, was waiting for her down below, surrounded by the Drujs who go to search for bodies and the Yatus who carry out their metamorphoses. And she advanced all alone, raising her faint candle toward the menacing night, like the symbol of liberating good deeds.

She thought about going back.

She told herself that it was already a good deal to be able to tell Aurelius and Socles about the existence of this corridor and staircase. But she reflected that the traces of the forcing of the doors would be discovered, that they would be guarded henceforth, and that it would doubtless be impossible to come back. By virtue of her audacious attempt and belated terror, she would have rendered the philosophers' projects unrealizable.

Then again, she was nearing the goal.

Perhaps the end of the stairway was behind the turning that she could perceive, and perhaps, if she went down a few more steps, she would see the glass coffin in which Alexander reposed...

Unsteadily, she descended.

But one turning succeeded another. The stairway was very long. The air was increasingly poisonous. As she leaned on one of the walls, she had a sensation of viscous damp on her hand. A sweat was escaping the stones, and sometimes a droplet ran over the granite, leaving a greenish trail behind it.

Touta felt dizzy. The spirals of the staircase were multiplied in her mind, and she had the sensation of descending into the depths of the earth.

Suddenly, a flow of fresh air passed and inclined the flame of the candle, which she protected with her hand instinctively. A stone that she had bumped with her foot resonated, and that resonance echoed like an appeal, like a burst of laughter, in an immeasurable, dismal, tenebrous extent that unfurled before her. That lasted for a few seconds, and Touta shivered, closed her eyes and thought that she was about to die.

Then silence fell again, but heavily, coming from high up and far away, implacable, charged with the ephialtes of the dead and the mist of their impotent desires.

Then, raising her candle, Touta gazed.

She sensed, rather than saw, great architectural masses that were stacked above her head. She distinguished colossal pylons, a cupola broken in several places, a balcony supported by stone caryatids, but which was not supported by anything at its extremity, as if it launched forth into the nocturnal space. There were files of obelisks that led to circular edicules, hermes, broken altars and fragile lotiform columns that were suggestive of young women, prisoners of a population of dead giants.

At hazard, she turned left. In the disarray of her soul, the vision of her goal persisted. She was almost walking on tiptoe, fearing the voices and laughter that might have greeted her appearance in that formidable realm of defunct stones.

Immediately, she almost collided with a black mass that barred her route. It was the immense statue of a goddess with the wings of an ostrich. On her head it bore a pointed bonnet, conical in form, and was holding out a pair of doves in her right hand.

She went around the statue and found herself in a hemicycle surrounded by niches, which she examined. Those niches, which numbered seven, contained the sacred animals symbolizing the evolution of inferior reigns. There was a serpent with a human head, a crocodile in the mouth of which the ivory of sharp teeth glistened, a bat with rubies in the place of its eyes, a jackal symbolizing Anubis, a crouching cynocephalus symbolizing the adoration of the rising sun, an ibis, the image of Thoth, and a winged bull, with its muzzle directed upwards and its wings deployed, to attest that matter must bring forth its greatest strength in order to rise toward spirit.

What were those great sarcophagi that the wandering Touta glimpsed, around which those mute divinities stood?

Perhaps the one where Queen Cleopatra and Antony reposed, united forever? Perhaps that of the divine Stratonicus? Perhaps that of Ptolemy Euergetes, the benevolent king? Perhaps that of Ptolemy Philopator, the debauched king who poisoned his father? But how could the gods that guarded them be consulted?

Never, in any temple built in the sunlight, had she contemplated faces as terrible, as closed to human prayers, as ravaged by the absence of pity, as consciously orientated toward evil! Did the perpetual shadow lie as heavily upon the gods as upon humans? Was it truly the case that they never heard prayers, that they never granted them, that they were merely companions in the darkness and brothers of the sepulcher?

Touta bumped into the knees of a bronze statue of Hathor, the cow-headed goddess. Mentou, the god of war, gave the impression of wanted to launch his blade at her. Horus resembled in his gesture the bronze sphinxes by which he was surrounded. The ithyphallic Khem threatened her with his attributes. Osiris extended the stumps of his broken arms toward her. Others, inclined, seemed to want to seize her in passing in order to crush her on the marble of their breasts. And she stumbled over fallen statues, climbed over the torsos of gods, and stepped over heads that seemed to want to bite her.

Where was the glass coffin for which she had come?

She had lost all presence of mind. She ran to the right and the left, sometimes retracing her steps, waving her candle, contemplating fearfully the pyramidal masses, the syenite columns, the rows of porticos with their cubic capitals, sometimes going through the arch of a portal that led to a new tomb, to a further infinity of mortuary darkness.

And suddenly, she stopped.

Her mind recovered all its clarity, but only to bring her new faculties of terror. She was not mistaken! A noise was audible in the empire of mute forms. She had woken up the slumbering powers. In the air, heavy with bituminous vapors that troubled her brain, a mysterious life now floated. It was a muffled murmur, a prolonged echo, a trailing voice.

Bewildered, she started to flee.

What monstrous figures were about to appear, what fantastic forms were about to reach out to seize her? She retained a gasp in the depths of her throat, and in the movements she made, the wax of her candle ran over her shoulder and arm, and that burn gave her the sensation of a touch emerging from the invisible. Her garment caught on a broken column and she uttered a howl, thinking that it was a stone hand that wanted to drag her to the ground—and a savage howl replied to hers from all directions.

She had launched herself into an avenue of obelisks. But to the right and the left those obelisks were agitating, rising and falling, leaning over and extending the mystery of their hieroglyphs toward her. A sphinx opened its human jaws immeasurably and stuck out its breasts toward her. Then, stone bats began to whirl around her head, fixing her with the beads of their ruby eyes.

She looked behind her and saw the troop of divine animals on her heels.

The cynocephalus was gamboling and grimacing, the serpent was unwinding its coils, and sometimes moving its sorrowful human face closer, the ibis was elongating is long legs and extending its ridiculous neck, the jaws of the crocodiles were moving, the rearing lions shook their manes, she was brushed by the flight of phoenixes with red-painted plumage, and winged bulls hovered above her head in the tenebrous air, like errant bolides.

She had wanted to violate the secrets of the dead, and she was irredeemably doomed. She passed through the same places without recognizing them, always more closely followed by her fears, and the sepulchral life became more intense and more prodigious.

Increasingly menacing Hathors succeeded one another, Astartes unfastened heir veils in order to envelop her in them. Isises and Osirises tried to crush her. Anubises with jackals' heads that presided over embalmings threw the black boxes that were their emblem at her. Apophises attempted to trip her with their forked tongues, Auta the female warrior with her buckler, Anhour the conductor with his rope, and the obscene Khem with his enormous penis.

And figures more mysterious loomed up between the steles and the obelisks. Royal mummies emerging from sarcophagi advanced their black, paltry, shrunken forms, attempting to envelop Touta with a circle of bodies wrapped in bandages, on which the heads seemed deformed, and they stared at her with their implacable gold masks.

Down the megalithic steps that were staged before her Touta ran, driven and lifted up by the endless horror of the monstrous images, the unnamable entities of the subterranean night, pursued by a procession of statues, by a procession of mummies.

She had penetrated into an enclosure, a darker and more silent place, and there, her legs exhausted, out of breath, devoid of consciousness, she fell to her knees.

Oh, if she had imprudently penetrated into the realm of Ahriman, the god of evil, she renounced he struggle. Let him take her! Let the Drujs seize her with their slender fingers, let the Yatus cut her up and crush her in the mortar of eternal change...

The paving stones on to which she had fallen were black marble, the walls were black marble, the arch of the vault was black marble with exceedingly thin white veins, like human tears in the night of the world.

Touta held up her candle again in her clenched hand. And she saw...

Blue-tinted and oblong in form, radiant and veiled, milky in places, the color of mat sapphire, the color of the moon rising on a autumnal evening, over the white jade pedestal sent from India by King Sandracottus, like the symbol of ideal qualities and inaccessible perfections, reposed the glass coffin of Alexander.

It was miraculous, serene, immortal.

In a second, Touta understood that she had reached her goal, and her vacillating light permitted her to glimpse the contour of the sacred mummy, and even the prominence made at its neck by the scroll for which she had come in search. But she had no joy in that, and not for an instant did she conceive the possibility of seizing it. The papyrus on which the truth was written seemed infinitely far away, separated from her by an infinity of perspectives and mirages.

Perhaps, in spite of her exhaustion and her distress, she might still have attempted to overturn bronze or marble, to stave in lead—but how could one touch that opaline transparency, that glaucous cloud, that lunar crystal so mysteriously blue-tinted?

And then, the distance was too great, in spite of the fact that she only had to put out her hand. And she felt so weary!

A great calm invaded her. She gazed within herself at a light that was born there and illuminated in waves her past existence. She had only lived in order to arrive here and die before the inexpressible blue of Alexander's glass coffin. It had been necessary for her to sacrifice herself and she offered her life joyfully. She would never see the light of the sky again.

She liked that. Men were pitiless and the gods worse. She preferred not to be among the victors, and to fall in darkness serving the only man who had ever been good to her. He was not of the triumphant race either. He was weak, human and sad. She would not bring him back what he desired.

"May the true light enlighten him as it enlightens me!" she murmured.

She sent him her last thought. She had descended the stairway of renunciation by the megalithic steps that had led her to the black marble room.

A voice repeated by a thousand echoes resonated in her ears like a tempest: "Touta!"

Yes, yes, she was ready! It was Yima, the master of the dead who was calling her. She was no longer afraid. Ormuz protects those who are able to give their lives for others; he throws his white robe over them.

"Touta!" called the voice, even nearer.

From the depths of her memory surged the formula of conjuration in the Zend language: "I have honored Ahuramazda, the holy and the veridical. By the grace of Ahuramazda, I am purified.

"Touta!" was repeated behind her.

She had stood up, lifting, in a hand that was no longer trembling, the flame of her candle, bluer in the rarefaction of the air, like the incarnation of her being, spiritualized by sacrifice.

And when Peter struck her from behind with his staff, with all his might, she entered thus into the realm of the dead, more luminous to the good than that of the living, of which Ormuz himself came to open the gates.

Peter considered Touta with surprise. After a long wait in his house, a suspicion had come to him. He had run to the church and had seen the door to the subterrain open. He had gone down the first staircase, found Touta's lamp in the presence of the debris of the second door and had gone into the gallery descending toward the tombs.

He regretted the body of the woman he had desired and had counted on enjoying. It was a wealth that he might have possessed and which was lost to him forever. But he knew how to sacrifice his pleasure to his interest. He found himself in the presence of even greater riches, the secret of which had just been revealed to him. A woman who knew that secret could not be allowed to live any longer.

The tombs of the Ptolemies! He had heard talk of their splendors and their burial.

How many jewels were there in the sarcophagi of kings! How many precious metals in the faces of statues! There were the eyes of Serapis, which were diamonds, and the teeth of Aphrodite, which were pearls! And all that could be his possession!

But Peter felt a sudden frisson. That dead woman at his feet, the putrefaction of the air, and the thickness of the darkness around him, suddenly chilled him and caused his knees to buckle.

He would see later! He would inform Bishop Cyril. Only holy men could triumph over the demons that must populate this pagan metropolis.

Then too, the candle with which he had equipped himself was almost extinct. Touta's had fallen on the floor. He hastened to relight it, and he placed it beside her.

Without looking back he drew away, and was only reassured after having climbed back up the spiral staircase and the subterranean gallery. He replaced the pieces of the worm-eaten door, went out of the church and, for the first time, he perceived that the stars projected an extraordinary light.

And all night long, in the crypt of black marble, next to the thin form of the dead woman, the candle burned.

The gods of stone remained immobile; the mummies did not awaken in the hieroglyphic sarcophagi. Yima did not emerge from the darkness to attest the violence and injustice committed in his empire. For in the sunlight of life or the darkness of the subterranean night, evil never has its immediate punishment and one cannot know at what belated moment of time the hand that strikes will be immobilized and there will finally be a loving word for the good.

When dawn appeared over the earth, the wick and the wax were consumed in the land of subterranean catafalques and the flame went out with a little sigh. And the body of the young woman, under the influences of gases and miasmas, commenced the slow, indefeasible labor of death, and became black with white furrows, similar to the marble on which it was lying.

XI. Amoraim's Luck

Every man has an occasional stroke of luck, and sometimes it seems to coincide with a date, a small event, or a familiar or ridiculous action, to which it is attributed.

It arrived for the unfortunate Amoraim.

When he burned his clothes soiled with Christian blood, he no longer had anything with which to dress himself but a few rags found at the bottom of an old chest. But a charm, a magic, undoubtedly resided in those rags.

He had made a firm resolution to remain henceforth crouched in the demi-obscurity of his shop, in order that no purchaser of candles would perceive his wretched appearance. That was what he did. But he could not stay there for long. For the first time in his life, the sunlight in the street inspired a singular admiration in him. He sensed, without knowing why, a lightness, an unaccustomed delight. Decidedly, he felt no shame for his patched and torn robe. He desired to run through the city and inform himself about new things.

"Ignorance is not wealth," he repeated to himself, that day. "To possess knowledge of the sciences and life and remain humble at the same time, that is the sign of a man's superiority."

He did not reflect that perhaps it was very late for him to enter into the path of study. No, curiosity passed through all the holes in his robe.

It was very hot. It was the middle of the afternoon. He closed his shop and he left the Jewish quarter, desirous of hearing news, of seeing monuments, of participation in existence.

The news was not good. There was no talk of anything but the death of Hieros, and the anger of the Christians was bursting forth in threats. But Amoraim was not interested in that. He did not want to think about the role he had played. He had done his duty, he had obeyed prudence. It was up to God to regulate the affair.

He went down to the port, walking tranquilly toward his first stroke of luck. Students went past him, arguing. He followed them, because there is always something to learn from youth. The group took the street of the Sema, arrived at the Museum, and went in.

The Museum! Amoraim knew that there were books accumulated there, and professors who debated. People spoke against the law there. But does not error make the truth stand out more clearly? He went in behind the students.

Certainly, he had entered with all possible modesty. He limped up a broad stone stairway and went through a door through which everyone was going. He hastened to sit down on a bench at the back, in a room full of listeners, at the very moment when a woman of marvelous beauty advanced on to a stage.

For a few seconds, Amoraim was able to think that his old bad luck had accompanied him, as usual. Curious faces turned toward him. People whispered, and laughed. Two people who were standing up near the door even made a movement in his direction. But then the woman who had appeared on the stage smiled and sketched a gesture that signified: *Let it go.*

And she began to speak.

Amoraim did not understand anything she said, but he felt penetrated by a strange sweetness as he listened to her. A wave of beauty reached him, and the meaning of the words was not necessary for him to be bathed by it. Then again, he was not mistaken. That astonishing magicienne, that elite individual, to whom God had made a present of the gift of the Word, had just distinguished the poor Jew Amoraim in the crowd. She fixed her great bright eyes upon him, and she almost made him a sign with her hand.

Amoraim left the Museum transfigured. He started to walk with his head high, like a young man who has had a beautiful amorous adventure. He was not astonished because a few young men pointed their fingers at him, and even followed him, imitating his limping gait. No, there was no mockery in that imitation, but rather admiration, and perhaps jealousy.

Had he not always been too humble? Would it not have been possible for him to conquer one of the foremost places in the world, if he had put himself forward?

And it was a few days later that he had his second stroke of luck.

On the fourteenth day of the month of Nizam, according to the Jewish calendar, the celebration of the festival of Pesach, in memory of the emergence of Israel from Egypt, commenced in the Jewish quarter.

According to the Torah, on that day God ordered the Jews united in the city of Ramses on the edge of the Red Sea to eat lamb standing up, girded by their belts containing all their riches, staff in hand, like travelers.

It was a Friday and, in the evening, all the Jews not ready to take their meal, with their money clasped against them and their traveling staff in their left hand. But beforehand, many believers went to the synagogue.

When the synagogue was full, the ethnarch walked through the assembly and said: "Who wants to open the commandments?" And the man who had paid the most for that honor was designated to open the Book, to recite the eighteen prayers and to sound the shofar, a kind of ram's horn, in memory of the horn the angels sounded when God descended over Sinai.

In spite of the sums received at the synagogue, however, the ethnarch Eleazer, who was a just man, strove only to designate every time a Jew whom he knew to have carried out a good deed.

That evening, he perceived in the front row, among the most honorable—moneychangers, merchants and commentators on the Law—the ragged Amoraim, standing there with his body slightly inclined to the left.

229

The ethnarch's first thought was astonishment that an individual as humble and timid as the candle-merchant occupied the first row. In truth, he might have dressed with more decency and have contented himself with a more modest place!

But the ethnarch considered the simplicity that was reflected on Amoraim's face. He remembered a tenebrous shop glimpsed in passing, a long life of poverty, labor and rectitude, the solid qualities of the race of Abraham.

Let the poor fellow be honored once in his life, he thought.

And it was Amoraim that he designated.

There were a few whispers, and then a great stupefied silence.

Amoraim advanced, limping, into the free space in front of the Book. Everything was spinning around him; he could hear his heart hammering in his breast. But he was sustained by a firm thought.

All the important men whose power and intelligence he venerated were there around him. They were showing him a signal confidence, via the ethnarch's choice. He had to show himself to be worthy of it. It was the recompense of his humble life.

He made a great effort and said, in a voice that was quavering slightly: "God has opened the doors of the heavens to us today, and will judge us."

Then his overexcited senses perceived beyond the closed doors of the synagogue a vast, unaccustomed rumor coming from all directions at once, as if God were coming with all his angels for the announced judgment.

That was also perceived by the audience, and they interrogated one another with apprehensive gazes.

"Play your role honorably, Amoraim," Amoraim murmured to himself. "Luck has come this evening; welcome it!"

And in a firm, even sonorous voice, he recited the eighteen prayers.

What was happening outside? Clamors resounds at the four cardinal points, mingled with cries of fear and cries of death, and only the majesty of the prayer prevented the Jews from running to the door.

Having concluded, Amoraim, who sensed calm descending within himself as the agitation of the assembly became greater, seized the ram's horn with a noble slowness, raised it to his lips and blew the three blasts that ought to be repeated symbolically seventy-two times, which corresponded to as many maledictions upon the seventy-two false beliefs.

From outside, as if the resonance of that horn had unleashed the enemies of Israel, a mighty shove opened the two battens of the door to the synagogue. Monks waving torches, who were carrying pikes and staffs, appeared on the threshold. The brown robes, the resolution and fanaticism of the faces and the voices that emerged from the increasing obscurity, had something terrifying about them. The first monks to appear began seizing the Jews and projecting them brutally into the street. Some tried to flee. Others prepared to defend themselves.

Then a voice rang out: an immeasurable, immense, thunderous voice, the like of which one would never have thought a human voice capable of producing. That quasi-divine voice drowned out the cries of terror, the savage shouts of the monks and the rumor of the revolutionized Jewish quarter.

It pronounced the last formula of the prayer: "Listen, Israel! The Eternal, our God, the Eternal is one!"

It reminded the Jewish people of their traditional virtues, prudence in danger, the religiosity that saves.

It was the voice of Amoraim.

He had just realized, suddenly, the role that God had fixed for him, and how he had been mysteriously prepared to play it. For the humblest man can have forces hidden within him that are precious, and can serve for the salvation of his race.

The redoubted hour, which had been announced as imminent for some time, had arrived for the Jews of Alexandria. The rumors that had run around were true. They were being expelled by force. But the God of Israel had selected the humble Amoraim to guide his people at that critical moment. He had forged his soul by means of years of silence. He had made the ethnarch choose him to recite the prayers, to the scorn of immemorial custom that put the rich ahead of the poor.

Amoraim contemplated momentarily the divine light that descended over his forehead, more radiant than the morning star.

He had taken the open Book in his hands. Clad in an incredible majesty, which immobilized the audience with stupor, he advanced, serene and tranquil, with a grave tread, toward the monks, who opened up before him.

Something supernatural escaped from his person. He emerged from the synagogue and started marching through the streets, followed by the ethnarch and the Jews.

He repeated, at intervals: "Listen, Israel! The Eternal, our God, the Eternal is one!"

And the cortege that followed him repeated it in their turn, and those who emerged from the crossroads, fleeing, and those who appeared at windows, also repeated it with a single voice, so that in the end, it was like an immense hymn that rose up from forty thousand mouths toward star-strewn night, affirming in the catastrophe the unity of God.

A few houses were began to burn, a few Jews who had tried to defend themselves were blocking their thresholds with their corpses. All the exits from the Delta quarter were guarded by armed groups save for the street that connected the quarter, via the city wall, with the region of sepulchers. By that route, all the Jews, robbed of their houses and their property, were to leave Alexandria by the end of the night.

And Amoraim advanced, with the principals of the synagogues now grouped behind him. He marched alone, because the law says that the prophet must lead and the people must follow and obey.

"Remember Hieros!" cried the monks and the crowd of Christians as he passed by.

Remember him! He could still feel the warmth of his blood running over his shoulder when he had transported him in order to aid him. This was the payment for his good deed! But he did not hate that Hieros, the cause of persecution. By the connection of events, that dead Christian had made him the reciter of the prayers, the sounder of the horn, the bearer of the Book, the conductor of the people, the equal of the prophets. At that moment he was Moses himself and he heard an interior voice soaking to him.

"Far from the city of the infidels you will lead into the desert the ever-wandering and persecuted race. You will make sure that the spikes of the tents are deeply embedded in the sand, and that the prayers are said, that the Ark is saved. And by invoking my name, you will also cause the manna of perseverance to rain from the sky and the pure water of the spirit that vivifies spring forth from the rock."

Amoraim, like all the Jews spread over the vast earth, knew that there existed in Alexandria sacred wealth more precious than human life He remembered that in the intoxication of his illumination and, still repeating with his formidable impressive voice: "Listen, Israel! The Eternal, our God, the Eternal is one!" he thought by virtue of a doubling of his mind of the admirable word of the Torah: "Be cunning in the dread of the Lord!"

And he went at a more rapid pace up the street where the house of the Hillels was, raising the Book above his head. From the other direction, under the guidance of Peter, groups of Parabalani were arriving, on whom it was incumbent to pillage that house, carefully designated by Cyril.

But in a second, all the Jews, those who preceded Amoraim, those who ware behind him, and those who were outside the doors, had understood.

Some lay down on the ground, others let themselves fall from windows. Around Amoraim, a compact mass, voluntarily inert, rolled and unfurled, which extinguished the torches and obstructed the door.

The Parabalani, rushing forward, striking with their pikes and swords amid plaints and howls, ended up fraying a passage, but it was too late. The torches were lit again, the door of the Hillel house was wide open. The crowd, like a mass, flowed further on, carrying its wounded and its dead, and also a few heavy coffers, wrapped in canvas sacks: the treasure of the Temple of Solomon, saved.

Guided by the prophet Amoraim, the Jews of Alexandria left the city and went toward another destiny.

The Christians were never able to explain how every inhabitant of the Delta, in spite of the suddenness of the attack, had been able to carry all his wealth with him. No gold or silver coins were found in the houses. That was because, on the fourteenth day of the month of Nizan, in accordance with the Torah, God ordered the Jews to eat lamb standing up girded by their belts containing all their riches, staff in hand, like travelers.

The Christians had found them ready to depart.

The greater number headed for Heliopolis, where Onias[35] had built a castle and a temple and founded a Jewish center. But the descendants of the Hillels and a few hundred of their friends and servants followed the inspired Amoraim and plunged into the desert.

Somewhere, under a mountain of gem salt, under an accumulation of stones battered by the simoom they hid the great candelabrum with seven branches, the miraculous almond-wood wand, the tablet in which the revelation made by Jehovah to Moses is engraved, and the talisman Thunim, formed by as many stones as there are tribes in Israel, and which provokes in its bearer a state of apocalyptic vision and communication with God.

There, the treasures of the Ark were to remain hidden until the prophecy is realized: "I shall bring from the Orient a bird, and from a distant land a man, who will execute my will."

---

[35] The Jewish high priest Onias IV built a temple in Leontopolis, not far from Heliopolis, in 150 B.C. or thereabouts.

XII. The Death of Hypatia

That morning, when the immutable dawn began to appear over Alexandria, many people woke up prey to desire, to torment, to hope and to fury. But souls are closed to one another, and evil is born of their incomprehension

In the cloister where he was lying in the midst of his companions, the monk Simon sat up. He was not numbed by the nocturnal chill, as on previous nights. He was light. A force lifted him up.

He looked at the other monks slumbering heavily on the flagstones. He had accompanied them to the Jewish quarter the previous evening. He no longer liked them. He was all alone now.

Oh, he understood that it was necessary to fight for the Church, that evil was triumphant everywhere, and that if one did not strike one was struck. The Jews had killed Hieros, they lived in the hatred of Jesus, it was perhaps a good thing that they had been expelled—but what had been prescribed for him to do this morning he refused to do.

His face suddenly lit up. Alone! He had been able to think that he was alone! Oh, no! He sensed an invisible presence to his right. The guide, the guardian angel, had returned, and was telling him to get up and act.

Silently, he stepped over the bodies of his companions, traversed the courtyard, penetrated into a kitchen garden and found himself at the foot of a wall, over which he climbed without difficulty. He was behind the Church of Caesarea. He could see the blue sea between the colonnades. He did not try to get his bearings. He launched himself through the streets, lightly, all the way to the Prefect's house.

Anxiety had kept the Prefect Orestes awake all night. Irresolution was devouring his soul. A month ago, foreseeing events, he had sent urgent letters to the Emperor in Constantinople asking to be given formal orders. None had come. He was not sure of troops almost entirely composed of Christians. He had sent the sole cohort on which he could count to the Delta quarter the previous evening. The commander Marcellus had sent word that to restore order it would be necessary to engage in a veritable battle with the Parabalani and the monks. He had hesitated; he had waited. Cyril had sent a messenger to him affirming that there would be no bloodshed. Finally, he had sacrificed the Jews.

He regretted it. He suffered from that injustice. He was a tolerant man, an inheritor of the old Roman tradition, respectful of all beliefs.

So, that morning, unable to sleep, faithful to his habits, he was trying not to think any longer out what was tormenting his conscience by burying himself in pleasure.

For him, pleasure was occupying himself with a marvelous collection of insects that he possessed, and which occupied the largest room in his house, classifying them according to their species and forms.

He had a specimen of every kind of butterfly and scarab known in the world, from the Acteon scarab, entirely covered in a fine down like the fur of cats, to the Jupiter scarab that bears on its back the image of a bearded man, from the Podalyre butterfly that has four wings the color of flame to the Alexander butterfly that has in the blue lunulae of its wings the design of the twelve signs of the Zodiac. And the best part of his time and his life was spent considering the variety of colors, weights, and the thickness of carapaces, and measuring elytrae and antennae.

He was about to put a drop of palm oil on a curious chrysalis when the porter came to tell him that a young monk was asking to see him in order to make him important revelations.

The porter was still half asleep and forgot to add that those revelations concerned Hypatia.

The Prefect Orestes was an admirer of the celebrated philosopher. He sometimes consulted her. It had even been claimed that he was secretly in love with her. If the name of Hypatia had been pronounced, he would have had Simon come in and added credence to his words. But events were of little account; the Prefect, with a burette in his hand, had a drop of palm oil to apply.

"Tell the monk to come back this evening," he said.

And the drop fell on the curious chrysalis, for his greater satisfaction.

Simon knew that the rich Palladius was the head of an organization of pagans that feared Cyril's partisans. He had been shown the house from which, at a given moment, groups hostile to the monks might emerge. It was at the other end of the city. He ran there. He went astray on the way and lost a good deal of time.

Long negotiations were necessary before he was admitted to see Palladius. The latter was in his bath. He finally appeared, draped in a green tunic, accompanied by two armed servants, who were ready to throw themselves on Simon, for Palladius believed himself to be surrounded by assassins, like a king, because of his importance. He went red at the name of Hypatia and began to tremble.

"Telamon will take charge of her defense," he replied.

And he made a sign for the monk to be dismissed.

The sun was already high in the sky. Anguished, Simon wondered what he ought to do.

"My God! How difficult it is to reach the hearts of men!"

And he started running in the direction of Hypatia's house.

In the courtyard of his house, Diodorus, bent double, was speaking in a hoarse voice to his children.

"The Patriarch wants the noblest families in Alexandra to be represented. The Parabalani have rendered themselves odious by their violence, so he wants a peaceful manifestation that will be the expression of the entire city. The grandchildren of the great Diodorus must be in the first rank. I'm too old and my legs are too weak for me to accompany you, but the wise Majorin won't quit you."

Marcus started to laugh stupidly, but Priscilla experienced a certain pride in having a small role to play in the battle between the Christians and the heretics. She drew herself up to her full height, touching the metal cross that she had around her neck, which Bishop Cyril had given her. On the very place where she was standing, her grandfather had once fallen, a victim of pagan fury.

Oh, yes, she was ready!

And at the same moment, Diodorus, who was looking at her, could not retain a movement of surprise. From that beautiful young woman, that creature of flesh, emerged a breath of life, an exhalation of pleasure that disturbed his old soul. The thick hair sprang in tresses from the head, her skin was an animated velvet, the strength of the young breasts elevated the tunic, and the entire young body was a hymn of sensuality.

Is that really my family? thought Diodorus, as the children draw away. *As long as God does not abandon it!*

The rendezvous was at the gate of the Sun. The city terminated there amid leprous houses and mariners' dives.

Peter had arrived first. He headed toward a wretched hovel, the door of which he opened. It was inhabited by a goitrous and idiotic beggar nicknamed Dionysus, well known in the two ports of Alexandria, where he served as a clown for the mariners.

He lived with his daughter Nausithoe, who was fifteen and had prostituted herself since childhood on the neories and around the barracks neighboring the Macedonia fortress.

Peter seized the beggar by his rags and pulled him outside vigorously. He explained to him what he wanted of him.

"Here! You'll never have such a good opportunity in your life. Ten drachms for a blow with a stick." And he tried to make him take the ten drachms.

It was a matter of ten drachms! What was money to Dionysus? He had always scorned it. Was he not rich without that? He did not want the ten drachms. He threw them on the ground, angrily.

Peter picked them up silently. He needed the beggar. He dragged him to a nearby tavern, where Parabalani were already sitting, arguing.

"Come on, you old fool," he said to him. "Have a drink with me. We'll see when you've had a drink."

But Dionysus darted somber glances to the right and left.

Peter started to laugh in order to make him laugh, and talked about his daughter.

"I know her well. She's the most beautiful girl in the port. But she gives herself too cheaply! I had her once for three drachms and there's a miserable velite who has her for nothing, and even takes her money."

Then Dionysus hurled himself at Peter, howling.

He knew full well that his daughter was a prostitute. What did prostituting herself matter? The essential thing was that she came home at night, even drunk and soiled. The essential thing was that he saw her, that he knew that she was alive. Last night, he had waited for her in vain. Where was she? It was that fat, sweaty and panting man who had murdered her.

He stated repeating: "Give me back my daughter!"

Peter wondered whether he ought not to knock the idiot out with a blow of his fist.

People formed a circle around them, and the tavern-keeper ran to lend Peter a hand.

But Dionysus widened his eyes and suddenly prostrated himself, his forehead to the ground.

"There she is!" he shouted. "By Our Lord Jesus Christ, there she is!"

Between Majorin and her brother, Priscilla advanced, radiant in her linen tunic, in the magnificence of her youth.

Dionysus got up, drew away a few paces, gazed at her, full of adoration, and calmed down, laughing and repeating to everyone: "It's not her! But that's how she ought to be!"

And a little later, he approached Peter and said to him: "You can give me the ten drachms now. I'll go with you, if she's coming too."

Groups appeared from all directions, so abundantly that the gate of the Sun was encumbered, and the carts of the market gardeners that were arriving from the country could not get through. A man dressed as a monk advanced, carrying a long metal cross and singing a hymn. The sunlight drew a sparkling flame from the cross and there was a murmur in the crowd because many wanted to see that as a divine sign. Then the taverns emptied. Cries resounded.

"Go fetch your staff," said Peter to Dionysus.

He made a sign to the Parabalani and they began to move along the Canopic Way.

The mathematician Theon kissed his daughter with more emotion than usual. He found her more beautiful than on other days. He felt vibrant and happy, and he was afraid of happiness because he considered it to be a sunlit force that causes souls to suffer by setting them ablaze.

He had perceived Hypatia walking in their minuscule garden planted with laurels and had come down from his bedroom to hug her in his arms.

Theon was a gentle and scholarly man, perpetually plunged in the study of mathematics and philosophy. He would have liked to say something to his daughter regarding the tender love that he had for her, but he had never been able to express himself on questions of that order. Oh, how much easier it was to write a commentary of Ptolemy's *Almagest* or to talk about eclipses than to pronounce a single word coming from the soul before a child as beautiful and as wise as Hypatia.

Perhaps for the first time in her life, Hypatia did not seem to comprehend the tenderness of his kiss, and she drew away, distracted.

She climbed the stone staircase that led to the terrace of her house and leaned on the balustrade, between a statuette of

Pallas Athene and a statuette of Aphrodite, which were facing one another.

Beneath her, the sun made the whiteness of the porphyry monuments resplendent, outlining against the azure the marble steeples and the syenite columns. On one side she saw sprays of red roses on bright terraces, on the other stages of hanging gardens with rows of lemon trees. In the warm and still air, a human rumor rose up. Hypatia felt ardent and weary, as if she had communicated with life through all the fibers of her being.

Am I about to commit a sin against the spirit? she thought. *It seems to me that I've already lost the beautiful intellectual solitude in which I lived as in a diamond palace. How demanding the gods are! It's necessary to serve them without reserve, and one second of weakness annihilates a lifetime of effort. Yes, the pythoness of Delphi was chaste. The symbolic fire was extinguished in the temple when the vestals betrayed their vow. Pythagoras and Apollonius both taught that one cannot, without chastity, attain the divine ecstasy that confounds us with the source of Being. And yet...*

She had inclined her face over her bare arm, and the warmth of her skin gave her a frisson. She gazed in turn at Pallas Athene and Aphrodite, mute, irreconcilable and omnipotent.

She was standing, anxious and alive, between the images of the two goddesses.

Unity of unities. Essence from which thoughts emanate, is it true that one cannot attain you without renouncing the brightness of colors, the beauty of sounds and forms? All of nature, with its suns and its gentle nights, would then be nothing but a vast trap to prevent humans, by the network of desires, from reaching the highest spirituality. That isn't possible. There must be a conciliation between the splendor of matter and the absolute reign of the spirit. A wisdom must exist that loves, a verity that has blood, which can only be embraced by terrestrial arms and only shows its true face through pleasure and pain.

It seemed to her that the face of Telamon was very close to her own and that she was respiring his breath.

She traversed the terrace and slowly descended the staircase.

Perhaps nothing would have happened if Hypatia had not let the entrance door of her house close abruptly behind her.

Her chariot was stationed in the street. She intended to go along the coast road, beyond the Gate of the Moon and the embalmers' quarter, in order to have the caress of the wind on her face.

She suddenly found herself in the presence of a howling crowd that blocked the street. She straightened up and mounted the chariot. She was already surrounded on all sides. But the majesty of the spirit is so great, when it is manifest in the gaze, that the Christians would have parted and perhaps nothing would have happened if the driver had whipped his horse and started the chariot in motion.

But the driver was a very young man. Either because he had understood the gravity of the moment by the fury of the faces or because he was gripped by an inexplicable panic terror, he threw down his reins, leapt from his seat and fled.

Then a clamor went up around Hypatia, standing and solitary, and a menacing circle formed. She was so calm and so beautiful that anyone endowed with reason would have been unable even to touch her robe.

But Peter shoved the goitrous Dionysus in front of him and murmured to him: "Go on!"

The latter was laughing and shouting without understanding, divided between joy and the ambient rage, intoxicated by the presence of Priscilla, whom he confounded with his daughter in his obscured mind.

He advanced and, at full tilt, he struck Hypatia on the head with his staff. He hit her on the jaw. Under the force of the blow, she tottered and fell on to the front of the chariot, and immediately, no longer maintained by the magnetism of her courage, the Christians fell upon her. Peter seized her by the legs and caused her to tumble on to the paving stones of the street.

"Take her to a church! Let her ask God's pardon for her sins!" said a voice.

The Church of Caesarea was not far away. Peter and another man set about dragging her there.

At that moment, a shrill voice was heard, saying: "Let me pass!"

And a woman of about forty who belonged to the high society of Alexandria cleaved through the crowd and stamped her heel twice on Hypatia's face, repeating: "There! Accursed one!"

Then she drew away, satisfied.

On the perron of the Church of Caesarea, Hypatia was thrown down brutally, and her head collided with a step with a dull sound. Her hair was undone. She recovered consciousness and raised herself up slightly, her jaw hanging down.

"Let her ask for pardon!" voices repeated.

Peter struck her in the breast with his fist and put her on her knees.

Then, suddenly, by a mysterious communication, an obscene madness took possession of the crowd. The Christians fell upon Hypatia and tore off her garments. Fifty hands pressed and struck her body. People spat on her. The hatred of beauty and intelligence that slumbers in the depths of base souls burst forth without restraint.

A haggard monk threw himself upon the assailants, his arms outspread, crying: "Wretches! What are you doing? Jesus Christ is watching you!"

He was knocked down, half-stunned. It was Simon.

A woman fell to the ground in a crisis of hysteria and someone threw himself upon her with so much violence that no one knew whether it was to help her or to rape her.

Then Peter who was holding Hypatia by the hair, raised his voice and said: "It's necessary to stone her." And he added, travestying the thought of Christ: "Let someone who has never sinned cast the first stone."

A stir in the crowd had pushed Priscilla, overwhelmed by horror to the front. Someone pointed at her and said: "There's the daughter of Diodorus! She's still a child! She's never sinned!"

And someone put a stone in her hand.

Priscilla was a few paces away from Hypathia, naked and soiled with dust. She distinguished the imprints of fingers on her shoulders and breasts. A little trickle of blood departed from her temple and descended inexhaustibly all the way to her lips.

Behind her, through a crack in the door of the church, the face of a fat priest appeared, animated by innocent curiosity, leaning out to see.

It seemed to Priscilla that a great silence had fallen around her, that she had become the center of the immobilized world.

Had she never sinned? She remembered the lips of a young man that smelled of honey and acacia. She had taken pleasure in remembering that kiss.

"Well, Priscilla!" people were repeating around her.

Then she participated in their Christian fury. Yes, the lies of the pagans must be punished, and also that beauty whose splendor was an outrage. She sensed a singular vigor in her arm, and she threw the stone with all her might, which hit Hypatia in the neck.

Priscilla saw the philosopher's eyes open very wide and fix themselves upon her. They were bright, cold and intelligent. They expressed astonishment, and the desire to understand that had always animated them. No pain, no reproach, no terror. A little sadness. It was only a flash, and that light, which Priscilla would never forget, vanished.

A howl burst forth. Stones began to rain down from all directions. And at least that fury permitted the neoplatonist to depart without an excess of suffering toward the regions of which, while alive, she had weighed the shadows and measured the mystery.

Priscilla had fled. There as a long battle around the body of Hypatia. The more moderate wanted to carry her body away and burn it in the country. But the others, armed with knives, tried to butcher it, saying that it was appropriate to set an example by parading the pieces triumphantly through the city. They hoped, in addition, to make the pagan suffer after death, believing that when a body is dispersed the double wanders or a long time, full of desolation.

It was the latter who were to win the argument, and a cobbler with a shop near the Diocletian column was to take pride for a long time in having conserved one of Hypatia's desiccated hands, which he had cut off with his paring-knife.

But they were all unaware that there would not be a plaintive double to wander under the porticos of the Museum, to lean on the terrace of the house in which her father Theon lived, or even to go and respire a perfume of crushed mint on the stone bench in the garden of the Gymnasium. For the spirits of the intelligent escape with death the appeal of terrestrial things, surpass without perceiving it the world of posthumous desires and leap into the ineffable abode of pure thought.

XIII. The Martyrdom of Abjection

Priscilla raised herself up on her elbow and darted a bleak glance over the furniture of her bedroom, vaguely illuminated by a night-light. Her hair undone, half-naked between the four ivory columns of her bed, she made sure that nothing had changed place, that the broad crimson curtains descended over the windows, that the oval bronze mirror sent back her confused image.

And yet, the top of her night-dress was torn and handing down over her young breasts, as if a brutal hand had attempted to tear it off. She felt on her arms and in her armpits a warmth of bruising, and in the demi-obscurity she thought she could distinguish blue marks in places.

She had a desire to cry out. What was the point? No one could have got through the blue-painted cedar-wood door, no one could have lain down beside her in her bed and embraced her so pitilessly.

The evil was within her. It was born of the epoch into which she had plunged, ruined by religion, shortly after the death of Hypatia, and since then it had only grown. The evil thoughts had multiplied around her as she had striven to drive them away. They were born of that, singular and obsessive. They had gradually taken on human form, borrowing the faces that, in life, inspired her with the greatest disgust and the greater terror.

By day, she succeeded in triumphing over them by activity or prayer; but by night, when she was alone in her bed, she could not escape them. So long as she was awake she confronted the danger. She fixed her thoughts on the image of the Virgin or that of Saint Mark, by whom she believed herself to be protected. But drowsiness extended over her against her will. She passed from wakefulness to an intermediate state that was not that of dreams, and in which she perceived the creations of her imagination as if they were reality.

How fatiguing the struggle was! Why was she the victim of these obsessions of evil? What had she done to deserve that? God was striking her cruelly!

But tonight, she was weary. Her limbs were heavy and worn out. She gazed at a thin moonbeam competing on the floor with the gleam of the night-light; she let her head, aureoled with hair, fall back on the pillow, and abandoned herself to the nocturnal torture.

Immediately, she had the impression of thick lips stuck to her mouth. It was a sticky, unspeakable kiss, the pollution of which penetrated between her teeth. She felt something soft and fleshy on her neck and she saw the goiter of the beggar who had been the first to strike Hypatia with his staff. Other hideous faces leaned over her, competing for her lips. But the frightful beggar held her in his inflexible caress. Then he dissolved and disappeared, and from the ceiling, rolled into a ball, her brother Marcus fell, who uttered a burst of stupid laughter and tore away the silk sheets in which she was wrapped.

Human forms filled the room. She sensed the warmth of bodies against her, hairy arms seized her, she was pressed by bony knees. In vain she resisted with all her might. An obscene human pullulation, a tide of rutting males, enveloped her, covered her and ravaged her. In the end, an opaque, diseased breath blew over her. Crushed and spread-eagled, she saw the monstrous Peter embracing her.

She woke up. She did not want to go back to sleep. Anything, but not that. Peter had disappeared from Alexandria on the same day that Hypatia had been stoned, in fear of the vengeance that threatened him; but for Priscilla, he was still present. The desire that he had had for her was the most terrible form of her nightmares.

As if to protect herself from caresses emerging from the invisible, she threw a garnet pallium embroidered with silver bees over her shoulders and she went to kneel down on her prie-dieu.

Then, far away, on a rising road, she perceived the leprous Christ who had haunted her dreams before. She distinguished on his tumefied face an expression of pitying sadness. He perceived her and he made her a sign to join him. She started to run and she saw to her right and her left sick, infirm and ulcerated individuals who extended their arms toward her. As she advanced, the infirm threw away their crutches, the lepers lost their scales, and the bearers of wounds became healthy. She, on the contrary, felt her muscles shriveling, she took on human deformities as she passed, and ulcers settled on her face like birds.

Priscilla meditated for a long time on the symbolic meaning of that dream. She thought she saw a revelation therein. It was because of it that she discovered the road to her salvation, and that road was to be singular and unexpected.

In that epoch there was rumor in Alexandria of the preaching of a mystic monk named Zosyma. It was said that the previous year he had occasioned disorder at Ptolemais by the vehemence of his tirades against the rich. No one knew precisely where he came from. He was only clad in an animal skin, like the anchorites of the desert.

He let his hair and beard grow and had immeasurable long fingernails. In the evening he refused the hospitality of pious people and wanted to sleep on the paving-stones of the street, exposed to bad weather, and the outrages of drunkards and pagans.

It was after sunset, at the most wretched crossroads in Rhacotis, that he began to speak. He abused the clergy, the Emperor, the Jews, the pagans: everyone. For some time it was fashionable in good society to go and listen to him, as one listens to an actor, and afterwards, everyone said: "He's a new John the Baptist."

Priscilla obtained permission from her father to go to Rhacotis one evening. Diodorus gave the authorization to her gladly. His daughter worried him. She was increasingly isolated, and had manifested the resolution to enter a convent.

Diodorus sometimes thought, not without remorse, of the distant convent from which his wife had not returned. He had resolved to find a husband for Priscilla. Now, he had learned that the monk Zosyma routinely criticized the monastic life as contrary to the teachings of Jesus Christ.

A young woman might be turned aside by a word spoken at the right moment, he thought.

He instructed Majorin and the slave Thoutmos to accompany her.

The streets of Rhacotis were so narrow that they could not advance three abreast. They went up and down and walked until they had difficulty going further forward because of the crowd that had gathered. In a little square, a trestle of planks had been set up, leaning on a brick wall. Zosyma was standing on the trestle. Bent over, his head forward, he was parading over the terrified audience eyes that burned like coals, and he seemed to be launching tangible maledictions with his hand.

Beside him, a fanatic was holding a torch, raising it and lowering it in order the people could see the prophet's face, and also a wound that he had beneath his rags, and which he uncovered proudly. Around him, the hovels of the poor raised up their small heaps of dirty stones. The lamp of a tavern blinked like a gummed-up eye. The noxious side-streets gave the impression of plunging into a perspective of misery.

Zosyma expressed himself in the Coptic language, with the result that not everyone understood what he was saying. But those who only spoke Greek read in his face and his gestures the terrible meaning of his words.

He cursed those who forgot God. He cursed all men. The most wretched members of his audience committed the same sin as the rich. There was no difference between them. They all lived like pigs, and what did it matter whether the trough was a little more of less full? The human beasts only pursued the enjoyment of their bodies, or that of their souls, which was worse. No one knew the narrow road that leads to God, which was the road of perfect and voluntary dolor.

Priscilla shuddered with hope. Zosyma's words celebrated her own horror of life.

A magnetic communication was established between the members of the audience, and she participated in it. Around her, the people aspired to suffer. What a sublime compensation, if the crushing burden of dolor procured eternal salvation! The wound covering Zosyma's breast was as radiant as a sun.

"Cast a glance into yourselves. Seek out what is odious and which arouses the disgust of the spirit, and strive toward that ideal of suffering. Let the man who takes pleasure in his house set fire to it! Let the man who is handsome disfigure himself! Let the man who cherishes his children live far away from them! The contemplative should break stones! The traveler should remain stationary! No wine for the drinker! No book for the man devoured by the desire for intelligence! And those who do not accomplish expiation during the rapid years lived on earth will be condemned to accomplish it during eternity."

The torch was suddenly extinguished, and the prophet was no longer anything but a silhouette gesticulating in the darkness, a bird of ill omen.

Men tore out their beards. Others cut themselves with their knives. There was a stir in front of a doorway. A woman whose limbs were agitated by a tremor pulled a crude cross out of her house, and, holding out a hammer and nails, she begged those who surrounded her to crucify her like Jesus.

Priscilla and her two companions returned through the streets.

Majorin let his ill humor burst forth in acerbic words. Priscilla kept silent and listened to the tumult of her thoughts.

She could see now, she understood. The monk Zosyma was right. What was it that inspired the most horror in her? It was the desire of men, the image of their possession of her virgin body. So? So?

She drew in her shoulders. Her flesh froze. But she recalled the Christ of her dream, the ulcerated Christ. He had only appeared to her with all the wounds of the earth and had only made a sign to her to indicate the path to follow.

And her resolution was made from that moment on.

As they were about to quite Rhacotis something strange happened.

A crouching form stood up, emerged from the shadow and ran toward Priscilla, who was walking two or three paces behind Majorin and Thoutmos.

Priscilla uttered a cry of terror.

But the goitrous Dionysus fell to his knees and attempted to kiss the hem of the young woman's robe, repeating: "My child! It's you, my child!"

Priscilla recognized him, heard the words that he pronounced almost tearfully, and distinguished that there was nothing in his attitude but humility and inoffensive admiration, but in spite of that, without knowing why, she cried: "Help!"

She stuck herself against the wall with the gesture of someone who is being attacked.

Thoutmos turned round and thought that his mistress was in danger. He leapt forward and struck Dionysus a heavy blow with a metal club that he had, attached to his wrist by a strap.

Dionysus, who had got up, collapsed into the gutter, vomiting blood.

"It's Dionysus," said Priscilla, very calmly, leaning over him while he repeated, in a desperate tone: "Oh, my daughter! You, my daughter!"

"He attacked you, Mistress?" said Thoutmos.

Priscilla did not reply.

She did not feel any pity.

"I think it's the jaw that he's broken," said Majorin, bending down. "The blow must have been terrible, and to judge by the spasms of his body, one can tell that he's going to die."

Priscilla stepped lightly over the body of the beggar, which was blocking the street.

"Come on," she said to the two men, and without looking back, she drew away.

Everything appeared facile to her, and it all unfolded with the ease of actions that one accomplishes in a dream.

Money? She only needed enough for the journey. She would always have enough. Clothes? She aspired to be naked.

The galleys that went from Alexandria to Constantinople were frequent. She took a place on one of them, which was laden with Ethiopian slaves destined for the service of the Hippodrome. Those slaves, lying on the deck, made a seething and howling mass that exhaled a heavy human odor.

Pricilla respired that odor with delight, savoring its nauseating effect more than the rarest of perfumes.

The emergence from the harbor took a long time because the galley had to row around the Heptastade and the isle of the Pharos. They were the only moments of anguish she had during her flight. She thought that her disappearance might have been perceived, that she might have been seen on the jetty, and that small boats might have time to overtake the galley.

She could see her house in the distance, the high windows, the great marble columns and the garden where she had played. Perhaps, by leaning over the side, she might have been able to distinguish the stooped silhouette of her father or the hesitant step of her brother Marcus. But she did not lean over.

The wind that began to inflate the sails also blew in her soul, bringing her the mystical hope of the fall of which she dreamed.

And when the large fig-trees and arborescent tamarinds of the isle of the Pharos began to decrease on the horizon, when Alexandria, with its towers, its obelisks, its acropolis and its triumphal arches was no more than a patch of white stone on the horizon, a great peace descended within her. She was in haste to open her arms, to be labored by caresses, purified by disgust, to attain God by means of the martyrdom of abjection.

XIV. The Phantom of Touta

Aurelius had passed through Antioch; he had reached the ancient city of Palmyra, built in the middle of the desert, and he had set forth across a region of sand and stones in order to reach the banks of the Euphrates.

He had dreamed of following exactly the same itinerary that Apollonius of Tyana had followed several centuries before, but he had not been able to find any trace of his passage in Antioch. Many temples were disaffected; others had been destroyed; the last priests were ignorant. The very name of Apollonius, once more celebrated that that of Jesus, was almost unknown.

Aurelius was now heading toward a temple consecrated to the goddess Derceto, which had been a celebrated center of initiation, and where a very ancient college of priests ought still to exist. Apollonius had stayed there while on his way to India. He had instructed the priests there in divine matters when he had returned from his voyage, bearing his message of wisdom.

Night fell. Aurelius' gourd was empty. He had eaten his last barley cake. He was exhausted.

He was about to lie down on the sand and sleep there, when it seemed to him that the wind, being less hot, must have passed over water and foliage that had refreshed it.

According to the indications he had been given in Palmyra, the trail he was following ought to lead him to a small agglomeration, doubtless the community of the temple of Derceto, and to a place where there was a bridge over the river. He climbed a ridge and in the twilight he perceived the blue sinuosity of the Euphrates. His strength returned, and he started to run.

When he had slaked his thirst and washed his feet and his face, he looked around.

Everything was silent. No prayer of neophytes turned toward the setting sun, no music of sacred flutes resonated in the air. No white robe of a hierophant in meditation appeared in the increasing shadow. He took a few steps and saw that he had to his right an entirely ruined village that seemed deserted. To his left, imposing masses of stone loomed up, a profusion of walls and columns.

He went there and recognized that the ancient temple of Derceto was no longer anything but a mass of ruins. He saw the skeleton of the porticos of the sacred enclosure, and the debris of the balustrade that preceded the place where sacrifices had been made. There was no longer anything but the framework of the lateral walls of the cella. He was walking over the grooves of pilasters and fragments of capitals.

He stopped. He was about to tread on the detached marble hand of a statue. Its lineaments were extraordinarily pure.

He noticed that it was turned toward the Orient.

He sat down on the ground and wept.

What if everything he believed was nothing but chimeras? Perhaps Apollonius of Tyana had not even passed this way. Perhaps he had never gone to India? Perhaps humanity was living at hazard, without any sage ever having guided it?

His head was empty. He was hungry. He was discouraged. He reviewed his past life and regretted it bitterly.

It was his dream of verity that had doomed him. He had not cultivated energy within himself. It would have been better if he had been an ordinary man with violent desires and the force that others put to work in order to realize them. He had loved a woman and he had done nothing to get her back when she had been snatched away from him! In Alexandria, a beautiful young woman who was his daughter had been instructed in the Christian faith, in which he did not believe, and he had done nothing to tell her that he was her father! He had always lacked courage. He had only shown any in order to head for an inaccessible country, abandoning a young slave who had loved him.

Then, through the turpentine trees that had grown between the colonnades, he perceived the form of a woman, standing still. It was a transparent apparition, slightly gray-tinted, which reproduced the face and familiar attitude of Touta when she came back from Alexandria binging him some news.

He thought immediately that it was a creation of his imagination caused by the intensity of memory—but, low and tremulous, coming from infinitely far away, a voice reached him.

"One doesn't suffer too much," said that voice. "One feels oneself diminishing, one dies a little more every day. One has difficulty remembering...fortunately! For if one remembered, it would be too sad. I've followed you in the cities, I've followed you in the sand, and I've followed you into these stones. Then I'll lose you, because I'll no longer be anything."

Aurelius knew that his slave Touta was dead, and he was stricken by grief. What he knew of the worlds of the afterlife made him think that perhaps that image had only appeared to him in order to formulate some posthumous plea. He was not unaware of the difficulty that the shades of the dead have in manifesting themselves to the living, and that it was necessary to hasten to grant such pleas.

"Can I do something for your repose?" he murmured. "Ought I to return to Alexandria to build you a sepulcher? Tell me quickly what you want."

But the shade of Touta became less visible. She was about to dissipate. A few words reached Aurelius' ears, but faintly and more distant. He heard: "Think of me...Priscilla...the roses in the garden...out there..."

That was all. There was no longer anything among the turpentine trees.

Aurelius remained in the same place for a long time in the hope that the image of Touta might form again before him. The stars had lit up in the sky. He waited in vain. Wrapped in his cloak, he lay down among the stones. He ended up going to sleep.

When he woke up the dawn did not take long to appear. His limbs were numbed by cold. He took a few steps and emerged from the temple. In the midst of the ruined houses that he could distinguish confusedly near the Euphrates there was the light of a fire. He ran toward it.

In a building whose walls were blackened and the roof disjointed, a tall man was sitting. He was clad in animal skins and hirsute, but beneath the hair that dangled over his face two soft eyes gleamed.

Aurelius interrogated him, speaking to him about the temple, the priests who had inhabited it, and the objective of his journey.

The man shook his head silently. He did not understand. He opened his mouth and showed the philosopher that his tongue had been cut out. With a gesture, he invited him to sit down, and to share the meal he was about to have, of barley bread and dried fish.

From the explanations he was given by means of gestures, Aurelius understood that at a time already distant, marauding tribes at war with the Palmyrans had set fire to the temple and the village, and massacred the priests and the inhabitants. The man had exercised the function of ferryman before the catastrophe occurred. He had survived the torture, and an obscure sentiment of duty had constrained him to remain, alone in the burned village, in order to continue to take travelers from one bank of the Euphrates to the other.

Alas, Aurelius would not have the consolation he had expected from the presence of learned priests, inheritors of the tradition of Apollonius. He would be obliged to continue his voyage with no other testimony or hope than his own faith.

The hirsute man had emerged from his house and had taken his guest as far as the bank of the Euphrates. A boat was moored amid the vegetation, near the piles of a destroyed bridge. He made him a sign to get in and took him to the other bank.

On the other side of the river there were more ruins. Aurelius made out a circular kiosk surrounded by columns, such as there had once been in proximity to important temples, where those who had a request to make of the divinities could deposit votive offerings.

The sun began to appear, making the Euphrates a long red streak, and illuminating the wild palms and the columns that were still standing with crimson. By means of that light, Aurelius, who was leaning over a fragment of fallen marble, read a name in Greek characters engraved with the point of a knife:

Apollonius of Tyana.

It was a small indication, but it was sufficient. His courage returned.

With his extended arm, the man showed him the way to the nearest town, Hanthis, in the direction of the rising sun.

Leaning on his staff, he set forth.

XV. The Brothel of Spartacus

The brothels of Byzantium pullulated along the enormous rampart built by Constantine They commenced at the Neorium and formed a quarter in which all the races of the earth became confounded at dusk.

The best-stocked were facing the fortifications. In accordance with the old Roman custom, they had before their doors either a phallus of painted wood or a copper plaque with an inscription, but the brothel-keepers attracted their clients by banging a gong, waving a lantern or shouting a joyful invitation, accompanied by the names and prices of the women. There were even brothels for the lowest orders hollowed out in subterrains in the fortifications, which were former food stores that had been disaffected and abandoned to prostitution.

When the sun set a human tide departed from the quays of the Golden Horn, the barracks quarter and the emporia and flowed toward the ramparts. Then the stevedores, the mercenaries, the stable-hands of the Hippodrome, the riff-raff of the port and that of the Sikhe district where foreigners lived mingled together. In a matter of minutes the silent boulevard and the side-streets that ended there were animated by an obscene and terrible life.

Drunken clamors mingled with the cries of the brothel-keepers, the clink of soldiers' swords and the screams of pursued women. Mounted on donkeys, merchants of watermelons went from group to group and sometimes sold their fruits by auction. Hairdressers and perfumers slid toward the doors brandishing bottle of curling tongs in order to be recognized, for there were fights in front of certain houses, which were more sought-after than others. Sometimes, a cataphract, with his horse, or a Patrician in a litter surrounded by slaves cleaved through the crowd in the midst of the tumult. Mimes gave performances by torchlight. Dancers with hairless bodies contorted themselves in lascivious poses. Procurers seized the best-dressed passers-by bodily and tried to drag them away by force, while whispering promises of little girls and boys.

When Priscilla disembarked on the Golden Horn the sun had not yet disappeared into the waves of the Propontida. She looked to the right and the left at the immensity of the quays, the wandering crowd going in and out through the Kharsian gate, and took at random one of the streets climbing up and around the seven Byzantine hills. The Church of Holy Purity erected its pink steeple and its colored architecture in the sky. From the narthex of a church floored with mosaics and surrounded by thin amaranthine columns a religious odor of dead flowers drifted toward her.

She went past a cortege of Kaloyeres in brown robes, which disappeared through the door of a convent murmuring prayers. She went down the street of jewelers through a magical landscape of topazes from the island of Taprobane, which sparkled in all the shops. She went up again along the streets of armorers, that of harness-makers and that of confectioners and emerged into the fish-market.

The stalls were being emptied and the dried seaweed swept away. In wooden crates, large soft, shiny, multicolored fish seemed to be gazing at her sadly with their insensible round eyes. She went down again by a wider street that ended at the tower of the Maganes.

Around her walked men in the most various costumes. There were Armenians with large embroidered dalmatics, Jews in black robes tightened at the waist by a yellow belt, Bulgars with leather braces, Scythians with long hair braided like that of women, Persians clad in silk with a fringed garnet shawl around the neck, and Byzantines with violet cloaks decorated with silver peacocks and fabulous birds.

There was a great rattle of armor because soldiers were numerous there. Latin mercenaries with their medallion faces, their tight-fitting knee-length gray garments and their short swords mingled with negro guards in violet garments of the same sort, Iberian merchants in red and Scandinavian mercenaries who were never separated from the rounded bucklers attached to their backs.

Priscilla saw before her the great shadow cast by the uniform line of the rampart, sometimes cut by a high square tower. She perceived the numerous brothels opposite with their low doors, their barred windows and the powdered and plastered faces of prostitutes crouching under Syrian bonnets and yellow robes. She understood that she had reached the place for which she was searching: the market of female bodies, the immense convent more redoubtable than the one in which her mother was tortured by thirst in the desert; the abode of penitence where no prayer rises toward God, where flesh is incessantly wearied by sickening dolor in a cell without solitude.

As she stopped she was surrounded by a group of Varangians of the Palace Guard. They were gigantic in stature and entirely clad in gold, from their conical helmets to their bulbous breastplates and belts. One of them, with a coarse laugh, plunged his hand between Priscilla's breasts. Another seized her by the waist.

She uttered a cry and pulled free. Arms extended around her to grab her. She fled. But the Varangians tried to catch up with her. Night had almost fallen. Priscilla slipped between the groups, which were becoming more compact. She collided with a bearded merchant who began to swear. Her youth, her fearful features and her white veils attracted the attention of the men she brushed past, and who attempted to caress her.

She had started running, still pursued by the gold-clad giants, who were gesticulating and laughing. The brothel-keepers on the thresholds called her filthy names because they hated streetwalkers who came to compete with their houses.

A mime who was spinning on one foot and beating cymbals made a few pirouettes around her. A hideous face breathed in her face in passing. A man with a wooden leg attempted to trip her up with it. Others started to give chase to her. Hands palpated her and grabbed her. She collided with the legs of a camel laden with gourds of wine and then, traversing and empty space, almost fell between the paws of a trained bear dancing to the sound of a flute.

A clamor of joy resounded. She bounded forward and, hunted like a beast, ran along the rampart. Corridors opened in places that led to the second enclosure. She threw herself into one of those corridors and reached the shadowed space that separated the two walls.

That formed a leprous avenue into which rubbish was thrown and into which prostitutes drew temporary lovers for rapid couplings. The obscurity was too great for anyone to be able to reach her.

She stopped. She took a deep breath. Suddenly, she felt remorse. Why was she fleeing that for which she had come in search? Was that people in rut not the force of God that was to labor and crush her body for the salvation of her soul? She had weakened at the first step. But she no longer wanted to recoil. Mute, her teeth clenched, she fortified herself in her resolution. Then she looked around. She would have liked a form to emerge from the darkness and possess her immediately, bruising her back on the stones.

She reflected that she would not suffer enough. She would not be able to see. She would not savor the torture. She started walking in the darkness. She stumbled over a couple lying on the ground and, extending her hand, felt the warm softness of a woman's breast. Around her there were murmurs and sighs. She perceived the sound of human caresses, mingled with oaths and arguments over price, in the midst of an insipid odor of sweat and putrescence.

Priscilla went around a tower and arrived at another opening in the rampart. Illuminated lanterns now gave a nocturnal pomp to the boulevard along which the crowd was passing. She plunged into it again, having partly covered her face with her veil.

Before a house more lugubrious than the others, where the bars on the windows seemed thicker and from which a heavy mildewed breath seemed to be emerging, a man more frightful than all those she had yet perceived was sitting.

He had an incandescent red beard, square and thick. Long hair like a mane sprang from his cranium and inundated his shoulders. He was enormously tall; his neck sank into his shoulders. Red eyebrows hid his round and stupid eyes almost entirely. And all that could be seen of his person—his breast, his arms and his hands—was covered with long red hair, so that he looked likes a human lion, posted to guard a brothel. He was the brothel-keeper Spartacus. It was him that Priscilla chose.

Having traversed the crowd, she let her veil fall over her shoulder, leaned over him and asked him in a low voice to welcome her among the women of his house. As she was unaware of the customs relative to such engagements, she hastened to offer the man the small bag of gold coins that she had brought with her.

The brothel-keeper Spartacus opened his eyes immeasurably wide. He had difficulty recruiting women. He had been obliged the previous year to go and buy Syrians in the market at Antioch. He had paid dearly for them and had not been able to keep them.

He did not understand at first what Priscilla was saying to him, for he was slow-witted. Nevertheless, he stood up at the sight of the gold and went into the house with her, letting the multicolored curtain that hung over the threshold fall back.

Then he rediscovered his professional knowledge of bodies. He took account mentally of the age that Priscilla might be, and marveled at her beauty, the quality of her skin, the abundance of her hair and the proportions of her form. He touched her breasts, he had a desire to make her open her mouth in order to see her teeth, as he did in the slave market.

At the same time as he appreciated those marvelous gifts he was gripped by a timidity, for, although he exercised his métier strictly, he was an innocent brute, a lion full of forbearance.

He considered with astonishment the resolute young woman, whose lips were trembling slightly, and made her repeat the objective of the visit several times. Certainly, he was ready to protect her if, gone astray into the quarter of prostitution, she had come to put herself under his safeguard. But no, there was no doubt about it. She was only an errant whore, weary of wandering, who wanted to enroll in his house and was offering him her fortune to keep. It would be folly to send her away.

"You know the customs," he said. And he tried to defend himself against his timidity by means of the thunderous sound of his own laughter.

No, she did not know them.

The first custom, when a prostitute entered into a house, was to give herself once, on arrival, to the proprietor of the brothel.

He pushed her toward a bed by the side of the door and tipped her on to it.

At that moment, a regular leapt down from a camel and attached it by a strap to a iron hook in the wall.

He shouted: "Spartacus!"

And he waited on the threshold.

The camel moved the striped curtain aside with its head and projected its long neck into the house.

And Priscilla, torn, found a little comfort in the fraternal melancholy of the animal's large eyes.

Priscilla was inscribed in the registers of the house of Spartacus under the name of Fabrilla.

A few months before, a young Armenian woman who bore that name had attracted a numerous clientele by her beauty and her appetite for amour. An eteriarch of scholars who was going to the Danube frontier had taken her away with him. Spartacus hoped by that similitude of names to let people believe that that Fabrilla had returned. So, when anyone asked for her, he called Priscilla. But the men were generally disappointed, for what they had liked about the real Fabrilla was a joyful humor that they did not find in the new one.

She was, along with the Jew Deborah, the only free woman in the house. The others were slaves. Spartacus had to pay a higher tax for free women, so he demanded more of them. When someone came at the hour when everyone was asleep, a little after sunrise, it was always Priscilla who was woken up; in any case, he found her docile and never weary.

The women lived on the first floor of the house, in narrow rooms that were all similar, which opened on to a corridor. They had their name inscribed on a piece of wood suspended by a cord from each door. The regulars went up directly to the corridor and penetrated into the room of the woman they wanted to see when the piece of wood was not inverted. Others had them come downstairs to drink palm wine in the low-ceilinged room on the ground floor or the courtyard behind the house. They often got drunk, for since the beginning of the world, the pleasure of drunkenness has been indissolubly combined with that of amour. Then the blows rained down, blood flowed, and Spartacus was obliged to intervene with his great leonine strength.

Priscilla's room had for its entire furniture a wooden bed, a stool, a chest, a sandstone water-trough with a tall two-handled pitcher and a carpet soiled by years of debauchery. The walls were covered with inscriptions. There was vermin in the mattress and black beasts emerged from the cracks in the floor-tiles when the light was extinguished.

During the day, Priscilla stayed in her room, sitting on her stool, her eyes fixed, waiting for someone to open the door. She wore the yellow robe of a prostitute and the square Assyrian bonnet.

In the evening she went down to the common room where people were drinking. Soldiers put her on their knees and made her drink by force, partly undressing her. She never showed any preference for one over another. She gave herself silently, complaisantly, without enthusiasm or disgust.

She did not suffer. But she was astonished not to perceive within herself the enlightenment for which he had hoped. In the drunken voices of street-porters and merchants, in the insults of men who played dice on her body and vied for her possession with punches, she often strove to hear the sweet music that ought to charm the ears of the elect. She did not hear it. No celestial dove came to fly toward her as a messenger, no angel of God appeared to her.

She did not have a dolorous disappointment in consequence, but she started to desire death ardently. She could not imagine that the existence she was leading could last for long. She expected death as the natural consequence of her sacrifice. She summoned it with all the sincerity of her soul.

It was forbidden for women in brothels to have an image in their room representing any divinity whatsoever. Those who infringed that prohibition could be condemned to flagellation, and the brothel-keeper subjected to a heavy fine. But the Nycteparch had instructed his functionaries to turn a blind eye to it and, in fact, the presence of gods above the beds of pleasure was tolerated. It was sufficient for a little curtain to hide them.

The women were almost all of different religions and each of them had a little hidden altar in her room. Seso, who was an Egyptian from the upper Nile had a statuette of Isis. The Babylonian Artystone had one of Ormuz. Cleobuline of Byblos adored Astarte. The Hindu Bagawali rendered worship to Indra, the transformer of things, who had seven arms to unite the parts of the heavens. The Roman Livia had a whole collection of different gods and accomplished a thousand bizarre rituals for them. She burned incense for Priapus and Comus. She offered flowers to Pilumnus, who protects women in childbirth. She poured water over Conisatus, who provokes sweat after amour, and wine over Tryphallus, who renders the body firm. And she did not fail to prostrate herself every evening before Genita-Mana, who protects against the pain that men can cause during coupling.

And other women simply had a phallus in bronze or gold, which they adored as the force generative of joy and life.

Priscilla placed in a niche above her bed, behind a piece of black silk bought for that purpose, a little wooden cross with a crude representation in ivory of the crucified Jesus.

That was the primary cause of the irrational, pitiless, delirious hatred that the Jewess Deborah, worshiper of the unique God without an image, had for her.

Priscilla was linked by amity with the tender Seso. She was a tender creature who gave the impression of carrying a secret within her. She taught Priscilla how to dye her hair with saffron in the Greek fashion; she took her to the shops where copper rings for the ankles and necklaces of colored stones to put round the neck were sold at a low price, and paints and powders for the face. She explained to her how many drachms she ought to demand from men and how she ought to demand more from those who were drunk. She showed her where to find the money-changer to convert drachms into gold besants, in order to have her fortune in the smallest possible volume and to be able to hide it more easily under a floor-tile in her room. She taught her what caresses she ought to make more willingly, according to whether she found herself in the presence of Greeks accustomed to amour or coarse barbarians. She taught her to fear the brutality of Cappadocians and the perversity of the men of Byblos.

Priscilla and Seso were both Egyptians, and the sound of their voices evoked for them the same landscape and the same sky. It was in the morning, when the house was deserted, before going to sleep, that Seso sometimes came to Priscilla's room.

They had equally weary bodies and buzzing heads. The sentiment of their misery penetrated them, but they found a tenderness in conversing in low voices and holding hands.

Priscilla talked about Jesus Christ to Seso and told her all the stories of the saints and martyrs that she knew. Seso told her the story of the death and rebirth of Osiris, and told her how Isis had searched for the fragments of his body on the banks of the Nile, how she had und them among the lotus flowers and how Horus, he luminous son, had grown in Abydos.

But while Seso listened distractedly to the marvelous lives of saints that Priscilla retraced with all her faith, the old Egyptian religion awoke dormant memories in Priscilla's soul. That was, above all, when it was a matter of the tenebrous Amenti, guarded by Anubis with the head of a jackal, where all the dead had to render. She believed that she would soon traverse that Amenti. Perhaps she would penetrate into the hall of truth and Hermes would unwrap before the Judge the tablets where all her actions were engraved. But what if the abandonment of her body to the most horrible torture was not sufficient to compensate for the evil that she had done? Had she not thrown a stone with all her strength into a face where intelligence was radiant? Was it not written that: *The only sin that cannot be forgiven is the sin against the spirit*?

In that case, Hermes would not give her the ring, the crucial sign of immortality; he would not permit her to climb into the boat of Isis to glide toward the realm without matter. Her soul unpurified, she would not be confounded with Osiris—or, rather, with Jesus Christ. She confused the two religions. She came back to her own with more ardor, but she remained troubled by the similarities they had.

And when, one day, Seso gave her a little statuette of Isis, she did not refuse it, because of the shadow of the Anenti, where she was afraid of remaining after her death.

The Jewess Deborah execrated in Priscilla, first of all, a creature who belonged to a religion that persecuted hers. She execrated, in addition, a woman more beautiful than her, for whom she experienced a natural antipathy, a physical repulsion.

Deborah had insensate fits of violence. Anger caused her to fall into crises in which she howled endlessly and in which white foam emerged from her mouth.

When the night was terminated, Spartacus sometimes shared her bed. She claimed that Priscilla was striving to attract him to her by means of hypocritical maneuvers.

Afterwards, she said that someone had stolen a golden comb from her, and that it was Priscilla who had accomplished that theft. Spartacus, fearing that she would make a complaint to the centurion of the quarter, visited Priscilla's room and found nothing.

Then Deborah adopted the habit of spitting with disgust every time she was in Priscilla's presence. She heaped her with mockery and insults and exasperated further every day the disdainful silence with which Priscilla enveloped herself like armor.

One evening, Deborah was visited by a coachman from the Hippodrome who sometimes came for her. All the women were in the common room, some on the knees of visitors, others waiting, painting their fingernails or putting on make-up in front of their little bronze mirrors.

A coachman from the Hippodrome was an important person, and Deborah felt an extreme pride in his visits. She stuck herself against him and unfastened her tunic all the way to the belly in order to show off her cleavage, which was beautiful. Having drunk to excess, she started to say a thousand foolish things, and to dance among the tables, and as Priscilla remained motionless in a corner she exhorted the coachman by way of derision to take the Christian immediately, in front of everyone, in order that he could compare the value of their mutual caresses.

The coachman, a taciturn man, did not budge, and tried to calm her down.

She then threw her arms round his neck, and shook him with all her strength, shouting: "If you're not a coward, to and give her a slap for me."

The coachman did not depart from his immobility.

Fury set Deborah ablaze, inflaming her face. And she went to Priscilla and slapped her twice.

A brawl followed, some siding with the Jewess, others with Priscilla.

Spartacus said nothing, out of respect for the coachman. He waited for the night to end. But when the door closed on the last of his clients he seized Deborah by the hair and dragged her, in spite of her screams, to Priscilla's room.

"Since you hate her," he said, "you can spend the night with her, in her bed, and you'll cure your hatred."

He watched the two women lay down side by side and he shot the exterior bolt of the door on them.

In the darkness, Priscilla remained immobile for a long time. She did not even hear her enemy's respiration, with the consequence that she eventually went to sleep.

And suddenly, two hands with bones as hard as stone seized her by the throat.

A merciless struggle was engaged. Priscilla fought with a surprising force. Breast to breast, the two women rolled on the floor. They got up, only to come to grips again, and to fall down again. Sometimes, holding one another by the shoulders, they remained motionless for some time, each waiting for some weakness on the other's part.

Priscilla felt the warmth of the body of the Jewess and divined, very close to her in the darkness, the expression of her furious face. She did not experience any terror, or veritable hatred. She had sensed, rising in her soul like a tide, the desire not to be vanquished by the force of evil that possessed Deborah.

She fought until sunrise, without crying out and without weakening. When the light appeared, it illuminated two disheveled, savage creatures with breasts scratched by fingernails and bites, equally inexorable. Then great spasms began to run the length of Deborah's body and she fell into one of the convulsive fits to which she was accustomed.

But her hatred was not appeased by her defeat. That same evening she announced to her confidante Livia, who repeated it to the other women, that she would stab Priscilla in the back when she was not expecting it. Ostentatiously, she sharpened a large double-edged knife that she possessed, sniggering and humming a Syrian song.

From that moment on, when she went downstairs, when she went to fetch water from the courtyard and when she

269

walked along the corridor, Priscilla had the sensation that the Jewess's blade was about to plunge into her back.

She had thought that she wanted to die. She perceived that she was mistaken and that it would be horrible to die like that. She kept on her guard. She spent her time watching over the existence that she thought she could no longer bear. That was a new torture.

Most of all, it was when she went down with her heavy pitcher on her head that she thought that she might be struck. She waited in order to go fetch water for moments when Deborah was with a man in her room. When she was in the common room and Deborah was drinking she did not lose sight of her, because it was especially when she was drunk that the Jewess was capable of anything.

But that obsession with murder gave her a strange appetite for life. She perceived that she participated in certain pleasures, that of breathing, that of perceiving soft light, that of receiving and sometimes giving caresses to unknown men.

She was conscious of that pleasure, but she had no remorse in consequence, and she did not ask forgiveness from God.

Toward that epoch, the body of the Babylonian Artystone, who was tall and graceful, sprouted smooth swellings. Her hair fell out, her skin split in places and symmetrical tumors appeared under her breasts.

She was placed in a damp cell at the back of the courtyard, which had once served as a pig sty. The cell was hermetically sealed at dusk, in order that no one would suspect that a woman afflicted by that disease was retained in the brothel. She stayed there all night, without air and light, forbidden to call out. Sometimes, out of pity, a woman went in the darkness to rap on the door, and she responded with an inarticulate cry that emerged with difficulty from her swollen throat.

They had doubted it at first. The Roman Livia, who claimed to know what to do because she had once lived with a student of the physician Archigenes,[36] had made her drunk an aster tisane that cured buboes and had applied cataplasms of boiled hyssop under her breasts. But it was gradually remembered that some time before, Artystone had spent an entire night with a mariner from Capua.

Capua was notorious for a hereditary disease that its inhabitants transmitted by the act of amour, sometimes even by a kiss, or even by the breath. According to what Artystone had said the next day, that mariner, simulating an exceptional modesty, had refused to take off his clothes in order to go to bed and, in spite of the heat, had kept a thick kerchief around his neck and his mouth.

The ceased to doubt when Artystone's face became coppery, when her lips swelled and hung down, when blackish excrescences and tubercles emerged all over her body.

Fear took possession of all souls.

Spartacus deliberated as to whether, in accordance with the prescriptions of the Nycteparch, he ought to go find the centurion in order for Artystone to be sent to an island near Zante where there were leprosaria and from which no one ever returned. Alone among the women of the brothel, Priscilla and Deborah consented to care for her and sometimes to sit with her.

In the afternoon, they went to sit down to either side of the unfortunate woman in the pig sty, the door of which it was necessary to close in order that the nauseating odor of the lesions would not reach the house. By the light of a candle they looked at one another in order not to see the frightful face that separated them.

Artystone repeated incessantly: "It's for my sins! It will happen to you too. It will happen to everyone."

Even then, Deborah did not abdicate her hatred. Priscilla sometimes thought that she was about to profit from the demiobscurity to throw the dagger whose handle she was fingering

---

[36] The eminent Greek physician Archigenes died in the second century, so this reference is anachronistic.

under her robe. Deborah undoubtedly thought about it, but dared not. Between then, the wretched body of their companion was like a wide abyss of dolor that rendered hatred impotent.

One night, a few men gathered in the low room of Spartacus' brothel drinking witnessed a strange and terrible sight. Unsteady on her feet, Artystone, who had not been seen standing up for several days, appeared in the doorway that opened to the corridor.

She had put on a large crimson garment from Persia, which she donned on feast days when she went to walk in the port. The garment fell to her feet; it was interwoven with gold thread and the lamplight gave it reflections of flame and blood. She had put her red Assyrian miter on her bald head and, thus clad, with her empty nose, whose bones had collapsed, her enormous lips and the two green-tinted globes of her eyes, her hand extended, on which there were no longer any fingernails, she seemed a accused queen, a goddess of the subterranean realms where prostitutes must suffer the torture of eternal debauchery.

Everyone was petrified by horror.

Then the unfortunate Artystone said a few words in a hoarse, quavering, absolutely unintelligible voice.

She thanked Spartacus for his humanity because he had kept her in his house. She thanked her friends for having cared for her. Everyone had been good. But she did not want to be a burden. She announced that all the listeners would be struck by a similar disease.

And suddenly, without anyone having dared to make a move, she disappeared like a nightmare.

All kinds of herbs were fetched to purify the places where she had put her feet, and Spartacus obtained promises from the witnesses that they would not say anything about that frightful scene.

Women who were hooking at the extremity of a street ending at the Golden Horn reported the next day that they had seen a spectral empress clad in crimson, an ambulant dead

272

woman who was staggering, a caricature of decomposition, throw herself into the stagnant waters of the port, which closed over her.

Many different men enjoyed Priscilla's body, but their caresses passed over her like wind over the sand, without leaving a trace. She forgot their faces and their forms. There were some who loved her and returned frequently. A man named Ibas who owned vineyards on Zante and chartered a boat himself to come to sell his grapes on Constantinople, acquired the habit, during each of his voyages, on spending his nights with her. Two soldiers who wanted her at the same time fought hand-to-hand one day, and she refused herself to the one who had been victorious. A crazy old physician proposed marriage to her and subsequently attempted to poison her because she had not accepted. A sadist offered Spartacus large sums of money for the right to flagellate her until death seemed good to her, but as she was not a slave the bargain could not be struck. A mime wanted to teach her to dance and a herdsman who was rich but who only paid Spartacus in kind gave her a dried sheep's head with glass eyes, which she hung on the wall of her room. A man condemned to death who was being pursued and who was drunk spent an entire night telling her about the pleasure he obtained from murdering women after having loved them. It was in her bed that the condemned man was arrested, and he declared on leaving that what he regretted the most in life was the pleasure he had had with Priscilla.

Once, a man clad in a white robe, like the philosophers Priscilla had once seen coming out of the Museum in Alexandria, opened the door of her room and sat down familiarly on her bed. He had bright eyes, and he started talking to her. To her great surprise, he made no attempt to take her. He stayed with her for a long time, sometimes caressing her forehead with his hand. Memories returned to Priscilla's soul. She recalled the Gymnasium, Hypatia, the sages in white robes, and Telamon's kiss.

The man quit her without even having kissed her lips. Shortly afterwards, Priscilla perceived with surprise that a dagger, which he had doubtless been carrying in his garments, had slipped out and fallen on to the floor.

She kept it, and hid it under her mattress, in order to return it to him if he came back. But he never came back.

And many days passed, bringing joys and pains, always more pains than joys. Priscilla's beauty developed mysteriously. She became slimmer, with a brighter gleam in her gaze, her hair more heavily twisted over her nape, into which the saffron dye put somber flames. She participated more in petty quotidian events. She took an interest in the quarrels of women, the brutality of men and the misery of all. Her intelligence awoke and grew. She was more desired and more hated. The sensuality that could arise and the dread of Deborah's knife added salt to her days.

She started to love life.

XVI. The Philosopher's Dagger

Spartacus was told one day that the Logothete of the Chrysargire taxes would come to his house in the evening.

That was a redoubtable event. The tax was levied regularly by subaltern collectors who taxed the brothels on the number of women who lived there. demanding more for free women than slaves, the former having cost the brothel-keeper nothing.

Spartacus had his registers in order and did not attempt fraud, but the coming of the high functionary that the Logothete was could only presage expense and annoyance.

The Logothete was reputed to be a venal and debauched man who extorted money from brothels by threats and who organized crapulously sumptuous orgies in them at their expense, for which he had a liking.

Spartacus was immediately obliged to threaten Deborah with the whip. The Jewess declared that she intended to throw the wine that was offered to her in the Logothete's face. She hated all the functionaries of the Empire that participated in the persecution of her race. Rumor of the expulsion of the Jews of Alexandria had spread throughout the world and that soul in revolt had extracted an excess of fury therefrom.

All the women had to put in their most beautiful tunics and their colored cothurnes, and arrange themselves round the tables in the low room as if on parade.

"I'll prevent him from going upstairs with her, if it's her he wants," said Deborah, indicating Priscilla to the other women. And she sniggered hatefully.

Priscilla's hand was extended on the table top. Swiftly, without anyone being able to stop her, Deborah took out her knife and delivered a great blow, intended to nail that white hand to the table. The blade plunged between Priscilla's fingers, vibrating. She felt the cold brush her.

Spartacus ran forward. The women got up and surrounded Priscilla, whose face had gone pale. At that moment, Livia, who was on watch at the door, shouted that the Logothete had arrived.

He irrupted into the room violently with three or four functionaries who were his companions in debauchery. He was already drunk. Enormous, under his gold dalmatic, he collapsed into a chair shouting to Spartacus that it was not a matter of taxation but amour.

"Have crowns of roses been prepared?" he demanded.

Spartacus had not thought of that.

The Logothete became indignant, and then started to laugh. "Let all the women strip naked!" he said.

The majority got ready to do so meekly, but they watched Deborah from the corner of the eye.

The latter clicked her teeth, trembling with fury.

But the Logothete swayed to the right and left, and leaned his bull-like neck and bestial head forward. His little eyes blinked. He looked at Priscilla with enormous attention.

And Priscilla, agape with horror, recognized Peter.

"What's the name of that woman?" he stammered.

"Fabrilla," Spartacus replied.

Peter repeated that name several time. "Fabrilla! Priscilla!" he murmured, in a low voice. He seemed bewildered.

Suddenly, he got up. He almost danced. He fell on to the breast of one of his companions, whom he clutched and embraced, repeating: "She resembles her! How she resembles her!"

Priscilla calculated the time she would need to bound to the door and reach the street. She braced herself. But she did not have time to put the project into execution.

Peter's large moist hands had seized her by the armpits and he squeezed her and lifted her up. He carried her to the staircase.

"Right away!" he shouted. "I want her right away."

Priscilla climbed the stairs with an apparent resignation. She counted on taking advantage of a moment of inattention.

There was none.

Peter shoved her into the room, turned over the placard and closed the door. He grunted with satisfaction and repeated to himself: "How she resembles her! How she resembles her!"

He had a new explosion of terrible joy. He sat down on the stool, laughing.

Priscilla took advantage of that to run to the door. She had opened it when he grabbed her by the neck and threw her back brutally into the room.

He was panting with wrath.

"It appears that I don't please you," he said. And he shook her forcefully.

Priscilla felt her energy dissolve and give way to fear: the frightful fear of a being delivered to a savage beast, the fear that makes one cry out for one's mother.

"Get undressed!" exclaimed Peter.

As she remained motionless, shaken by sobs, he ripped her long linen chemise in two.

"Kneel down before me!"

Terrified, Priscilla knelt down.

"Kiss my feet!"

Humbly, Priscilla kissed the cothurnes stained with dust and wine.

Then Peter started laughing, enormously, and he let himself fall on to the bed, but while still holding her by a fistful of hair. He spoke, for he had a need to exteriorize his satisfaction verbally, and while speaking he moved his head closer to Priscilla's head, exhaling a winy breath over her.

"You please me. Why did you want to run away? I'll give you all the money you want. You're a girl named Fabrilla, aren't you? From what country? Alexandria, perhaps? Ha ha! In Alexandria, they wanted to murder me. But one doesn't murder Peter like that. I'll go back there one day and march over them. I'll go back with you. Do you know the Church of Saint Mark? Yes, everyone knows it. But there's only me who knows what's underneath it, under the ground. There are incalculable treasures, with a cadaver that guards

277

them. I'll give you jewels that have slept for a thousand years in sarcophagi, necklaces that Cleopatra wore around her neck. But you're going to lie down here, beside me."

Priscilla listened as if in a dream, and internally, she formulated the most ardent of prayers.

Oh, let Jesus Christ free her from Peter thus minute! Doubtless he wanted to punish her for having allowed herself to lapse into bodily enjoyment. She would accomplish unprecedented penances. She would follow another path. It was her mother who was on the true one. She too would go into the mysterious convent in the middle of the sands and would let herself die there of thirst. But let her be delivered from the pollution that has no name.

Peter's voice was thick and Priscilla had seen so many men struck with torpor while drunk that she hoped that he would fall asleep.

He was still holding her by the hair with one hand, with the other he sometimes caressed her body, moistening it with the dampness of his palm, and he spoke, stirring his memories.

"You want to deceive me. Your name isn't Fabrilla but Priscilla. You're the sister of the idiot and the daughter of the woman who was taken into the desert because she'd had a child by another man than your so-called father, the imbecile Diodorus. How many things one never knows! Me, I didn't know that I'd end up having you. But I'll have you. You're going to lie down here beside me."

There had been so many miracles! The one that Priscilla was asking of God was not very difficult. Let slumber weigh upon that man! But not this abomination!

"Oh, that Priscilla! I went to prowl around her house by night. She might have been fifteen years old then. She was so gentle. If I'd held her in my arms I'd have killed her afterwards, so that she wouldn't be anyone else's."

Peter had softened; he was almost weeping.

But suddenly, he straightened up and cried: "Bitch! You, you're nothing but a whore for soldiers."

And he knocked her down on the bed, striking her.

Priscilla had a second to invoke Jesus and also the other gods whose images she knew to be nearby in the other rooms. She appealed to Isis the merciful, the white Ormuz, Indra with the seven arms. She would belong to the one who saved her.

But she was not saved. Peter gripped her sides with his arms, pressed her against him, crushed her. He possessed her, insulting her, and she submitted to him as she had submitted to others. But this was too much. This surpassed the measure of horror that a soul can contain.

While that caress ravaged her, her soul screamed. She uttered toward Jesus Christ a clamor of revolt. Why had he wanted this? Had she not immolated for him her youth and her life? If he had permitted his creature to be lying under this caress, it was because he could do nothing about human action, it was because he was impotent for good as for evil. She no longer believed. Faith left her like an unhealthy humor that has long maintained the dolor of a wound, extracted by the surgeon's knife.

After the pleasure, the man fell asleep.

Slowly, Priscilla moved away from him in order no longer to feel the contact of his skin. She was against the wall and she could not think of getting out of the bed without waking Peter. But she did not even think about it. She was devoid of strength. She fell into a demi-slumber.

And suddenly, it seemed to her that a voice shouted nearby: "The one who has never sinned!"

And she came forward.

There was a great assembly of people in front of a church. She saw prelates in golden miters, cavaliers, and the people of Alexandria. The Patriarch Cyril was about to celebrate a marriage. That marriage was her own. She had been chosen by Peter as a spouse. Her father Diodorus, her brother Marcus, the monks, the Parabalani: they were all there. The door of the church, which was the Church of Caesarea, opened and she saw the face of a fat priest appear, with the same innocent expression as the one she had seen on the morning of Hypatia's death.

And she had become Peter's wife. She shared his bed. She felt the warmth and odor of his body, she was moistened by his sweat. Thus, all that there was on earth of the abject had been for her. Jesus Christ had bought her to the brothel in order that she should have, as the aliment of her soul, the hatred of Deborah, and as bodily pleasure, the putrefaction of Artystone and Peter's caress.

Now she was lying beside the man she had feared since childhood. That was the terminus of her mystical youth.

Was that possible?

She was almost tempted to wake Peter up in order to belong go him again and see whether she could go any further along the road of her absolute misery.

She emerged from her demi-slumber and it seemed to her that the room, which was only illuminated by a smoky lamp hanging from the wall was filled with a sudden brightness. She saw with sharp clarity all the events of her life unfold, her journeys to Zenobia's convent, the piety of her childhood, the stone that she had thrown at Hypatia, and the nullity and the stupidity of her entire existence appeared to her.

For her to be here, lying ignominiously next to that repulsive male, various causes had been necessary. She pictured her grandfather, stubborn and fanatical, her limited father, and Bishop Cyril, who had weighed upon the destiny of her family like the stone of a sepulcher on a creature buried alive.

Everything had pushed her toward evil.

Evil was the stone of hatred that she had thrown; evil was ugliness and debauchery; evil was the man snoring beside her.

And evil was triumphant everywhere. The weak were crushed, the pure were soiled and the gods did not intervene, and Jesus said: "Turn the other cheek."

And she had been cowardly enough to let herself go, to get down on her knees, to throw the stone, to listen to the monk Zosyma, to open her body, to sacrifice her beauty.

So the evil had just entered into her. She had felt it profoundly in her loins. It had labored her. She was covered in filth.

But in that extremity, it seemed to her that she had traveled a kind of circle and had returned to her point of departure. She glimpsed a new faith. A task appeared to her, for which she had been chosen. She began to understand the meaning of her life. She associated the death of the beggar Dionysus, who had allowed himself to be killed almost voluntarily, with the presence of Peter asleep beside her.

Yes, that was it! It was for her to cut the throat of evil, to be the instrument of justice. She felt pure. She had never sinned. What was material was of no account. With the pollution of Peter she had just received an ignoble baptism, but it had spiritualized her soul.

At that moment, far way along the ramparts, the trumpets sounded of cataphracts who were leaving the city for exercises. For her, it was like an announcement of the Last Judgment. She shivered. The divinity to which she no longer gave a face was perhaps about to demand that she account for actions she had not yet accomplished.

She raised herself up on her elbow. But no. No hatred! She had plenty of time. She knew from experience the duration of those heavy drunken slumbers. It was necessary to reflect. It was necessary to preserve her precious life. She felt vigorous, active, and cunning. She imagined everything that would follow. Everything would succeed. She was invincible.

Cautiously, she slid her naked arm under the mattress. She grasped the knife that was hidden there and drew it out of its leather scabbard. It was astonishingly sharp. She remembered. The man who had dropped it from his cloak was a philosopher in a white robe whom desire had not pushed toward her. He had scarcely brushed her forehead with his hand. He had only come, by virtue of an enchantment of mysterious things, to leave that weapon in her hands.

Oh, how she would have liked to make Peter suffer! She wondered whether she ought not to put his eyes out, or castrate him. But he would cry out, someone would come. She would not be able to escape. She was determined to preserve the treasure of admirable life.

And she remembered that the Hindu Bagawali said that in her religion, the most unfortunate were those who die abruptly, because they were dragged, without being prepared for it, into the region she called Kama-Loka, where the dead despaired. That Kama-Loka must be the Amenti of her country, perhaps also the Christian Hell.

Let death be abrupt for that accursed man!

She searched for the location of his heart. The folds of the raised dalmatic hid it.

Then she delivered an immense thrust to the throat, for she thought the flesh more resistant than it was. The blade plunged in to the hilt and penetrated quite profoundly into the wood of the bed, so that the man was nailed to it.

Scarcely had she struck than Priscilla took the gilded dalmatic in her fist and stuffed it into Peter's open mouth, as he gasped. She held it there until the spasms of the body had stopped.

She leapt out of the bed, strangely calm and lucid.

Blood was flooding over the floor-tiles, and was so abundant that it might pass under the crack of the door and stream into the corridor. She leapt toward the pitcher, which was empty. She put on a light chemise, red in color, in order that no one would see the stains by which her body was soiled, put the pitcher on her head, and went downstairs.

She stopped for a few seconds on the threshold of the low room. Spartacus was asleep. Two of Peter's companions were in the same state but the other two were still drinking with Livia and Bagawali, who had stripped naked.

Laugher and gibes greeted her. Priscilla replied to them joyfully, pointing to the pitcher she was carrying. She caused water to flow from the fountain noisily. She reappeared again outside the low room and stopped, putting her pitcher on the floor, or further pleasantries. She took care to close the door of the room before going upstairs.

With her torn chemise, dipped in the pitcher, she staunched the blood that was flowing. She washed herself, and put on a tunic and a cloak. She wrenched the philosopher's dagger out of Peter's throat, wiped it carefully, and put it in her belt. Perhaps she would need it again. Woe betide anyone who tried to get in her way!

One last glance at the room where she had suffered without hope. The ivory Christ before which she had prayed so much had fallen from its niche by virtue of the shock of the dagger-thrust. She looked at it for a second and, with her toe, she pushed it into the blood.

No one saw her slide along the corridor and open the door to the street. Outside, the boulevard was deserted. The brothels were dark. Only the windows of the square towers in the ramparts cast glimmers of light at intervals. It was the indecisive hour when the night is coming to an end but the sun has not yet begun to appear.

It seemed to Priscilla that the landscape was new and mysterious, full of the multiform riches of life. She had never looked at the world in which she lived. The towers appeared to her for the first time with their signification of force and war. The brothels revealed to her the enigma of their nameless misery. The prowler drawing away to the right was a silhouette of crime, the one drawing away to the left a silhouette of despair. The houses, the earth and the sky were full of correspondences and signs. On all sides there was danger, hatred and amour for her but she no longer feared anything. Was she not an Exterminating Angel?

In any case, she knew where she was going. Ibas, the merchant from Zante, was in Constantinople and would set sail in the morning. He had told her the day before that he would sleep on his boat and that the boat in question was moored at the extremity of the port. Priscilla calculated that Peter's death would be discovered within an hour. She also calculated that an hour after that the port would probably be closed and all the boats searched. She remembered the rapidity with which, a few months earlier, the Nycteparch's police had acted after the murder of a less important individual than a Logothete of taxes. She had two hours in which to find Ibas, tell him everything and persuade him to set forth. That was just enough!

She started to run in the direction of the port.

Priscilla had more than two hours before her to flee, in consequence of an event that cast all the inhabitants of Spartacus' brothel into a stupor.

The centurion of the quarter had just arrived. He had had the house surrounded by his soldiers and he had gathered everyone who was there on the ground floor in order to interrogate them. It was evident to him and everyone else that it was Priscilla that had committed the crime.

Then, howling, agitating her curly hair, Deborah launched herself toward the centurion.

"It's me who killed the Logothete! It's me! It's me! I cut his throat with this hand! I'm ready to do it again!"

In vain, Spartacus swore that it was impossible, since Deborah had not quit a laborer from the quays of Neorium, who had left almost at the moment when Peter's murder had been discovered.

Did Deborah want by accusing herself to glorify herself with the admirable action that the murder of a high functionary of the Empire was because she was jealous of not having accomplished it herself? Was she thinking, in her hatred for Priscilla, of stealing such a dangerous honor from her? Or, by an abrupt reversal caused by admiration, did she want to save her enemy by giving her time to escape?

She he could never explain it to herself.

Confronted by her formal confession, the centurion had her wrists bound and kept her out of sight until the arrival of the Nycteparch.

Daylight had appeared by the time he came.

He was a very small man, old and wily, who seemed never to look at anyone but saw extraordinarily far into souls, beyond the appearances of gestures and words.

284

He had the whole affair explained to him, listened to Deborah's renewed confessions and immediately said, when she had finished: "Fifty lashes for this woman for having accused herself falsely. No more. She isn't an accomplice."

Then he gave rapid orders to be transmitted to the gates of the city and the jetties of the port.

It was too late. The boat of the merchant Ibas was already heading for the open sea.

XVII. The Crown of Narcissi

Isidore of Gaza lifted his thin finger toward the star-studded sky as if to take it as a witness to the prodigies with which the earth was full, and he said: "I had two extraordinary dreams last night of a prophetic character. Listen."

Around him, extended on the carpet in the Greek fashion or leaning on the marble balustrade of the terrace, were grouped the philosopher Proclus and his former master Eunapius: Asclepigenia,[37] a young woman renowned for her knowledge of magic and theurgy: the Chaldean priest Cerinthus; Antagoras, an extraordinary individual renowned for his eccentricities; and young Telamon, among others.

The villa of Palladius was situated not far from the port of Cenchreae on the Saronic Gulf, at the foot of the ruins of the temple of Venus. It was in Corinth that Palladius lived now for preference, and it was there that he reunited in his villa the philosophers of the Museum, who had almost all deserted Alexandria, in the wake of Cyril's persecutions, for the various cities of Greece.

Palladius was striding back and forth agitatedly, often looking in the direction of the gardens in order to see whether any further guests were going to appear. Pale under the mauve of his tunic, his fine head leaning on his arm, decked with bracelets, Telamon's misty eyes were staring in the same direction.

Satisfied by the silence, Isidore of Gaza spoke.

---

[37] The presence of the Athenian philosopher Asclepigenia, the daughter of Plutarch of Athens, is anachronistic; although there is some doubt about her dates she was probably born in 430. She was certainly not contemporary with Eunapius, an earlier Athenian philosopher, who cannot have known Proclus, although Asclepigenia did. The Cerinthus cited cannot be the first-century Gnostic of that name.

"At the bottom of a great mass of stone that might have been the pyramid of Cheops, a temple or a hill, two young women, two sisters of great beauty, were walking side by side. They wore a blue ribbon around the forehead with a golden hawk—which was, as you know, the distinctive sign of the ancient priestesses of Nephtys, the Minerva of Egypt. That also makes me think that the dream might have been the image of an anterior life rather than a scene from the mediocre existence that we are living.

"One of the two sisters, the younger, showed the other a young man who was drawing away, and by whom she was loved. The elder sister persuaded her younger sister forcefully that it is shameful for a priestess to yield to the love of a man, and exhorted her to chastity by the powerful radiation of her will. Now, the elder sister had, in my dream, the face of Hypatia, while the other resembled the daughter of Diodorus, that Priscilla, whose intelligence amazes us, whose life appears to us to be an enigma, and whom we all love, albeit to different degrees."

It was in seeing the impassioned face of Palladius that Isidore of Gaza added the last words, with an ironic half-smile.

For me, dreams are more mute than tombs," said old Eunapius. "And if they sometimes speak, they are more deceptive than the clouds and the wind."

"The time is not far off," said Isidore of Gaza, shrugging his shoulders with an indulgent pity, "when, thanks to me, everyone will know the future as well as the past. It will suffice to make the ablutions that I indicate, to say three prayers whose formulae I will give, and by means of an ineffable communication with the invisible powers, one will be in confrontation during sleep with the great tableau of events of life, which contains all possibilities and all fatalities."

"Excuse my short sight," said Telamon, "but I don't see why the dream you've had merits being reported."

Isidore of Gaza started to laugh at such ignorance. "My dream is marvelously symbolic," he said. "It explains what has

287

astonished us all, it answer a question that we have posed. How was a young woman endowed with reason, even though she was a Christian, able to participate in the stoning of Hypatia? How, so few years thereafter, was she to show such an amorous admiration for that same Hypatia? That amour has caused her to renounce her religion, to raise her intelligence to the point that the philosophy of Plotinus is accessible to her and she can discuss it with us. It even seems that that amour is reflected in the plasticity of her features, since I believe I can sometimes distinguish a certain resemblance between Hypatia and Priscilla."

"Is it also because of that amour," said Asclepigenia, ironically, that Priscilla can live with a man as vulgar as that grape-merchant named Ibas?"

"The faculty that is superior to all others, enthusiasm," said Proclus, "can as well be found under the dense form of a grape-merchant as that of the most elevated of philosophers. It appears that this Ibas spends hours in the temple of Minerva alongside the port of Lechaeum and that he begs to goddess to render him more intelligent. He strives to read and to comprehend, I don't know whether he'll succeed, but I find that very touching. The only time it has been given to me to see him, he reminded me of those extremely faithful dogs that gaze at their master with a fixed stare in which one perceives the enigma of all nature making progress toward more thought and more love."

"It's a pity," said Asclepigenia, "that he has such pretentions to elegance. With his embroidered cloaks and his appearance of a Zantean peasant, he always seems to be a ridiculous travesty."

"In any case, Priscilla lives with that Ibas like brother and sister," said Palladius, becoming very red, while Asclepigenia uttered an ingenuous bust of laughter.

"I still don't see," Telamon added, "how Isidore's dream can..."

The joy of explaining a dream made Isidore of Gaza's eyes sparkle even more.

"I've seen in my dream a scene from the past that illuminates the present and the future. In a previous life, Hypatia and Priscilla were sisters and loved one another tenderly. Hypatia then deflected Priscilla from amour, doubtless in order to consecrate her to the religious life of the temple of Nephtys, of whom they were both priestesses. In doing that, she caused an injury to her sister by depriving her of the happiness to which she aspired, from the superiority that she might have acquired by means of pleasure. Every injury receives its punishment in one life or another, and the stone that Priscilla threw was merely the payment of a debt engendered by imprudent advice in a previous life. For everyone must remain free in one's actions and create one's own destiny, good or bad. The debt having been paid, the anterior love reappeared, and it's a sister that Priscilla is mourning without knowing it."

"That explanation is very subtle," said Proclus, getting up and advancing toward the edge of the terrace, outside the luminous circle of the torches, as if he had suddenly been attracted by the shadows of the night. "What does the chain of events that links us to one another matter? The essential thing, in the sadness of these times, is that those who are linked hold one another's hand faithfully. The memory of Hypatia is like a pure flame that illuminates us, and perhaps the powers by which we are ruled have sent the beautiful Pricilla to us in order that she should be its living representation among us."

In the distance, on the rocky path that snaked around the ruins of the temple of Venus there was a flickering light. A man carrying a lantern whose flame the wind threatened to extinguish was descending toward Corinth. The little glimmer seemed to be struggling against the darkness and gave the impression that it was about to expire at any moment.

"Alas," said Proclus, again, following his train of thought, "the reign of the mind is over. Yesterday, the emperor ordered the destruction of the books of Porphyry. Tomorrow, we'll no longer be safe, either in Corinth or in Athens. Behold the image of our epoch: a man with a lantern that is about to go out, descending the hill where the ruins of the temple of Venus are."

Footsteps resounded. A voice pronounced the formula of Greek salutation: "Rejoice!"

It was Priscilla,

She was wearing a blue-tinted veil with silver spangles, like the one Hypatia had been accustomed to wear, and her light step was not exempt from a certain majesty. Clear and rapid, her gaze posed on all the faces.

Palladius had hastened toward her. He was almost stammering. He piled cushions on top of one another and made her a sign to take her place.

Telamon was staring at Priscilla, but he remained impassive.

"Palladius," said Isidore of Gaza, leaning over the poet's shoulder and drawing him toward him. "You haven't asked me about my second dream. It has a symbolic and prophetic range, however, which concerns you. Well, you can be less agitated. I've seen you in a closed room. You were holding Priscilla in your arms and you had a bed behind you. And as it's a matter of a dream that I had just before sunrise, its realization is very imminent."

Then Telamon, who had overheard involuntarily, half-closed his wide eyes, and lay down as if he were going to sleep.

Sitting on the deck at sunset the merchant Ibas was covered with sweat.

He was the captain of his own ship and he only had six crewmen. The sea had been rough in the vicinity of the isle of Seriphos and he had hardly slept. In the morning, within sight of the rocks of Aegina, the wind had dropped and it had been necessary to row. For several hours Ibas had rowed ardently, but now a favorable breeze was blowing and driving the ship, with all sails hoisted, toward the port of Corinth.

The sweat that bathed his forehead was caused by a greater effort than the one that he had required to avoid the reefs or ply the oar forcefully. He was holding Plato's *Symposium* in his hand and striving, for the hundredth time, to decipher its mysterious meaning.

Alas, he did not understand the ancient Greek in which the book was written very well. There were scholarly words in it that he had never pronounced. But even when the words were comprehensible, the thought escaped him. He sensed it close to him, marvelous, invisible and winged, but he strove to pursue in vain.

H got up. He smiled in a melancholy fashion at a hope that was drawing away. His resolution was made. He had just made one last attempt, which had failed. The die was cast. He gave up. He would never understand philosophy. He was renouncing many other things more precious than the works of Plato. Since he was only a poor limited merchant, that was what he would remain. Perhaps he would become even more limited.

He took the thick scrolls of papyrus and, with all this might, threw them into the sea. There was not even a fleck of foam when they disappeared.

Then Ibas considered his garments, and found himself extremely ridiculous. An hour before, when he had distinguished the patch of white stone that the Acropolis of Corinth made on the horizon, he had changed his trousers and his chiton of coarse cloth for a dalmatic with grandiose embroidery representing a fabulous mythical bird. He had thought himself very handsome in that dalmatic, and had marched with pride through the streets of Alexandria because of it, but now the dalmatic weighed upon him, inconveniencing him. The fabulous bird was sinking its golden claws into his breast. Then too, he divined the contained laughter of one of his mariners, who was considering him, creasing his eyes. The mariner was a brute whose judgment he would have scorned the day bore. Since the books of Plato had disappeared into the sea, the brute had resumed his importance, with a hidden gaiety.

He ran to the low cabin that he had between the decks. He took off the dalmatic. He took clothes out of a chest. He picked up a patched tunic, but dropped it. No, that was still too fine. He put on one that was uglier. He resembled the slave of a grape-merchant rather than a merchant himself. That is because one descends again far more rapidly than one had climbed.

The sun was about to disappear when the ship moored in the harbor. The humble captain ordered the crew not to go far; they were going to depart again shortly.

Rapidly, he traversed the yards where triremes were under construction and he quays encumbered by ivory from Libya, leather from Cyrene, incense from Syria and carpets from Carthage, and hastened toward the road to Cenchreae, where the house was that he had bought for Priscilla after the flight from Constantinople.

Priscilla had never been as beautiful as she was that evening.

All the shades of blue from sapphire blue to the pale blue of the early morning sky were mingled in her garments and harmonized with the milky oval of her face. Her hair, once tinted blonde in accordance with the custom of Byzantine prostitutes, had resumed its natural color and made an ardent black mass under a fine golden network.

She was walking along the only path in the minuscule garden that surrounded her house, respiring an acacia branch, in the perfume of which she was trying to recover a memory.

Ibas appeared before her abruptly.

She could not retain an exclamation of surprise.

He was not longer the slightly vain, taciturn and good merchant who had once me to visit her in Spartacus' house and how had saved her life one morning with so much joy; he was no longer the faithful companion who had respected her sudden intoxication with chastity, whom she had made to share her love of study; he was no longer the silent confidant, the friend concerned for her happiness.

He was a servant, a poor servant—not even that, a slave.

He fixed his eyes on the ground. "I've just got back from Alexandria. I did everything you asked. Your father Diodorus believed you to be dead. He forgives you and would like to see you before dying."

And he fell silent.

He hardly said anything more. He only responded briefly to Priscilla's questions.

Oh, yes, certainly, he had seen it, his palace overlooking the sea, he had seen the slaves, the marble staircase, the onyx colonnades, and he had been shown the ships in the port four times as large as his, and the formidable cargoes that belonged to Diodorus, Priscilla's father!

What he had been told was nothing. It is necessary to see such things!

And he, who had been so proud of his boat, his six crewmen and the extent of his transactions!

The sight of omnipotent wealth, the face of a true master sitting in the depths of his palace had rendered Ibas a sense of reality. He had been abruptly returned to his place as a former peasant to whom a petty commerce had given a petty ease. In passing through Diodorus' great portal his forehead had been curbed toward the earth, and had not risen again since. For a man born on the stony hills of Zante, where there is nothing but sun and vine ceps, a man emerged directly from the rude earth, cannot march with impunity into rooms where there are precious mosaics and rare Oriental carpets, crimson magnificence and the sumptuousness of mirrors, without retaining an imperishable dazzlement.

Iban no longer had anything to say to the heir to the age-old fortune of Diodorus, except to ask her whether she had any orders to give him. He was leaving Corinth. He would not come back. He would go, as before, from Zante to Constantinople and from Constantinople to Zante. He would not complain about that. To each his life. And above all, no more philosophy! He had never been able to understand it. Minerva had not granted his prayers. He was returning to Jesus.

In vain, Priscilla tried to retain him.

They walked for a long time in the falling night. They perceived, in the end, that they had arrived without suspecting it in the vicinity of Palladius' villa, where Priscilla was awaited.

She was late. They would be astonished by her absence. It was necessary to part. It was Ibas who said that first, and Priscilla acquiesced immediately.

A bright light emerged through the open portico. In the garden, lamps were hanging in the trees, and by their light, the branches gave the impression of being cut out in pieces of jade. Under the torches of the terrace, white robes could be seen that were agitating, the profiles of philosophers with prominent temples, sculpted by intelligence.

And when Priscilla bid him adieu and drew way under her veil, like a fragment of blue sky, the peasant from Zante remained in the shadow, motionless, for a long time, gazing at that forbidden universe into which the woman who had been the beauty of his life had just disappeared.

"They'll all tell you that you resemble her," said Palladius, in a voice that passion rendered tremulous, as he inclined his curly head over Priscilla's shoulder, "but you're more beautiful than her! In your gaze there's a love of life that she didn't possess. Your voice has a warmth that never animated the marble of her words."

Palladius and Priscilla were walking along a path that bordered the sea. The sky, moonless but streaming with stars, illuminated the garden dimly. Behind the curtain of sculpted spindle trees the voices of philosophers were audible, debating, mingled with the distant voices of boatmen and the songs of belated passers-by.

Sometimes Priscilla turned round abruptly as if to see whether someone was following them, but every time she saw nothing behind them but the whiteness of the deserted path, like a young woman asleep under a tunic of gilded sand.

"I've always been more loved than I have loved myself," Palladius went on, "And I didn't know what it was to suffer from amour. But since I've seen you, that has changed. I'd like to take you away to a land where no one will know the syllables of your name and where I alone will have the right to look at you."

"You say that because you're able to forget," Priscilla replied, smiling. "Forgetfulness is easy for some, difficult for others. I wish I were like you."

"To what are you alluding?" stopping and plunging his eyes into those of Priscilla, who did not turn away.

"Haven't you loved already, more than you love me?"

"Who?"

"Hypatia, perhaps?"

Palladius' face altered, shrank, becoming gray for a moment. A surge of anger had invaded him. He recovered his self-control and uttered a little bitter laugh, repeating, scornfully: "Hypatia!"

Priscilla contained her amazement. "Why deny it? I know it. You loved her more than me." And there was a hint of melancholy in her voice.

Palladius protested with all his might. He had never experienced before what he felt for her. His life had no other goal henceforth but her amour.

While walking they had almost made a tour of the garden and they had returned to the extremity of the terrace. They perceived the silhouette of Telamon, who was gazing at the sea.

Then Priscilla leaned on the balustrade and remained motionless, as if she were lost in a reverie.

"Why are you looking at Telamon like that?" said Palladius.

"He's younger than you. Perhaps he's never loved..."

"So what?" said Palladius, gritting his teeth in fury.

"So nothing. But I have one regret."

"What?"

"You loved Hypatia. I would have liked to encounter you before you loved her. Now, it's too late,"

Palladius exploded. He had never loved Hypatia. Perhaps he had desired her, at first, but he had ended up hating her. Her virtue had been exaggerated. Her genius had been exaggerated. Love Hypatia! Him! He had demonstrated clearly that there was nothing of the sort.

"Oh, if you could prove to me that what you're saying is true....," murmured Priscilla, staring at a point in the sky.

Palladius lowered his voice. "I could have tried to save her, and I didn't."

He stopped.

"Explain," said Priscilla, softly her eyes still lost in space.

"Yes, the morning of her death, a monk came to warn me what was in preparation. I've often reflected since that it was already too late. I didn't have the time to gather the students of the Museum and arm them. By jumping into a chariot I might have been able to arrive in time to stop her going out. But she had irritated me. I've always noticed, in any case, that misfortune overtakes those I don't like. I've sometimes regretted my inaction. At other times I've thought that great pride is always punished and that the death of Hypatia, in its unjust form, was inevitable. No matter! I only love those who love me. Hypatia loved Telamon."

Priscilla's gaze quit the sky to contemplate the face of Palladius.

Either because of the memory he had evoked, or because of his physical desire for Priscilla, Palladius appeared to be enveloped by a material aureole of baseness. His eyelids were fluttering; his lips, protruding slightly, were thicker, and allowed the sight of his gleaming teeth. He had the air of a lustful sheep that has the jaws of a wolf in order to bite.

Then Priscilla made a large movement full of spontaneity. She placed her hand on Palladius' arm. He shuddered.

"I'm not promising you anything, but perhaps..."

She stopped. He was agog with attention.

"You know my house on the road to Cenchreae?"

He nodded his head.

"There's a narrow window that overlooks the road. To-morrow, at the sixth hour of the night, come to stick your ear to the shutter. I'll tell you then through the crack in the cedar-wood what I dare not tell you now..."

Palladius put out his arm to embrace her. He saw more in that rendezvous than the promise of a word.

"Be careful," said Priscilla, "Telamon, over there, is watching us. He loved Hypatia, you say. He might be jealous."

"Oh, I hope so! I can't imagine a greater joy. He must desire you because you're beautiful, and perhaps he's told you so. I'd give my entire fortune for him to suffer because of me."

And Palladius made another movement to clasp Priscilla's body against him.

But she slipped away, lightly.

And she came back into the light of the torches, her eye-lids half-closed, with an expression in which there was not the slightest trace of emotion.

Women! thought Palladius. *They're all the same!*

"Look," said Proclus, vaguely indicating the shadow that was opposite the terrace. "The man descending with his lantern has just disappeared. Even so, a star is casting a little white gleam on the fronton of the temple of Venus."

"You ask me," Proclus relied to Priscilla, "why the goddess Nemesis is always represented with a crown of narcissi. Nemesis isn't vengeance. Nemesis isn't justice. She's a law of cause and effect. The evil that one accomplishes inevitably engenders a similar evil, which strikes you. But when one receives the punishment of a sin, one had always forgotten the sin. The narcissi, whose perfume has a narcotic effect, symbolize that forgetfulness."

"But why? Why?" said Priscilla, avidly. "That law is unjust. The person who is being punished ought to know why."

"The law appears unjust because our vision of things is restricted. It's only from a certain height that one can perceive the equilibrium of the world. Then again, humans couldn't have the merit of making progress if they knew with rigorous exactitude that Nemesis would render every parcel of good and every parcel of evil that they have done. But when and in what manner that retribution will occur, neither the Chaldean priests nor those of Egypt informed the initiates of their mysteries. The law is so great in its effects that it isn't susceptible to measurement."

"Oh, the goddess Nemesis is too slow! When it's a matter of certain crimes, don't you think that one ought to strive with all one's might to hasten the punishment?"

"The crown of narcissi has two meanings," said Proclus then. "The man who is guilty forgets his fault. The one who wants to punish ought to forget too."

The following day, toward the fifth hour of the night, surrounded by perfumes and sparkling with jewels, Palladius emerged from his villa and headed for the road to Cenchreae.

At that moment, in Priscilla's bedroom, the bronze lamp suspended from the wall began to burn lower. As if she had been woken up by the shadow, Priscilla raised her heavy head, which was resting on Telamon's breast and showed him a bottle placed on a small shelf.

He got up, took the bottle and poured its contents into the lamp, whose flame revived. Then he resumed his place by Priscilla's side on the narrow bed of sculpted olive-wood.

"It's with the eyes that one sees ones happiness," he said. "The lines of the human body contain the greatest sum of beauty that there is in the world. It has never been given to me to contemplate such perfection in the form of a woman. I need to see you in order to be certain that you're really here and that I'm not dreaming."

And having enlaced Priscilla with a gesture simultaneously voluptuous and indolent, he pressed his lips to hers for a long time.

Her hair had spread over her shoulders. She sensed a heaviness in her eyelids and a lassitude in her loins. All of her flesh was numbed by abandonment, but her mind was singularly alert. She ran through memories, built edifices of hopes. She only stopped in order to be astonished by what had happened.

Certainly, she was not surprised to be lying in Telamon's arms. It was her who had wanted him to come. She had met him in the public gardens at the bottom of the road to Cenchreae, where the philosophers were accustomed to gather at dusk had had not had any difficulty making him understand, for reciprocal desire has a mute language that is clearer than that of words.

She knew that he would come into her bedroom and that she would be his, but she had not understood that she would be able to belong to him in that fashion.

So many arms had enveloped her, so many caresses had run over her body. She confounded all those pleasures and she had not believed that there could be any more profound. Physical amour had been for her at first the suffering of a martyr, and then the sadness of a task accepted with resignation, and then a quotidian function, neither good nor bad. Now, abruptly, she had discovered that that state of dream, that joyous impulse to offer oneself, that ineffable complaisance of the flesh, which desire gives the senses when it is mingled with the sympathy of the heart.

It was as if she had been lifted up by a warm wave, carried away in the arms that were kneading her. She had wanted to lose herself like a child in a forest, to evaporate like a perfume in the sun.

"Do you remember when you kissed me," she said, "in the garden of the Gymnasium in Alexandria? There were white laurels in bloom and jets of water in onyx basins. How I detested you afterwards! How I love you now!"

The lamp threw off a more vivid light and Priscilla's eyes wandered at random over the tiles of the room, which represented designs of flowers and birds. It seemed to her that the flower-bed in question was animated; sandy paths slid between clumps of spindle trees that had just been watered and she saw brilliant droplets in the foliage, like pearls. A jet of water sprang forth between branches of white laurels and swayed in the middle of the room like an animate individual. Climbing roses on the walls shed their petals around her, raining down on the table encrusted with ivory, on the little lather rug embroidered with silver thread. She was naked and intoxicated in the garden of the Gymnasium of Alexandria. She rediscovered on Telamon's mouth the perfume of honey and acacia that had tortured her with remorse and desire.

In the middle of the room there was a silver tripod supporting a bronze tray, and on the tray an Arab perfume was burning, the smoke of which rose up, swirling, in a blue-tinted spiral.

As she gazed at that smoke, Priscilla thought she could see the glint of a sapphire there, and a confused face, which was that of Hypatia. There was no reproach in that face, no sadness of jealousy. It seemed to be saying:

Be happy with one another. Thought is multiplied by the desire that beings have for one another. Every harmonious sensuality in a useful note in the concert of the earth and is amplified in echoing indefinitely. In the afterlife, where my intelligence lives, our pleasure permits me to communicate with you subtly. Amour is one of the roads that lead to the spirit.

The things that surrounded her seemed to Priscilla more laden with mystery and beauty. Her from was radiant with life. She read its history in its reliefs and in its color. The little leather rugs at the foot of the bed came from so far away! She saw the caravans in which long black files traversed the gray desert to bring them from Gandhara. Elephants had died in forests in order that the oval doorway facing her, leading to the atrium, could be framed in ivory. She could hear the song of the women of Jerusalem reducing the wood of the Sandalis tree to powder and kneading that powder into a cone in order that the one could intoxicate with its blue-tinted smoke. The flame of the bronze lamp that was reddening over the crimson of her bed and over her nudity, would burn endlessly, like the eternal lamps that watches over the tombs of the Emperors of Rome. She felt that she was enveloped by talismans and spells. King Solomon, Hermes and Zoroaster had combined the power of their magic in order that she should be here, on an enchanted bed, against the warm and naked body of this young man, whom she loved.

She had always loved him. She identified him with all the men whose embrace she had felt.

Every time that, for a minute, she had forgotten the horror of life, in Spartacus' brothel, it was because he was pressing against her loins. He had borrowed the face of a puerile mariner from Carthage, that of a cataphract with blue eyes; he had been the Illyrian adolescent who came to see her with a guzla, which he played to charm her. He had never quit her since the evening of the first kiss.

She huddled against him and she told him again that she loved him.

"Don't speak so loudly," said Telamon, smiling. "The goddess Nemesis might hear you and come running. As soon as humans have too great a sum of happiness, she hastens to snatch it way from them."

Then Priscilla remembered. The goddess Nemesis was present. She had summoned her to punish. The sixth hour of the night had passed and on the road, with his ear stuck to the shutter, Palladius must have heard what Telamon had said. The bed was next to the window. The rustle of their skin, the creaking of their bones, must have reached him. Every plaint, and every word, had been like a stone hurled at his vanity. He had just been subjected to an invisible lapidation whose wounds would not heal.

"I thought I heard a human respiration behind the window," Telamon said. "Someone passing on the road must have stopped at the sound of our sighs."

"You're not mistaken," said Priscilla. "Now there's the sound of heavy footsteps drawing away. I won't say any more to you except in a low voice, but I believe that the goddess Nemesis has gone."

Telamon had just thrown his cloak of light silk over his shoulder. He was about to leave. The rising sun was brightening the room with pink. Priscilla had just opened the ivory-framed door opening to the atrium and, with one hand placed on her lover's shoulder, she was breathing in the fresh air.

Telamon hesitated. He looked at her. He seemed to be searching in her bight yes for vanished images.

"Would you love me more," she said, "if I told you about my life since the day when I fled Alexandria?"

And without waiting for his response, gripped by a sudden great need to tell her story, to reveal herself, she drew Telamon into the bedroom, and closed the door again.

"Listen...," she said.

But he shook his head. "No. Later, perhaps. Not now. I don't want to know what you've done, or who you've loved. When I was fifteen, I dreamed of being the lover of a statue of Aphrodite that I had seen in the temple of that goddess in Byblos. I imagined that her marble footfalls were about to resonate on the mosaics of the vestibule and that she would come to lie down in my bed, beside me. I would have liked her lips and her torso only to be animated in order to caress me, and that all her possibilities of amour would be enclosed again afterwards in the mystery of the stone. You're as beautiful as that Aphrodite. A part of my dream has been realized. But I prefer not to know the weaknesses and pleasures of the goddess, and not to know whether many unknown hands have profaned her beauty."

"But what if I were suffering," said Priscilla, "what if I had a secret that weighs upon me, a heavy burden of the soul to set down..."

The expression of Telamon's gaze became more distant. With a slow gesture, he arranged the pleats of his cloak. In an atonal voice he said: "Suffering is the error of those who have understood nature poorly. It's necessary to strive toward joy. I only want to know your beauty."

Priscilla withdrew her bare arm from the ray of sunlight that illuminated it and, as if she had suddenly been gripped by modesty, she hid it under her veil.

"I'll come back this evening," said Telamon then, "but you'll remain the Aphrodite of my dream. Later, only then, you can tell me..."

"Yes, only later," said Priscilla, looking at the sky above Telamon's head. "You're right. Everyone is born for one thing. Your part is beauty, and that's the most beautiful. Mine..."

She stopped. Telamon did not invite her to continue.

"Don't come this evening," she said. "I'm going to leave for Alexandria. My father wants to see me again. You can join me out there, or I'll come back here. At any rate, the statue will be devoid of dolor for you."

She offered him her cold lips.

Telamon drew away.

That evening, in the public gardens at the bottom of the road to Cenchreae, the Alexandrian philosophers, when they met, announced two news items to one another.

The previous night, the poet Palladius had returned to his villa like a madman. He had broken his statues, and trampled his works of art underfoot. He had just embarked for Antioch, without saying adieu to anyone.

At the same time, Priscilla had boarded a ship that set sail for Alexandria.

Antagoras, who was going along the quays at dusk, had seen the two ships leave the harbor at the same time. He reported that Palladius, having perceived Priscilla, had shouted a coarse insult at her from afar, and that she had replied, with a smile on her lips: "It's in order for you to remember Hypatia."

XVIII. The Death of the Convent

The funeral of Diodorus had just taken place, with an extraordinary pomp. No one knew of what he had died. His mind had weakened during the last years of his life and it seemed that it had been extinguished by a lack of will.

It was at his funeral that the Christians of Alexandria whispered to one another, for the first time, the news of the unexpected return of his daughter Priscilla. The disappearance of the young woman a few years before had caused a great fuss. Some had believed her to be dead. According to the most widespread opinion, however, she had satisfied, unknown to everyone, the mysterious demands of her nature and had gone to bury herself in one of the convents of Palestine entirely closed to the world, which were not subject to any religious authority and from which one never emerged once one had passed through the door.

Thanks to his fortune and the protection of Bishop Cyril, Diodorus had had enquiries made in all the communities of women, even those on the shores of the Red Sea, which were the most celebrated for the rigor of their rule. He had not found any trace of his daughter but, at length, in accord with the Bishop, he had allowed the rumor that she was in a convent somewhere to be accredited.

It did not appear extraordinary that she had reappeared in order to be present at the father's last moments. It was said that she had arrived when Diodorus had entered his death throes and that he had hardly recognized her.

She was not seen at the funeral. In any case, the curiosity awakened by her return was eclipsed by another event. Cyril had just returned to Alexandria after an absence of a year. It was at Diodorus' interment that he appeared in public for the first time.

He had been obliged to go to Constantinople to justify his violence against the partisans of Nestorius. He had entered into a conflict with the Patriarch of Constantinople, Nestorius, and the Empire, impassioned by theological questions, had been divided into two camps. There had been fighting in Ephesus, Antioch and Constantinople because Nestorius affirmed that there were two persons in Jesus Christ, while Cyril maintained that there was only one.

The Emperor Theodosius,[38] not knowing which to support, had had Nestorius and Cyril imprisoned, but the Council of Ephesus had decided in favor of Cyril. He had been freed, and put back in possession of the patriarchate of Alexandria. He had returned to his city, triumphant but devoured by hatred against his enemies, desirous of crushing the Nestorian heretics definitively, and especially of causing the death of the former Patriarch of Constantinople, who had fled to Arabia and was hiding in a convent there.

Cyril had aged, and, contrary to what happens to the majority of men, the evil sentiments that possessed him had given rose to an exaggerated corpulence. He was bald, his jowls were jaundiced, and his enormous blue eyes bulged even further from his head, only to express pitiless thoughts. Evil had accumulated in his fat body and seemed to ooze out with the sweat of his brow, which he mopped incessantly.

He was acclaimed by the Christians of Alexandria.

Not one week! Not one day! She did not want to wait. The iron fittings of the tents had rusted? It was necessary to run to Alexandria to replace them. There were no camels available? They would find as many as they wished at the market at the Gate of the Sun. Guards for the journey. They were unnecessary. Armed slaves would suffice. And Priscilla

---

[38] Theodosius II, Eastern Roman Emperor from 408-450, should not be confused with Theodosius I, cited in the early chapters of the novel. The Council of Ephesus, which he summoned to settled the theological dispute between Cyril and Nestorius, was held in 431.

gave the order to Thoutmos to choose them carefully from among those who were not Christians.

Her father's funeral celebrations had not yet concluded when Priscilla already had the authority of a redoubtable master in her house. That authority was exercised first upon Majorin.

The former tutor of Priscilla and Marcus had become a kind of majordomo-in-chief for Diodorus. The weakness of the latter and the incapacity of Marcus had enabled him to acquire the habit of command. A mean and religious spirit, he practiced intolerance toward those whose Christian sentiments appeared to him to be lukewarm. Afflicted by a disease of the liver, he hated everyone who offered an image of health and took pleasure in having the youngest and most vigorous of the slaves whipped under futile pretexts.

That day, the servants occupied in removing the funereal hangings from the staircase saw Majorin emerge from Priscilla's room and run down the stairs, with her in pursuit, whip In hand.

"Sacrilege!" he cried.

He had seen Priscilla snatch from the walls and throw on the floor the statuettes of saints that were in the four corners of the room. He had attempted to oppose it, and had raised his voice, invoking the name of Bishop Cyril.

The air had whistled around his face, and he hastened to flee.

"Throw in the gutter his clothes and all the objects that belong to him," Priscilla said to the slaves.

Then Majorin had made a gesture of supplication.

Cracking her whip, Priscilla added: "Call me if he crosses that threshold again."

Marcus, dazzled by his sister, made no objection to her will and watched with a bewildered gaze the preparations for departure that she was making.

No, she did not want to wait one hour more! In addition to Thoutmos, six vigorous slaves were sufficient to provide an escort.

The cavalcade traversed Alexandria and the quarter of catacombs like a whirlwind and hurtled along the road that ran alongside Lake Mareotis. Priscilla was in the lead, disdaining to look at the landscape, in which she did not want to find reminders of the past.

She saw, however, as if in a dream, the plantations intercut with canals, the hexagonal houses with their varied colors. Late in the night the little caravan arrived at the dilapidated palace of the time of the Ptolemies in which the steward of Diodorus' cotton plantations lived.

They rested there for a few hours.

Priscilla had decided that they would leave again at first light. Thoutmos reminded her that it was there that they had previously loaded the camels with the provisions of vegetables and fruits that were presents for Zenobia's convent.

Priscilla shook her head.

But the wind was blowing with an extreme violence. The herdsmen guarding the livestock on the bare hills that preceded the region of sands had come back to shelter in the villages. A caravan had arrived from the desert the previous evening and the camel-drivers had reported that the simoom was blowing there tempestuously.

All day they traveled through whirlwinds of sand. They traversed immense plains strewn with stones, they passed the place known as the "waterless sea" because the waves of the Nile had unfurled there long ago. It was necessary to stop at every well to refill the water-skins, for the air was so hot that it dried up the water through the leather. White powder blinded the eyes, inflamed the throat and covered the men and camels entirely, which gave the impression of carrying shrouds of a sort and made it a cavalcade of specters.

In the evening the wind eased slightly and they camped in the middle of the sand, in an abode of lions. They were no longer very far from their objective. They departed before sunrise, fearful that the tempest might recommence with the daylight.

Then, as if there was a secret communication between them, the animals and he men were gripped by a malaise, an inexplicable anxiety. It did not come from fear of the elements, for as they advanced the wind seemed to die down, the gusts of hot sand fell back, and an extraordinary calm seemed to spread over the desert. It was an internal apprehension that took possession of souls.

Lions that roared in the distance fell silent and the silence aggravated the anxiety. The light of the sun had not yet appeared, but the sand had recovered a uniformly ruddy hue, the floating dust became ocher and the shadow was a dirty red. The oldest of the slaves, overtaken by weakness, tottered on his camel and began to weep. Another, claiming that he could see menacing forms in the air, uttered cries of terror at times. A discouragement that no one expressed in words showed the progress of the caravan.

Suddenly, Thoutmos, who was in the lead, stopped.

An entire pack of jackals had just fled. The swarming life of those desert scavengers caused everyone to shudder.

There were the bones of a camel mingled with human bones. They were dispersed and mixed up, and some were broken and partly splintered by the teeth of the beasts. Thoutmos recognized by their whiteness that they were not very old.

They set off again. And it was then that the anguishing silence that covered the expanse was troubled by an imperceptible plaint: a quavering, cracked, desperate voice; a frightful appeal, that began to grow and then became a murmur again; the voice of the dead expressing the nameless terror of the beyond.

Priscilla recognized the timbre of the bell that she had heard in the same place in her childhood and she made a sign to her servants to hasten their pace.

A wan, sickly light that preceded the dawn illuminated the bleak stone silhouette of the convent of thirst.

When they arrived at the bottom of the hill, Priscilla ordered one of the slaves to stay there and guard the camels. The others, with Thoutmos, would go up to the convent. Perhaps they would be necessary.

And she commenced climbing the zigzags of the path. But at half way she thought that the slaves would not be necessary and there would not be any violence to employ.

A breath of desolation, a pestilential exhalation of horror, emerged from the door of the convent like a palpable phantom in putrescence, which advanced along the path. The bell was still ringing, and everyone fortified their souls in advance.

When Priscilla, taking a short cut, had reached the wall of the convent and had passed through the door, she found herself in the presence of a terrible and singular spectacle.

A skeleton of tall stature covered with yellow-tinted skin, from the skull of which sprang white hair of an extraordinary vivacity—a feminine and living skeleton covered in vague rags—was agitating the bell-rope frenetically with all her might, with bizarre laughter and dance-like contortions. Several birds were flying around her head, making her a sinister aureole and watching for the first moment of immobility in order to strike with their beaks.

In that demented creature, Priscilla recognized the Syrian Zenobia.

But she did not stop to consider her. Mastering her horror, she only darted a hateful glance at her, and she ran into the courtyard rapidly.

To begin with, she could not distinguish anything in the ruddy auroral twilight but the flapping wings of a great flock of vultures that rose into the air, circling.

Several half-consumed cadavers lay in the sand, outside the cells. The tortured expression of what remained of the faces, and the jutting bones, indicated a death from hunger and thirst after indescribable suffering. One head had taken between its teeth the wood of a door and life must have fled with that illusion of nourishment.

One woman was kneeling, her hands joined, in an attitude of invocation, and her plucked-out eyes attested to the manner in which divine aid had been manifest for her.

Another, prey to madness, had scaled the wall of the enclosure and set herself astride it, and death must have struck her while she was miming a caricature of flight on horseback.

Priscilla divined the drama that had occurred.

In the tempest that had been raging for several days, the nuns charged with going to fetch the provision of water for the week must have died. Doubtless a delivery of food supplies had also been delayed, and the few miserable creatures who had escaped until then the torture of the solitude had succumbed one by one to thirst and hunger.

The birds swooped down again, gliding.

Priscilla took a few steps into the courtyard, and it seemed to her that she heard a faint groan. She saw a woman on the threshold of the chapel, the door of which was open. The woman was lying face down and protecting her face with her arms, which she was holding tightly over her eyes. Priscilla understood that she feared the thrusts of the vultures' beaks, and she made a sign to the slaves to advance and drive them away by agitating their cloaks.

She wondered why that woman had preferred to struggle in the dark against the carnivores, beside her dead and decomposing companions, rather than drag herself inside the chapel and find shelter there by shutting herself in.

Gently, she raised the head of the unfortunate woman, whose plaint trickled like blood from a wound, and leaned over her.

What a fleshless, emaciated, exsanguinated face! It almost had the same mortuary appearance as the madwoman who was ringing the bell. The gaze seemed dead, and did not revive. Only fear sometimes caused a glimmer to be reborn there.

In the gleam of the eyes, however, in what remained of the features, within that vestige of humanity, Priscilla thought that she recognized her mother.

She brought the face close to hers and repeated, several times: "I'm Priscilla! I'm your daughter!"

But that did not seem to evoke anything for her. She stammered, very faintly, a name unknown to Priscilla: "Aurelius!"

And as she was still raising her arms to hide her face, in the dread of the vultures, Priscilla called Thoutmos and they both carried her under the narrow vault of the chapel.

But then, Priscilla's mother, vaguely perceiving the coolness of the stones, was reanimated, sat up, and uttered a frightful clamor of terror. She attempted to flee, to escape the altar and the cross, and, struggling, she pointed at an invisible image by which she thought herself menaced and she repeated: "There he is! The Bishop! Bishop Cyril! Pardon!"

It was necessary to take her back to the threshold of the church. She preferred the odor of cadavers, the presence of death and the devouring vultures to the calm chapel where her ever-terrified soul discovered the evil genius of her life.

And she expired a few minutes later, when the first ray of sunlight posed upon her.

The slaves had taken the bodies of the dead women down to the bottom of the hill in order to bury them.

The birds were high in the sky.

Priscilla darted one last glance at the convent of desolation and death. She looked at the bare cells, the mute chapel, and the walls of that pitiless tomb of ascetics.

And before the Christ devoid of ornamentation she said: "A curse on your religion, which kills happiness, which uproots from exalted souls the love of life, and does not even give in exchange the particle of justice that they have the right to demand. A curse on you, whose worship distances people from the spirit instead of bringing them closer. You wanted the mother to be locked up here in a prison where prayer was futile, and the daughter to be locked up out there in a convent where pleasure was devoid of hope, in order that their bodies should be broken and their souls martyrized by an equal dolor. You have engendered nothing but self-destructive revolt. Be-

311

cause of you I am animated by an inexorable thought of vengeance that will not perish with my life."

The sun now illuminated the hill and the horizon of sand with a taint of ardent flame.

Zenobia the Syrian was still hanging on to the bell-rope, and Thoutmos had tried in vain to extract it from her hands.

"Should we take her away by force?" he asked Priscilla.

She laughed bitterly.

She approached the fanatical guardian who had invented that tortuous way of life and had made other women share it with her against their will. For if there had been mystics who had come to suffer and die there of their own free will, there had also been weak creatures whom she had maintained in that Hell by her authority and her religious fury.

And her mother was one of them. Priscilla would have like to slap her, to fight a duel with her. She gazed at the skeleton agitated by convulsions without experiencing any pity.

"Leave her," she said to Thoutmos. "Let her die where she wanted to live."

The caravan had not gone far along the trail that led toward Alexandria when the sound of the bell quavered and was interrupted, and then rang out again, more cracked, and then expired.

The little troop emerged from the shadow projected by the hill of stone, and only then did the camels raise their heads again and the men breathe more easily; and as if a malevolent influence had dissipated, anguish ceased to oppress their souls.

XIX. The Severed Hand

It was no longer a secret for anyone that the cobbler Theonas possessed a desiccated hand, one of Hypatia's, which he had cut off himself in front of the Church of Caesarea after the stoning of the philosopher.

At first, fearing reprisals, he had only shown it to his friends, but now he drew vanity publicly from that possession. He had hung it up on a nail in his shop and he showed off his knife with pride, saying: "It was with this tool. I only had to slash once. The hand came away and I cut it."

He also explained, obligingly, the method by which he had dried it in order to conserve it, and he pointed with one of his fingers at a slight circular depression, which was the trace of a ring. He had sometimes prided himself on having that ring in his possession.

Theonas was a colossus with a dense brain. He scarcely left his shop in Rhacotis where he worked leather and wove sandals of palm-fiber. He slept on a meager bed at the back and a nauseating odor of tanned hides and human dirtiness escaped into the street.

He fell ill. He had eaten corrupted meat. He had fits of vertigo and vomiting. It was the first time in his life that he had been afflicted in the strength of his body. He did not get out of bed. He allowed himself to fall into the dejection that the fear of death causes.

Three whores from a small brothel next door to his shop came to care for him. They took turns to bring him tisanes, and when night fell, they lit a lamp beside his bed. They did not love him, but in exchange for their bodies they sometimes obtained brodequins with straps.

The one with whom he had gone most frequently was a Nabataean named Sara. It was her who penetrated into his shop on the evening of the third day of his illness, lit the lamp and placed next to the bed the cakes made from flour and hon-

313

ey that the proprietress of the house next door had prepared for him.

He thanked her with an unaccustomed mildness and he drew from the horrible sheets on which he was lying a small object wrapped in a greasy cloth. It was a ring with a blue stone of an extraordinary purity. He showed it to Sara and he said: "One day, I'll give you this jewel if you care for me and if you love me."

It was that same evening that Bishop Cyril decided to go and see Theonas.

The death of Hypatia had caused a surge if indignation throughout Christianity. Cyril had had a great deal of difficulty disculpating himself and distancing himself from the horror of that crime. It had been necessary for him to buy the testimony of Count Candidianus,[39] charged by the Emperor to carry out an investigation. He did not want any further mention of Hypatia. He had been informed by several sources that a cobbler was glorying in having in his shop a desiccated hand that was that of the philosopher. It was a subject of scandal to which it was necessary to put an end. Times had changed. Such memories could only throw discredit upon his triumph. It was appropriate to give a sepulcher to that accusing hand.

He had the Parabalanus Paulin accompany him, who knew where the cobbler lived, and he set off on foot for Rhacotis.

"It appears that he's an obstinate brute, said Paulin, on the way, "and the presence of the Patriarch himself might not be sufficient."

The back street into which they had just penetrated was sordid. They bumped by turns into piles of rubbish or women crouched in doorways muttering obscene invitations as they passed. Sometimes, luminous liquid fell from a window. The night was dark and the two men were almost feeling their way.

---

[39] Several documents refer to Nestorius being placed in the custody of this individual prior to the Council of Ephesus, but nothing more seems to be known about him.

"I think this is it," said Paulin, indicating a door that stood ajar. "Theonas!" he shouted.

There was no response. Then he pushed the door and stood aside before Cyril.

The latter took a step forward, but remained immobile, struck by the offensive odor of leather and dirty linen, with which a strangely insipid and repulsive perfume was mingled. His eyes adapted to the demi-obscurity and he uttered a fearful exclamation.

Above a small wooden table bearing the cobbler's tools, Cyril saw a hand attached to a nail by a piece of lambskin. But it was not the hand he had imagined. This one was a large, hairy hand of a man, with square fingers and blackened fingernails—a hand freshly severed, for a drop of blood sometimes dripped from it and fell on to the table. Cyril perceived with horror the minuscule sound of that regular drip.

At the back, on the bed, the cobbler was lying. As if it were as heavy as lead, his head made a profound depression in the bed, into which it was plunged. His left arm was dangling, frightfully mutilated. It had been sectioned at the wrist and a flood of blood had escaped from it, soiling the wooden floor of the room. That arm must have been twisted and broken by a brutal grip, for it was swinging slowly, like something deprived of all resistance, inert and limp.

Cyril approached and saw that the cobbler Theonas was dead.

He understood immediately that he was in the presence of a belated vengeance of the death of Hypatia. He saw the danger that there was for him and the church if that affair were resuscitated by a scandal. It was necessary to reflect. He made an imperious sign to Paulin to close the door.

It was too late.

There was a woman on the threshold. She uttered exclamations and raised her arms to the heavens, repeating: "I knew it! He's been murdered!"

Cyril seized her by the arm and dragged her inside. He intimated an order to explain to him in a low voice what she knew.

She knew everything. She had warned Theonas personally several times. The dead sometimes come back. She knew many examples of those returns. Theonas was not a very bad man, but he was devoid of judgment and prudence. Three days ago, the malady had weakened his mind. He had been well cared for. She had made pastries herself with his intention. And yet life was hard, one was heaped with taxes. Men broke glasses, even broke stools while fighting with one another. She had three women in her house, but they were scarcely beautiful and were only desired by mariners and camel-drivers. Theonas sometimes gave footwear, but never money. It was known, however, that he possessed a valuable jewel hidden somewhere in his mattress. He had shown it to her sometimes.

Because of that it might be claimed that thieves had murdered him; but no, it wasn't thieves. Why would they have cut off his hand? Thieves kill and flee, and don't hang a severed hand on a wall. Anyway, she had seen. She was on her doorstep, as usual, to appeal to passers-by and indicate the price of the women—a very modest price! She had seen two shadows gliding past. But one of them was a woman and she believed that she had recognized her...

She had recognized Hypatia.

The two shadows had gone into the cobbler's shop. She had wanted to listen, but she had not dared. She knew that it was Hypatia, who was coming to reclaim her hand. She had told Theonas many a time that it would happen. He laughed. Now, he was dead. There had been cries. He must have tried to avoid giving back the ring. He hadn't struggled. He was so weak! The two shadows had departed without haste. The dead woman marched ahead. The second shadow, that of a man, gave the impression of being the slave of the first. Can the dead have slaves?

"Were there other people than you who knew that Theonas was ill?" asked Cyril.

316

"Certainly. Neighbors, the three women in my house, especially the Nabataean Sara, who brought him my cakes.

"No one would be astonished, then," said Cyril, "if they learned that Theonas had died tonight of his illness?"

"No one except me."

Cyril uttered a sigh of satisfaction. The affair could be stifled. He would buy this woman's silence. The commander of the night watch was a good Christian who was devoted to him, and by whom he could have the cobbler's body carried away as if he had been afflicted with a contagious disease.

The first thing to do was to go with the woman to the centurion of the quarter and to inform the commander of the watch.

A vengeance, he said to himself, on the way. But whose? Perhaps simply thieves. And he repeated, in order to convince himself: *The dead don't come back.*

XX. In the Shade of the Bodhi Tree

Accompanied by his master Nanda, Aurelius had quit the Buddhist community of Palibothra and had started walking, clad in the yellow robe of pilgrims, toward the confluence of the rivers Niladjan and Mohara, to reach the place where, in the shade of broad-leaved mahouas, among sansar and bir bushes, the Buddha had discovered the truth.

They had both traversed the village of Senani, which looked like a cluster of thatched huts surrounded by a crown of palm trees and they had climbed a small ridge. An immense forest commenced there.

Indicating a marvelous tree, taller and bushier that the others, Nanda said to his companion: "That is the Bodhi Tree under which, a little before daybreak in the one hundred and third year of the Eatzana era, on the day of the full moon of Katsou, the Buddha sat down, cross-legged, and where he found within his spirit the divine science by means of which humans can escape the wheel of eternal reincarnations. The foliage of that tree will never fade again. The water of the stream that flows past it is charged with aromatic juices that give those who drink from it a facility of ecstasy, and the air that circulates over this hill is impregnated with wisdom."

Nanda and Aurelius slaked their thirst in the aromatic stream, put down their staffs, sat down cross-legged under the branches of the Bodhi Tree, and looked into themselves.

Snakes slid among the starry flowers of white and gold Champaks; gazelles approached and considered them fearlessly; butterflies and hummingbirds fluttered around them, and the sun went down.

Evening came.

Then Nanda emerged from his meditation and touched Aurelius on the shoulder.

"Has calm returned to you now?" he asked.

Aurelius shook his head sadly, indicating that it had not.

"Since I've arrived in this sacred place," he said, "contrary to my expectation, I've been more anxious and more troubled, and my thoughts wander with more ardor among the things of the past. It seems to me that I'm held by a powerful chain, which a human creature, who is linked to me without knowing it, is pulling from afar."

Nanda stood up, picked up dry leaves and a few branches of dead wood, took his briquette from his pouch and lit a small fire. Thick smoke rose up from it. Then he started to chant a kind of invocation. Afterwards, he extended his hand, placed his thumb between Aurelius' eyes, and said: "Look!"

In the white spirals of smoke that were rising before him, Aurelius saw, with a gripping reality, without being able to discern whether what he was seeing was close at hand or distant, a miserable room with a bed. On that bed, two nearly naked human forms were lying. One of them was that of a stout man who was sleeping heavily, and whom he did not know. The other, slightly raised on one elbow, was that of Priscilla. He saw her straighten up further. She leaned over the man, her face full of passion, hesitated, and suddenly, with a great sweep of her hand, armed with a dagger, she traversed the man's throat, which she pinned to the wood of the bed.

The cloud of smoke became the color of blood, and Aurelius uttered a cry of horror.

At the same instant, another image appeared. It represented a white cell whose door had an opening in the form of a cross. In that cell, a woman was sitting who was gazing obstinately at the ground. Her face was ravaged, furrowed by wrinkles. Her hair was sparse and white. She was not praying. She had no expectation. Her lips murmured a name: "Aurelius!"

And she gazed obstinately at the ground.

Then Aurelius hid his head in his hands. Then he got up, and he stood in front of Nanda, who said to him: "We are chained to life, and we multiply our chains by our actions and by our thoughts. You loved a woman, and you created by that love a Karma of which you will receive the good and evil retribution. A child has been born of you and the actions that

319

child accomplishes are indirectly yours, and if she sheds blood, you will pay the price of it in your future lives. The search for wisdom is not sufficient reason to flee the consequences of what you have done, and there is a manner of aiding those one loves that takes you further along the perfect path than the wisdom of the most sage. In any case, that wisdom is the jewel hidden in the heart of the lotus, to which a man can only pretend when all debts are paid, all duties accomplished, all amours purified."

"It is still very far away from me," said Aurelius, sadly.

"Perhaps. But perhaps you'll discover soon that you carry it within you without suspecting it. The seed that requires an entire winter to germinate under the earth sometimes only requires an hour to enable its stem to appear in the sunlight, on certain spring mornings. Go, return to the country from which you came. Since the evening when I encountered you, naked and exhausted, on the bank of the River Ganges, and when I took you to the convent of Palibothra, I have taught you the fruit of transmitted knowledge, the illusion by which we are enveloped, the seven human bodies, Tanha, the force of desire that drives us to be reborn in new lives, inexorable Karma, the four noble virtues the practice of which leads men to nirvana, the end of change and perfect repose. You have slept in the cell where Apollonius slept and you have just meditated in the place where the Buddha meditated. But your mind has always been tormented, dragged down, and when you receive the highest teaching you demand material proofs, not knowing that the higher a truth is, the less, perhaps, it can be verified by the senses."

"That's true," said Aurelius. "I have had the dream of seeing the wise men who direct humanity, those with whom Apollonius conversed. You've told me that they quit Palibothra a long time ago in order to go beyond those high mountains, which seem to close the earth, into the Gobi desert which surrounds the subterranean city of Shambala with its uncrossable sands. You've told me that one of them sometimes returns to Palibothra and that you have conversed with him. I hoped ardently to kneel before him, to kiss his robe, to collect an immortal robe—in vain. Often, I've woken up at night in my cell, to listen, in case the light tread of an ascetic is brushing the stone of the corridor. But no, the convent of Palibothra has not received the marvelous visit."

"How do you know?" said Nanda. "All eyes do not see, all ears do not hear. You will end up seeing and hearing, but only when there is no longer an image or a sound on the earth that makes you tremble."

"Shambala in the Gobi desert is much further away from the Egypt where I might perhaps succeed than Palibothra. Do you think, all the same, that one day...?" asked Aurelius.

"Distance does not exist for them. When the time comes, they will be beside you."

Nanda had risen to his feet. He drew Aurelius away from the shade of the Bodhi Tree. They went down the hill. Night had almost fallen. After the last thatched huts of the village of Senani there were two roads that intersected.

"It's here that we're going to separate," said Nanda, "but for a mendicant monk, the journey is too long and too dangerous. Take this."

He handed Aurelius a small bag that he took out of his pouch, and which was full of gold coins.

"The sharaff of the next town will change these ancient coins into current money. It is via Taxila, the city where King Asoka lives, that you must reach the Indus and descend as far as Caumara, on the edge of the sea. There, ships belonging to the Jewish colonies depart frequently for the Red Sea, with cargoes of spices, aromatics and ivory. Embark on one of them and you'll shorten your voyage to Yanavapura, which you call Alexandria, by at least a year."

He hugged Aurelius in his arms and strove not to let any emotion resulting from that separation show.

"Amity also chains us to the wheel," he said then, so softly that Aurelius was not sure that he had heard him.

Several times, when they had parted, Aurelius looked back to see the stooped silhouette of the old sage decreasing in the shadow.

But the old sage did not look back.

XXI. The Chain of the Dead

Thoutmos preceded Priscilla long a narrow street in the Necropolis quarter. The heat was overwhelming, in spite of the darkness that had fallen, and an odor of putrescence rose from the ground.

"It was almost at the same hour when we passed this way on the day of your grandfather's death," said the old slave. "That was many years ago! Do you remember it?"

Did she remember it! She had often relived in thought the hours spent in the home of the embalmer, had often heard in her memory a low whispering voice that did not express itself by means of lips and which had said: "Priscilla it's you, Priscilla!"

She had never forgotten Sebek, the embalmer with the triangular beard, and his wife Khepra, the Rhacotis prostitute who had stared at her with moist glaucous eyes and had placed a little stone between her breasts while she slept, the contact of which had burned her.

At the moment when he was about to push a wooden barrier giving access to a patch of waste ground strewn with rubbish, Thoutmos stopped.

"She makes a beverage with male hemp and palm wine," he said. "Often, she drinks too much of it. Don't be astonished if she says extravagant things. She always remains lucid with regard to what you want."

They traversed the waste ground and Thoutmos knocked on the door of a low house.

A shrill voice shouted: "Who's there?"

The judas grille allowed a glimpse of glaucous eyes, and the door opened immediately.

Priscilla did not recognize the woman who was standing before her. Khepra had aged extraordinarily, and most of all grown fat. Her face, furrowed with wrinkles, was enveloped by unhealthy yellow fat from which the eyes emerged, secret-

323

ing an impure water. With her bushy red hair, her fleshy lips, her breasts sagging over an enormous belly, and legs that seemed frail, she gave the impression of a tragic beast, whom desire had bloated and rendered similar to a wineskin.

Behind her, the colored bottles, the sachets full of perfume, the tongs, the knives the minuscule tools that served for embalming, and the aligned golden masks with enamel eyes, added by their enigmatic assembly to the strangeness of her form.

It was for pleasure that Khepra had practiced prostitution in Rhacotis all her life, for the embalming gave Sebek a certain ease. Now, she could no longer find men, even for nothing. So she went to prowl the cemeteries by night, where she ended up coupling with some thief or runaway slave.

On perceiving Priscilla she uttered a savage cry of admiration.

Thoutmos had no need to provide an explanation. Yes, it was the little princess who had slept there once! How she had grown! How beautiful she was!

And suddenly, she guffawed. She sat down, shaken by enormous laughter.

Khem! The god Khem! He must have thrown her on her back! There had been no lack of men! That was why she had become beautiful!

Priscilla looked at her uncomprehendingly.

"You don't remember the little stone Priapus that I put between your breasts. He never misses its goal. You must have received pleasure and you must have rendered it, and done it over and over again. Ha ha!

And she continued laughing.

But Thoutmos intervened. It was a matter of something else. She could ask for any sum of money she wanted. The figure was unlimited provided that the secret was kept.

"I understand," said Khepra, exultantly. "It's a matter of amour. You did well to come to find me. I have roots from Ethiopia, Arab mandrakes and the famous blue hellebores from the land of Serica. If there's a man who has refused you,

you'll have him in your bed whenever you want. I'll even make him swoon so often against you that he'll die of exhaustion. I exercise influences by means of perfumes, ointments, potions, poisons, light, strings that are made to vibrate and mirrors on which one spits. I'm at your orders, little princess of amour!" And with a sudden alteration in her features and a hoarser tone in her voice, she added: "Me, I'm just an old and worn-out carcass, which no one wants whatever I do."

Priscilla shook her head and made a sign to Thoutmos to indicate that she wanted to remain alone with old Khepra.

"Death is easier to transmit than amour," said Khepra, when they were alone. "Speak, Whose do you want?"

No, it was not that, yet. Death was perhaps a great good. It was to favor a man who had been evil to deliver him from life.

"I want him to suffer as much as the suffering he has caused," Priscilla murmured, her eyes fixed.

"I can do anything, thanks to them. They will aid us with their strength." Khepra pointed to the low door at the back, framed by canopic jars covered in hieroglyphs.

"Who?"

"You're lucky," Khepra went on. "The embalmed are numerous at the moment. Men want to live the life of their double, miserable as it might be. There are even Christians! Come and see—the room is full. I'll make them work for you."

And Khepra drew Priscilla into the next room.

She was struck by the same sensation of sad and stifling perfumes and occult life that she had experienced before. Here was a tremulous little oil lamp. To the right, the more recent dead were lying in stone sarcophagi and bathing in natron water. Those on the left has passed the forty days prescribed and were wrapped in bandages, covered in gold leaf, or already bore the mask with enamel eyes that was to be their face during eternity.

And all of them, invisible, were there.

325

"Have you any object belonging to the one you want to make suffer?" asked Khepra.

Priscilla had heard mention of these magical practices, which the recent emperors had punished with so much severity and had been the pretext for cruel persecutions. Just in case, she had taken from her brother's room a little sachet containing a fragment of the mantle of Saint Athanasius that Bishop Cyril had worn round his neck for a long time, and had given to Marcus at the moment of his father's death.

She handed it to Khepra.

"I can distinguish a miter, a priestly costume, bulging eyes and a beard... It's the Patriarch!"

She picked up a piece of black wood that had a vaguely human outline and, with five nails in the form of a cross, she nailed the relic to the simulacrum of the head.

"Don't move," she said to Priscilla, "and concentrate your life on this piece of wood. With the rhythm of the seven syllables that penetrate into the Amenti and command the invisible forms, I'm going to create the chain of the dead that will draw the man you hate in spite of himself and will make him penetrate this emblem by force."

Rapidly, she had set fire to blocks of charcoal on a little tripod and she poured a red powder over them that spread a suffocating odor.

"It's the same perfume that makes the doubles live next to mummies," she said.

Priscilla was about to ask what "concentrating her life" meant, but the witch began circling the piece of wood to which the sachet was nailed and cried: "See! It's necessary to see!"

Than Priscilla pictured the image of Cyril forcefully, and concentrated her mind upon it.

From Khepra's throat a bizarre modulation emerged, a series of sounds that did not form words and sometimes resembled a prayer and sometimes an imperious summons. Her huge belly agitated on her little legs, she threw her arms in the air, her wrinkled face took on an ecstatic expression, and she gave the impression of a caricature of a drunken frog.

From time to time she shouted to Priscilla: "Look hard!" and she spun more rapidly. Sweat trickled from her brow.

That went on for a long time. In the end, Khepra let herself fall on the ground. Her body was agitated by convulsive tremors. Her face had a terrible expression.

"He's entered into the chain of the dead. He's resisting, but it's necessary. The dead have taken him. Now he's there. You can do whatever you wish to him."

She took several deep breaths, with difficulty. Then she wrapped the piece of black wood in a rag and handed it to Priscilla.

"There are people on whom one can't cast a spell, but very few. Those who are pure! Cyril isn't one of those. And also those who are strong. He's that even less. You can make him suffer as much as you want. You only have to pass the piece of wood over gold or ivory and put a mirror beside it. Then imagine what you want the man to experience and look, not at the piece of wood, but its image reflected in the mirror. You won't have to make a great deal of effort. He's caught in the chain of the dead. The others will come running. If you knew how rapidly the dead communicate with one another! And there are few of them who forgive!"

Priscilla hid the object under her robe. She went out of the room of the sarcophagi. She summoned Thoutmos.

Khepra was tottering. She seemed very weary. In her slack yellow cheeks there were two wrinkles more profound, more sorrowful.

On the threshold, Priscilla took off one of her rings and handed it to her.

Khepra hesitated. A flame passed through her eyes. She considered the ring, whose diamond flashed.

"You're not afraid?" she said.

"Of what?"

"There is in that ring a little of the fluid of your life, just as the sachet I pierced with nails contained Cyril's."

Priscilla had come to consult Khepra at hazard. She only half-believed in the power of magic. Nevertheless, she regretted her imprudence, but it was too late.

Suddenly, Khepra became furious.

"Perhaps you think I love you," she said, in a low and hoarse voice, "because you're young and can have all the men you like. Well, you can do your utmost, but you'll never have as many as me. I don't want your ring. It will force me to torture you one day. In any case, you'll grow old too. You'll have a fat belly, a sagging chin and you'll go to the cemetery to wallow on the tombstones among the beggars who stink of sweat."

She threw the diamond on the ground and shut the door behind her.

XXII. At the Doors of the Tombs

Socles was about to attain his goal. It was the final wall that he was attacking. He put down his pickax and sat down beside his lamp.

For years he had been struggling in the dark to reach Alexander's tomb. Everything had taken a long time. Menalchos had obstinately refused to sell his house. It had been necessary to wait for him to die and engage in interminable negotiations with his son in order to buy it, in exchange for a large sum of money.

Then a subterranean life had commenced for Socles. Not wanting to confide his secret to anyone, he had resolved to accomplish by himself, all alone, the task he had set himself.

But he had run into unexpected difficulties. He had indeed found in Menalchos' cellars a corridor that connected them to an ancient aqueduct, disaffected for centuries. But, either by virtue of the effects of time or because of the earthquake that had ravaged Bruchium, roof-falls had been produced in the aqueduct and had obstructed it. Socles had undertaken the exhausting task of fraying a path through the middle of the rubble and following the aqueduct to the place that was parallel to Cleopatra's Mausoleum.

He had just reached that point. He had already attacked the large blocks linked by dense cement with his pickax. He knew that Cleopatra's Mausoleum communicated with the tomb of Alexander. His dream was about to be realized.

But that dream no longer had the same marvelous attraction that it had once had. For a long time, Socles had given no further thought to the papyrus that Alexander, the initiate of action, had received from his brothers in the temple of Ammon, in which human wisdom was written. The subterranean struggle against the collapses and the stone blocks of the ancient walls had become the true objective.

He was no longer the same man. His muscles had developed; his chest had expanded; a long thick beard had sprung from his face. He ate abundantly the nourishment prepared very day by two faithful servants, he drank a great deal of wine, and when he stopped working, physical fatigue enabled him to fall into a dreamless sleep.

He had difficulty resuming his old philosophical speculations. His brain became less active as his body was more so. He scarcely thought any longer. He dug, he carried stones, he filled in foundations, and he shored up the vaults behind him with pine logs in order not to be buried. He shifted the earth joyfully, but he had acquired a certain repulsion for shifting ideas.

And gradually, in the darkness in which he lived perpetually, a secret amour for the sun was born in him. A new ideal had come to him, of which he was not yet conscious. In the heavy air charged with unhealthy exhalations, he dreamed of the pure light of the sky and, while gazing at the melancholy star of his lamp, he imagined the clarity of true stars.

Now, he was sure of having reached the region of the royal tombs. The wall of the aqueduct no longer rendered the same full sound when it was struck. But he was surprised not to be in any hurry to finish, no joy in realizing a project meditated for so long.

The sole desire that he experienced was to puncture the wall with great blows of the pickax, to make use of the new strength that he had in his body. But whether it was here or elsewhere was of scant importance! What he wanted was to make a breach in some wall or other, to transform matter by making the blows of his powerful arm fall upon it.

He got up and took up his pickax.

He thought about the convicts who were sent to the mines in Numidia and who, once they had entered a mine, never emerged again. Was he not like them?

And why was he there, in sum? To reach a papyrus scroll hung around the neck of a mummy. Another few hours of effort and he would probably have broken through the wall, traversed the tombs, and be standing before Alexander's coffin.

He thought that it might be the middle of the day.

Then he saw, clearly, one of those the vast farmhouses, with its flat blue-panted roof, and the immense spray of a palm tree outside the door, unusual in its regularity, which expanded and spread a broad shadow. He saw the transparency of the water of canals coming from Lake Mareotis, the narcissi and the violets that grew on the banks, the slender boats on which people traversed them, the fields of barley and rice alternating with fields of clover. It was the time when the lemon-trees were heavy with lemons, when the acacia and the henna were in flower, when the dates fell, when the carobs formed blood-stains. He was gripped by an immeasurable desire to see the color of things, to contemplate the light of the sun.

He owned large plantations, vast fields of all sorts, and this labor, from which he could derive bodily joy, he could do in the light. Why not admit it to himself? He had found happiness in his ardent labor. He would continue, but up above, beside the water, among the plants, in the midst of what was beautiful and alive.

He would not see Alexander's glass coffin. The papyrus on which the great verity of the world was written was not worth an hour of darkness.

He picked up his lamp. He marched along the aqueduct. He was tranquil and joyful. He knew what he ought to do. He would sow, he would labor, and he would carry large baskets of oranges on his back. He would still lift up stones, in order to build a house, but in the sun! In the sun!

He had found the truth.

On the far side of the royal tombs, in the crypt of Saint Mark's Church, Bishop Cyril was standing in front of the door that Peter had once closed behind him, and which no one had opened since.

At the time when the church was closed to the faithful he had dismissed the caretaker and had descended alone by the stone stairway behind the altar with a torch and an iron implement for opening the door.

He had decided to verify the confidences that Peter had made to him when he had left Alexandria precipitately in order to flee reprisals after the death of Hypatia. Since then, the struggle against the pagans, the heretics and the Jews had absorbed his life. Councils had summoned him to distant places. It had been necessary to appear personally in all the greatest cites of the empire in order to combat Nestorius. Then the Emperor had imprisoned him in Constantinople. But now he was victorious, he was triumphant. His religious authority was greater than before. He was the master of Alexandria. He was about to be able to satisfy the passion by which he was dominated, the love of riches.

And as he raised his lighted torch in the crypt, he suddenly stood still. He had felt a hand pulling him gently by the sleeve.

It was almost nothing. He looked. There was no one there.

"Come this way. Come with me," whispered a voice in his ear.

And he thought he saw, for a second, the transparent form of an old man to whom he had given extreme unction a few days before and who belonged to an ancient Egyptian family. He had had occasion to think about him several times because he had been informed by his police that after his death, his son, although a pious Christian in appearance, had secretly transported him to the Necropolis quarter in order for him to be embalmed there.

It's an illusion, he thought.

But he felt dizzy and he leaned against the wall.

"I'm being devoured by the natron water. I no longer have my brain or my eyes," said another victim, very softly. "Come, come!"

And Cyril perceived around him other light, desolate forms, which were passing through the walls and were pushing him, and lifting him up.

He had the sensation that he was transported into another place unknown to him, where he saw with clarity a strange caricature of a woman who was dancing among aligned sarcophagi. A detestable face was staring at him. It was that of Priscilla, the daughter of his friend Diodorus.

She had refused to see him a few days before. He knew from the steward Majorin that she had profaned images of the saints, that she had lost the faith, that she was avowed to evil. He intended to have her imprisoned soon, under an accusation of sacrilege.

Priscilla's face was immediately effaced, and Cyril passed a trembling hand over his brow. He thought he had divined what was happening. He was the victim of some diabolical practice organized by that Priscilla. It was necessary to defeat it. But he felt singularly weak. He had difficulty gathering his ideas. He would visit the royal tombs another day.

Slowly, he went back up the stairway of the crypt, traversed the church, and extinguished the torch.

He had he sensation that something had happened to him, but he did not know what it was. He started walking toward the Serapeum. The street of the Sema was full of people. He pulled the hood of his monk's robe over his eyes in order not to be recognized.

Sometimes, he stopped. He sensed that he was in danger. He murmured to himself: "Magical practices! The pagans have always had terrible secrets in their possession! It's not in vain that Valens and Valentinian pursued so rigorously the execrable ceremonies and he infernal rites to which they devoted themselves. Death can be sent from afar!"

He remembered certain inexplicable deaths. He frightened himself. And suddenly, he was struck by an idea. The nightmare was about to disappear.

"Adamantius! Adamantius has studied all these questions. Only Adamantius can deliver me from this."

Adamantius was a celebrated Jewish physician. At the moment when his forty thousand coreligionists had been expelled, he had been the only one to accept baptism in order to escape the expulsion, and Cyril had protected that unique renegade, whose great medical science had rendered him illustrious.[40]

The Bishop felt better when he had reached the Serapeum. He had scarcely opened the door than he shouted to the first servant he perceived: "Adamantius! Go fetch Adamantius immediately!"

And in her closed room, where there was no longer any sacred image on the walls, Priscilla had placed the piece of black wood in human form, bewitched by Khepra, on a gold plate.

She took a bronze mirror and wiped it carefully, in order that it would be as pure as her will.

Then articulating each syllable forcefully, because thought takes its impetus from sound, she said: "Let him suffer as he has made others suffer!

"Let the demons in which he believes terrify him!

"Let him see the evil he has done and let remorse devour his heart in this existence as well as after death!"

---

[40] The historical Adamantius, who was indeed a physician known for an early work on physiognomy and a few surviving fragments of other texts, actually left Alexandria during the expulsion and went to Constantinople; it was there that he was persuaded to embrace Christianity, although he did return to Alexandria thereafter.

XXIII. Distance Does Not Exist For Them

Oh, quicker still! The wind was not inflating the triangular sails strongly enough, the oars were striking the water too slowly!

Sitting on the deck, Aurelius gazed at the banks of coral, the sandy creeks bordered by red reefs of the Arabic coast, and in front of him, the horizon of the sea, where the two white columns ought to appear that stood at the entrance to the port of Arsinoe.

His journey had lasted even longer than he had expected. He had had great difficulties in making his way through Nepal and the land of the Seven Rivers. Among the monks of Palibothra he had learned the Sanskrit language in order to converse with them about matters of science and philosophy, but that language was no longer spoken by the Brahmins in the cities he had traversed, so he had had great deal of trouble reaching Taxila. There he had fallen ill. A Buddhist priest had taken him in and cared for him in a small pagoda in the pariahs' quarter. Scarcely had he recovered than he had set forth again, descending the Indus to reach the sea.

He had contemplated things so extraordinary that now he was sitting among men expressing themselves in the Greek language he wondered whether he had not dreamed them.

From the height of a ridge, in a gigantic valley open at his feet, he had seen by the light of the rising sun hundreds of motionless elephants raising their trunks toward the sky, as if to address a mute invocation to the dawn.

Once, he had penetrated into a forest whose trees were as straight as pillars and so tall that they seemed to rise all the way to the sky. The trunks of those trees, the soil from which they emerged, and the foliage that formed their distant vault, were a despairingly uniform red. Overwhelmed by the sentiment of his smallness, Aurelius had had a desire to lie down and await death. Then a white deer had advanced with majesty, had stared at him with its moist eyes and had passed on. And his courage had returned.

Another time, he had seen an immense city surge forth in the middle of the jungle. He had walked over the paving stones of its avenues, past palaces bordered by pilasters and temples with jade cupolas, and descended staircases that led to series of superimposed basins in which, in increasingly blue waters, lotus flowers abounded. But no human being inhabited that city, doubtless abandoned as a result of some religious malediction, for there was no trace of pillage or conflagration there. The open doors allowed the sight of beds of repose in teak wood, and tables made with sheets of ivory and bearing the story of Rama engraved in Sanskrit characters.

The statues of the gods were in the temples, and in one palace, more splendid in its architecture than the others, Aurelius had seen a golden throne surrounded by other, less elevated thrones, as if for the assembly of a king and his councilors. But a monkey with a tuft on its head was sitting on the throne, another was playing with a scepter of sculpted bronze, a symbol of royal power, and others were suspended by the tail from the arms of an immense stone Brahma. Tree branches had sprouted in the enameled faiences of the walls, lianas had invaded the porches, climbed around the balustrades and overburdened the monolithic columns at the crossroads, on which royal edicts were traced. Crocodiles were basking in the sun alongside the basins. Snakes were glistening on the marbles.

And Aurelius had continued on his way.

After a great deal of time and difficulty, and after going astray frequently, he had reached Caumara. But there was no longer a single foreigner in that city. The Jewish trading posts that Nanda had mentioned no longer existed; there was no commerce with the Occident.

Fortunately, a ship coming from Taprobane and carrying a cargo of ivory was obliged, after a tempest, to put in to Caumara in order to renew its supplies of food and water. It belonged to Greeks who had established a trading post at Arsinoe and carried out a considerable commerce via the Red

Sea with the cities of India, those of Taprobane and even those of Serica.

Aurelius had embarked on that ship, and now he was waiting anxiously for the moment when he would set foot once again on Egyptian soil.

He had changed. He resembled an old man. His eyes sparkled. A breath of sanctity was disengaged from his person. Although he did not wear a cross on his breast and did not murmur prayers of any sort, the Christian sailors on the ship solicited his blessing and kissed the hem of his torn robe respectfully.

But he sounded the horizon anxiously. When would this interminable voyage end? When would he finally be able to meet his daughter Priscilla?

Every day, every hour was developing the force of evil in her. He knew that by virtue of the image that Nanda had caused to appear to his eyes. She had devoted herself to a task of vengeance, and every action that she accomplished to punish someone would strike her in her turn, either in this life or another.

It was necessary to reach her, to explain to her the immutable law, which is modified neither by prayer, nor by remorse, nor the desire for justice. It was necessary to tell her that evil engenders evil, that the suffering caused to someone gives rise to suffering that they cause, and that that was determined, unchangeable and inexorable, like the figures in a book of accounts. Evil is perpetuated endlessly in the same proportion, until the moment when the will of a good and clear-sighted human being intervenes, which breaks the chain with a deliberate thought. The desire for vengeance was the most solid bond attaching the spirit to matter and thus condemning it to successive incarnations, in order that it can receive once again the dolor it has caused. The goal of the universe, which was the liberation of the spirit, could only be attained by the knowledge of the Law.

Finally, the white columns of Arsinoe appeared on the horizon. The ship penetrated into the port.

The captain and several ivory merchants who had spent many hours listening to Aurelius' stories and had developed an amity for him, insisted that he ought to come and rest for a few days in their house before going on to Alexandria.

He refused. He took his leave of his companions. He did not want to lose an hour. He set out in quest of a boat to descend Ptolemy's canal.

He perceived then that the gold coins that Nanda had given him were exhausted, and that what remained was not sufficient for him to reach Alexandria either via the Nile and the Canopic branch or by buying a camel and joining a caravan.

He went to the trapezites of the port. They all knew his name and that of Mucius, the Alexandrian trapezite who was managing his fortune, but in the presence of the ascetic with the shining eyes and the wretched clothes, none of them was prepared to believe that they were dealing with Aurelius, the rich Alexandrian who had departed on a voyage a long time ago.

Aurelius feared being imprisoned as an impostor and thought that it was better to go to Heliopolis, where he could have himself recognized by several of his old friends who lived in that city.

The boatman to whom he addressed himself displayed amazement when he learned the objective of the voyage. Aurelius was obliged to give him everything he possessed in order to persuade him. It was also necessary to agree that they would not go as far as the city but that the journey would conclude when they perceived the high walls in the distance.

Scarcely had the boat set off than Aurelius experienced the afflictions of the illness that had struck him in Taxila. He was cold in spite of the stifling heat. The waters of the canal seemed to rise up in front of him and he was precipitated as if from the top of a waterfall. He felt exhausted. He remained speechless and ate almost nothing during the several days that the descent of Ptolemy's canal, and that of the Pelusiac branch of the Nile, lasted.

Night had fallen when the rowers stopped abruptly. A series of fires was perceptible in the distance that succeeded one another and formed a circle. On a hill, a somber mass dotted with lights had to be Heliopolis.

Aurelius questioned the owner of the boat about the road he had to follow to reach one of the city's gates and the significance of the fires visible in the distance. Only then did he learn in what accursed place he had arrived.

A large number of the Jews expelled from Alexandria had come to swell a Jewish community installed alongside Heliopolis and had formed a city there. Thanks to the tolerance of the Prefect Orestes, the Alexandrian Jews had obtained the reopening of a temple once constructed by Onias, on the model of the one in Jerusalem, which had been closed for a long time by imperial order. Scarcely had that temple been reopened, however, than the plague had become manifest in the new Jewish city. It had made terrible ravages.

Many of the Jews had loaded their possessions on to donkeys and camels and had fled along the roads. But the epistratege of Nome, attributing the origin of the disease to the detestable Jewish blood and wanting to prevent contagion, had sent legionaries to surround the Jewish city and to kill any inhabitants who attempted to get out of that circle of death. They only attempted it by night, so the legionaries built great fires, and patrols of cavaliers traveled the intervals incessantly.

The high city, the ancient Heliopolis, where the Christians lived, was closed as if for a siege. There were watchers on the towers and guards at the gates, who launched stones and arrows at any stranger who approached it.

The boat that had bought Aurelius disappeared into the darkness, and the latter started waking painfully along a road leading north, leaving behind the two cities of Heliopolis inexorably closed by terror, contagion and death.

He only stopped when he could no longer see the legionaries' fires when he turned round. He was exhausted by fatigue. He looked for a place to sleep. Near the road he perceived sections of the walls of a destroyed and abandoned house. He went there to look for a shelter. He passed under a porch that was still standing, walked over paving stones where grass had grown and lay down, using a stone for a pillow.

But he could not sleep. He was tormented by too great an anxiety. He told himself that Alexandria was still a long way off and that his strength might perhaps betray him before he arrived here.

Fatigue and fever excited his mind. He recalled Nanda's words: "Distance does not exist for them."

He sat up and formulated an ardent prayer: *Wise men, lights of the spirit, doubtless you can read my thoughts and you have witnessed my ordeals from the depths of the Gobi desert where you live. I believe in you, I have searched for you, I have loved you. If I commenced in error, I have striven afterwards toward the truth. Bring me the aid of which I have need, for in the extreme misery where I am, an evil greater than the others has just descended upon me. I doubt your existence, I doubt the wisdom that I learned in India, and I am wondering whether the goal that I am pursuing is not a worthless chimera. Give me a visible sign, give me real evidence. If only for a second, appear, in order to console someone who has appealed to you so often.*

Aurelius heard groans around him and opened his eyes wide in order to see by the faint light of the stars whether an unexpected apparition was about to surge forth.

And he perceived a low voice nearby, which said to him: "Are you there, my son?"

"I'm here," he replied.

"Are you suffering?" said the voice.

"I have suffered, but I'm no longer suffering at present," he replied again, and he felt a profound joy animating him.

And the voice spoke again, in a tone of delight. "Perhaps God wishes you to escape! May he be praised! Would you like to recite aloud the Schemoneh Esrei, for your brothers and sisters?"

Hen Aurelius, on hearing those incomprehensible words, remained mute with astonishment. Someone dragged himself over the ground, there was the frisson that hands make running over a face, and a loud cry resounded, "My son is dead!"

Groans responded to that cry, and human forms agitated round Aurelius.

"But if my son is dead, who has just responded to me?"

Aurelius understood that a Jewish family afflicted by the plague, who had doubtless been able to escape the surveillance of the legionaries had, like him, taken refuge in the ruins. He was more upset by disappointment than by horror.

He had stood up. He was surrounded by a group of specters. Confusedly, he made out heads covered with black scabs and breasts bared because of the buboes that had burst forth under the armpits.

So, it was with that frightful vision that his great hope of communicating mentally with the wise directors of humankind had concluded! He had a desire to hug one of the plague victims in order to be struck by death immediately.

"A curse on you who have come to turn our misfortune to derision," proclaimed the one who appeared to be the oldest among the specters, "and may that curse fall upon your children!"

Aurelius ran toward the porch of the ruin, went through it and started running along the road.

For days he went on as if in a dream. He was scarcely conscious of the places he passed through. He was so detached from things that the proximity of Alexandria did not cause him any joy.

Night had fallen a long time ago when he passed alongside the marshes of Shedia.

If he had turned right and walked for a few moments, he would have perceived the roof of reeds under which his friend Olympios was leading the life of an anchorite. Perhaps he was in the process, by virtue of the force of his meditation, of rising into the air, as he said he often did when he was alone. Perhaps he had died a long time ago. Aurelius would have liked to know, but it was much further that he had to go.

The sycamores made a slight sound of foliage over his head. Now he was going alongside Lake Mareotis. The stars were sparkling over the waters.

Oh, faster still!

When a whiteness rendered the azure of the sky paler and announced the dawn, Aurelius went past his house at a rapid pace.

Scarcely a glance at the locked door, scarcely a glance to observe that there were no longer any white roses above the wall!

It was the hour when the gates of Alexandria were opened. A few market gardeners leading donkeys were already advancing along the road. Aurelius stumbled several times and nearly fell. Beside him, someone advised him to sit down and rest a while. A woman in a great striped burnoose like those Arabs wore shouted from the back of the camel on which she was crouched: "Can't you see that he's drunk?"

Faster still! He was going very slowly. The Gate of the Sun, which he had thought closed, was much further away than it appeared. He finally arrived there.

But he no longer recognized the city. The houses had a foreign, hostile aspect. They were tightly grouped together as if to block his way. The Canopic Way unfurled infinitely and on the two sides the colonnades of monuments had the effect on him of two corteges of white monks who were about to extend their arms and immobilize him by the power of prayer.

He sensed his strength diminishing. He was weaker than a child. If he had fallen, he would not have got up again. Priscilla's house was at the other end of the city. He wondered whether he ought to take the quays of the port of Magnus and go as far as the port of Kibotos or follow the Canopic Way, in which he was already engaged.

And now, with marvelous precision, and in extraordinary detail, he saw once again memories of childhood that he had forgotten completely. There was a series of unexpected, absurd, exact images that unfurled rapidly, and which he could not avoid.

342

Do not those who are about to die have similar reminiscences? he thought.

He went passed churches, obelisks and the perspectives of rows of sphinxes. He leaned on the truncated pylons of the temple of Isis. He caused doves to fly away amid the laurels of the temple of Poseidon.

He hesitated after the street of the Sema and as a porter came to open a door he said to him, in a voice as light as a breath: "I'm going to see Priscilla, the daughter of Diodorus. Indicate her house to me."

The porter made a gesture, pointing at a street.

Aurelius had never imagined that she might be married, or have left Alexandria. The porter's gesture confirmed his certainty. He was about to see her, to bring her the message.

He was about to see her, if he did not die beforehand.

A deserted street illuminated by the first rays of the rising sun and an immense cedar-wood door, as high, as closed and as impenetrable as the one that separates imperfect humans from the abode of pure spirits...

One last effort to go along the street, one last effort, and he reaches the door.

He touches the thick wood, and considers it, but from below, for he is now lying on the pavement of the street.

How to open it? There is a means, but he no longer has a clear idea of what it is. He searches, He cannot remember. He makes desperate efforts.

Priscilla is very close. He only has one movement to make and the door that separates him from her will open. What is the necessary gesture?

And time passes and death comes, for it is a very long time since he has eaten, or slept, and a heavy shadow is beginning to invade his brain.

Suddenly there is a light. He remembers! It is necessary to lift the bronze knocker, let it fall back, and slaves will come running, and the immense door will open as if by enchantment. He will be in Priscilla's presence.

Where is that bronze knocker?

Aurelius raises his head and perceives it, very far away and very high, at an infinite distance. He cannot make an effort sufficient to reach it. In vain he raises himself up and extends his arm.

With the extremity of his trembling fingers he touches the bronze, but that is all. He falls back.

He will not try again. He starts to laugh bitterly. A determined injustice has followed him in his voyage, and is going to make him perish at the exact moment that he has reached his goal, after so much difficulty!

It is too much! No good intelligence rules the world.

He closes his eyes, denies his faith, and aspires to enter into an annihilation of darkness.

Then he heard a voice, which said: "Are you there, my son?"

And in spite of himself, he responded: "I'm here!"

And he opened his eyelids slightly.

But he closed them again immediately. It was the trap of hope. No, no, he did not want to see the plague-ridden old Jew with his pustules and his open buboes. He sensed around him the specters he had already glimpsed near Heliopolis. They had followed him. Let them go away! May they let him die in peace!

"Are you suffering?" said the voice.

And in spite of himself, he replied: "I have suffered, but I'm no longer suffering at present."

And the voice said again, as it had out there: "Perhaps God will permit you to escape."

But it had a graver, more profound tone than the voice that had resonated in the ruined house.

Escape to what? To the obscurity of the mind, to the desiccation of the heart, to the absence of love, to what had been evil for him?

What did it matter to him now to attain the blissful peace of the sage, to achieve his salvation, as the Christians put it, if he left his daughter prey to hatred, if he could not bequeath to her his heritage of truth?

He opened his eyes wide. The sun was radiant with a resplendent light, such as he had never seen before.

"Distance does not exist for them."

They had come. They were around him. He saw on their noble features and expression of serene goodness. Aurelius believed that he recognized them. One resembled Pythagoras. The one who was short and completely bald must be Apollonius. The one who was dressed like the Jews of Jerusalem and wore his beard in three points must be Jesus, and in the tallest, the one who had the yellow robe of Hindu monks and a complexion he color of clay he rediscovered the features of the Iarchas whom Nanda had often described to him.[41]

To him, humble messenger that he was, the law of Retribution had not given the hour of strength he still needed to complete his task. Perhaps he had not merited it. But the law was mysterious and the message would arrive anyway.

He was quite tranquil now. It was not worth the trouble of lifting the bronze knocker. The cedar-wood door could remain closed, and inside the dwelling, the slaves could stay asleep. Priscilla would awake up to listen to the voice of the divine masters.

Aurelius saw, distinctly, the master who resembled Apollonius of Tyana make him a sign that signified: *Come!* and with an inconceivable lightness he launched himself forth to join him.

He was dead.

---

[41] In Philostratus' *Life of Apollonius of Tyana*, Iarchas is the leader of the sages who receive Apollonius in India. History has no other trace of any such individual.

XXIV. Bishop Cyril's Last Night

In his large armchair, before the table on which the pages of his *Anathematism* lay,[42] Bishop Cyril straightened up.

In order not to think, he had started to write and had doubtless let himself fall asleep while writing. He opened his eyes wide in order to examine an extraordinary spectacle. His perception was amplified. A story that had been told to him and to which he had not added credence took on the proportions of an exact reality before him.

In a landscape of rocks and sandy hills a few hundred men were gathered. He recognized them by their robes, their bonnets and their curled hair. They were Jews. The setting sun inflamed their energetic and tenacious faces. They were praying. In spite of the extent of the desert around them, however, they were strangely huddled together.

At the center of their group was a large coffer at the extremities of which Cyril distinguished two solid gold cherubim. In front of the coffer was an immense candelabrum with seven branches, and behind it, a motionless young man was lifting a golden lamp so luminous that Cyril thought that it must be the sacred lamp that, according to Solomon, cast more light than the morning star.

An old man of short stature, his body slightly inclined to the right, had a book in his hands and was reading prayers that everyone around him was repeating.

So the accursed race had not been vanquished! They had departed with their treasures, which he, Cyril, had not been able to steal; they had carried them away like the symbols of their insatiable, rebellious, indestructible soul.

---

[42] Cyril's prolific writings do not appear to include a book actually entitled *Anathematism*, but one of his diatribes against Nestorius includes a section knows as the twelve anathemas, and they are sometimes individually cited as "the first/second/third anathematism," etc.

If those few hundred Jews were huddled together, shoulder to shoulder, it was because they supposed themselves to be enclosed within the walls of an invisible Temple, which their minds had built. Tracked by simooms and ferocious beasts, uncertain of the morrow, they were nevertheless accomplishing, around the holy Ark that they had saved, the age-old rites prescribed by their law.

Before that fanaticism, equal to his own, Cyril, understanding for the first time the vivacious force of his enemy, and felt weary and discouraged.

Immediately, however, another image appeared to his eyes just as clearly.

In the shadow of the great red ramparts of Heliopolis, he saw the Jewish city constructed on the terrain once ceded to Onias, the tragedy of which had recently been recounted to him.

A poor city, whose inhabitants had been obliged to struggle from the first day against despair and hunger! The land that had been put into cultivation was not sufficiently vast to nourish so many people and it would take time for commerce to become prosperous.

Cyril contemplated that mute city in which the plague, it was said, had emerged from the temple that the prefect Orestes had imprudently allowed to be reopened.

In a white and empty street he saw a man walking. He recognized him. He was the former ethnarch of Alexandria, thinned by anguish and privations. He was carrying a long staff on his shoulder at the extremity of which, attached to it by a hook, was a jar, at the bottom of which there was a broth of barley and rice. Having arrived at a house whose door and all of the windows but one were nailed shut by large beams in the form of a cross, he shouted a name. At the only window that was not condemned, a livid face appeared, marbled by black patches. The ethnarch held out to the plague victim the wretched nourishment at the end of his pole, intimating an instruction to close the window quickly, for the wind transported the germs of the disease with the exhalations of the sick.

Cyril saw men planting stakes at the extremity of certain streets. The plague was in all the houses of those streets and the inhabitants there were condemned to the contagion after having known the terror of the contagion, more terrible than the disease itself.

At the entrance to those streets, the ethnarch, increasingly thin and defeated, brought the broth of barley and rice. But he no longer made use of a pole. He set down the jar with his own hands, for the danger, in becoming more menacing, had only developed his courage, his pity and his scorn for death. And men twisted their hands, others begged, and others were praying, on the thresholds of those closed and accursed streets.

And Cyril saw other terrible images unfurling before his eyes.

A cart, preceded by a man holding a torch, traveled through the city by night and collected the cadavers, which were then thrown into a profound ditch that had been hollowed out to receive them. But the ditch had been filled rapidly, and only an insufficient layer of earth had been thrown on top of the corpses that were overflowing it. That overfull ditch, from which hands and heads emerged, was a nucleus of pestilence, but no one dared any longer to approach it in order to complete the burial, with the exception of one wretched demented woman who ran around it repeatedly, and whose frightful screams could be heard for several days.

His gaze was transported then to the marketplace, in front of the temple. Men who had not felt any visible affliction of the disease but who were being eaten away by it internally without being aware of it were abruptly stricken.

He saw one of them who suddenly tore his robe in two, considered his naked breast, and then fell to his knees crying: "Get away from me! I have the disease! May the Lord protect me!"

And a great circle opened up around him.

He saw another who was running hither and yon, weeping and saying: "Kill me! I'm suffering too much!"

Then a crowd gathered in the temple and outside it, on the steps of the threshold. It was the day of penitence and expiatory prayers. The ceremony of Rosh Hashanah was being celebrated. Every Jew advanced toward the Temple holding a candle fabricated with seven wicks, in which his sins were supposedly enlaced, in order that they would burn with the flame. On that day, God, seated on his throne, in the presence of Satan the denunciator, judged each man and determined is fate.

But his decision was known in advance, for at the extremities of the city the weapons of the legionaries could be seen glinting, and the plague was everywhere, in all the streets, and in all the houses.

"Be blessed, Adonai, who has chosen us among all peoples!" chanted the Jews, with a single voice, raising their candles.

But when the moment came for the assembly to repeat seven times the forty-seventh psalm: "People, clap your hands! Rejoice!" the Jewish people measured the derision of those words, their hearts broke and there was no longer anything but an immense sob rising toward the God that had abandoned his own in order to condemn them to an unspeakable misery.

And Cyril then saw the eyes of the pale and courageous ethnarch fixed on him with a heart-rending expression of reproach. All the dolorous and sobbing faces turned in his direction, and all the Jews of the plague-ridden city looked at him. There were not only those assembled before the temple, there were those wandering in the sealed streets, those who were agonizing in the houses with their buboes and pustules, and also the dead, who were lifting themselves out of the full ditch to stare at him.

Cyril took his head in his hands. He heard a slight sound behind him. He turned round. The door of his room opened. Pale and sad, the ethnarch was standing before him.

349

Cyril did not reflect on the impossibility of that advent. His knees buckled. He fell, his arms outstretched in front of him to protect himself.

It was the physician Adamantius who picked him up.

He apologized profusely for arriving so late. He had not been at home and had come as soon as he had acquired cognizance of Cyril's message. He was at the Bishop's orders.

But his obsequious politeness died away and dried up as Cyril explained his trouble, recounted the strangeness of his visions, their reality before his eyes, and how he thought he had seen the ethnarch when he, Adamantius, had appeared at his door.

His gaze lit up, his face took on a grave expression, and he stared at the Bishop for a long time, as if he had been in front of the temple himself, holding a candle with seven woven wicks and intoning the forty-seventh psalm: "People, clap your hands! Rejoice!"

He savored all the irony there was in the fact that it was him, the renegade, the only one of the forty thousand who had accepted baptism, who was a witness to the punishment of the execrable persecutor of the Jewish people.

He was a man of great science, who had put himself above religions by the absence of faith, but who remained forcefully attached to the race he had betrayed. He had difficulty not allowing a terrible joy to burst forth.

Cyril's words indicated that his mind was completely unhinged. He could speak to him as to a child.

"No, these visions are not pure imagination. They are a reality transmitted by hostile thoughts. A physician is powerless for that."

"But after all," moaned Cyril, "I'm not the cause of that frightful epidemic. Was it not on the very day of the reopening of the Temple that the epidemic became manifest, by virtue of an ancient malediction? It's the Epistratege of Memphis, not me, who is responsible for the measures taken to prevent the disease from spreading."

"What was the first cause of the evil?" Adamantius asked, gravely, as if he were searching his memories. Then, after a pause, he went on: "Who ordered the expulsion of the Jews from Alexandria? That was you."

"That was me," Cyril replied.

"Who sent secret orders to the Bishop of Heliopolis for him to oppose any commerce between Christians and Jews when the latter were building their city? That was you."

Cyril lowered his head.

"It was you who thus aggravated their misery, who provoked famine among them, who rendered them too debilitated to struggle against the epidemic. It's your hatred that is the cause of everything."

His voice had become grim.

Cyril looked at him fearfully.

"And besides," Adamantius went on, "have you heard that there were plagues in Egypt before this one? How was the scourge born? This year, the Nile flood has been higher than usual; it reached many cemeteries in the region of Heliopolis and has disturbed them. From the putrescence of cadavers exposed to the light, the germs of the plague were born. That is happening for the first time, because once, the wise priests who directed this land had the dead embalmed in order to protect the living from the dangers of their decomposition. How long have people been punished for obeying the salutary law of embalming? Who is the fanatical Patriarch who has obliged the living to be poisoned by the putrescence of the dead? It's you. It's your religion that is the cause of everything."

As he spoke, Adamantius measured the terror that he was creating and the faculty of reaction that Cyril might still have. He must have judged it negligible, for he took him by the collar of his robe, shook him, and said to him in a pitiless tone full of delight:

"There is no remedy: none. You are destined to die in frightful torments. You ought to wish with all your might that there is nothing beyond life, for if there is a Hell, you will suffer there eternally."

Cyril fell back into his armchair, and Adamantius hastened to disappear.

On the morning of that same day, Cyril had listened with satisfaction to the story of the frightful death of Nestorius, transmitted by desert nomads and brought by a monk.[43]

In Syria, to which he had fled, Nestorius had been sent to the great oasis that was the most rigorous place of exile. The extreme solitude had caused him to fall into a state of melancholy dejection. One evening he had marched straight ahead and had gone to sit down beside a marsh where savage beasts drank. On the first two nights, the lions had roared close by and had come to sniff him without attacking him, but on the third evening, pastors had seen one of them seize the motionless head of the enemy Patriarch between its teeth and lacerate him with its claws.

Cyril saw his enemy Nestorius distinctly, sitting beside his table, making the gesture of stirring sand with his hand and looking at him with is bright eyes. He had a triumphant expression and he said: "There are two persons in Jesus Christ."

Another voice immediately resonated.

"It's Apollinaris who is right. The body of Jesus Christ is not consubstantial with ours."

Cyril saw the Archimandrite Eutyches,[44] who had been condemned by a synod in Constantinople. He was tranquil, full of faith, sure of his verity.

---

[43] The historical Nestorius is thought to have died in or after 450, surviving Cyril by at least six years, but exactly when and how is unknown; that uncertainty might license the advancement of the event and the melodramatic imagination of its manner by the present narrative—in which, in any case, the rumor reported to Cyril might have no truth in it. Cyril's death also appears to have been brought forward from the generally-accepted date of 444, but that too is speculative.

[44] Eutyches (c380-c456), the superior of monastery near Constantinople, played a leading role in the Council of Ephesus in

Immediately, other voices resonated, and Cyril perceived that he was surrounded by the heretics against whom he had fought throughout his life.

They were all there, some in monastic robes, others in the white mantles of philosophers, raising pastoral crosiers or theurgical staffs, all affirming their religious idea, obstinate illuminates ready to die for the point of dogma that had been the passion of their existence.

Cyril recognized the false prophet Elci who had lived under Trajan.[45] He was brandishing the book that an angel had put into his own hands, and he said: "Jesus Christ has come to earth many times before. I knew him personally in four former lives."

He recognized the monk Eustathius, condemned in Paphlagonia, whose sanctity was so great that no pleasure and no sensual excess could tarnish it, with the consequence that he devoted himself to all of them with impunity.

He recognized Pelasgius by the fur that he had over his shoulders, because he was always cold. Shivering, he said:

431, where his vehement denunciation of Nestorianism became so extreme as to provoke his own condemnation as a heretic.

[45] This obscure individual seems to have been introduced to French readers by a curious book entitled *Publication d'un ancien manuscrit containing précis curieux des hérésies qui ont le plus alarmé l'Église* [Publication of an Ancient Manuscript Containing Brief Summaries of the Heresies that have Most Alarmed the Church], published in 1840, which credits mention of his sect to Origen, with no apparent warrant. The 1840 text credits Elci with the assertion of Christ's repeated appearances since the beginning of time, to which the present text adds various embellishing details. Magre must have used the book as a source because the other bizarre heretics cited, and the traits attributed to them, are mostly featured in its text; some do not appear to be mentioned anywhere else, apparently having been invented by the anonymous author.

"There was no original sin. It was Augustine, the imbecile bishop of Hippo, who invented it."

By her shaven head and her long teeth he recognized Quintilla, the prophetess of the Pepusians to whom Jesus had appeared in Phrygia. She repeated:

"Eve is superior to Adam because it was her who ate the fruit of the tree of knowledge first."

Sabbathius displayed his atrophied left hand with pride. He claimed that men ought to be horrified by it and let it dangle at the end of his arm like a dead branch.

"Only one hand is good," said the Sabbathians behind him.

"Tatian was indignant against the mass because wine was served there that came from the devil, and Seleucus was indignant against baptism because use was made therein of water, which is an impure element.

And Cyril saw the disciples of Simon Magus appear, whose perverse smile betrayed the abominations they were preparing to commit; the Tocodrugites who, by virtue of an affectation of meditation, inserted their second finger into one of their nostrils; the Abelians who, as a symbol of their continence, wore an iron grille over the loins; the Adamites who lived naked in order to recall the original innocence and only had intercourse with women in public; the Antidicomarianites who claimed that he Holy Virgin was not a virgin and had several children by Saint Joseph, the names of whom they knew; the Artotyrites, who made use of cheese for the eucharist; the Barborians, who claimed that Christ had be created from the joyous humor of a female spirit named Barbeliote; the Cainites, who venerated Cain and Judas; the Passolorhynchites, who became mute by dint of maintaining silence; the Hesyrastes, who considered their navel; the Musorites, who rendered worship to mice because they spread through houses like the Holy Spirit through souls; and also the Paulianists, the Celicoles, the Origenians, the Noetians, the Cerdonians, the Cataphrygians and a thousand others, equally possessed by their errors and inflamed by their follies.

All of them showed him the finger. They were united by one common thought, which was the scorn they had for him. Those irreconcilable sectarians no longer hated one another, and had even been brought together by a sort of fraternity. All those fanatics were poor. Consumed by theological arguments and the search for religious truth, they had disdained material wealth and had voluntarily stripped themselves of it.

When Nestorius, raising his ravaged face, turned his insensate eyes toward Cyril and proclaimed: "Behold the man who bought the Council of Ephesus with gold! Behind the man who paid the Emperor's entourage in order that I might be condemned!" an immense cry of reprobation rose up from all sides.

The saints, the prophets, the doctors, the commentators on the laws, the extravagant anchorites, and the mad ascetics moved away in horror. They opened a great circle around Cyril and drew away, as if he had just been afflicted by the plague of Heliopolis; they recoiled into the shadows or plunged into the walls, and there was no longer anything but a few eyes that continued to shine with a expression of disgust.

And Nestorius started to snigger, crying: "I prefer the lions! Let them come and eat my face! The so-called Patriarch of Alexandria is nothing but an incarnation of Mammon!"

Cyril closed his eyes. He had often exorcized the possessed. Demonic possession, the strange mystery of evil taking over a soul, had always troubled him. He knew that the demon could slip into you easily, during sleep, at certain times of the year, in places where the pagans had long celebrated their religion. He had often said that Theophilus had committed a great imprudence in constructing the Episcopal palace on the site where the temple of Serapis had stood, and employing the same materials with which it had been built. Had the age-old gods of Egypt not ended up bewitching him?

Mammon, Nestorius had said: the demon of wealth! As far as he could go back in the remembrance of his life, he saw that the desire for wealth had always held the foremost place there. He had loved gold, he had acquired it, and he had made use of it in order to obtain more of it. If he had had the statues of temples melted down, it was to have the ingots transported to his coffers. If he had closed the churches of the Donatists it was because they were full of ornaments and he had pillaged them. If he had expelled the Jews from Alexandria it was to steal the treasure hidden in the house of the Hillels. Yes, he had bought the Council of Ephesus, and he had bought the advisors of Theodosius. He had always bargained and trafficked in order to acquire more.

But why? He scarcely had any needs. The books in his library were sufficient for him. His only love was refuting, by means of his pen, the heresies of false doctrines.

So, he had persecuted, tormented and had people killed in order to have wealth that did not serve any purpose for him. That was because he was possessed by Mammon. Nestorius was right. He had identified himself without being aware of it with the demon. He was the demon personified.

He had fallen on to his hands. He found himself on all fours, and he stopped moaning in order to think that he was like an animal. He had gone backwards. The demon had brought him back to the condition of a beast. The disorder of his soul was so great that he was tempted to roar in order to frighten Nestorius, to croak like the crows that devour the dead, or to writhe while hissing like the tempter Serpent. A great bloodstain bathed the floor tiles in front of him. He advanced his head in order to lap that refreshing liquid with his tongue.

He perceived that it was the first ray of the rising sun.

A face of supernatural beauty was very close to his. A blue jewel cast a light in her hair, parted in the Greek style. Cyril saw the birth of a woman's shoulders and he would have distinguished the grace of her body if he had dared to look.

He had just recognized the features of Hypatia. They were imprinted with a marvelous comprehension. She gazed at him, she understood him. She measured his savage fanaticism, his hatred of free discussion and everything that contradicted the limited dogma of his religion, his blind conviction and his incommensurable love of virtue,[46] which had been mysteriously expressed in him by avarice, persecution and crime.

"Love of virtue all the same," she said. "I forgive you because I have arrived at a degree of intelligence that permits sight and penetration of the mind, and the sincerity of your faith shines like a lamp tarnished by ordure, but which nevertheless projects a tiny eternal glow."

Cyril got up painfully, sat down, and wept.

It was at that moment that, between the four ivory columns of her bed, Priscilla had just woken up.

Sitting upright, her dark hair flowing in two sheaves over her breasts, she gazed avidly at her bedroom, blanched by the morning, and was astonished to be alone.

She had, therefore, only had a dream. Men whose faces expressed wisdom and purity had previously grouped around her bed and had spoken to her. She could not remember their words. They were tender, confused and admirable.

On reflection, she told herself that it had been more than a dream. She wondered who those men could have been, and how they had come and gone after having indicated to her what she ought to do. But she was never to know that.

She leapt out of bed, ran to the wooden figurine that Khepra had given her and gently, carefully, detached the little sachet that was nailed to it.

Then she threw a cloak over her shoulders, went out of her bedroom, went down the marble stairs and ran to the portal that gave access to the street.

---

[46] The French word *bien*, here translated as "virtue," has many more meanings than any single English word can contain, which include both "good" and "property," hence licensing an elaborate ambiguity in this assertion.

XXV. There is a Way for Everyone

Beneath his hut of reeds in the marshes of Shedia, Olympios had arrived at detachment from all things.

The men who drained the salt and those who cut the wild plants in order that they did not encumber the salt-pans gave him the bananas and rice necessary to his life in exchange for a few words that they did not understand but to which they attributed a meaning of benediction.

He only walked slowly, in order not to crush insects under his footsteps, because his wisdom informed him that it is necessary not to destroy life even in the humblest forms; and he only picked up dead and desiccated branches for his fire, in order not to attack vegetable life.

One day, a young monk named Simon had come to build a hut of reeds like his, not far from the place where he lived, and had installed himself therein.

At first, Olympios had been fearful of that proximity, for he knew the intolerance of Christians wearing dark robes. At first he had expected furious anathemas or subtle attempts at conversion. There had been nothing of the sort. The monk Simon was gentle and sad, and gazed suavely into his soul.

First, they had exchanged a few words on the subject of the Nile flood, which, when it was high, made itself felt as far as the salt-pans, with the consequence that the water could invade their huts. Then a narrower relationship had been formed because of a fire that one of them had been unable to light and for which the other had lent his briquette, in exchange for barley cakes, which they shared. They had acquired the habit of coming to visit one another every day, and they talked about divine things.

Although they departed from the most opposed points of faith, there was no contradiction between them. Olympios translated the terms employed by Simon internally. When the latter talked about his guardian angel and looked to his right,

Olympios knew that it was a matter of the entity that he had labored to create within himself, and which Socrates called his familiar daemon.

Their goal was common, and they educated one another reciprocally on means to achieve it. They both sought perfection by ecstasy, and the monk's ecstasy and the philosopher's ecstasy were similar; they each permitted the human spirit to be confounded by love with the divine unity.

Sometimes, there were loud vocal outbursts on the threshold of Olympios' hut. That was Socles, who had not forgotten his friend, and came to visit him. Slaves unloaded a basket of provisions, and Simon was always invited to the meal they took together in the shade of a sycamore.

Socles laughed noisily and mocked his guests because of their sobriety. He drank the wine that he had brought alone and proudly showed off his muscular arms and laborer's calluses. He had just constructed a house himself in one of his fields, and he was going to build another. He was happy. Physical labor had given him mental serenity.

"There is a way for everyone," said Olympios, softly.

And when Socles asked him, ironically, if he still rose up into the air, he shook his head negatively, for since he had sensed that power of levitation within him, he no longer took pride in having it, and no longer exercised it.

One evening, all three of them were sitting under their familiar sycamore and Socles was recounting the news of Alexandria to the two anchorites.

Bishop Cyril had declared to his entourage that he was renouncing the patriarchate of Alexandria and was going to go on foot, clad in the robe of a mendicant monk, as far as the great oasis, where he would end his days in solitude. People had tried in vain to deflect him from that project. It was doubtless when he began to realize it that he had been struck by death. He had been found lying on the steps of the Serapeum with a beggar's wallet and a pilgrim's staff.

An event had turned the house of Diodorus upside-down. One morning, on opening the door to the street, the porter had found a man in wretched clothing who had just died. At the same moment, the beautiful Priscilla came running. She had the body of the unknown man washed and perfumed and had him carried to a villa she possessed outside Alexandria. Public rumor said that she had had a sandalwood and lemonwood pyre built and, scorning imperial edicts, she had had him solemnly burned. Then she had collected the ashes in a solid gold urn.

Socles remembered ancient confidences that had once escaped Aurelius. He had often thought about his friend, departed for the abode of the wise and had been afflicted by his absence. He wondered whether it might be him who had come to die on the threshold of Priscilla's house. He had made enquiries, interrogated the servants. He had intended to go see Priscilla herself. But he had learned that she was completely ignorant of the identity of the traveler. He could not explain the funeral honors that she had rendered him.

"Perhaps it was Aurelius," said Olympios, pensively. "Certain beings communicate by means of a wordless language during sleep and don't remember it when they wake up."

And as they were conversing about their friend's destiny, a man who was passing along the road perceived their little group, and climbed the path that led to the place where they were seated.

He was limping, and he was very weary, although of joyful humor.

He did not hide the fact that he was hungry. He was immediately invited to sit down and Socles served him copiously, insisting that he drink some wine in order to make him feel better. He drank some.

His name was Amoraim and he mingled the greatest pride with the greatest simplicity. He explained that his life had been divided into two parts, the first tormented by bad luck, the other illuminated by an unparalleled good fortune.

The essential thing was to see the world and educate oneself. Sometimes he mentioned a little shop where he had sold candles, sometimes he confided that he was Moses and that he was charged by God with teaching the law. In both cases, however, he had spread light. He could not imagine that any human life might be more beautiful than his. He was in a hurry because he had learned that his coreligionists were in misfortune in Heliopolis, and he was going to that city in haste in order to save them. No, it was necessary not to insist. He could not stay longer. Moses does not stop when his people call him.

He thanked his hosts very humbly for the meal hey had offered him. He almost prostrated himself. But he adjusted his petty stature immediately, uncertain as to whether his quality as a prophet permitted him to bless men who appeared to be full of sanctity themselves.

"The eternal, our God, is one!" he said, by way of adieu, and he drew away repeating in the darkness in an increasingly loud voice the formula that had saved the Jews of Alexandria from the massacre.

A little later, when Socles left, Amoraim's voice was still audible in the distance among the arborescent tamarinds and the violet pistachio trees of the marsh.

"The Eternal, our God, is one!" murmured Olympios, turning to Simon, who was also about to leave. He showed him with a gesture the opposite directions in which the two men, so different from one another, were heading, and he added: "There is a way for everyone—but only one truth, however."

XXVI. Hypatia's Sapphire

"There's a saying from which my mind can't detach itself," said Priscilla to Telamon. "I think about it incessantly, and yet, it's impossible for me to remember who said it to me."

"What is it?" asked Telamon.

"That it is only by means of love that one can stop hatred." Priscilla remained silent for a moment, and then went on: "Yes, love is the greatest force there is in the world."

She held out her hand to Telamon and gazed at the sea. They were leaning on the marble balustrade of Diodorus' house, and behind them, the heavy heat of the finishing afternoon caused the immense garden of rare flowers to live with an animal life, swelling the bulbs of violet-tinted irises, making the calices of foxgloves burst forth, drawing white sudations from the velvety petunias and rendering the stamens of the pelargoniums more incandescent.

For a long time, Telamon had waited in Corinth for the message from Priscilla that would summon him to Alexandria. That wait had increased his amour. The liking he had for beautiful statues, luminous landscapes and works of art sculpted in precious materials was summarized in the ideal of a human beauty that had the form of Priscilla's body. He had yielded to his impatience and had embarked for Alexandria.

He had found Priscilla at the moment when the ashes of Aurelius' pyre, lifted by a light breeze, were dispersing in a fine gray mist on the coast of the sea. They had given themselves to one another with a hectic ardor. Spring and summer had passed without their being able to quit one another even for an hour. They both had a physical need to be with one another. Desire had made their eyes brighter, and made their faces paler, rendering them more beautiful.

"Oh, perhaps you, who have known Synesius, and have lived in the intimacy of Proclus and Eunapius," Priscilla said, suddenly, with a passionate impulse, "can resolve the problem that often torments me. Why accomplish one action rather than another? By virtue of what law do we do good or evil? What is the force within us that links us to certain beings? It seems to me that the hours I have spent loving you were marked in advance on a mysterious tableau and that they had to elapse for me as ineluctably as those I employed in avenging Hypatia."

"Do you remember what Isidore of Gaza said, who explained everything by dreams?" Telamon replied. "He put forward the hypothesis that you were, in a former life, Hypatia's younger sister, and that she turned you away from the love of a young man in order to consecrate yourself to the service of the gods. Perhaps I was that young man, and we are now realizing the desire of old, for human love is imperishable."

"Perhaps," said Priscilla. "But in that case, every life is a perpetual recommencement, and every action, good or bad, entails a recompense or a punishment. That would have no end. And I, who would like to repose eternally in your arms, am already weary in thinking of everything to which it might be necessary for me to submit by virtue of the reaction of my actions."

"Didn't you say just now that love stops hatred. We know very little. The balance in which everything is weighed in order to be reproduced is invisible and unknown. Every kiss that our lips give, every spontaneous impulse that impels us together is perhaps inscribed to our count in the book of immanent justice. The love of a man and a woman for one another is the most elevated in the hierarchy of amours, and the one you experience will doubtless tip the balance in your favor."

The sun would soon disappear over the horizon. Priscilla wanted to go along the road to Paroetonium in order to contemplate the gigantic clumps of rhododendrons in flower that were blooming a short distance from the villa and the colors of which were splendid in the twilight.

The two lovers had mounted a chariot with two seats which Telamon drove. As they came back, they went past a group of children playing. They were young Christians. They recognized Priscilla and Telamon and they shouted insults. A little girl even followed the chariot at a run and, with all her might, threw a stone that struck Priscilla on the temple.

Telamon stopped the horses in order to look at the wound, but there was only a tiny trickle of blood, which stopped flowing immediately.

"It's nothing," said Priscilla.

They went back.

It was only later that Priscilla felt weak, gripped by vertigo. She perceived then that she had been stricken by a kind of paralysis that immobilized half her body.

Slaves left for Alexandria immediately with the order to fetch a physician, Adamantius in preference to any other.

Priscilla wanted to be carried on to the terrace, in front of the sea, in the midst of flowers. She felt ill, and was having difficulty breathing. Her memory was fading.

She asked for an ivory casket that was on a shelf in her bedroom. She took a sapphire out of it, which she gave to Telamon.

"Keep it," she said. "It's Hypatia's sapphire. It's stained by a little blood. I haven't washed it because of the verity of the symbol."

And as Telamon looked at her in surprise she murmured: "It's better thus. The blow that I dealt before has just been returned to me. Fortunate are those who pay for their faults in this existence! They arrive in the following one exempt from debts."

Now she could no longer move. Thoutmos was weeping, saying that blood must have flowed internally and that the best thing to do was to bleed her.

Telamon preferred to wait for Adamantius. He wanted to remain alone with Priscilla. He had placed the sapphire between her two breasts.

The moon had risen. Priscilla was lying on a bed of repose hastily placed under a clump of parasol pines, from which a gilded needle was detached.

She struggled internally against the departure of memories. She clung on to one of them, and was able to say, in a low voice: "Your first kiss in the Gymnasium of Alexandria..."

It seemed to Telamon that the aromas of the garden, in becoming confounded, gave him a spiritual intoxication of which he was not the master. The moon was high in the sky. The pine needles rained down in silence.

Adamantius did not arrive.

Priscilla, beneath the serene night, had never been as beautiful. Telamon wondered who she resembled. That marble visage was like that of the Aphrodite he had once contemplated in the temple of Byblos. Only the lips were less full, and tighter, the nose thinner. But the breasts, the hollow of the hips and the long legs were more perfect. That white form lying on the whiteness of the terrace, with the life of the spread hair, and the delicacy of the hands, really was the beauty personified that he had pursued all his life, and which was his veritable religion.

He was so penetrated with admiration that it was only when dawn appeared that he perceived that Priscilla was dead.

He uttered a cry.

Like a star illuminated by the rising sun, pure of all pollution, Hypatia's sapphire projected a sparkling blue light.

SF & FANTASY

Adolphe Alhaiza. *Cybele*

Alphonse Allais. *The Adventures of Captain Cap*

Henri Allorge. *The Great Cataclysm*

Guy d'Armen. *Doc Ardan: The City of Gold and Lepers; The Troglodytes of Mount Everest/The Giants of Black Lake; The Abominable Snowman*

G.-J. Arnaud. *The Ice Company*

André Arnyvelde. *The Ark; The Mutilated Bacchus*

Charles Asselineau. *The Double Life*

Henri Austruy. *The Eupantophone; The Olotelepan; The Petitpaon Era*

Barillet-Lagargousse. *The Final War*

Barbot de Villeneuve.*The Naiads/Beauty & The Beast*

Cyprien Bérard. *The Vampire Lord Ruthwen*

S. Henry Berthoud. *Martyrs of Science; The Angel Asrael*

Aloysius Bertrand. *Gaspard de la Nuit*

Richard Bessière. *The Gardens of the Apocalypse; The Masters of Silence*

Chevalier de Béthune. *The World of Mercury*

Albert Bleunard. *Ever Smaller*

Félix Bodin. *The Novel of the Future*

Pierre Boitard. *Journey to the Sun*

Louis Boussenard. *Monsieur Synthesis*

Alphonse Brown. *City of Glass; The Conquest of the Air*

Émile Calvet. *In a Thousand Years*

André Caroff. *The Terror of Madame Atomos; Miss Atomos; The Return of Madame Atomos; The Mistake of Madame Atomos; The Monsters of Madame Atomos; The Revenge of Madame Atomos; The Resurrection of Madame Atomos; The Mark of Madame Atomos; The Spheres of Madame Atomos; The Wrath of Madame Atomos* (w/M. & Sylvie Stéphan)

Jean Carrère. *The End of Atlantis*

Félicien Champsaur. *Homo-Deus; The Human Arrow; Nora, The Ape-Woman; Ouha, King of the Apes; Pharaoh's Wife*

Didier de Chousy. *Ignis*

Jules Clarétie. *Obsession*

Jacques Collin de Plancy. *Voyage to the Center of the Earth*

Michel Corday. *The Eternal Flame; The Lynx* (w/André Couvreur)
André Couvreur. *Caresco, Superman; The Exploits of Professor Tornada* (3 vols.); *The Necessary Evil*
Gaston Danville. *The Perfume of Lust*
Camille Debans. *The Misfortunes of John Bull*
Captain Danrit. *Undersea Odyssey*
C. I. Defontenay. *Star (Psi Cassiopeia)*
Charles Derennes. *The People of the Pole*
Georges Dodds (anthologist). *The Missing Link*
Charles Dodeman. *The Silent Bomb*
Harry Dickson. *The Heir of Dracula; Harry Dickson vs. The Spider*
Jules Dornay. *Lord Ruthven Begins*
Alfred Driou. *The Adventures of a Parisian Aeronaut*
Odette Dulac. *The War of the Sexes*
Alexandre Dumas. *The Return of Lord Ruthven; The Man who Married a Mermaid* (w/P. Lacroix)
Renée Dunan. *Baal; The Ultimate Pleasure*
J.-C. Dunyach. *The Night Orchid; The Thieves of Silence*
Henri Duvernois. *The Man Who Found Himself*
Achille Eyraud. *Voyage to Venus*
Henri Falk. *The Age of Lead*
Paul Féval. *Anne of the Isles; Knightshade; Revenants; Vampire City; The Vampire Countess; The Wandering Jew's Daughter*
Paul Féval, *fils. Felifax, the Tiger-Man*
Charles de Fieux. *Lamékis*
Fernand Fleuret. *Jim Click*
Charles-Marie Flor O'Squarr. *Phantoms*
Louis Forest. *Someone is Stealing Children in Paris*
Arnould Galopin. *Doctor Omega*; *Doctor Omega and the Shadowmen* (anthology)
Judith Gautier. *Isoline and the Serpent-Flower*
H. Gayar. *The Marvelous Adventures of Serge Myrandhal on Mars*
Louis Geoffroy. *The Apocryphal Napoleon*
G.L. Gick. *Harry Dickson and the Werewolf of Rutherford Grange*
Raoul Gineste. *The Second Life of Doctor Albin*
Delphine de Girardin. *Balzac's Cane*
Léon Gozlan. *The Vampire of the Val-de-Grâce*
Jules Gros. *The Fossil Man*
Jimmy Guieu. *The Polarian-Denebian War* (2 vols.)
Edmond Haraucourt. *Daah, the First Human; Illusions of Immortality*
Nathalie Henneberg. *The Green Gods*

Eugène Hennebert. *The Enchanted City*
Jules Hoche. *The Maker of Men and His Formula*
V. Hugo, P. Foucher & P. Meurice. *The Hunchback of Notre-Dame*
Romain d'Huissier. *Hexagon: Dark Matter*
Jules Janin. *The Magnetized Corpse*
Gustave Kahn. *The Tale of Gold and Silence*
Gérard Klein. *The Mote in Time's Eye*
Fernand Kolney. *Love in 5000 Years*
Paul Lacroix. *Danse Macabre; The Man who Married a Mermaid* (w/Alexandre Dumas)
Louis-Guillaume de La Follie. *The Unpretentious Philosopher*
Jean de La Hire. *The Fiery Wheel; Enter the Nyctalope; The Nyctalope on Mars; The Nyctalope vs. Lucifer; The Nyctalope Steps In; Night of the Nyctalope; Return of the Nyctalope*
Etienne-Léon de Lamothe-Langon. *The Virgin Vampire*
André Laurie. *Spiridon*
Gabriel de Lautrec. *The Vengeance of the Oval Portrait*
Alain le Drimeur. *The Future City*
Georges Le Faure & Henri de Graffigny. *The Extraordinary Adventures of a Russian Scientist Across the Solar System* (2 vols.)
Gustave Le Rouge. *The Dominion of the World* (w/Gustave Guitton) (4 vols.); *The Mysterious Doctor Cornelius* (3 vols.); *The Vampires of Mars*
Jules Lermina. *The Battle of Strasbourg; Mysteryville; Panic in Paris; The Secret of Zippelius; To-Ho and the Gold Destroyers*
Maurice Level. *The Gates of Hell*
André Lichtenberger. *The Centaurs; The Children of the Crab*
Maurice Limat. *Mephista*
Listonai. *The Philosophical Voyager*
Jean-Marc & Randy Lofficier. *Edgar Allan Poe on Mars; The Katrina Protocol; Pacifica 1, 2; Robonocchio; Return of the Nyctalope;* (anthologists) *Tales of the Shadowmen 1-13; The Vampire Almanac* (2 vols.)
Ch. Lomon & P.-B. Gheuzi. *The Last Days of Atlantis*
Maurice Magre. *The Marvelous Story of Claire d'Amour; The Call of the Beast*
Camille Mauclair. *The Virgin Orient*
Xavier Mauméjean. *The League of Heroes*
Joseph Méry. *The Tower of Destiny*
Hippolyte Mettais. *Paris Before the Deluge; The Year 5865*
Louise Michel. *The Human Microbes; The New World*

Tony Moilin. *Paris in the Year 2000*
Michael Moorcock's *Legends of the Multiverse*
José Moselli. *Illa's End*
John-Antoine Nau. *Enemy Force*
Marie Nizet. *Captain Vampire*
Charles Nodier. *Trilby and The Crumb Fairy*
C. Nodier, A. Beraud & Toussaint-Merle. *Frankenstein*
Henri de Parville. *An Inhabitant of the Planet Mars*
Gaston de Pawlowski. *Journey to the Land of the 4th Dimension*
Georges Pellerin. *The World in 2000 Years*
Ernest Pérochon. *The Frenetic People*
Pierre Pelot. *The Child Who Walked on the Sky*
Jean Petithuguenin. *An International Mission to the Moon*
J. Polidori, C. Nodier, E. Scribe. *Lord Ruthven the Vampire*
P.-A. Ponson du Terrail. *The Immortal Woman; The Vampire and the Devil's Son; The Police Agent*
Georges Price. *The Missing Men of the* Sirius
René Pujol. *The Chimerical Quest*
Edgar Quinet. *Ahasuerus; The Enchanter Merlin*
Jean Rameau. *Arrival; in the Stars*
Henri de Régnier. *A Surfeit of Mirrors*
Maurice Renard. *The Blue Peril; Doctor Lerne; The Doctored Man; A Man Among the Microbes; The Master of Light*
Restif de la Bretonne. *The Discovery of the Austral Continent by a Flying Man; Posthumous Correspondence* (3 vols.); *The Fay Ouroucoucou* (2 vols.)
Jean Richepin. *The Crazy Corner; The Wing*
Albert Robida. *The Adventures of Saturnin Farandoul; Chalet in the Sky; The Clock of the Centuries; The Electric Life; The Engineer Von Satanas*
J.-H. Rosny Aîné. *Helgvor of the Blue River; The Givreuse Enigma; The Mysterious Force; The Navigators of Space; Vamireh; The World of the Variants; The Young Vampire*
Marcel Rouff. *Journey to the Inverted World*
Marie-Anne de Roumier-Robert. *The Voyage of Lord Seaton to the Seven Planets*
Léonie Rouzade. *The World Turned Upside Down*
Han Ryner. *The Human Ant; The Superhumans*
Henri de Saint-Georges. *The Green Eyes*
Louis-Claude de Saint-Martin. *The Crocodile*

Frank Schildiner. *The Quest of Frankenstein; The Triumph of Frankenstein; Napoleon's Vampire Hunters*

Nicolas Ségur. *The Human Paradise*

Pierre de Selenes: *An Unknown World*

Norbert Sevestre. *Sâr Dubnotal: Vs. Jack the Ripper; The Astral Trail*

Angelo de Sorr. *The Vampires of London*

Brian Stableford. *The Empire of the Necromancers (1. The Shadow of Frankenstein; 2. Frankenstein and the Vampire Countess; 3. Frankenstein in London); The Wayward Muse; Eurydice's Lament; The Mirror of Dionysius; The New Faust at the Tragicomique; Sherlock Holmes and The Vampires of Eternity; The Stones of Camelot* (anthologist) *News from the Moon; The Germans on Venus; The Supreme Progress; The World Above the World; Nemoville; Investigations of the Future; The Conqueror of Death; The Revolt of the Machines; The Man With the Blue Face; The Aerial Valley; The New Moon; The Nickel Man; On the Brink of the World's End; The Mirror of Present Events; The Humanisphere*

Jacques Spitz. *The Eye of Purgatory*

Kurt Steiner. *Ortog*

Eugène Thébault. *Radio-Terror*

C.-F. Tiphaigne de La Roche. *Amilec*

Simon Tyssot de Patot. *The Strange Voyages of Jacques Massé and Pierre de Mésange*

Louis Ulbach. *Prince Bonifacio*

Théo Varlet. *The Castaways of Eros; The Golden Rock.; The Martian Epic* (w/Octave Joncquel); *Timeslip Troopers* (w/André Blandin); *The Xenobiotic Invasion*

Pierre Véron. *The Merchants of Health*

Paul Vibert. *The Mysterious Fluid*

Villiers de l'Isle-Adam. *The Scaffold; The Vampire Soul*

Gaston de Wailly. *The Murderer of the World*

Philippe Ward. *Artahe; Manhattan Ghost* (w/Mickael Laguerre); *The Song of Montségur* (w/Sylvie Miller)

Victor Margueritte. *The Bacheloress; The Companion; The Couple*

www.ingramcontent.com/pod-product-compliance
Lightning Source LLC
Chambersburg PA
CBHW031144050726
47495CB00018B/527